CRACKED & CRUSHED

THE SACRED HEARTS MC BOOK THREE

A.J. DOWNEY

COPYRIGHT

Text Copyright © 2014 by A.J. Downey

~

ISBN: 978-0692333907

Edited by Barbara J. Bailey

Book design by Maggie Kern

Cover art by Dar Albert at Wicked Smart Designs

Model - Chase Ketron

Photographer - Furious Fotog

DEDICATION

To the real Hannah Hossler and Tonya Annon, for bouncing ideas and jumping on promoting the first book in this series in exchange for a couple of cameo appearances. More specifically, for not getting pissed off at your character selves! It was a riot writing you guys into this book. I hope I get to do something like it again.

PROLOGUE

Hayden...

The weather was perfect, the setup had gone smooth as silk and as I turned to walk down the aisle, I couldn't help but smile broadly. My father patted my hand where it rested in the crook of his arm and smiled down at me proudly. My bridesmaids were positively beaming. Ashton looked radiant in lilac satin, Everett, Shelly, and Chandra equally beautiful in their sleek pewter gowns.

Andy looked so nervous! He stood so still and so straight, his brown eyes a little too wide, and I felt a little bad for him. His four fraternity brothers looked dapper in their gray long-tailed tuxedos, the pewter satin stripe down the pant legs matching the bridesmaid's gowns to perfection. The best man wore a lilac vest and bow tie and stood behind Andy with a carefully-schooled blank look.

I started down the aisle, the music swelled, the hundred or so guests turned to watch me, and I felt a little nervous myself. I had wanted a small, intimate wedding, but, as always, my mother had her way in things. Most of these people were business associates of my father's and of Andy's. I scanned the crowd for someone, anyone, familiar to me and my gaze fell on Reaver and Trigger. My breath caught slightly in my throat. Trigger looked amazing, the big man standing head and shoulders taller than almost everyone else – but it was Reaver who stole my breath away.

He wore a shirt and tie and light-grey pair of slacks. I'd never seen him in anything other than casual wear before. The dressier clothes made him look stiff, but delicious... *which is so not a thought I should be having about another man on my wedding day!* I thought. Still, I couldn't help but look my fill; the shirt was crisp and white and the blue of his slim tie matched his icy blue eyes to perfection. It was in the high eighties out here on the manor's back lawn, but the moment his wintry gaze fell upon me, I felt like it cooled fifteen degrees.

His expression was shuttered and closed, a mystery wrapped in a delicate bow of an enigma. I liked that about Reaver. I could never tell what he was thinking when he looked at me unless he wanted me to. I tried a smile on him and he smiled thinly back, but it wasn't a happy one. I wanted to know why; some small part of me yearned to stop and ask him, but too soon, my father and I swept by. There was no turning back now and I could still feel his eyes on the open back of my gown. It was simply cooler where his gaze slid along my skin. I had never been hyper-aware of another person like I was of Reaver. That included Andy, but I loved Andy and had agreed to marry him before I had ever had the chance to really know Reaver.

I gave an involuntary shiver from the press of that wintry gaze and my dad chuckled, misreading it. "Steady," he said under his breath. I rolled my eyes up to him and smiled sweetly. I adored my father, was the epitome of a daddy's girl.

He handed me to Andy who took my hands in his. His palms were sweating and I tried to give him a reassuring look. The pastor had his say, I said my vows, and I looked up at the man I had just pledged the rest of my life to.

"I can't," he said. I blinked. *I can't?* He couldn't what? He couldn't remember his vows? Was he that nervous? The poor thing! I felt my face fall into lines of confusion when he simply stood there, an agonized look upon his face. Our guests were muttering and murmuring among themselves as the silence stretched on.

"Andy?" I asked, when he'd been silent for just far too long. He dropped my hands abruptly at the sound of his name.

"I can't," he repeated and I stood there speechless and blinked stupidly.

"You can't, what?" I asked, my heart heavy with dread, weighted in my chest, crushing the air from my lungs. I held my breath.

"I don't love you Hayden, you're not the one for me... I can't marry you." His frat buddies snickered behind him; the murmurs among our guests, our families, thickened.

My whole world, my future, my life of the last four years, all of it came crashing down on me... What was I supposed to do?

1

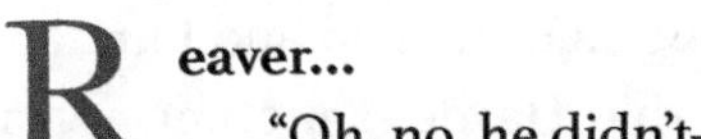

R eaver...

"Oh, no, he didn't–" I said.

"Yeah. Yeah, he did, buddy." Trigger sounded murderous but he was going to have to get in line; I called dibs on putting the hurt on this asshole. Hayden looked like she was desperate... no... more like, she was drowning. She stood stock-still, her green eyes showing way too much white and I couldn't stand it. I had to save her, but fucked if I knew how to rescue someone from something like this.

I pushed out from the row where Trig and I were seated and he had my six all the way up the aisle. Ashton was standing just behind Hayden, her golden eyes wide and incredulous as some of the douchebag groomsmen behind the douchebag groom started cracking up. The silence crept in on me and it was all I could do to leave my knives where they were. I felt like putting somebody's eye out. Trigger and I reached the front and I gently handed Hayden over to Ashton, Everett, and Shells.

"Take her inside," I told Trigger's Sunshine Girl and she nodded a bit rapidly. Hayden's eyes were welling with tears and it simultaneously cracked my heart in two and aroused me. God, she was even prettier when she cried. I'd never seen her do it before. I shook the latter thought off and turned on Andy, the douchebag groom, who was trying to push past me and Trig to get to Hayden; he was babbling something about being sorry. I called out over my shoulder to the girls.

"Get her inside!" I didn't want her to see, but as Andy became more insistent with his shoving, I balled up my fist and brought it up and under, connecting solidly with his solar plexus. His breath whooshed out of him and he doubled over. There were cries of dismay from the prim and proper crowd, and I looked up at a blur of grey motion beside me, into the green eyes of Hayden's father. He looked at me grimly and nodded.

"Thanks," he said, and then, "You beat me to it."

"No problem," I replied.

The older man was around Trigger's height but was almost painfully thin by comparison. He jerked his head towards the house.

"I don't want to leave Hayden to her mother," he said and I understood. I knew from watchful experience that Hayden's mother was a piece of work. Truth is, I wasn't sure why her pops put up with the woman. I nodded and he took long strides in the direction of the mansion.

He'd rented the place for the wedding, I think. Some old-money joint that sat on a farm where they trained racehorses. It was a nice place to have a wedding, but right now, the only thing I was really interested in was carving up the man who'd just humiliated my girl in front of all of their wedding guests... Fuck. Wasn't that a brain-twister?

Andy was still trying to relearn how to breathe; his frat-buddy douche-canoe groomsmen were all eyeing me and Trig, four to our two. If they wanted to dance, I was more than happy to do-si-do. I unbuttoned my cuff and started rolling back my sleeve. One of them glanced at my face, his eyes drawn to the corner of my eye, and I felt a real unfriendly smile curve my lips. His eyes shot to my hands and widened a little at the tattoos on them. It was the stilettos on the insides of my forearms that decided them against taking any retaliation.

"That's what we thought," Trigger said and crossed his arms, his suit jacket straining just a bit at the shoulders. I finished rolling up my sleeves, smiled saccharine-sweet at the five of them, and nodded once.

"Pussies," I declared and walked backwards towards the mansion. Trigger followed my lead and we turned only when we were sure none of them had any designs on taking a cheap shot when our backs were presented.

"What're you going to do, Brother?" Trigger asked me as we crossed the grass in our fancy dress shoes.

"Playin' it by ear, Trig," I said, and he grunted.

"Tread lightly," he suggested.

I snorted. "No shit. I just watched Mount-fucking-Everest drop on her head. I'm not about to push one of my fucked-up agendas right now, Brother, but somebody's gotta look out for her." We caught up to her dad just as he pulled open the door on the wrap-around porch. We all three grimaced in unison as Hayden's mother's voice floated from inside the mansion somewhere, berating her daughter.

"I mean, honestly, Hayden! Who does that without just cause? You must have done something to upset him! Said something? The embarrassment! Surely you know how this is going to reflect on your father–" She didn't get another word out.

Hayden's pop's mouth thinned down into a grim line of steel determination and he barked out "Margaret! Let that girl alone!"

We trailed him up the hall and rounded the corner into the room that was set aside for the bridal party to get ready. Some kind of sitting room or parlor, it had built-in library shelves and antique Victorian furniture scattered around. A dressing screen was in the corner, one of those tri-fold deals, gold with swans on a lake on it. The image was too serene for the tempest going on inside the room.

Hayden sat stiff as a board at a little dressing table, hands folded primly in her lap, but mottled and shaking with how hard she gripped the balled-up Kleenexes in them. Mascara dripped to her chin and her bright green eyes seemed all the brighter from the shine that the tears put on 'em. Her dark lashes were clumped together with moisture and her chin trembled. She looked frail and about to fly apart any second and I thought she was so beautiful it physically hurt me: a sharp, fractured, aching feeling deep in my chest.

"Sunshine," I said, and Ashton's golden eyes snapped over to me, "You're the maid of honor, so it's up to you to go out there and wrangle the guests." She nodded and Trigger held out his hand to her.

"C'mon, I'll help you," he said and she went to him, the light in her eyes saying that as long as she were with her man, anything was possible. God, I'd give anything for Hayden to look at me the way Sunshine looked at Trigger. I turned back to the room.

"Irish, get her out of that dress and into some street clothes. Make 'em sturdy," I said to Everett and she nodded once and stooped beside Hayden, speaking gently to her in that sexy-as-hell Irish accent of hers that sometimes came out when she was drinking – or stressed out. Dray had picked a fine match with that girl.

Shelly looked at me with her cool, assessing gaze, so like my own, right down to the color, and things passed between us, unspoken but loud as hell. I clearly communicated to her what I wanted. She gave me her smart-assed little secret smile and went over to Hayden's bitch of a mother.

"C'mon Mamma, let's help smooth things over with the guests." She led Hayden's mom out of the room and I turned to her dad, who was looking me over with an assessing gaze of his own.

"A moment alone, sir?" I asked him, not used to being all polite and shit. He smiled at me in a way that said he knew it and led the way into the hall. We closed the door to the drawing room behind us.

"This is going to be a circus," he said with a sigh, and pulled at the knot in his tie. I stuffed my hands in my pockets and gave him a shrewd look.

"Honeymoon's paid for isn't it?" I asked.

He cocked his head to the side and considered me.

"What you got in mind, son?" he asked me.

"Hayden doesn't need to be around for this," I said.

He nodded slowly.

"Can I ask you something?" he asked me and I smirked.

"Believe you just did, but I get you. What do you wanna know?" I asked him back.

"Just exactly who or what are you to my daughter?" he asked and I barked a bit of a crazy laugh. Good question. I was the guy that loved her on first sight, but that wasn't going to get me anywhere. I looked at the many varied truths in front of me to pick from and settled on what I thought would get me from point A to point B fastest.

"I'm just a dude that's BFFs with her BFF's dude." I shrugged and said something entirely different with my expression, willing him to pick up what I was puttin' down with my eyes: that Hayden Michaels meant the world to me and had for well over a year. He nodded slowly.

"I see. Is that why you looked like I was leading my little girl to her execution rather than to her future husband?" he asked, grimly. I smiled and rocked back and forth on my feet like he'd caught me. His green-eyed gaze roved over me, lingering, briefly, on the ink on my inner forearms and longer on the teardrop tattoo near my eye.

"You been to prison?" he asked me suddenly.

"Jail a few times," I answered honestly. Not enough evidence to send me to prison, although I probably should be rotting there. I didn't volunteer that information, though. He leaned in real close, and I went stock-still.

"Would you ever hurt my daughter?" he asked me. I thought: *Only if she asked me really, really nicely...* I'm pretty sure he didn't want to hear that, so I simply looked at him and let the silence and ice of my gaze do the talking for me.

He nodded slowly. "If someone were to hurt my daughter–"

I didn't let him even get close to finishing what he was going to say. I cut him off sharply.

"I'd kill them before they even got through thinkin' about it." It was about this time I realized how bizarre this conversation was getting. At the same time though, I'd pretty much do whatever it took, up to and including kidnapping her lovely ass, to get her some distance from this shit-storm. Her father produced a credit card and held it out between his fingers, pow! Just, there, like magic. He was a fast fucker for a guy bordering on geezer. Still, I snorted.

"I got my own money and I take care of my own shit. Put that away." I barely kept myself from adding 'old man' to the end of that sentence. Shit, if I was gonna take care of Hayden, *I* was gonna do it. I didn't want or need his charity for this or any other matter. He looked me over as if I had just done something interesting, but he put the credit card away.

"You know where she's honeymooning?" he asked.

Hell, yes. I wasn't about to admit how stalker status I'd gone on Hayden's beautiful ass though, so I simply nodded. She'd told Ashton everything and in turn I'd wheedled every bit of information I could out of the small woman. Granted it hadn't been tough. Ashton loved me like a brother from another mother, just like Trig.

"You keep her safe, away from the media..." he said and I held up two fingers in the classic Boy Scout salute. Too bad I'd never been one, but, details, details... I meant to keep my word just the same.

Irish poked her head out the door. "Okay," she murmured.

We went in. Hayden was curled up in a ball on the little couch, her face buried in her knees, arms around them, her small shoulders hitching in silent sobs. She had on jeans and a boat-neck tee, a black cardigan hanging loose around her frame. Her daddy sat down next to her and pulled her against him. Shells came back in the room and I gave her a chin lift. She put two fingers against the side of her head, put her thumb down like the dropping hammer of a gun, crossed her eyes and nodded her head from side to side. Yeah, I'd want to kill myself too, if I had to spend longer than ten minutes with Hayden's mom. I went over to my cousin and spoke low and even.

"Find her bag, the one she packed for her trip, bring it here, and Shells, I'm gonna need your jacket. You'll get it back in a few days." She nodded and didn't even bitch, a record for her. She brought the items to me just as a haggard-looking Ashton re-entered the room.

"Mom's headed this way," she warned. I shot an apologetic look to Hayden's pops, said "Get the bag," to whoever was listening, and scooped Hayden up. She was only like three inches taller than

Ashton and just as slender, so carrying her like this was no problem. She was maybe a buck-ten, buck-twenty... I didn't really think about it as I strode through the house, Ashton, Irish, and Shelly on my ass. We found Chandra out front, smoking a cig with the limo driver.

"Figured you'd need an out, so I went and found him," she commented dryly.

"That's why you're the best." I pecked her on the cheek and climbed into the back of the car. Ashton got in with me, and Trigger came out of nowhere and climbed in with her.

We could hear Margaret's raised voice and I watched Shells stiffen. "I'm about to knock her ol' ass out," Shelly complained, as Chandra swung the door shut. Ashton had the suitcase and Shelly's jacket was on the floor between the seats. Good girl.

"Where to?" the driver said, wide-eyed. I gave him the address to the clubhouse.

"Where you going?" Trig asked, gently.

"Away," I said softly, over Hayden's crying, smoothing a hand uselessly up and down her back. "You cool without me for a few days?" I asked.

"Do what you gotta do," he said grimly. Good 'ol Trig. I knew he'd have my back. Ashton's golden eyes were shut down with concern as she gazed at her friend's tiny form balled up in my lap. Her gaze trailed up to my face, and she nodded grimly, too. Shit. She knew I'd take care of her, but fuck if I didn't feel like maybe a little too much faith was being put into me here.

The driver pulled up the steep gravel drive into the lot at the top and stopped. Trigger tipped him well and I got out of the car with Hayden still balled up in my arms. She wasn't crying anymore, but I think that was more because she just didn't have anything left in her. Well, that was too bad. We had like an eight- or nine-hour ride ahead of us; I damn sure couldn't get on a plane with my knives and truth be told, I liked both feet planted firmly on the ground. The thought of being that high up gave me the creeps in a big way. I set Hayden to her feet and she wiped her eyes with her sleeve.

"What are we doing here?" she asked miserably. I tipped her face up to look at me, my hands on either side of her head.

"Do you trust me?" I asked her softly.

I'd asked her the same question before. The first time I'd ever taken her for a ride, the first time she'd ever been on the back of a bike. Her eyes glowed with a fierce green light.

"Depends. Are you taking me away from here?" she asked. I nodded slowly.

"Then, yes. Of course, I trust you, Reaver." I smiled and resisted the urge to kiss her.

"Gimme a few minutes." I let her go abruptly and shot over my shoulder at whoever was listening, "Put her shit on the bike."

I went to my room in the clubhouse and pulled down clothes and my spare helmet off the shelf. I pulled off the stupid monkey suit and threw a tee shirt over my head and pulled on some jeans. I took the fancy wallet out of my slacks pocket and transferred the essentials back into my scruffy old one that attached to my belt by a chain. I pulled on my boots, figured since the ride was going to be a long one, I'd best throw on my chaps, and went back out with some more clothes, my spare helmet, my jacket, and my cut bundled in my arms.

Back out front, I knelt opposite where Ashton was packing Hayden's things neatly in one of my empty saddlebags. I dumped my shit into the other one and stuffed my running shoes on top. I shrugged into my jacket and cut. I felt more human, more myself in minutes.

I held out Shelly's jacket for Hayden and she shrugged into it. Shelly may be taller than Hayden but she is rail thin, so the coat fit the smaller woman like a dream. I eyed Ashton, squatting in her matron-of-honor gown and her strappy high-heel matching sandals and I wanted her to hurry the hell up. I kept my cool though, and let her finish and checked out Hayden's footwear. Running shoes. Meh, they would have to do.

Ashton flopped the top of the saddlebag closed and fastened it. I buckled my spare helmet on Hayden, who was watching Ashton, though her green eyes were distant. She wasn't really here. That was okay – for now. I intended to fucking exhaust her. She wasn't used to a long ride and I had every intention of taking it in one shot. She'd sleep well tonight – and she needed to.

I felt like killing the douchebag all over again, but at the same time I was glad for her that she didn't only finally see him for what he was ten, fifteen years down the line, after she had really given him the best parts of herself. He didn't deserve 'em. Truth was, I didn't either. Hayden Michaels getting tangled up with me would bring her a whole new lesson in pain, a variety of hurts she never knew existed, but fuck if I wasn't drawn to her like a moth to the flame. I got on the bike and Trigger helped her up after me.

Ashton hugged her and I started the motorcycle up. My best friend and his girl both backed away and I pulled my sunglasses from my inside pocket and slipped them on. I tied my grinning skull bandanna over my nose and mouth and felt myself grow hard when Hayden's arms twined around my chest.

"Where are we going?" she asked suddenly, right before we pulled out.

"On your honeymoon," I answered grimly, and caught her startled expression in my side view.

"But that's in Flor-!" I pulled out and she bit out a yelp and hung on tighter. I didn't give her a chance to really acclimate, caning it instead... er... that's riding aggressively to keep her off-balance. I wanted her to focus on the ride, on me, and yeah, on holding on for dear life, for as long as possible. Why? Because focusing on any of those things would keep her brain on anything but the abject hurt and humiliation she'd just endured in front of her friends, her family, and even some of her clientele.

Hayden tucked her head and rested it against my back and I took my hand from one of the controls just long enough to pat her hands reassuringly where they were fisted in the front of my tee shirt. It was going to be a long ride.

Somewhere around nine and a half hours later it was drawing on towards full dark and I was winding my way through the streets of some small beachfront town in Florida. Twice in the last three hours

I had felt Hayden's grip on me start to slacken, her energy reserves running on empty. Both times I had placed my hand on her knee, found the right spot and squeezed the pressure point there. I knew how much that shit hurt and both times I'd had to be ready for it.

Just as I expected, she jerked, then held on for dear life, but not before throwing the balance of the bike off a bit. I compensated, but that shit even scared me! I kept us going and was better prepared for it when the cycle repeated. Now, I was tired, sweaty, felt grimy from the dust of the road, and was starting to get pissed that I couldn't find the right fucking house number for this retarded bed and breakfast she'd booked for the two of them. I stopped and looked it up on my phone. Fuck, I'd passed it.

"Hang on beautiful, we're almost there," I told her. She held on and I got us there, pulling into the tree-lined drive. I killed the bike in front of the Victorian mansion and had to admit, the place looked pretty spiffy. A woman in a salmon-colored fitted tee and khaki capri pants descended the front steps.

"Mr. and Mrs. Richardson?" she asked with a broad smile. I got off the bike.

"Naw. Reaver and Ms. Hayden Michaels who is supposed to be Mrs. Richardson. Place is paid for right?" I asked, and she looked taken aback.

"Why, um, yes," she said as I helped Hayden off the bike. I left the helmets with it and turned back to the woman.

"Cool, I'll explain later. Which one is ours? She's had a rough day." Hayden swayed a little on her feet. I slung the bike's saddlebags over my shoulder and steered her into the house behind the hostess lady.

"I'm Miranda Pernell, I own the house. I'll need ID and..." I listened to the woman prattle on and handed her my driver's license.

"Say nothing," I said, and gave her a stone-cold look. She blushed faintly, looked from me to the square of laminated cardboard and back to me.

"This is really real?" she asked skeptically.

"Yeah. It's real. You mind? She's fallin' asleep on her feet." She sped through the paperwork; I signed this, that, and the other, and she pulled a key down from the rack of 'em hanging behind the old fashioned check-in desk.

"Right this way, Mr. Butler," she said, and I scowled.

"Reaver," I corrected her.

"Of course." She pursed her lips like she wanted to say something, but wisely kept her mouth shut.

"Thanks," I told her and shut the room door in her startled face. So, I was being a dick; she was getting paid and, from the looks of things, she was getting paid really well.

The room was all antique furniture and Egyptian cotton bedding done in whites and blues. I turned Hayden by the shoulders and looked at her. I steered her into a chair and she sat. I went in the bathroom and ran the tap, wetting a washcloth and returned, cleaning up her face. I loved to see her cry but the aftermath of smeared makeup and eight or nine hours on the back of a bike going across the big slab? That was a shitty look for anybody.

Next, I went through the saddlebags. Ashton had thought of everything. Hayden's pajamas were right on top. I raised my eyebrows at the matching set. The fact that they were flowery and pink was the only thing that kept me from thinkin' they were Andy's. Nope. No, and hell no. I pulled out a clean tee shirt from my side of the bag. Next came the hard part. I got her changed for bed without copping a single feel. I was the picture of gentlemanly efficiency except for, you know, throwing her pajamas in the trashcan by the door.

She'd fallen asleep sitting up. I tucked her into the big king-sized bed and took a shower before getting in on the other side. I thought to myself that three days and four nights like this might kill me, just before sleep overcame me. Truth was, I was probably just as exhausted as she was.

2

Hayden...

I woke with a start in an unfamiliar bed in unfamiliar surroundings. I gasped and sat up sharply, the light of false dawn casting soft, barely-there light in the room through the floor-to-ceiling windows, the breezy white curtains hanging open. I listened; the only sounds were the distant rhythmic roar of ocean waves upon the shore and the persistent hum of the old house's modern air conditioning unit.

The rhythmic sound of deep, even breathing filled the intimate space and I looked down beside me to the bare, muscled back nestled in the covers, a relatively smooth expanse of skin, but laced with sweeping lines of silvery scar tissue from long-ago altercations. I traced a finger over the warm skin. Memories of the day before, all of them horrible, rushed to the surface. I took my hand away lest I wake Reaver, and closed my eyes against a hot flood of tears. I took in long, slow, deep, and even breaths and forced the floodwaters back down, my face burning with the humiliation of it all.

I got out of bed, slipping off the side carefully and went to my knees by the open saddlebags. I was in one of his tees. I didn't know why; I had packed pajamas – then I spotted them in the trashcan by the door and smiled. Apparently, Reaver had an opinion about them, like he did so many other things. I rescued the PJ's and set them aside for tonight. I swallowed hard, and gathered shorts, a tee shirt, and fresh underwear and tiptoed into the bathroom.

I stared at myself in the mirror for a long silent minute before starting the shower. I was sore from the long hours cramped in an unfamiliar position on the back of his motorcycle. I hadn't realized his intention to bring me all the way here, to my chosen honeymoon destination, until we were pretty much already underway. I couldn't decide if this was a good idea or a bad one, and right now I didn't want to put too much thought into it.

I thrust my face under the hot shower spray and scrubbed it with my hands. I felt tired, grimy, and icky and I wasn't sure it was all something I could wash down the drain, but I was going to try anyway. I used the little hotel soaps and shampoo and conditioner, grateful my hair was so short that the little bottles would work. The smell of gardenias hung heavy in the little bathroom and I wrinkled my nose. I wasn't partial to the smell, too flowery for my taste, but beggars couldn't be choosers. Maybe I could find something more to my taste later. I sighed. I wondered why he did it, brought me all the way here. I didn't much want to be here, alone with my thoughts. There was really nothing good going on inside my head. Nothing at all.

I finished my shower and plucked the fluffy towel off the bar, drying myself briskly. I dressed quickly in a pair of women's olive-green short cargo shorts and a white fitted tee and ran a comb through my short hair, parting it on the side and sweeping it down by my opposite ear. When I had seen the short hairstyle on Robin Wright in the Netflix series *House of Cards,* I'd instantly fallen in love with it.

Though she was blonde and my hair was dark, I'd immediately taken a picture of it to my stylist, had my hair cut just like it, and had never looked back. My hair had been this way for two years and I loved it! At most, it required just a little hair gel to keep it in place and that was totally acceptable. For now, I just let it dry naturally. I didn't want to use the little hairdryer and risk waking Reaver, partially because he looked more at peace than I'd ever seen him when he slept, and partially because I wasn't quite ready to deal with his sheer force of personality yet.

He had this undefinable way about him. If I had to put it to words, I would have to say Reaver had presence. He knew just what to say and how to say it to put me on edge without ever even opening his mouth... if that made sense. I peeked into the room and he was just as I had left him, sound asleep. I got back into the bag with my belongings and rooted around in it. I found my smartphone and my wallet. I slipped some cash out of it and stuck it in my back pocket. I stuck my phone into one of my hip pockets. It was turned off and I wondered if it even had a charge.

I looked for the charger but didn't find it, but I did find a pair of flip-flops and I took those as well. I went quietly out of the room and let Reaver sleep, padding barefoot down the stairs. I could smell food in the kitchen and my stomach roiled in an unpleasant manner. I didn't feel like eating and I didn't feel like company, so instead, I found my way out the back door and onto the wraparound porch.

I breathed deep the salty air and let my gaze roam across the small backyard. A flagstone path led from the porch's bottom step and wound artfully through the grass to a little back gate which was beautifully arched to either side by swaying trees and greenery, a portal of lush flora that guests could look through to white sand beaches and the rolling surf beyond. The sight was beautiful and I looked away from it just long enough to start up my phone. It started, fully charged but turned off, so it would seem. I dropped my thongs to the painted porch surface and shrugged my feet into them. I wanted sunshine, needed the warmth on my skin. I went down the steps as my phone buzzed through the startup screen.

As I let myself out through the gate, a slew of messages buzzed through. Forty-three missed calls, nineteen voicemails and so many text messages my phone crashed twice before I could get it to stay on. I sighed. Most of them were from Andy, the rest from my mother; only a very few were from miscellaneous clients and guests. I know they meant well with their messages of well-wishing, some angry on my behalf touting what a jerk Andy was, but none of it was really helping. I trudged through the sand towards the water and deleted messages and just generally cleaned up my phone.

The voicemails were all from either Andy or my mother. Andy wanted to talk to me; my mother wanted to get a few more licks in on her disappointing daughter. I groaned and deleted them without listening to more than a few words of each.

My phone started buzzing in my hand. I stared at Andy's smiling face on the screen and debated answering. I mean, what could he possibly have to say to me? My curiosity won out and I silently made up my mind that I must be some sort of emotional masochist when I slid my finger across the screen to take the call.

"Hello?" I said softly.

"Hayden?" His voice sounded like he didn't believe I'd answer.

"What do you want, Andy?" I asked, and closed my eyes, huddling in on myself.

"Where are you?" he demanded.

"You don't get to know that. Now, what do you want?" I asked.

"Well, do you know when you'll be back?" he asked, and his righteous tone irked me.

"No, Andy, I don't! What do you want?" I repeated for a third time.

"I wanted to let you know I'm going to be picking up my stuff from the townhome..." he said.

"Fine, good, you do that," I said, and I couldn't keep the bitterness out of my tone.

"Don't be like that, Hayden," he said softly.

"Are you kidding me? You left me at the altar Andy, in front of everyone, in front of my family, in front of our friends! After I forgave you! I thought we were fine! What is the deal with you? Why? I want to know why!" I dashed at the tears in my eyes and sniffed.

"I don't know why. I just... froze... I looked at you and I... shit, I couldn't do it!" He sounded like a little boy who'd been caught with his hand in the cookie jar, not like a grown man who'd just humiliated the woman he was supposed to profess his love for, for forever and ever.

"Why did you even ask me to marry you?" I asked tiredly.

"I don't know, because you expected it of me?" he answered and I scoffed.

"Are you seriously asking me? Jesus, Andy! Take responsibility and own this and just tell me why... I really need to know! I mean, did you ever love me at all?" I couldn't keep the pleading out of my voice. The second the words were out of my mouth I knew they would lead nowhere good, but it was too late. They were out into the ether and I couldn't take them back.

"I don't know..." he said and I felt my heart plummet in my chest.

"You don't know what, why you asked me or if you ever loved me?" I asked, voice hollow.

"I don't know why I asked you and I don't know if I ever loved you. I guess you were just... convenient. You know? You were the next expected evolution, go to college, get a good job, marry the girl... I don't think I really felt one way about you or the other; I was just doing what was expected of me and it didn't hurt that you were hot and your dad and my dad played golf together..." His voice buzzed on in my ear but I'd stopped listening. His words crushed me. If my heart were made of glass, it was nothing but finely ground powder now, finer than the sand I stood on. Long, deft fingers plucked the phone from my hand and I turned and looked up into cool sympathetic blue eyes. Reaver put the phone to his ear.

"Yeah, hello?" he said, then, "Never mind who this is, what did you say to her this time?" Reaver's voice was low and controlled.

"I think that's a good idea. You have until the weekend is up." His eyes searched my face and narrowed at whatever Andy said on the other line.

"Nope. Don't bother contacting her again either, you do and you'll pay for it. I'll make sure of it. Nope, not a threat, just a very real promise there, junior." He ended the call and looked me over.

"Yeah, fuck. No more of this," he said and held up my phone. I reached for it and he turned and flung it in a high, sweeping arch into the surf. I stared, open-mouthed at the shiny glint of a splash the phone made as it entered the water.

"Are you serious?" I cried and rounded on him. "Do you know how much that thing cost?"

"Buy you a new one later, sweetheart."

"Not good enough! All of my clients were in there! My calendar! Oh, my god, why couldn't you have just turned it off? What is the matter with you?" I railed at him. He simply stood there impassively, a slightly-bored expression on his face.

"Your clients will reach out to you. If I just turned it off you'd find it and turn it on again, and I'm not going to let you torture yourself over the next four days. Between that douche-bag and your mother, you would seriously lose your shit. As for what's the matter with me? Good question. When you figure it out, will you let me know?" And then the bastard grinned. My jaw dropped, incredulous at his audacity, and his smile got bigger.

"You're fucking unbelievable!" I shouted.

"Oooo, such a dirty mouth. I like it," he said.

I turned around and gave him my back, staring out to where my phone had gone in the drink.

"Hayden," he said and I turned; the serious look on his face jolted me a bit.

"Stop, baby. It's a phone. Just stop obsessing, stop stressing; stop worrying. I brought you out here to get you some distance. Put some healing on yourself. You only got a few days before you gotta go back to it. I can't protect you from it forever, though Lord knows, I would if I could." I blinked at him, speechless and before I could stop myself, the question was out of my mouth.

"Why?" I asked.

Reaver simply smiled a mysterious little Mona Lisa smile and lifted a shoulder in an indelicate shrug. I swallowed. It was about this time I realized he was shirtless, wearing only a pair of brown cut-off cargo shorts that fell just below his knees. The hot sand could not be comfortable on his bare feet but he didn't seem to notice.

"Come on, you need to eat breakfast," he said gently.

"I'm not hungry," I responded miserably.

He grasped me by the shoulders and turned me, propelling me back to the bed-and-breakfast.

"Didn't ask if you were hungry, baby. Don't care. You need to eat something." I really didn't feel like eating, but damn. Reaver was being so nice to me, taking a genuine interest and was trying to take care of me. It was so unexpected and so... confusing.

"Why are you doing all of this?" I asked him again, as we trudged through the sand towards the B&B's back gate.

"Because I can," he said enigmatically. I sighed.

The dining table was set for six when we got inside and one other couple was already seated, newlyweds by the look of things. I took a seat beside Reaver and tried not to look at them. They were leaned in over a tourist map and talking excitedly about what to do first.

"Ah, there you are!" The hostess set a platter of pancakes on the table and I tried not to wince.

"Did you sleep okay?" It took me a moment to realize she was talking to me.

"What?" I asked and blinked, "Oh, yes!" I tried a smile and it felt so artificial I abandoned the effort pretty quickly. The hostess gave me a sympathetic look and turned to Reaver.

"Mr. Butler, may I please impose upon you a little and ask that you put on a shirt at the table?" she asked gently, not a single note of admonishment in her tone.

"Yeah, sure, and it's Reaver. Be right back." He got up and took the stairs two at a time. The couple across from where we were seated looked up from their map and after Reaver, puzzled.

"That's your husband?" the woman asked and I grimaced.

"No..." I said softly, but didn't expand on things. The hostess gave me another sympathetic look. Reaver came back to the table and I looked at him curiously.

"So your last name is Butler?" I asked him. He scowled at me, his blue eyes gone wintry and predatory. He didn't say anything, just started loading his plate.

"Wait until I tell Ashton," I said, and smiled a real smile this time, albeit impish. His eyes thawed just a little.

"You tell Sunshine, I can't promise I won't retaliate in horrible ways," he said and the way he said it had my toes curling under the table. Not in an 'oh my god that was so hot' way but more like an 'I feel like I'm five years old' almost exactly like the time I spilled almost all of my daddy's expensive cologne. Rich upper-crust family or not, I'd had to pick my own switch off one of the orchard trees that day. I grimaced at the memory. Not so much at the memories of the licks I'd taken but more that I disappointed my father. I turned my head and looked out the windows, my eyes misting with fresh tears.

I still didn't know what I'd done, but I felt fresh awful well up at the sharp memory of my mother's words the day before, that I had disappointed my daddy all over again by driving Andy away. Gentle fingertips grazed my chin and I looked up into steady blue eyes the color of the sky outside, as warm as I had ever seen Reaver's eyes get.

"Eat something. Try not to think about it right now," he urged gently, and the couple across from us exchanged looks. I nodded and wiped at my eyes and tried a bite of pancake.

"Eat some protein," Reaver ordered, and after I swallowed the pancake I took a bite of eggs. He smiled.

"I'm Marcy," the woman said and I smiled, but it was weak. She was tan, tall, and thin with brown hair and kind brown eyes. She wore an aqua-colored sundress that looked lovely on her figure.

"Hayden," I said and complimented her on her dress.

"Aww, thank you! This is my husband, Tom," she said.

"Nice to meet you," Tom said and took a bite of bacon. He was handsome, blonde-haired and brown-eyed and filled out his red and white striped rugby shirt like he might actually play.

"Reaver," Reaver said by way of introduction, and took a bite of food.

"I don't want to sound rude, but what kind of name is Reaver?" Marcy asked and she looked apologetic.

"Road name," he answered shortly and I elbowed him in the ribs. He put a hand on my knee and before I could figure out what he was up to he squeezed in a place that shot pain through the joint. I jumped and yelped and remembered him doing it on the bike. I slapped his shoulder and scowled at him. He grinned ferally at me.

"I take it the bike outside belongs to you then?" Tom asked.

"Yep," Reaver answered and eyed him speculatively.

"Oh, my God. Reaver, stop being rude!" I snapped and he looked at me. "I apologize, apparently social interaction isn't the caveman biker's strong suit," I said, getting thoroughly annoyed. Reaver barked a laugh.

"Yeah, what she said," he said grinning, "Sorry, man."

There was a lull in the conversation.

"What is it?" Marcy asked curiously.

"What's what?" Reaver asked.

"Your motorcycle. What is it?" she clarified. Reaver beamed at her.

"Baby is a 2011 Harley Davidson Heritage Softail Classic," he answered with pride.

"Oh, it is a Harley?" she asked.

"Yep."

"How come it doesn't have any logos on it?" she asked.

Reaver shrugged. "I laid her once doing some stupid shit. When I got her fixed, I got her skin repainted the glossy black and decided I liked her better with no logos, so I kept it." He smiled and gave a one-shouldered shrug and shoveled some more eggs into his mouth.

"Where you all from?" Tom asked. I opened my mouth but Reaver cut me off before I could answer.

"Around eight, nine hours north," he said. I looked at him. That could be anywhere! He gave me a cool warning look that said he had his reasons and I let it go. I drank some orange juice.

"I got to take this," he said and I looked at him. He pulled his cell from his pocket and sure enough it was buzzing. He answered it with, "What have you got, Prez?" as he got up from the table and wandered a short distance away.

"Yeeeah, got in towards nightfall, she was falling asleep on the back of the bike. Didn't even think about it, came riding onto their turf flying colors with no heads-up..." He sounded rueful; someone, I assumed Dragon, was speaking on the other end of the line.

"I figured I was seen when I saw you was callin'. They take it the wrong way?" he asked.

"Shit. Best get ahead of it before shit goes sideways. Who do I need to go talk to?"

"Seriously? Who the hell is a Kraken?" he asked, and Marcy looked up and answered his question.

"A Kraken is a mythical creature in seafarer lore. It was said when a ship was lost inexplicably at sea it was taken by the Kraken, a giant squid-like beast. All aboard were then committed to Davey Jones' locker. He was said to be a frightening figure, akin to death." She smiled; Reaver had turned around and was looking at her blankly. The voice buzzed out of his phone.

"Just got a lesson on what a Kraken is and who the fuck Davey Jones is. Kind of bad-ass, but still, who the hell names their MC after a giant squid?"

Dragon's familiar laugh boomed out of the cellphone. "Who the fuck cares, Reaver? Just make it right!" We heard it all the way over at the table, and I swallowed hard, feeling a little guilty.

I had an inkling about how dangerous and cutthroat the world of motorcycle gangs could be. A little over a year ago, I'd provided Ashton with a safe place to stay and helped with an alibi for Reaver and Ashton's man, Trigger, as well as some other Sacred Hearts members when Ashton's husband had ...committed suicide.

I looked at Reaver. It was easy to forget with his typically-easy smile and laughing manner that he'd killed at least one man that I knew of. Granted, that man had deserved it; I still couldn't shake the images of the bruises staining Ashton's slightly-smaller body. They'd made her look so frail.

Reaver's eyes were on mine when he said, "Got it, boss," and hung up the phone. I instantly felt lousy with guilt. Had him bringing me here gotten him in trouble? Would these people hurt him?

"Do you want me to go with you?" I asked.

"Not only no, but hell, no. I got it handled." He dropped into his seat to finish his breakfast. Marcy and Tom exchanged a look and looked Reaver over. He smiled his most disarming smile and reached for the bacon.

Ten minutes later he came down the stairs dressed to ride. I looked him over. He'd traded the shorts for jeans and a white tee shirt. His white Adidas were on and he left off his jacket and simply wore his vest, or cut, over the tee.

I studied the vest. On the left side it had a small patch that said 'Sacred Hearts,' blue on a white background, up on the breast; below that was a bar of a patch with our state on it. On the same side, a patch they called a 'rocker' splayed out along his ribs; the patch was dirty and white with big blue letters spaced evenly that said S.H.M.C. which, of course, stood for Sacred Hearts Motorcycle Club.

On the opposite side of the vest there were two small patches up on the breast that matched the left side in size and shape, except the top one read 'Reaver' and the bottom 'Treasurer'. Below them, neatly stitched on were six switchblade knife patches in a row. The one at the bottom was ragged, but markedly newer than the rest.

That one, I was pretty sure, belonged to Chadwick. Dray had one put on his vest around the same time, though his patch was of a modern-looking assault rifle. Either way, they meant the same thing: the men had killed for the club. Reaver had told me when I'd asked one night when we'd all been out drinking. The stillness that radiated from his eyes, which had iced over at the question, had left me breathless and frightened. My reaction had, strangely, warmed his expression with a very different but no less primal heat, and that, in some ways, had thrilled me, and in others, terrified me even more.

It was never boring around Reaver. That was for sure.

The rocker below the switchblade patches bore the geographical location of where his chapter was located and a square patch below that bore the letters SHFFSH, which meant 'Sacred Hearts Forever, Forever Sacred Hearts'.

He smoothed down the hair along the top of his skull between his eyes, and I sighed inwardly. After a year of knowing him I knew his tic for being agitated or nervous and that was it. He picked up his coffee cup and slugged the rest of it back. Marcy and Tom were staring at his vest unabashedly.

The back might have had have fewer patches, but, truth be told, I always found it to be more impressive. The top rocker proclaimed the name of the club loud and proud, white background, dark blue letters like the patches on the front.

Below it, though, set on a white circle, was a red human heart veined in blue. The heart was wreathed in silver barbed wire and the valves of the heart morphed from tissue to steel tailpipes which spewed fire, hovering over the image in a bastardized version of the Catholic's Sacred Heart of Jesus. Beside the disc, that the rough and tumble men called the club's 'colors', on the right was a square white patch that bore the letters MC in thick letters in the same blue script as the top and bottom rockers.

Of course, the bottom rocker on the back of the vest also declared where Reaver came from, all though I had seen some men bear the word 'Nomad' on their bottom rockers. I always thought it was sort of neat that the club's colors were red, white, and blue.

"C'mere," Reaver said and I went to him. He led me out front of the bed and breakfast, out of earshot of the other couple.

"Might come back with a bit of an ass-whoopin' on me, might not. Depends on my winning personality." He grinned and I felt myself frown.

"Why are you telling me this?" I asked softly.

"You look worried," he said.

"Of course, I'm worried," I said, and he touched a finger to my lips to hush me. My lip tingled from the touch and I closed my eyes.

"I also need you to know that whatever does happen, it's through no fault but my own." I opened my mouth to speak and he fixed me with a stern look.

"Stop," he said, and the one word was full of steel.

"No one's fault but my own," he repeated, and when I didn't speak, he dipped to meet my gaze with his.

"You get me?" he demanded. I searched his face and finally gave him what he wanted to hear.

"Fine, I get you," I said, and it sounded petulant even to me.

"Do what you wanna do, but stay close around here. I should be back by lunch; if I'm not, then by dinner. You got money?" he asked.

"Yes, but without you here, I don't have anywhere to go," I said.

"Bullshit, there's plenty inside walking distance," he said.

"You just told me to stay close to here!" I objected, and he grinned.

"Good, wanted to make sure you were listening to me." I glared up at him and suddenly felt way more tired than I ought to. Keeping up with Reaver's thought patterns was maddening on a good day, the half-cracked bastard.

"Be back soon," he said and went down the steps and got on his Harley. He put on his helmet, didn't bother with the chinstrap, and checked his phone before sliding it into an inside pocket of his vest.

He gave a wave and pulled out of the old brick circular drive and I watched the fade of his tail light as he went below the shade trees and out into the street.

"He's a character," Marcy commented dryly from behind me.

I made a noise of agreement and went back up to our room to lay down. I suddenly had a headache and no interest in social interaction of any kind. All I wanted was a nap.

3
———

R eaver...
I found the clubhouse for the Krakens fairly easily. The town wasn't that friggin' big and once I saw the bikes it wasn't that tough to deduce this was them. Their clubhouse wasn't much to speak of as far as clubhouses go. It was just a hole-in-the-wall bar that I was pretty sure more than one unsuspecting tourist had stumbled into. Likely they were made so uncomfortable with scowls and looks they quickly finished their drinks and GTFO'ed. Actually, looked like some fun times.

I parked out front, setting Baby apart from the rest of the bikes so as not to step on any toes, and took off my helmet. I smoothed my hair down and got off the bike, nodding to a prospect keeping watch over the bikes just outside the door. He gave me an unreadable look from behind the fiery orange-and-red lenses of his black-framed wraparound sunglasses.

"'Sup? Boss-man in?" I asked him.

The man was older, maybe late-forties, early-fifties with a salt-and-pepper handlebar mustache. He wore jeans and black chaps, and a black tee with the sleeves cut off. He was a beefy motherfucker, with his arms crossed over his broad chest and an ample beer gut. He had on a black do-rag of faded, thicker material, and screamed 'do not fuck with me' by the set of his body language alone. I found it odd that a dude who looked like he'd been there and fucking done that would be prospecting at his age.

He jerked his head behind him, indicating the man I sought could be found inside.

"Thanks," I said and barely kept my smartass in check. What I'd really wanted to say was 'Thanks, Silent Bob,' but I really didn't feel like taking a bunch of these m'fer's out. Pissin' off their MC, pissin' off my MC, and comin' back and putting a worry on Hayden wasn't on my list of priorities for the day. So I went into the dimly-lit interior of the bar and peeled off my own sunglasses, putting them around the back of my head for later. I was stopped by a hand on my chest just inside the door.

Oh, so they wanted to play it this way? Okay, I was cool. I assumed the position, arms out, feet shoulder-width apart, and submitted to their pat-down, and wouldn't you know it? They missed every single damn one of my blades – and I carried a lot of fucking hardware.

The Kraken's Sergeant-At-Arms stepped back and I got a good look at him. He was in his fifties too, long steel-gray hair curling past his shoulders, orange bandanna wide across his forehead. I glanced back down at his cut and noted his name... Tiny. Really? He was pretty beefy, like the dude outside, minus the beer gut. Kind of reminded me of the way Dragon was built, except this dude was white with blue eyes.

"This way," he said and I nodded, following him. Their cuts weren't half bad. The top rocker was a white background with black letters and read 'Kraken' of course, bottom rocker read the town's name, so they were pretty limited geographically but strong enough to hold their own against all comers. Good to know.

Their colors were actually pretty rockin'. It featured one of those big brown wooden ships with sails on the open waves, a giant orange octopus with big yellow discs for eyes wrapping strong tentacle arms around it. The ship was broken in two and going down. All in all, pretty bad-ass, and appropriate for the beachfront town.

Tiny led me back past some pool tables into a back area. I shit you not, an electric chair, probably a real one, sat against the wall on a raised dais. The president of the Kraken MC sat in it nonchalantly, a beer in one hand, a leg draped over one of the arms, his phone in his hand, thumb flying across the lower part of the screen as he texted away.

Dude was in his late-thirties, early-forties, built like me, which was to say, muscular without being bulky. He had long brown hair in a loose ponytail that curled down the back of his cut. It was going gray at the temples, as was his close-trimmed goatee. Smile lines bracketed his mouth and the corners of his eyes, but the look in the hazel orbs as they were trained on his phone said that the smiles he gave weren't always of the friendly variety. He glanced a sidelong look in my direction and hit the switch on his phone that made the screen go dark.

"So, you're him!" he said, straightening up and putting his worn motorcycle boots to the concrete below the chair. The heels made a sharp sound.

"I'm him," I agreed.

"So, what you doin' in my town?" he asked, and smiled at me, and I was right, not a friendly smile. I gave him one as good as I got, my smile going a little wider when I caught sight of his road name on his cut. Cutter. Ha, sweet! His eyes narrowed.

"What's so funny?" he asked.

"Pleased to meet you, Cutter, my name is Reaver," I held out my fist, Cutter smiled a genuine smile and glanced at my cut; his smile got wider just as mine had, and he reached out and bumped fists.

"All pleasantries aside," he said, "I'll ask you again. What are you doing in my town?"

I sighed and eyed his beer.

"Mind if I sit? This is a bit of a long story." Cutter looked me over and nodded grudgingly. I pulled a chair out from a table and dropped into it facing him on his fucked-up-but-cool-as-shit little throne on its raised slab of concrete.

"So, yesterday mornin', I'm at this wedding–" I start.

Cutter gave me this look and said, "This almost sounds like you're pullin' my leg and are about to tell me some dumb-assed joke!", and the look said it all: Don't waste my time or I'ma have your ass whooped. Seen that look around a million times before.

"Swear on a stack of bibles, may the big man strike me down where I sit, this is the story of why I'm in your town, flyin' Sacred Hearts colors like some noob jackass without checkin' in with you first," I said.

He nodded and said to someone over my shoulder. "Get him a beer." I nodded my thanks and got down to it.

"So I'm at this wedding and the happy couple is about to exchange vows… she goes through her bit, and is lookin' up at him all expectant-like and he drops a thermonuclear bomb in her lap. Says he don't want her. She ain't good enough for him."

Cutter let out a low whistle and a laugh. "How does that bring you to my town?"

"I've been in love with the girl getting married since the day I saw her a little over a year ago. I was standing there, along with all the other guests, while she was getting her heart ripped out. She'd picked this town for the honeymoon and the shit was all paid for and so I grabbed her up, popped smoke and brought her down here to get her out of the shitstorm." I leaned back and crossed my arms; a beer got handed to me and I took it and drank deeply, downing half the bottle in one go.

"So that was the little bit you came into town with, huh?" he asked.

"Yep. I should have stopped, should have phoned in or at least come in slick-backed. I was havin' some trouble, she was out-and-out exhausted and turning into a liability quick. Damn near fell asleep on the back of the bike twice at the tail-end of the ride. I was a moron comin' in flyin', but I swear to you, I'm not on a run and had every intention of comin' around for a sit-down like this one." I finished off the beer. Cutter looked me over and nodded slowly.

"I believe you, Reaver," he said finally, then added, "Welcome to Kraken territory." I felt myself relax some and nodded.

"Good to be here, brother. You got a sweet little town," I said.

"Whereabout you stayin'?" he asked. I told him the name of the B&B and he nodded.

"Good deal," he said.

"I promised Hayden, that's the girl, I'd try to be back in time for lunch, or barring that, dinner," I said and got to my feet.

"Right, well, I don't have a problem with you flyin' your colors now that we know what you're about. Shouldn't make a habit of comin' round other territories, though." He came down to my level and held out his hand; I clasped it.

"Trust me, man, I feel like a right dumbass," I said.

"Should come by later," he said.

"I wouldn't mind it," I said, grinning. "It's always nice hangin' with like-minded folk."

He grinned back. "Tell you what, give me your digits. We got a beach party tomorrow night, might be the thing Li'l Bit needs to get her mind off things. Like to see what you got when it comes to an edge." I nodded and gave him my number.

"Thanks for being understanding," I said, and I meant it.

"Your P. helped smooth things over before your arrival. Pretty much told me what you did; if you'd been lyin', I would've had your ass beat, then turned you over to your own crew." He smiled and again, it wasn't what you'd call friendly.

"Noted," I said, and smiled back.

"We'll see you tomorrow night, then." He let me go and I nodded.

So far, these guys weren't half bad. I rode back to the B&B feeling like at least one disaster had been averted, which wasn't too bad.

I slipped into the room Hayden and I were sharing and didn't feel so fucking good about myself anymore. She lay on her side in the pajamas I'd tossed the night before. Her hands were tucked beneath her cheek and she looked like a fucking angel when she slept. Unfortunately, it was one tired, wrung-out, and sorrowful-looking angel.

The girl looked pitiful. There were deep dark circles under each eye, her skin was pale, and with her deep, chestnut-brown hair, it made her look ghostly. Though she slept, it wasn't an easy one. A wrinkle of distress lay between her eyes. I bent, I couldn't help myself, and kissed her cheek lightly. I straightened and my tongue flicked out over my lips unbidden, and brought the salt of her dried tears with it.

She sucked in a tremulous deep breath and her beautiful, bright green eyes flicked open and snapped to me.

"You're back..." The sound of her voice was the sweetest thing I'd ever heard. I plucked at the sleeve of her pajamas.

"I threw these away," I said. She rolled her eyes at me.

"And I rescued them from the trash," she argued back.

"No dice. Take 'em off," I said, and smiled serenely.

"They're my pajamas, Reaver," she persisted, and I raised an eyebrow.

"I said take 'em off..." She looked at me and tried to change the subject.

"How did it go?" she asked.

"Got us invited to a beach party tomorrow night," I said, and it was her turn to arch one delicate, dark brow.

"I see. So your winning personality won out this time, huh?" she said and I laughed softly.

"I'm waiting, Hayden," I said.

"Well, you're going to be waiting a long time," she quipped and stuck her tongue out at me and I sailed right over the limits of my self-control. I kicked off my shoes and let my cut fall to the floor. Yeah, the floor, the motherfucking floor, my cut, which we treated better than our country's flag. I bounded onto the bed and trapped her between my knees.

My cock was straining against my jeans but I didn't want that, not yet. No, I couldn't help myself – I wanted her fear. Her eyes flashed wide and she put up her hands and I easily captured both her wrists in one of my hands and pinned them both to the bed up over her head.

"Reaver! What are you doing?" she asked, her voice high and breathy with panic, and I drank it in like fine wine, letting it soak into every one of my senses. Her heart beat rapidly inside the cage of her ribs, so hard, so fast, like a little rabbit's, fluttering against the insides of my thighs through the thick denim there.

I looked down on her impersonally. All personality, all feeling bled from my eyes, my features slack and expressionless and I met her eyes with those of my stone-cold killer's. Her fear ratcheted up a notch and she bucked beneath me.

"Shhhh," I soothed and it had the opposite effect of the intent of the noise, just like I knew it would. She gasped and went very still when I showed her what I had in my other hand.

"I'm a fucked-up individual, Hayden," I said and waited for a moment. "Do you believe me?" I asked her.

"Yes and no," she said softly, her eyes glued to the black and silver handle of the switchblade in my hand. Her answer perplexed me and would bear further scrutiny later, but right now I wanted to play. I needed to play.

"Do you trust me, Hayden?" I asked, and my voice was cold and deep. I expected her to say no, to struggle, to begin to cry, but again she surprised me.

She swallowed hard, her expression became resolute, and she told me, unequivocally, "Yes."

It was all over her face, in the deepest facets of her eyes, holy fucking shit... She was going to let me do whatever I wanted. I had to test my limits with her. I always had to test my fucking limits... I flicked the switch and the sharp blade came free of the knife's handle. Hayden sucked in a breath as sharp as the blade, and went very, very still. She trusted me, sure, but that didn't keep her from being afraid, and I lapped that shit up.

"I don't like these pajamas," I told her and snagged the front with the tip of my blade. She looked down her body at me and I carefully punched a hole in the pink cotton. I ran the knife tip along the inside of the material as far as I could go. Up the chest, all the way up the arm, the material parted smoothly before the blade, gaping behind it to give me glimpses of her silky smooth skin.

Hayden moaned, she mother-fucking –moaned–, and I nearly jizzed in my fucking pants from the sound. Her breast showed through the gaping material, the nipple dusky, a deeper nude against her creamy skin and I wanted so badly to take it into my mouth and turn that little moan into something deeper, throatier... decadent-sweet, a sound I could suck on and have melt on my tongue like fine chocolate.

I captured her eyes with my own and gave her a dark, wickedly sinful smile and cut the rest of the ugly-ass pajama set off her lithe and sexy body. She glistened with moisture at the apex of her thighs and I wanted to taste her, finger her and tease her into an orgasm, bury myself balls deep inside of her but I did none of those things. Instead I folded the blade back into its hilt. I relinquished her wrists and backed off both her and the bed abruptly, pulling myself back from the brink, but just barely.

My breath came hot and heavy, and I swept her beautiful body with my eyes and wrestled the beast back into its cage. She covered her chest with her arms and curled up, hiding her beautiful pussy with its barely-there wisp of hair from my sight.

"I'm... I..." I was sorry, but not in the way she would think. I couldn't bring myself to say it out loud. I didn't want her to think I didn't want her because, holy motherfucking balls, I wanted her so damn bad it felt like my nuts were in a vice right now.

"I'll buy you something different, baby, I promise," I said, and like a jackass, I bolted, leaving the door swinging wide behind me. I needed distance; I needed away from her right now, because what I just did was so not cool, not after yesterday, not with the hurt that had been put on her.

Holy fucking shit, what the fuck did I just do?

I needed to get a grip and fast.

4

Hayden...

I didn't know what the hell that was, but I had never been so aroused, or so shaken, in my life. I stared wide-eyed at the open bedroom door that Reaver had just disappeared through, stunned by what had just transpired. I felt so many things all at once and I shook as I got off the bed, leaving the ruin of my pajamas behind on the expensive sheets. I padded barefoot and on shaky legs to the door and shut it before any of the other guests happened by.

What was that? What the hell was I feeling? I took several deep breaths.

I didn't understand.

Ashton had told me about the time she had let Trigger and Reaver share her, about how gentle, patient, and amazing both men had been and I confess, I had listened with rapt attention. I'd daydreamed about it, had even fantasized about it on more than one occasion during Andy's long absences while he was away on business.

I colored faintly. When I say I had fantasized about it, I didn't mean about Trigger. Never about him. When I closed my eyes it was always Reaver I saw in my fantasies, in my dreams... I admit, shamefully so, I had even pictured Reaver behind my closed eyelids a time or two when it had been Andy sucking on my neck, moving inside me.

I scrubbed my face with my hands as tears welled. Not because I was upset about what happened or how I'd just been treated... the fact that what had just happened didn't bother me was a conundrum for another time. No, what bothered me was that he had left. That Reaver didn't stay with me.

What was I doing so wrong that I sent every man who came to my bed running, practically screaming, for the hills?

Well, by god, I aimed to find out and I would be damned if I would take any vague half-truths from Mr. Butler. I yanked on the pair of shorts from earlier and didn't even bother with underwear. I pulled the tee over my head, tossed the ruined scraps of cotton in the trash and shrugged my feet into my flip-flops, striding purposefully for the door.

The footwear made an angry slapping sound against the soles of my feet as I strode quickly to the back door and bounced lightly down the back steps. I found Reaver just the other side of the B&B's back gate; his head was bowed, his long-fingered hand palming the back of his neck.

"Hayden I am so sor..." the words died in his throat when he caught sight of the angry tears glistening in my eyes.

"Why did you stop?" I demanded and he looked taken aback. "What is it, Reaver? Huh? What is so wrong with me?" I demanded and my voice broke on a devastated, angry, pain-filled sob.

"No, baby, no... no no no no no," he repeated and he came at me. I took a violent step back, bogged down in the soft sand and fell on my ass. That was it. My humiliation was complete. I cried like I have never cried in my life before and Reaver's strong arms went around me and pulled me unceremoniously into his lap.

"I am such a fucking failure," he crooned above me.

"I don't understand. Why?" I demanded.

"Fuck, Hayden. I've made such a giant mess of things, I don't even know where to begin!" he said and let out the most frustrated sound I've ever heard come out of someone.

"I don't understand..." I said again, and he tipped my face up to look at him and all I saw in his eyes was gentleness and a deep-seated hurt.

"Baby, I've loved you from the first moment I saw you. All I've ever wanted since that day was to see you happy and I thought..." He squeezed his eyes shut and bowed his head, turning his head to the side. I put my hands on either side of his face and forced him around to look at me.

"Tell me," I demanded, because I really, really needed to hear this. My soul was thirsty for it.

"I thought you were better off without me. I thought you were better off with him and as time wore on I tried so hard to let it the fuck go but I just wanted you more and more and what that fucker was doing to you... The fucking neglect, benign at first, maybe... but what he did to you yesterday, don't you understand?" He looked at me and the desperation in his clear, wintry blue eyes was almost too much to bear.

"I've killed men for a lot less, I've killed them for a lot more... I'm one seriously-twisted fuck and you deserve so much better than the likes of me!" he said harshly, when it was clear to him I wasn't getting it.

"All I wanted to do was bring you out here to protect you, but then I go and do that, and shit, Hayden, I just don't know if I can protect you from the monster inside of me." He tucked my head under his chin and held me, rocking me, I think, as much to comfort himself as to comfort me.

This was the man that Ashton had described to me. The one I fantasized about but, I think, a few minutes ago I had learned there were other things to fantasize about. A delicious shiver went up my spine and he held me tighter.

"So you don't think I'm repulsive?" I asked weakly. I felt pathetically insecure but I think I had a pretty good reason to be.

"Baby, you're more addictive to me than smack," he said.

I knew that about him already, that he'd had a heroin addiction. It was how he and Trigger had met. Both of them addicted. Both of them desperate for something else, something different. Trigger had craved the stability, the structure, of a brotherhood, one like he'd had in the military. It was his idea to replace the military with the motorcycle club. He had convinced Reaver to join with him.

The club had helped them both get clean and they'd been inseparable, best friends, ever since, despite their nine- or ten-year age difference. Reaver even wore Trigger's dog-tags in among the myriad of other necklaces and charms around his neck.

"You just had happen to you what happened, and here I am, losing my shit, doing things I have no fucking right to be doing... I'm your friend before anything else, Hayden. I don't want to fuck that up. I want to keep you in my life." I looked up sharply, and sure enough, his deep blue eyes were welling with tears.

"Please, tell me I did not just fuck that up?" he said and the begging, the pleading in his voice damned near broke my heart.

"No. No, you didn't, I promise," I said hugging him, crushing myself to him. "I promise, we're okay," I said and my voice shook because, honestly, the thought of no more Reaver in my life made me want to wade out into the surf and drown myself.

We stayed like that, for how long I don't know, but eventually he stood up with me cradled in his arms and I let him.

"Where are we going?" I asked softly.

"We're going to get cleaned up, and then I'm taking you to dinner, if that's okay?" I nodded and looked at him.

"I'd like that, and maybe look around town?" I suggested timidly.

"Sounds good," he said.

"Reaver?" I asked after a long silence; he stopped mid-stride across the backyard to the B&B.

"Yeah, Doll?" he asked me.

"Am I completely fucked up... you know... for liking what you did in there?"

He sucked in a breath and shuddered, closing his eyes.

"No, Doll. No, you're not, but can we please not talk about it for a while?" he asked.

"Sure, yeah! No, I get it." I shook my head as if clearing it. "Too soon," I said and he nodded and set me on my feet on the back porch.

"Yeah, too soon," he agreed.

We went inside and cleaned up, and by cleaned up, I mean I hopped in the shower and rinsed off the sand and found some freaking underwear and redressed. When I came out of the bathroom, Reaver looked perfect. His boots were back on and his cut was off the floor and back on his body. I gave him a brave smile and he smiled back.

"Not sure I like you riding in shorts and a tee shirt," he said, frowning. I pulled my ID and my American Express credit card out of my wallet and added it to the cash in my back pocket. I shrugged.

"Yolo," I said.

"Yo-low? What the fuck is that?" he asked, and his expression was priceless. I laughed and spelled it out.

"Y-O-L-O. It stands for You Only Live Once," I explained. He grinned and his arm snapped out and hooked around my neck and shoulders. He pulled me into his side and hugged me, laughing, and this felt like the old Reaver, the Reaver and me that were friends all those times Andy was out of town and I was blessed enough to hang with Ashton and the MC, even if I did sometimes feel set apart or branded as 'other.'

We went out and down the stairs, locking up the room behind us.

"What was wrong with those pajamas, anyway?" I asked him as we went out the front door. I couldn't help thinking about it. He raised an eyebrow and the small teardrop tattoo by his eye rippled with the movement.

"Baby, you have a bangin' body. Those were old-man pajamas," he said.

"They were pink!" I said.

"They were a shirt-and-pant set that grandpas wear as they shuffle in those weird half- slipper things down the nursing-home hallway," he declared and got onto his bike, Baby.

I got up behind him and he handed me the half-helmet. I put it on and smiled. I'd never ridden with anyone else. Just Reaver. He didn't know it, but he was the only one I trusted with my safety enough to get on the back of a motorcycle with. I'm sure there were others in the MC that were trustworthy enough and that I would be safe enough with, but Reaver was the only one I felt safe with.

"What you thinking about so hard back there?" he asked.

"Nothing!" I lied.

"Yeah. Okay," he said, like he didn't believe me, and started up the bike.

The air was hot and heavy outside and felt delicious moving against my skin. Reaver rode easy, obeying all the speed limits, which, predictably in a small tourist town, were slower than molasses in January. I looked around, for the first time since getting here, through the polarized lenses of my sunglasses.

"What sounds good?" he called over the bike's engine and I realized that, finally, I was hungry.

"Fish and chips!" I called back and he nodded once. We lived in a landlocked state, so when in a coastal town, you got your sea fish while the getting was good. It was nothing but trout and catfish back home.

He backed his bike next to a line of them outside a beachfront bar. There was a sandwich board out front proclaiming the best fish and chips in town. We'd passed another bar proclaiming they had the best drinks in town and the second-best fish and chips. There had been an arrow on their sandwich board pointing the way to the best. This bar proclaimed the second-best drinks in town and the best fish and chips, with an arrow pointing back to the bar we'd just passed for the best drinks. It was funny, and Reaver and I shared in some laughter over the signs. Way to help each other out!

"You good?" he asked, after I fussed over my hair a bit in the side-view mirror.

"I need some gel," I said, and made a face.

"We'll stop and get you some," he said, and steered me in the direction of the bar.

It was crowded inside, but open and airy. The tang of frying fish filled the air and my stomach rumbled. We waited and were seated at a four-person booth. I didn't miss the curious stares of a lot of the natives when Reaver walked past in his cut. I chewed my bottom lip thoughtfully and sat down.

We ordered drinks; I asked for something tropical and fruity while Reaver just got a beer. We smiled at each other across the well-worn table, and it was a little bit awkward, but not too bad.

"So, when you planned this trip what did you have in mind?" he asked over the din of the bar.

"A lot of things, actually," I told him, sipping my drink, which was frosty, perfect, and tasted like coconut.

"Gonna have to elaborate, Doll," he said and winked. I smiled at him.

"I wanted to try snorkeling —" he nodded. "And I heard there's a lighthouse up the coast a little ways that's supposed to be haunted. I wanted to see that!" I said and he raised his eyebrows.

"You like a good ghost story?" he asked and I nodded.

"There's, just, something so beautiful about them you know? Everyone's story is different. I feel a bit sorry for them, being trapped like that... Unable to let go. There something hauntingly sweet about the lighthouse ghost." He laughed at me.

"What?" I asked.

"You just described a ghost as 'hauntingly sweet,' Doll," he said dryly, and took a sip of his beer.

"So?" I asked.

"So it's a ghost! Doesn't that mean, by definition, that it's going to be haunting?" I blinked at him, well, of course, he was right, but my attention was suddenly drawn to the wall of black beside our table. I looked up at two men dressed in leather.

"Aren't you hot?" I blurted, without thinking. The two men laughed and Reaver stood up and stuck out his hand to one of them. He had long, medium-brown hair pulled back into a ponytail, and a goatee. He was going slightly gray at the temples and in his facial hair but he seemed handsome enough. His brown eyes almost perfectly matched his hair in color and it was sort of striking. He smiled down at me while he shook Reaver's hand.

"Hayden, this is Cutter, president of the Kraken motorcycle club. Sorry, I haven't met you." Reaver held out his hand to the other man. I looked over to him.

He stood slightly taller than Reaver and Cutter, so to me, he was pretty much a giant. Reaver was six-foot-three to my five-foot-three, but then, I've been petite all my life so I was pretty much used to it.

He was a blond, his hair so light and cut so short it gave the illusion that it was dandelion fluff rather than hair. His eyes were just as pale, so clear and so light it was as if you looked into his soul through a slightly dirty window pane.

"Pyro," he said and shook Reaver's hand.

"You weren't kidding about those eyes," Cutter said, his gaze fixed on me.

"You should see my friend, Ashton's," I said, "Here, I'll show you," and I reached for my phone – that was no longer there. "Oh, wait. I can't, because Reaver threw my phone in the ocean." I scowled at Reaver who grinned bigger at me.

"Relax, Doll. I told you I'd buy you a new one," he told me, and I felt my lips twist in a wry grin.

"Do I even wanna know why you threw the woman's phone in the ocean?" Cutter asked, grinning. Pyro didn't look like he ever smiled.

"No," I said, my smile fading. Reaver looked me over and smoothed down his hair. An uncomfortable silence ensued.

"I'm sorry that happened to you," Cutter said, and I looked sharply up at Reaver, my expression likely murderous.

"Had to tell him why I was on his turf, baby," Reaver said and had the grace to look apologetic. I nodded solemnly and sucked down some of my drink.

"Mind if we join you?" Cutter asked. Reaver looked at me and I nodded softly. Cutter gave me a megawatt smile and slid into the booth beside me before Reaver could or before I could get up and switch to Reaver's side of the table.

Reaver didn't look happy about it, and I stilled him with a slight smile. I believed in him, despite his repeatedly telling me he wasn't worth it.

"You good?" he asked me anyway.

"I'm good," I said, as our waitress returned and set down our food. Pyro and Cutter placed their orders while Reaver and I began to eat. Cutter looked over his shoulder and down at me and I tried not to blush.

"You want to call Sunshine?" Reaver asked. I looked up.

"Can I?" I asked, then looked at the two other men, "Would you mind?" I asked.

"Not at all!" Cutter said and smiled down at me. Pyro gave me a chin lift.

Reaver slid his phone across the table at me and I picked it up. He smiled and I hit the switch.

"Fifty-one fifty. She's listed at 'Trigger's girl'. Put it on speaker," he said and I tapped in the numbers. Five one five zero. I scrolled through and dialed the number. Ashton's smiling face filled the screen. Cutter gave a low whistle.

"Told you," I said and put it on speaker.

"Reaver, I swear to god! Why haven't you called me?" Her lyrical voice floated out of the phone.

"Well, I would have called you by now, but he threw my phone into the ocean!" I said.

"Oh, my God, Hayden! How are you doing?" she asked. I heard Trigger's low rumble of a voice ask a question but I couldn't make it out.

"Trigger wants to know if Reaver pitched your phone because you were talking to the douche-canoe," Ashton said.

"Yeah!" Reaver called out.

"Oh, in that case, I'll buy you a new one. You know I'm good for it," she said. I made an incredulous noise.

"You know, you were the sweetest thing before these two barbarians got a hold of you!" I cried, joking. I heard kissing.

"Hey, you should try these two barbarians. I might be willing to share my Viking." There was a shriek and a giggle and I felt my face fall. I wondered for a brief second if I would ever have what Ashton had with Trig. My eyes met Reaver's and his gaze was unreadable.

"Hayden?" Ashton asked.

"Yeah, I'm here," I said, but my voice trembled, giving me away.

"Awww, honey, I'm sorry! Reaver, you take care of her!" Ashton called.

"On it, babes. See you when I get home," Reaver said.

"Keep the shiny side up brother!" Trigger called out, and Reaver ended the call. I closed my eyes but it was too late. The meltdown had started.

"Aw, sweetheart," I heard from my side and I closed my eyes and dragged in a breath, then another and another but I suddenly felt like I couldn't get enough air.

"Excuse me," I heard Reaver say and suddenly the unfamiliar presence at my side was replaced with Reaver's somewhat-familiar one.

"I'm sorry! I'm sorry! I'm sorry!" I repeated and the tears flowed. I didn't know what was happening, I couldn't breathe and my pulse raced and I felt hot and shaky.

"Breathe, Baby Doll, breathe for me." Reaver captured my face between his hands.

"What's wrong?" he asked and his voice was calm.

"We had everything planned," I keened. "School, work, when the time was right married, kids... all of it... and he just decided all of a sudden I wasn't good enough for any of it! It hurts!" I cried. "It just hurts so damned much that he never loved me! Every time he said it, every time he looked me in the eye, every time he kissed me, he was lying! It was all lies and he let me get up in front of all those people before he told me so!" I was talking a hundred miles an hour and I couldn't get enough air. Reaver crushed me to his chest and held me tight.

"Shhhh, baby, it's okay. Shhhh," he said.

"It's not okay! What's happening to me? What's wrong with me?" I cried, but it was muffled by his chest.

"You're having a panic attack, babes, but it's okay. Okay? It's okay. I'm here." He held me tight.

"But it's not okay!" I cried and sobbed. Reaver pulled back and looked me in the eye.

"What'd I tell you on the beach? Hmm?" he asked me and his angry tone made my brain scramble for the answer. I didn't want to disappoint him, too... not like Andy, not like my mother.

"You said you wanted me to be happy," I said.

"What else?"

"That you wanted to protect me."

"Uh-huh, and what else?"

"That I was more addictive than heroin?" I felt like I was failing him, I wasn't giving him the right answer.

"Okay, close, what else, baby? What else did I tell you?"

"That you loved me from the first time you saw me..." I said – and the world snapped back into place.

"Bingo. And I'm not about to stop now." He smiled at me and pulled me tight against him. I closed my eyes.

"I really don't deserve you," I said miserably.

"Naw, babe, you deserve much better," he said.

"I dunno, you seem like an all-right guy to me." Cutter said from across the table, a serene little smile on his lips.

I felt myself blush to the very roots of my hair.

"S'okay, Li'l Bit. You've had a real shitty couple of days, I get that," he said.

"Uh, thank you," I said. Pyro had disappeared. The rest of the bar seemed oblivious to my little melodrama.

"He went out to smoke. He can't handle emotional women. Especially pretty ones," he explained and smiled thinly. That so did not make me feel any better. I felt like such an asshole.

"Surprised you held it in this long," Reaver said and popped a fry from his plate into his mouth, chewing thoughtfully.

"I feel like I've completely lost my mind..." I said, dully.

Cutter pushed my drink at me.

"Drink up, numb it out for now. You look like you could use it," he said dryly.

"I am so sorry..." I started.

"Don't be," he said, and Pyro returned.

"Where you guys live?" he asked us. I answered him without even thinking. Reaver didn't seem bothered by it, though. Pyro mulled it over, nodding to himself.

"Want me to kill him?" he asked and my green eyes got really wide. Reaver went really still and quiet beside me.

"I was only kidding!" The blond man put his hands up. I blushed faintly.

"Reaver didn't earn those switchblade patches playing checkers," Cutter said quietly. Pyro's eyes got wide.

"Missed that," he stated mildly.

I shook as if waking from a bad dream and drank down more of my sweet drink. Pyro got up again and returned with another and set it down in front of me.

"On me," he said, and I smiled across the table at him.

"So, what do you do?" Cutter asked me and the conversation turned to much more low-key, much more normal things.

It turned out that Reaver did drywall installation and general construction. I hadn't known that and that had made me think about it, I mean really think about it, and I was surprised to realize that after more than a year of knowing him, I didn't know very much about Reaver at all. I mean he was attractive, in that bad boy sort of way that made my heart pick up pace whenever I looked at him. I knew he worked out regularly at the YMCA because that's where I'd met him.

I knew that he was in the Sacred Hearts motorcycle club and I knew he was, um, sexually adventurous, from what Ashton told me. I knew he used to be addicted to heroin and how he'd gotten away from it. I knew he liked vanilla over the taste of chocolate and his favorite beer was an IPA. I knew he liked knives and abhorred guns. He said that guns were too impersonal.

I listened politely to Cutter, who was a maritime salvage operator, whatever that meant, and thought to myself that, okay, maybe I did know a few more things than I thought I did about Reaver. Still, how did you know someone for a year and more and not know what they did for a living?

"What are you thinking about so hard over there, Li'l Bit?" Cutter asked me and I started, my train of thought came to a violent and sudden end.

"I didn't know what you did for a living," I said, addressing Reaver.

"Didn't?" he asked, surprised.

I shook my head and his mouth turned down at the corners.

"Meh, it's a job... a way to pay the bills. Guess I never thought about it," he said.

"I just thought it strange that I've known you over a year and yet never knew what you did for a living... I don't know. I guess maybe I was closed-off? So busy planning my wedding and things I just never..." It was incredibly sad and more than a little embarrassing that I didn't know. God, what kind of self-absorbed...

"Don't," Reaver said softly, and broke me out of the familiar downwards spiral of thought I'd been about to go down. I dashed at my eyes.

"I should have been a better friend. Taken some interest, not been such a self-absorbed..." His clear blue eyes went cold as winter's ice.

"I said, don't," he said, and I swallowed. I felt confused and Cutter finally helped me out.

"Don't talk bad about yourself, girl. Psychoanalyze yourself later. Right now you're supposed to be having a good time," he said.

"Was I?" I asked, bewildered.

"Yep," all three of them chorused.

"What does a maritime salvage operator do?" I asked Cutter, turning the conversation away from me.

"Well, for right now I'm a little sidelined by injury, so I spend most of my time at the helm and at the radio, but we generally go out and tow disabled boats and ships back to shore, or raise vessels that have sunk off the bottom," he said and gave a stretch.

"It's fun," Pyro said with a grin.

"Pyro, here, is on my crew," Cutter smiled.

"Sounds like fun," Reaver said.

"Can be. Can also be a real pain in the ass..." Cutter went on to tell us about how there were a lot of maritime salvage operations in the area and how fierce the competition could be. Apparently it was also a really expensive operation to run.

Reaver and I listened and I polished off my second drink. The fish and chips had been amazing, and I was full and, between the large meal and the alcohol, growing sleepy. When there was a lull in the conversation, I poked Reaver in the ribs.

"You still owe me something to sleep in."

He smiled down at me and said, "So I do."

"Oh, this I gotta hear," Cutter said, and folded his hands behind his head, leaning back in the booth.

"Nope. Not your business," I said and shook my head. Reaver smiled and squeezed my knee.

"Any place around here sell sleepwear?" Reaver asked.

"My girl clerks at a boutique up the street. Three blocks down. Might have what you're looking for," Pyro suggested.

Reaver scooted out of the booth and I followed. Cutter's brown eyes followed my movements.

"What'd you want to do while you were in town?" he asked before we could get away.

"She wanted to try snorkeling, and check out some haunted light-house up the coast," Reaver said. Cutter grinned broadly.

"Tell you what, come by the marina around four tomorrow, I'd be happy to take you out for it. I have all the equipment. We can do it from the beach the party is gonna be at. You guys can hit the light-house early in the day." Reaver checked with me with a look and I nodded. It sounded good to me.

"Okay," Reaver said. They all traded numbers and Reaver and I left, following Pyro's directions up the street to his girl's boutique. It was still midafternoon so we had time to look around before things started to close. I needed to walk off our heavy meal and sober up some before trying to ride anyways.

Sultry Nights was the name of the shop and I blinked in surprise when we walked in. I mean, I don't know what I expected, but this was a straight-up sex-shop! It had nightgowns and some of them were beautiful and classy but still sexy, which may be what Reaver had in mind. I looked up at him dubiously, but he was smiling at what was on offer. He plucked something purple and satin off a rack and handed it to me.

I eyed him critically, then looked at it and decided that, holy cow, it wasn't bad. It had wide straps of the same material as the body that tapered down where it attached to the gown itself. The gown was shorter than anything I would normally wear. I mean, I was raised to be modest, by my mother at least. My father had tried to instill his sense of adventure into his only child.

I remembered a time I had tried a sexy teddy on Andy, and he'd told me not to be crude, that I was better than that and to have some modesty. I chewed my bottom lip while I looked over the satin night-gown in my hand. It was short, yes, but it was also solid satin; the whole thing. There were no lace accents, just sleek shiny material, and it covered everything. My gaze flicked to Reaver, whose expression was shuttered as he watched me, assessing, calculating, like the way you look at the scattered pieces of a jigsaw puzzle searching for the next piece to bring more of the image together into a cohesive whole.

"What?" I asked.

"That one, I figured, would make you comfortable. So I'll get that one for you, but the next one is for me, Doll," he said, and the way he said it made me shiver.

"I only need one," I said softly.

"It was a two-piece pajama set," he said simply.

"So?"

"So I'm going to get one for me. Something I want, and you're going to save it for when you want to wear it for me. You get me?" he asked.

I felt my brows wrinkle in confusion.

"I'm not sure I do," I said honestly.

"I'll explain it later," he said with one of his cryptic smiles and held out his hand for the nightgown in mine. I handed it to him and he nodded, jerking his head towards the door.

"I'll be right out," he said with an enigmatic smile. I eyed him with mistrust and suspicion but I left the little shop and went next door.

'Next door' was a jewelry shop, but it had some unique offerings. I slipped into the air-conditioned coolness, relieved after the stifling heat and crushing humidity of outside. I stared into the case at what had caught my attention.

"You like?" the shop owner, a balding man with leathery brown skin and an ample spare tire around his middle asked. He was decidedly from not-America though I wouldn't hazard a guess as to his country of origin. He could be African, he could be Middle Eastern, I just didn't know.

"Where is it from?" I asked.

"Ah, that is a Spanish four-Reales coin, set in fourteen-karat white gold," he said.

"A real Spanish coin?" I asked, fascinated.

"Yes, it was salvaged off of the São José. Went down off the coast of Mozambique in 1622." I looked at him.

"How much?" I asked. There was something beautiful about the misshapen coin; it was set with a cross but so worn around its edges that the towers and lions set in the four quadrants made by the cross were nearly indistinguishable. I couldn't even tell you what was on the back of the coin.

"Ah, you cannot afford," he said looking me over. I blinked at him. Rude!

"How much?" I repeated.

"One thousand, two hundred and fifty dollars," he said. Reaver spied me through the shop window and I smiled faintly. He came in, and the man frowned.

"No, you leave! You leave now!" he told Reaver, and I was really stunned by his audacity.

"Relax!" Reaver said, putting up his hands.

"He's with me!" I said, over the older man's protests that the biker get out of his shop.

"Then you leave, too!" he shouted.

"But I want to buy the necklace!" I said and he scoffed.

"You cannot afford! Out! You leave–" he stopped when I held up my black AmEx.

"Yes. I *can* afford it and I want to buy it," I said calmly. Reaver looked at me and grinned, a bit of pride shining in his true-blue eyes. The man went to the window and got the pendant down and took the card from my hand. He wrapped the pendant carefully and rang me up.

"I don't spend my daddy's money often," I muttered, and Reaver grinned.

"You don't have to justify yourself to me, babe. You buying it because you want it that bad, or to shut the old man up?" he asked me.

"I think, a little bit of both," I said honestly, and signed the receipt. The man had been eyeing me suspiciously while he'd slid the card, like he didn't expect it to go through. Then he looked at the back and saw my picture on it and his eyebrows went up.

"Thank you, and let that be a lesson to you!" I said and took the little bag from him. He stared after us, wide-eyed, as we left his shop.

"What exactly did you get?" Reaver asked. I opened the box and showed him, and he gave a low whistle.

"That looks both old and expensive," he commented.

"I like old things." I shrugged a shoulder. "It's about the only thing my mother and I have in common. Antiques," I said.

Reaver snorted as I put my little prize away.

"Your mother *is* an antique," he said. I finally took a look at the rather large bag in his hand.

"What did you get?" I asked. Whatever it was, it was a lot bigger than two nightgowns.

"Someday I'll show ya. If you're really, really nice to me." He smiled and I laughed. That was the Reaver I knew and loved, a joker and incurable flirt.

"Ready to go back?" he asked.

"Yes, but not to turn in, it's too early for that. I thought it might be nice to take a walk on the beach."

"Sounds good," he said as we walked back to his bike.

"Can you hold these without peeking?" he asked.

"I can't make any promises." He fixed me with a cold look and I felt about three inches tall, like the biggest disappointment in the world.

"I won't look. I promise." The words were out of my mouth and I wasn't at all surprised that I meant them. He smiled at me and ruffled my hair and I rolled my eyes and scoffed.

"You're going to have to teach me that trick!" I complained.

"Mmm, nope. All mine," he said and I smiled. "C'mon, Doll." He held out the helmet and we made the ride back to the bed and breakfast.

I went into the bathroom and changed into my bikini. It was white, and I slid my olive green shorts back on over the bottoms. I threw on a light tan crocheted cover-up on and let it hang off my shoulders. Really, I just wanted to have it in case the wind coming off the water got too cool.

Reaver met me out in the bedroom, a pair of cut-off green camouflage pants slung low on his hips. I realized he had tattoos along his hip flexors, the very top of them peeking above the waistband of the low-slung pants.

His hands went to the fly and he started to undo it. My eyes snapped up to his face, alarmed. He gave me the most devil-may-care grin and said, "I'll show you mine if you show me yours..."

I scowled at him. "One, I don't have any tattoos, and two, you've already seen mine," I told him. His smile faded around the edges.

"Trust me, baby, I'm not going to forget it so long as I live, either. Still happy to show you mine." His smile lit back up and I smiled back.

"Only if I can put it in my mouth," I said, taking a step towards him. I thought maybe I could catch him off guard, that maybe, just maybe, I could beat him at his own game. No dice. His expression turned frosty and imperious and he sucked in a breath. I felt my smile fade around the edges and he asked me in a too-quiet voice,

"Do you want that? Because I really, really want that," he said. I opened my mouth to reply and the look in his eyes stilled me. "I want you to think about it, baby, really think about what you're going to say, because once you say it, there aren't any take-backs," he said, and I felt a little thrill of fear. Reaver played for keeps. I knew that, but it was easy to lose sight of the forest for the trees, and Reaver was like that, too.

It was easy to forget how intense he was under his laughing affectation. Reaver ran deeper than any man I'd ever known. He was complex, and layer after layer of mystery. I closed my mouth and looked at him solemnly.

"I don't know what I want," I told him and it was the truth. He nodded.

"That's okay, too," he said.

"Right now, I want to go for a walk. Feel the sun on my skin..." I said and he smiled, just like that, the intensity of a moment before whisked away as if it had never been. He held out his hand and I tentatively took it. We went out the door and down the stairs, out to the beach. The sand was unbearably hot on my feet at first, but then I grew used to it.

We walked along the water's edge, bare feet cooled by the warm surf. Reaver held my hand and I held his with both of mine. We were quiet, soaking in the beauty and serenity. Letting the water pull the stress from just... everything... out to sea.

"How can you love me? I mean, how do you know?" I asked and he looked down at me. He stopped for a second and considered me, and then continued our walk.

"The moment I saw you it was... I don't know... It was electric. I had to know you. I just knew." He smoothed his hair down over his forehead, head bowed. "I don't know how to describe it. You'll just have to trust me." He looked at me and stopped our stroll. "Do you?" he asked me.

"Do I trust you?" I asked, a smile curving my lips.

"Yeah."

"You know I do," I said, my tone slightly chiding.

"Why?" he asked me.

"I don't know, I just... I just feel like I can," I said, and tilted my face up to his. I cocked my head to the side and considered him.

"Will you talk to me?" I asked.

"About what?" he asked.

"Anything. Everything. About yourself... I feel like I hardly know anything about you but you dropped everything for me. Brought me here... who does that?" I asked.

He shrugged and started us walking again, and was silent for a long time.

"I..." he stopped and I waited patiently for him to start again.

"Hayden, baby, you've got to understand I'm a fucked-up individual..." I stopped and pulled on his arm.

"If I'm not allowed to talk bad about myself, you aren't either," I said.

The look he gave me was one of sorrow. "Can I ask you for something? You can say no... but..."

"Ask me," I said.

"Can I kiss you? Once, before I tell you what you want to know," he asked and his blue eyes were cracked wide open, the truest emotion I'd ever seen out of him rushing through their depths.

"I... I would like that," I confessed. He smiled and tipped my face up with gentle fingers beneath my chin.

His lips hovered over mine, his breath fanning across them, a whispered promise of things to come. He breathed me in and closed his eyes, and mine slipped shut as well. When his mouth grazed mine it was like fireworks went off behind my eyes, the sparks fizzing from my mouth, along the surface of my skin in a pleasantly buzzing current of electricity. I gasped and he took it as an invitation, deepening the kiss, his tongue sweeping past my lips.

I sucked it into my mouth and moaned, melting against him. His arms folded around me and pulled me snug against him. I wrapped my arms around his neck and marveled that a simple kiss could feel so good. His hands smoothed up my back from my hips to my shoulders and back down until he held me by my lower back.

He drew back from the kiss slowly, as if waking from a dream, and chastely kissed my lower lip, then top lip, with these sweet little pecks before straightening. We were silent for a long time, searching each other's eyes. He smiled faintly at whatever he saw in mine but then his expression darkened, growing distant and cold.

"I have six patches on my cut but I've killed seven men," he said at last, swallowing.

"Okay..." I said, very still. "Why?"

He blinked at me as if he hadn't considered my asking.

"I grew up in a trailer park." He started us walking again. "My mother crawled into a bottle... booze bottle, pill bottle... didn't matter. Her husband, my stepdad, was a dick. She hooked up with him when I was one. No fucking clue who my real dad was. Anyways, Rick would tie one on and... Well, when he got done beating on my mom, he'd start in on me. Wasn't pretty. He'd use whatever was handy, most of the time his belt." He was quiet for a really long time and I continued to hold his hand in both of mine.

"The scars on your back?" I asked softly.

"Yeah, him," he answered and sucked in a long breath. We paced forward along the water's edge and he continued his story.

"He was always telling me how fucking worthless I was, how fucking stupid, and it got old. Watching my mom turn into what she is... it got old. Thing was, when Rick got started on me, he was always on about how it was going to make me a better man. How he was going to toughen me up."

We continued along at a leisurely pace across the wet sand and I closed my eyes. I had seen the scars and, though faded, they spoke of a brutality that I didn't want to even imagine a young Reaver going through.

"He never counted on me taking his lessons to heart," Reaver said and I looked up sharply at him.

"What do you mean?" I asked.

"I learned to cope. Internalized all his garbage. Something inside my head just finally cracked and one night, when I was in the kitchen, he was piss-drunk off of something and he started in on me. I was seventeen. My mom was pulling the late shift at the bar and Rick started in on me about how I would never amount to shit." He paused.

"I played football in high school, and hooked up with this girl Aimee. She was sweet and kind and just everything I wasn't used to. I got her pregnant and Rick was really on a roll about that. Anyways, I was fucking scared about being a dad, I mean, what the hell did I have to offer a kid? Look at how I was raised." Tension radiated down Reaver's arm and I bowed my head, waiting patiently for him to continue. When he didn't right away, I asked a question.

"Why did you ask me if you could kiss me?" I asked softly.

"Because I'm pretty sure when I finish telling you this, you're not going to want to have anything to do with me," he said. I looked up sharply and the look in his eyes said it all. Whatever he had to say, it was going to be bad, really bad, and I was almost afraid to hear it.

"I wanted to know what it was like, just once, if it was going to be the only thing I got to hold onto of you for the rest of my life," he said and I think my heart broke a little, from not just his words but the raw anxiety in his face. I nodded in understanding, and he swallowed and pressed on with his story.

"Anyways. Rick didn't think I was listening to him. I was doing my damnedest to ignore him and that pissed him off. The next thing I know he's got me from behind and has me pinned face down on the kitchen counter and I just... I cracked." His voice cracked and I squeezed his hand.

"I picked up a knife and swung it back and around and I caught him up under the ribs, babe. He was hurt and he was hurt bad, but if I had called for help, he probably would have lived but... But I didn't. He's on his knees in the kitchen, his hand pressed to his side and the fear is just coming off of him in waves and ...I liked it." He smoothed down his hair with the hand I wasn't holding and scrubbed over his face with it.

"I got up behind him and pulled his head back and looked down into the fear shining out of his eyes and didn't feel a goddamned thing but satisfaction when I ran the blade across his throat. His skin parted like water, I remember that, so smooth and perfect. I remember thinking it was beautiful. There was blood, but not a whole lot. I cut to sever his windpipe and vocal cords. I wanted him to die slowly, and he did."

I was staring up at him, wide-eyed and fearful. He was serious. I knew it when I saw it, and he was completely serious. I knew this about him. I knew he had killed, I had even aided and abetted him in the murder of Ashton's husband, who everyone thought had committed suicide, by hiding Ashton in my home while they went out and did it, by reinforcing the boys' alibis with text messages from Ashton's phone.

Ashton's husband had been a monster. I'd seen what he was capable of twice, and felt no remorse that he was gone, but Ashton and I had been spared the gory details. I looked up at Reaver now, my mouth slightly open, and realized that he was a monster too, but a very different kind. Still... I don't know... I felt all mixed up inside at this revelation. I didn't want to hear more but at the same time I needed to. I chewed my lip and made up my mind.

"Go on," I said, and he looked halfway defeated.

"He died slow. I disposed of the body and cleaned up before my mom got home, told her he'd gone out for a pack of smokes. He was gone, his truck was gone, and he just never came back. My mom crawled into a bottle harder than ever. I crawled into a bag of weed, and a bottle myself." He palmed the back of his neck and looked over at me.

"I don't feel guilty about killing him. I liked killing him. I've enjoyed every kill I've done. No, what I feel guilty about is the fact that I don't feel anything, one way or another, about what I did to Rick, to Chadwick... To any of them."

"What... what happened with Aimee?" I asked.

"Oh, God, I loved her," he sighed. "Loving her became almost a way of atoning for what I'd done... She had a boy, but still, the things I'd done, they haunted me. I wasn't sleeping, then when I did sleep

I'd have these dreams. Not about Rick, but about Aimee, about my baby boy, about carving them up, and I'd wake up and..." He took his hand away from me and used both to scrub his face.

"I got into speed to keep me up, keep me working so I could support them. Then I got into H to sleep... and let me tell you, that shit was the sweetest oblivion." The look on his face, for a fraction of a second, spoke of a longing for a lost love.

"That's how I met Trigger. We scored from the same dealer. We'd get high together and he told me about Over There. You know?" I nodded.

"Anyways, one night, it all came spilling out and I told him everything I just told you and he told me some secrets of his. Things I won't tell you, because they aren't my secrets to tell." I nodded in agreement.

"What happened?" I asked. He turned us around to start the surprisingly long walk back to the bed and breakfast.

"It made me feel better, knowing that we had something in common. We joined the MC not long after that and shit... well, shit had fallen apart with Aimee because of the drugs and so I stopped giving a shit. She moved out and took my kid, and I went all in with the club. I was nineteen... It was back when the shit was heavy, and I decided if I couldn't beat the monster, I might as well embrace him." I looked at him a little wide-eyed.

"That's how I started killing for the club. I'd gotten heavy into blades after Rick, spent countless hours with all manner of 'em. Got obsessed... got really good. I fed the monster and sold off bits of my soul to the devil every time." He looked tranquil – sad, but tranquil. He'd somehow made peace with what he'd done and by the looks of it, some time ago. I didn't know how I felt about all of what he'd told me.

Part of me wanted to run but it was the tiny, primal, prey part of my brain. If there was one thing I knew about Reaver, one very important thing that I had learned in the last year – hell, in the last couple of days – it was that the man he had been describing, the cold, drug-using, depraved killer... that sure, it may be a part of him, but it was just that... a part.

Still it was a part that gave me serious pause. I had to make one observation and see where it led. "You don't seem to be that man anymore..." I said and he looked down at me, and a flash of something –hope, maybe?– crossed his face.

"Part of what tripped my trigger into falling headlong into the abyss was losing Aimee. Loving her, being with her and my boy, it's what held me together, but she couldn't hold on. Not with a three-year-old and a man forever getting into trouble, coming home fucked-up," he said.

"I mean, I know it doesn't help, but three of the patches are men responsible for Tilly. We loved her. She was like a mother to us all. Not just Dray. When that shit went down it sobered us up, but quick. Me and Trig detoxed the hard way with Dragon's help. We reformed the club. Went on the straight and narrow, and part of that was I learned how to feed the monster in other ways." He said.

"How?" I asked.

"Figured out what it was. It wasn't the killing that did it for me, Doll, it was the fear. It was having that power, that control, that was doing it for me, so I found other, more consensual, ways to feed the beast, so to speak," he said.

I mulled that over.

"Like what happened earlier today?" I hazarded a guess.

"Yeah," he said, and had the grace to look embarrassed.

"Hey, don't," I said and swinging myself out and around, to stand in front of him, I gave him a hard look. "Don't be embarrassed. Please?" I begged and his eyebrows went up in surprise.

He put his hands on my shoulders and smoothed his thumbs in a light caress in the hollows below my collar bones. "Why?" he asked.

"Because if you're embarrassed, what does that say about me liking what you did?" I asked, troubled.

He chuckled and gave a one-sided smile, "Says you're my kind of woman."

I chewed my lower lip and gazed out over the water. Finally, I sighed and wrapped my arms loosely around his waist. I laid my head against the center of his chest and closed my eyes, listening to the steady thrum of his heart. His arms slid loosely around my shoulders and he held me like that for a long time, not saying anything.

I had so much to think about, so many feelings and so many paths in front of me. So much new stuff had come up in the last two days that I didn't know what to do, and I felt so small and so vulnerable in the face of it all. So, for right now, I cleaned off my metaphorical desk. Swept an arm across it and dumped everything to the floor in one violent swipe.

Reaver sighed; I rode the rise and swell of his chest and pulled away when it ebbed, taking a step back.

"Thank you. I needed that," I said and he smiled.

"Anything for you, Doll," he said and I smiled too, because deep down I knew, beyond a shadow of a doubt, that he meant it.

5

————————

Reaver...

I didn't dare hope but I couldn't help myself. Hayden pulled back from me and thanked me for holding her. Thanked me. Which put me into a pretty intense thought-pattern of my own.

The afternoon was growing late and I could tell that, with the heaps of things piled on her narrow shoulders, Hayden was about at her limit. She looked tired. Truth be told, I was tired myself. Emotional exhaustion tends to take its toll like any other type of exhaustion out there.

We walked leisurely back to the B&B in silence. She held my hand and I let her. Truth was I never wanted her to let it go. It was one of the lifelines giving me hope that trusting her with my fucked-up past was the right decision.

I'd decided a long time ago that the thing that really ripped me and Aimee apart was the lies, more than any one thing. It was what she'd always bitched about, more than anything. Hell, the only thing she complained about more was the drugs.

The ocean breeze ruffled Hayden's short cropped hair, the longer side-parted bangs skating across her forehead in such a way I had to actively resist the urge to brush it back into place.

When we returned to the bed and breakfast's back gate she let go of my hand, and I felt the loss keenly. I opened the gate and she slipped through ahead of me and I felt this fractured ache of panic in my chest that I'd lost her. She was so quiet and so somber. Lost inside her own head. We went up to our room.

"I'm going to grab a shower," I said.

"Okay, I'll go after you," she murmured.

"Sure, okay." I grabbed a fresh pair of comfortable basketball shorts to sleep in out of my saddlebag and plucked out my shower and shave kit with it.

"May I call Ashton back?" Hayden asked before I went into the bathroom. I smiled.

"Don't even need to ask, Babe." I tossed my phone into the center of the made, but turned-down, bed.

"Thank you," she murmured and I took my time with a hot shower and shaving off my five o'clock shadow. I hated being scruffy.

When I came out, Hayden was sitting on the bed looking thoughtful, turning my phone over in her fingers.

"You doing all right?" I asked and she startled. She didn't say anything but she nodded. I smiled and fished in the bag for her new purple nighty, and held it out to her. She took it, her lower lip clasped between her teeth and murmured her thanks. I accepted my phone as a sort of trade.

She slipped into the bathroom, the weight of the world on her mind, and showered. I heard the hair dryer from under the sink start up but it was short-lived. She came back out, looking fresh, her hair dry, but her expression was weary. Fuck though, I'd nailed it with the purple. The color made the green of her eyes fiercer and the satiny material clung to her body in all the right ways, like a preview of coming attractions.

I wanted so badly to take one of my blades to it. Reveal her creamy smooth skin one slice, one knick, one cut at a time. I wanted to watch the fear blossom in those pretty green eyes. I wanted that intense connection her trust brought and I wanted to do everything in my power to rock her world for giving me her fear and her trust in equal measure. I denied myself those things for now. She wasn't in a place to give them without running the risk of breeding anger and resentment in their wake and those were two things I never wanted aimed in my direction. Not from her.

I lay on my side of the bed on my back, my hands clasped behind my head, while she climbed up onto hers. She settled onto her side, facing me and I rolled onto mine to face her. I tucked one arm up under the pillow, propping my head onto it. She folded both hers under her cheek. She looked so damned angelic.

"Feel a little better?" I asked.

"Yes and no," she answered somberly.

"What can I do?" I asked her.

"Honestly, I don't know... you've already done so much, I can't..."

"You can ask me anything," I said, knowing right where she was headed.

"It would be selfish, especially given that I don't know where I stand within myself," she said gently.

"Hayden, Baby, what do you need?" I asked gently.

"I don't know," she said, but I could see the lie. She knew what she needed but she was afraid to ask for it. I tried a different tack.

"Tell me what you're feeling? Huh?" I asked.

"I don't know that either." Truth this time. "Just so many things, all at once, I don't... I don't know where to begin." Her eyes misted with tears and I thumbed one away before it could drip down her cute little nose. She gave a shaky laugh. "I'm embarrassed, I'm afraid, I feel so horribly guilty..."

"Guilty. Why?" I asked, picking up on that one.

"I don't know what I did wrong. I don't know why Andy did what he did. I don't know what I did to push him away. I feel guilty because I embarrassed my dad, my mom invited all of these business people of his to the wedding and–" I placed a finger against her petal-soft lips and stopped her right there.

"Hold up right there, baby," I said gently, and her green eyes became inquisitive.

"Replay what you just said in your brain and tell me something," I said, my finger still on her lips. I watched her do it, her brow wrinkling in confusion.

"Now tell me, why do you get to own any guilt for the feelings of the people your mother invited to your wedding? I hear you didn't even want those people at your wedding. You wanted something small, yeah?" She nodded, and when I was sure she wasn't going to speak I took my finger away.

"So, why do you give two fucks about those people? Let your mom work herself into a tizzy over it. Fuck them and fuck her for what she said to you!" I said. Her eyes got wide. "Yeah. I heard her, carrying on like some harpy at you. Not cool, Baby Doll. She's gonna spend at least five minutes in hell for the way she treated you after Andy pulled the bullshit he did." She blinked, perplexed.

"Oh, and while we're on that subject. What makes you think it was anything you did? Because of that toxic spew coming out of your mother's mouth? Andy was the one to do it. Him. No one else. This is his shit and you don't get to own his BS either," I said and she finally opened her mouth.

"Why?" she asked. She was forever asking why and it was something I loved about her, her inquisitiveness.

"Why don't you get to own it?" I asked.

"No, why did he do it?" she asked and I knew it bothered her more than anything in the world, I knew it was eating at her like some kind of cancer, but this one I didn't have an answer for. Well, not true. I had my suspicions, but no way to confirm them.

"I don't know why he did it," I said truthfully. I couldn't resist stroking her upturned cheek with my thumb, a gentle caress. I knew I was out of bounds but the way her eyes slipped shut, the way she subtly turned into my hand...

"Did that man ever show you any affection?" I found myself blurting. Her eyes flashed open, wide and wider still; I'd taken her aback with the question, pretty hard.

"Andy wasn't really... Um, he wasn't really like that. He was all business," she said, flushing a gentle pink.

"You can tell me to shut it any time from here on out, you don't have to answer a thing, but I can't keep myself from asking... Did he ever hold you?" I watched her face and hoped like hell she would answer me.

"Um, sometimes, in the beginning of our relationship," she said. Fuck me. That was four years ago.

"When was the last time you had sex together?" I asked, and I half-hoped she would tell me to shut up and half-hoped she would trust in me enough to tell me.

"Uh, about six months ago..." she said, and was really blushing hard. Fuck, I appreciated that she trusted me enough to answer these questions, she really didn't have to.

"What the hell was wrong with him? Couldn't get it up?" She laughed but her expression darkened. I wasn't going to like this answer, I could feel it.

"He worked a lot... was tired a lot, and out on business a lot..." I closed my eyes and counted to ten. A man loves his woman and is pulled away from her on business? The first thing he did was come home and fuck her brains out... unless he was one of two things: gay or getting a piece on the side. My suspicions were looking to be right on the money.

"He was cheating on me for some of it," she said miserably, and my eyes snapped open. Suspicion fucking confirmed but wait? She knew?

"What the fuck? And you were going to marry him anyways?" I asked, outraged partially at her and partially on her behalf.

"I kicked his ass out but then my mom found out. She took me aside and explained it was a common thing for couples to go through, that I should give him a second chance, that if it ever got out it would look really bad, and that, you know..." She shrugged and seemed to fold in on herself.

What was the deal with her mother? Was the woman seriously all about how good she looked at the country club, over the emotional well-being of her daughter? I kept my mouth shut; I didn't want Hayden to hurt any more than she was hurting and I wished like hell I'd been a better man and seen what the hell was really going on.

Hindsight was always fucking 20/20 and I'd been blind as a mother-fucking bat.

"So I did, and things were, you know, really good after that. He was attentive and it was like the beginning all over again and he asked me to marry him and I said yes and then business pulled him away and it was all about planning the wedding for me and now here we are."

I looked her over. "Jesus, Doll. This is not you. None of this is you. You're a bright, shining, confident woman. I don't fucking understand these people, your own mother included!" I searched her face for an answer I didn't think I was ever going to get. I was pretty sure she didn't even have one but I was going to get one. Somehow, some way.

"I know what you're going to say," she said.

"Oh, yeah?"

"You're going to say you don't know how I could let them do this to me... Am I right?" she asked.

"That was my next question." I replied honestly.

"Truth?" she asked.

"Always, between us," I answered.

"I don't know either... I guess I just got tired. My mother, Andy, they just have this way of turning what I say I'm feeling back on me. Like it's no one's fault but my own. Andy would tell me I was being unreasonable and he always had these arguments that made me wonder, and I'd spend days picking it apart in my head and..." I placed a fingertip on her lips.

"Andy was covering his own ass, babe. Your mother, I don't know what her fucking excuse is, but I'm starting to hate her about as much as I hate my own. I don't know why your dad is even with her." I took my hand away and let it rest on my stomach.

"I don't think he loves her anymore. I think he feels, I don't know, responsible for her..." she said and cringed.

"Only good explanation. Do you see what's happening here?" I asked her. Her face fell and she sighed out.

"Honestly, the whole thing makes my head hurt and makes me really, really tired," she said miserably.

"I can imagine," I said soberly.

"You know how you asked me what I needed?" she asked and her voice sounded timid and small.

"Yeah," I said, encouragingly.

"I really need a hug," she said and I smiled. I got up and finished turning down the blankets right from under her and got back into bed. I hugged her close and she settled with her head on my shoulder and it felt so good.

"Where has your dad been in all of this?" I asked her. It was the one thing that was bothering me.

"I love my dad; I didn't want him to worry. I thought I could handle things on my own, and I really did think that things were okay between me and Andy," she murmured.

"Were you happy? I mean really happy?" I asked her.

"I thought I was," she said, quietly.

"What changed your mind?" I asked.

She was silent for a long time. I fought the urge to ask her again. Finally, she sighed out and I realized she was sound asleep. I sighed myself and put a hand behind my head, staring at the ceiling, my other arm around my beautiful girl.

I wanted her like I've never wanted anything in my life. I wanted her to feel safe, and happy – well, except for when I intentionally scared the hell out of her for my own gratification. I had told her I was her friend before anything and I meant it. Tomorrow I would be just that, her friend, but at the same time, I needed to try and figure out a way to hold and touch her as much as possible. Not for me, but for her... though it was a huge bonus for me, too.

The poor woman was as touch-starved as I'd ever seen anyone, myself included. She was abused just as surely as I had ever been, too. Granted, she may not have been beat-to-shit like me or Ashton, but a person can only endure so much vitriol. She'd been berated and gaslighted into thinking it was all her own fault for so long that she was like a delicate flower crushed under her mother's stilettos and Andy's wingtips.

Her own fucking family. I wished I could say I was surprised, but rich, poor, it made no difference. Douchebags came in every color of the rainbow, were every race, creed, and sexual orientation. There were good people and bad people from any and every walk of life, and then there were some of us who walked the center line between both lanes.

On a good day, I was one of those. On a not-so-good day I was squarely in the black. I was trying very hard to have more good days than bad, and for the most part I'd been pretty damn successful. Hayden made me want to try even harder than I already did, and I was already trying really damn hard for my boy.

He was ten going on eleven. A good kid, into sports like his dad. His mom had met and fell in love with a guy when he was six. You better believe I vetted him, looked into him; I stalked his ass for months. I needed to make sure my son, and yes, even his mother, no matter how much she hated me, were going to be safe. I couldn't find anything on the guy. He was as decent as they came, and I thanked god for that every day, even if the big man and I weren't on the best of terms.

Connor was a good kid and we had a good relationship. Aimee had taken him with good reason when he was three; by the time he was four, I was deep in the land of self-pity and barely saw him; by the time he was five, I was on the road to getting my shit together; and by the time he was six, I was clean and I took Aimee's ass to the mat for the right to see him on the regular.

Never, not once, did I ever not pay my child support; no matter how fucked-up I was, I always provided for her and my boy. I still did, even though she'd remarried. Connor was my kid and I worked my ass off to get them the money they needed to be comfortable. I'd missed out on way too much, and I'd be damned if I'd miss out on any more.

Another point of pride that I held. I had never, not once, laid a hand on either of them. No matter how pissed off I got.

I looked down at Hayden's angelic face, her edges soft and smooth in a deep and dreamless sleep, and for the thousandth time, worried that I was doing things all wrong where she was concerned. I had to admit to myself that she was still here. I didn't know what that meant, but I had to hope that it meant something good. I closed my eyes and tried to sleep but it was an elusive bastard. Finally, I settled into it and when I woke up in the morning it was to an empty bed. I felt a moment of panic when I spied her purple nightgown across the room's chair. I got up quickly and threw on the same shorts I'd worn last night and a tee over my head. I padded downstairs and stopped when Miranda, the hostess lady for the B&B, called out to me.

"Mr. Butler!"

I turned and gave her my best scowl. "Reaver," I corrected her.

"Yes, well, Ms. Michaels asked me to tell you that you could find her on the beach," she said with a smile.

"'Yes, well', nothing. It's 'Reaver'. 'Butler' is the name of a man I never met and never care to, who left me in the care of an abusive fuck who destroyed mine and my mom's lives. Don't say it again." I fixed her with a hard look, then told her, "Thanks for telling me where she's at."

I headed out the door, leaving Miranda with her mouth agape, her eyes a little wide, but the bitch deserved it as far as I was concerned. I'd tried polite. At least polite by my standards.

Hayden was out in the sun, sitting in the sand staring out at the water a ways between the mansion and the sea. I went out to her but she was a million miles away lost in her own thoughts. I sat down in the sand behind her and eased up so my legs were to either side of her and let her be. I sat with her cradled protectively in front of me without touching her, and kept my knees bent, my arms on the outsides of my legs, just content to be here with her.

I watched her as she watched the gently-crashing waves and honestly, there wasn't anything more peaceful, more tranquil than this right here. It was as good a way to start the morning as any.

6

Hayden…

I woke before Reaver to find I was snug against him, my back to his front, though I was free to move. One of his arms lay atop his body, over his hip and down his leg; the other was curled beneath his head. I slipped out of bed and dressed quickly in my swimsuit and shorts from the day before and slipped on my crocheted beach cover-up, hugging it in front of me.

I craved sunlight and time to think, to meditate on the last few days, and so I slipped out and down the stairs. I found the hostess in the kitchen and told her if Reaver should come looking that I could be found on the beach. I didn't want him thinking I'd taken off.

I walked out a ways and sat down in the sand to do some reflection. My eyes staring blankly at some distant point over the water, my breathing deep and even, I sat, legs in front of me, hands on the front of my ankles. It wasn't the traditional cross-legged position for meditation but I'd learned a long time ago that meditation required that which worked for you, not what was the generally-accepted standard.

My thoughts turned to Reaver. He had told me more than I had ever bargained for last night and in turn I suppose I had done the same. I hadn't even told Ashton of Andy's cheating.

I turned over everything Reaver had said to me about my ex and my mother in my head, studied it, really thought about it, and I sighed. I didn't know whether to feel relieved or duped. I knew my mother had problems, was narcissistic to an extent, but never in a million years did I think I was as weak as I had been where she was concerned. I was disappointed in myself and I vowed from here on out to be stronger-willed.

Reaver had asked me if I'd been happy. I thought I had. I wasn't naïve, I mean, relationships of every kind required hard work and dedication right? But now, looking back, I realized it required the work of both parties. Both needed to be invested and one couldn't bear all the weight or they'd be crushed... Which is what I had allowed to happen to me.

I had tried to follow the silly notions that my mother had put in my head. That to be a good and dutiful wife was to be silent and endure, which was laughable, really. I mean since when had Margaret Michaels ever silently endured anything? Let alone her daughter.

I sighed.

I had always been my daddy's girl and had spent most of my childhood in the care of a nanny. My mother had been far too busy with her social clubs and garden parties. The only time I had been included was more as a doll, as a point of pride only in what a pretty and well-behaved daughter I was.

And I was. Completely and unfailingly polite, never a hair out of place, I strove so hard to be the perfect daughter for my mother in hopes that she might somehow notice me, take more than a passing interest in me. But when dad was home, oh, that was when I truly lived. If it was one thing my dad was good at, it was lavishing me with attention when he managed to be home.

He didn't always get me everything I wanted but I didn't care as long as he spent time with me, which he did as often as he could. In retrospect, it was probably to make up for the time my mother missed out on. Once the party was over it was like she put me back on my shelf until the next time she needed to pull me down to impress someone.

I saw it now. Clear as day... and not only did it hurt, it made me angry.

I huffed out another great sigh.

And then there was Reaver.

Reaver, who looked at me every time as if I mattered, who bent over backwards to keep me happy, to keep me safe all while knowing that I belonged to another man. Reaver, who pushed me in all the right ways to work through the ugly inside my head, who took on my burdens as if they were his own. Reaver, who saw the real me and not my daddy's money, who didn't care about my daddy's money!

Reaver, who harbored such deep and ugly hurts mine absolutely paled in comparison, who held a dark and sordid monster inside his head and did everything in his power to keep it in check.

Dangerous, attractive, cracked, and scary Reaver, who killed men and liked it.

No, not quite. He'd said that hadn't he? That he liked the –fear– part of it. Not necessarily the killing... although maybe some of that too. The way he'd described the path of the knife... I shuddered involuntarily.

I'd called Ashton last night and I'd asked her something.

How did she cope knowing that Trigger held a stone cold killer inside his head?

Her answer was simple. She loved him; good, bad, and in-between. He'd never given her any reason not to love him, and that she knew beyond any shadows that they were meant for each other. Then she asked if Reaver had opened up to me. I'd told her yes, and she'd said that he'd never told her anything about himself, just Trigger, and that I was likely the only other soul he'd ever confided in.

Her earlier comments had both helped and didn't. Her final comments brought with them some semblance of understanding.

Reaver confided in me. Reaver trusted me and I... Well, I knew I trusted him. I knew I had no reason not to trust him. I saw it in his face and in his eyes, even when they were coldest winter skies. I'd seen the killer peeking out and I felt, down to my bones, that while it was healthy to fear that part of him, that I didn't have to. Parts of Reaver terrified me but he would never hurt me. Not once. Not ever.

He would never humiliate me in public, at least not on purpose. He would never berate me or make something my fault that wasn't really my fault. Reaver was safe, despite the monster I sometimes glimpsed that lived inside his head.

I swallowed and came back to myself, a little steadier, a little calmer than when I'd gone. I felt more centered than I had in a while, and when I came back from my internal musings, it was in the protective cage of Reaver's body. He sat behind me, legs to either side of mine, a hair's breadth from my back, so close I could feel his body's heat and his still, quiet energy enveloping me. I closed my eyes and leaned back into him and cuddled close, pulling his arms around me and he relaxed.

I could feel the relief swirl through his aura and I felt surrounded by his love as much as his cool, still influence.

"Welcome back," he said, and I smiled.

"Thanks," I said softly.

"I thought for sure the things I told you would be too much," he said and his voice was cautious.

"At first it was but we all have some sort of past and you've never done anything to hurt me... Quite the opposite." I looked up at him and he looked down at me.

"I'd never hurt you, at least not on purpose," he said echoing my earlier thoughts. I nodded. He shuddered and held me tighter and I tipped my head to the side.

"Is this okay or is it too confusing?" I asked.

"What?" he asked.

"Holding me like this," I said.

"Hayden, baby, I told you, I'm here, for whatever you need," he said, and rocked me gently from side to side.

"Okay, because it's really nice... being held by you like this," I confessed. He smiled.

"Yeah, it is," he agreed.

"Reaver, is it okay that I'm still confused? That... that I don't really know how..." He stopped me with a gentle chiding look.

"Baby, just because I love you doesn't mean I expect you to know what to do with it, doesn't mean that I expect you to love me back. I have to earn that, and you know what? Not sure I can. Not sure I deserve something as sweet or as wonderful as you are." He shrugged. "Doesn't mean I expect you to jump right back into dating, doesn't mean I expect you to want to date me." He kissed my forehead and my eyes drifted shut. The touch of his lips on my skin made me feel all glowy inside.

"I just want to be a part of your life. I'm happy to just be your friend, be in your orbit for now. No expectations. I just like being near you," he said, his breath warm against my skin. I opened my eyes and smiled.

"Promise to tell me if any of that changes?" I asked.

"I promise," he said.

He cradled me and we stared out over the water for the longest time. The silence was comfortable and I was grateful. I finally felt like I was mere feet away from being back on solid ground.

Reaver pulled his cell from his pocket and looked at the time.

"C'mon, Doll, let's go get some breakfast," he said, and helped me to my feet.

I smiled, "Sounds perfect," I said.

We ate quietly for the first few minutes until Marcy and Tom joined the table. The other couple arrived as well. Alice and Joe weren't newlyweds, though. I glanced up at Reaver and caught a flicker of motion under the table. His hand found my knee and I gave him a dirty look.

"Don't you dare!" I threatened, remembering the unpleasantness he wrought with a mere pinch of his fingers.

Both couples looked at us sharply. Reaver started grinning.

"Relax, Doll," he said and patted my knee. I snorted.

"That'd be folly around you," I said.

"You know it!" he affirmed and popped a bite of bacon into his mouth. He chewed and sighed. The other couples went quietly back to their conversations.

"So, where's that haunted lighthouse at you wanna see?" he asked me. I smiled.

"Up the coast about forty-five minutes. Can we go?" I asked.

"Does the Pope shit in the woods?" he asked. I laughed. Alice gasped and looked affronted. Reaver winked at her.

"Mr. Reaver!" Our hostess admonished from the kitchen doorway.

I wondered how he'd gotten her to stop calling him Mr. Butler. Reaver smiled the beatific smile he and his cousin Shelly shared when they were trouble-making and I stifled a giggle behind my hand.

"I'd like to remind you that there are other guests at my table! Such language is not appreciated," she admonished, and Reaver shrugged.

"Guess now we're even, aren't we, Miranda?" he asked with one of his icy-cold looks. She scowled at him and nodded curtly, then disappeared into the kitchen.

"What was that about?" Marcy asked and, with a flick of a switch, Reaver's warm smile and charming side was back in place.

"What was what about?" he asked pleasantly, and Marcy smiled and shook her head ruefully.

Alice, a woman in her early thirties, gave Reaver a disgusted look. Technically, she and I should have been cut from the same cloth. By that, I meant that she had money or came from it. Her clothes were designer and perfectly tailored. She had on linen slacks and a rose-colored silk blouse with a creamy cardigan. A string of pearls graced her throat and the diamond wedding set on her finger sparkled. The stone in the main setting of her engagement ring was a cushion-cut diamond as big as my thumbnail.

She wore her dishwater-blonde hair in a severe French twist, and her husband, Joe, was just as stuffy, in dress, if not attitude. He wore pressed gray slacks and a crisp white button-down shirt. Expensive black loafers were on his feet. His shirt was at least undone at the collar by the top two buttons and his cuffs were undone and turned back midway up his forearms.

He was going prematurely gray at his temples, the white standing out against his milk-chocolate-brown hair, which was perfectly styled just like his wife's. Joe's only saving grace was the sparkle of mirth in his grey-blue eyes whenever Reaver irritated his wife. He reminded me of a younger version of my dad that way.

They hadn't introduced themselves at all when they sat down; Miranda had done it for them. Reaver and I were hardly worth their notice until Reaver did something uncouth enough to garner Alice's ire. Once he realized that his lewd, crude, and tattooed ways got to her, he dialed it up a notch, which made me smile. He was incorrigible in all the right ways in my opinion.

Life was just way too short.

I chewed thoughtfully on Miranda's French toast.

"Reaver?" I asked quietly.

"Yeah, Doll?" he asked.

"Why do you think you love me?" I asked him, and speared him with my gaze. He looked right back at me a slight smile curving his mouth.

"I don't think I love you, babe. I know I do," he said and crunched into another piece of bacon. I frowned. "And to answer your question, I think about you all the time, I can tell just by looking at you if you're happy or you're sad and it's a deciding factor on how I feel on any given day. The thought of anything happening to you wrecks me, and when you smile at me, sort of like you're smiling at me now, my whole world falls into place and I can almost pretend that I'm not as big a bastard as I am."

Alice snorted in disgust and looked appalled. I looked over at her and said "Shut up. Jesus!", to which Reaver barked out a laugh that boomed through the dining room and had Marcy and Tom and even Alice's husband Joe joining in.

Reaver hooked an arm around my shoulders and pulled me against his side, kissing the top of my head before letting me go. Alice stood up with an angry scrape of her chair and stalked out of the room. Joe remained seated and smiling, continued eating his breakfast.

"I'm sorry," I muttered, embarrassed.

"I'm not," Joe said, good-naturedly. "She's my wife and I love her, but she had it coming. I keep telling her, you can't treat people that way." He shrugged.

"So, we couldn't help but overhear you say you were going up to the old Acantilados Cortos lighthouse," Tom said.

"Is that what it's called?" Reaver asked me.

"Yes," I said softly.

"Then, yeah, that's where we're heading. Why?" he asked.

"If it's all right, we'd love to join you!" Marcy said.

Reaver and I exchanged looks.

"Kind of hard to fit four on my bike," he said, with a grin.

Marcy laughed. "We'd follow you of course!" she said.

"Up for some company, Doll?" he asked me, and I smiled.

"As long as I get you to myself at some point during this trip," I said before I even realized what was going to come out of my mouth. I smiled at Reaver and the look of sheer delight that lit up his handsome features, causing his eyes to glow from within with a boyish glee, well, that made what I'd said entirely worth it.

While I hadn't done everything with Andy all wrong, I was willing to admit that I hadn't done everything entirely right either. I didn't know what exactly it was that I was doing with Reaver, especially just two days after being unceremoniously dropped on my ass at the altar by Andy.

Everything my upbringing had taught me was screaming at me "What are you doing, Hayden?" but simultaneously I felt more relaxed and more, just... I don't know; safe, appreciated, cared for, loved –pick an adjective– in Reaver's presence than I had whenever I was around Andy, be it in the beginning, middle, or end of our relationship.

Reaver took every notion I had, about life, love, and family, and turned it on its head and honestly, it scared me but not in that way that made me want to run for my life, but more in that way you get stepping onto a roller coaster for the ride of your life.

I tuned back in to the conversation just in time to hear Tom say, "That's great, we'll see you back down here in ten," as he and Marcie got up from the table. I smiled and nodded and looked to Reaver who was studying me with his steady, cool blue eyes.

"You've been thinking awful hard today, Doll," he said softly.

"I have, haven't I?" I said ruefully.

"Yeah," he said and he looked me over again.

"What?" I asked.

"Nothin'," he said and I could taste the lie of the single word.

Joe coughed and excused himself, and Reaver and I were suddenly alone in the dining room.

"Having second thoughts about me?" he asked quietly, and I was shocked to detect a little bit of fear in his tone.

I stood up and did something I wouldn't ever normally do. With a false sense of bravado, I straddled Reaver's lap. His hands went automatically to my hips to steady me, and his eyes gently, but silently, questioned me. He held me lightly on his lap and I put my hands to either side of his face.

He let me, watching me fascinated as I lowered my face to his.

"Doll?" he asked and the breath from the one word utterance brushed across my lips sending an erotic frisson up my spine in a tingling wave.

"I still don't know what I'm doing," I said softly, and let my eyes slip shut.

"I get you," he said, his voice strained, and I kissed him.

I touched my lips lightly to his and it was as if my blood turned to fine champagne, the bubbles rushing and fizzing through my veins in a subtle pleasurable sensation that engulfed me. Sound stopped, sight stopped and the whole world narrowed to my lips on his, my hands cupping the heat of his face, the warmth of our mingling breaths on our skin heady. I drank him in. He tasted masculine and brisk, a hint of the bacon he'd consumed lingering in the background. He pulled me forcefully and tightly against him, and I could feel at the apex of my thighs that he was very, very happy to have me in his lap.

His length was intimidating even through the combination of my shorts and his. I could feel myself moisten in my bikini bottoms as our tongues stroked against one another, clashing and dancing as we languidly took each other in, each exploring the other's mouth with intrepid curiosity. I let my hands smooth down the rough stubble on his cheeks and along the sides of his throat. I caressed his shoulders through his tee shirt and marveled at the swell of muscle in his bicep, sculpted to perfection from his long hours spent at the gym, and possibly from his line of work as well.

His hands drifted to the slight swell of my ass and his long, strong, sure fingers gripped me there, tight and tighter pulling me up against him, crushing our pelvises together. I rode him, sliding my hips up and down his length and he moaned into my mouth. Things were quickly heating up, slipping outside my control and I didn't care.

Finally, Reaver reared back, his eyes glazed with passion, and sucked in a shuddering breath as if he were a swimmer too long under water. He shook himself and pushed me back off of him a bit.

"Baby, my self-control isn't absolute," he said and I bowed my head, resting my forehead against his shoulder, half-disappointed we'd stopped. He pushed back firmly but gently on my hips and I slid from his lap and got to my feet, a little unsteady.

"Go get dressed to ride, babe," he ordered gently.

"Reaver I'm..." I began but he cut me off.

"Hayden, baby, just please, go... or I'm going to fuck you right here on the dining room table." His voice was low and controlled but still gave the impression that the order was barked. I felt things low in my body coil with wanting at his admission but his tone had me taking a step back, none the less.

I left him sitting alone and obviously hard in his shorts in the dining room and ascended the stairs on quivering knees. I did as I was told and dressed in jeans, slipping them on over my swimsuit as I had with my shorts. I pulled on a slightly oversized button-down blue women's oxford shirt on and buttoned it most of the way.

Reaver entered the room as I was lacing up my running shoes over low socks. He went about getting better clothes together to ride in, and I slipped off the bed and to my feet. I picked up Shelly's jacket, but his voice stopped me with my hand on the door handle.

"Baby, I didn't want to stop," He swallowed hard. I turned to look at him and he looked worried. I frowned.

"I didn't, either," I said.

"I get why you're pushin'," he said.

"Am I?" I asked, surprised.

"Yeah, babe, you are, and it's okay. I'm not going anywhere, but I gotta ask... why'd ya kiss me like that?" He looked me over, and I swallowed and told the truth.

"Because no one has ever kissed me the way you do... Because I like it and I... I know it's selfish but I wanted to feel good and I feel better than I ever have before when you touch me, when you kiss me." I bowed my head and fixed my eyes on the floor, my cheeks heating with embarrassment at my admission.

It was true. He kissed me and the whole world tilted on its axis. It was crazy, like something out of a romance novel or a movie, the kind of thing you always heard talked about and dismissed as a pure flight of fancy.

"One of these days we're going to dance, Doll," he said to me, a very audible smile tinging his voice. I looked up and met his eyes, which were sparkling with good humor. They cooled with a flip of the switch.

"Before we do, we have to talk because sleeping with me... it comes at a price," I swallowed at the ominous words.

"Wh-" I cleared my throat, which was suddenly a little tight. "What kind of price?" I asked.

"You planning on something I should know about?" he asked me. My eyes snapped up to study his face. He was smiling that incorrigible, rakish grin of his at me and I bit my bottom lip.

"I want you," I blurted.

"I want you too, baby, but I want you when you're really ready, not when you think you're ready. You want to feel good? I'll make you feel good but you don't get me, all of me unless you're ready for it. I'd rather you get some rebound sex from Cutter or one of his guys first." I balked with an audible noise. His eyes were cool, somber and distant.

"Are you serious?" I demanded.

"As a heart attack." He stalked to me and his fingers curled around the back of my neck, his thumb smoothing under my jaw and over the pulse-point in my neck. I felt my heart rate pick up.

"You forget what kind of monster I am," he said carefully, and all semblance of warmth, all emotion leaked from his eyes and was swallowed whole by their glacial crystalline depths. I heard a slight snick and I jumped when the cool metal of the blade kissed the skin at the side of my throat, not cutting, not yet, but one slight move on my part or his...

I went very, very still, the coppery tang of fear coating my tongue. Reaver let out a shuddering breath.

"Oh, yeah, there it is..." he said and he bent, slowly but surely, his mouth hovering over mine.

"There's what?" I whispered, barely breathing, but I knew the answer. I was both fearful but at the same time... oh my god, this was hot! Crazy, but totally erotic!

"You want this, don't you?" he asked, his breath hot against my lips.

"I want you, Reaver... and I'll take you whichever way I can get you. You..." I swallowed hard and felt the sharp edge of the blade against my throat as it expanded minutely with the motion. "You scare me some times, when you do this, but I trust you, and maybe I'm crazy, but you make me feel alive." I meant it. I was surprised that I meant it.

"I'm not going to add my malfunction to the pile sittin' on top of your chest, but one day, we're going to finish this and I'm going to taste you and make you beg me for more before I'm done. You get me, Hayden?" he asked me.

"I get you, Reaver," I said, trembling.

"Good girl," he murmured, and he kissed me, a gentle, almost-chaste press of lips. Sometime during the kiss, I heard the blade snick back into its handle, and when he pulled away it was simply gone. His hand was empty, as if it never was there. I'd never even seen it. I felt the hair raise on the back of my neck and I shivered. Reaver shook himself and turned away from me.

"Don't," I said.

"Don't what?" he asked, with a wry curl of his lips.

I went to him and dropped Shelly's jacket onto the bed.

"I don't want you to beat yourself up. You are who you are, Reaver. I don't know what that is, I don't know if I'm crazy but..." I swallowed. This was the most brash and crude thing I was likely ever going to do...

"But?" he asked.

I unbuttoned my jeans and lowered the fly and snatched his hand from where it rested at his side. I slid his hand against my body, between my skin and my bikini bottoms. His eyes went wide in his face with surprise and when his fingers found the wetness his lips curled into a slow and feral grin.

I closed my eyes and relished the feel of his fingers against my sex. He withdrew his hand and smiled his rogue devil-may-care grin down on me.

"Oh, yeah, we're going to finish this," he said, in no uncertain terms.

"Okay," I said and smiled.

"We got folks waiting on us, Doll," he reminded me gently and I startled. Oh god! I'd forgotten all about Tom and Marcy!

"See you downstairs," he said and turned around. I zipped and buttoned up and snatched Shelly's jacket off the bed, going for the door. Reaver's soft laughter followed me into the hall until I shut the door on it.

He turned me upside down and inside out and left me so rattled!

And I would be a liar if I said I didn't love every minute of it.

What did that make me?

7

———————

R eaver...

I shook my head and pulled a plain white tee shirt on. It was snug in the chest and shoulders but would work. I pulled on my jeans and my boots and threw on my cut. I sighed and adjusted myself. My cock was standing at attention and it had taken just about everything I had in me to not fuck Hayden into next week for what she did.

The perfume of her hot, slick, wet pussy still clung to my fingers and I went into the little bathroom, and roughly and regretfully, washed my hands. I couldn't have her there, not and maintain my self-control. As it was, I was barely holding on to the strings of it which, with the way she cuddled into me, the way she held my hand and stood inside my personal space, may be just better left to fray.

I didn't think we were going to make it out of Florida without having sex. I didn't really know how I felt about that. On the one hand, I wanted her with a deep-seated, gnawing ache that made my desire for my next fix of heroin back when I was addicted seem like a paltry thing in comparison. She was in my blood, on my mind, in my heart, and like the other half of my soul within a blink of the eye and I didn't understand it.

I didn't want to.

There were some things in life, some people you met and connected with that just fit. Like peanut butter and jelly, we went together. I felt it in the deepest part of me. When we were together it was fated, meant to be; and when we were apart, that gnawing angry desire that pushed me to find her and be with her, near her, hovering over her and protecting her was too strong to ignore.

On the other hand I didn't want to break us before we had a chance to get started.

There was a lot to this life of mine, to the life of being an Old Lady to one of the MC brotherhood. I didn't want to put her in over her head and have it break her in two. I wanted her scared, but I didn't want her scared away. I felt like I was walking this tight-wire act with her. I wanted so many things, and yet, everything that I wanted came at a steep cost.

Not for me, but for her.

I combed my hair forward and tugged on my cut, checked for wallet and keys, and, satisfied, I headed downstairs. Hayden was talking with Marcy; Tom was across the circular cobblestone drive, swinging the back door on a dark blue Mazda shut.

Hayden's body language said it all. She stood, completely unaware of what she was doing, but she was hugging herself despite the oppressive heat. Her shoulders were rounded in, as if to hold all that wild chaos of what she was feeling inside, and even though her face was smiling, even though she laughed at something Marcy said, I could see the hurt just there below the surface and I wanted to take it away. Unburden her narrow shoulders...

I wanted to see those light emerald eyes of hers spark fire again. I wanted to see the happy, confident woman who stepped out of the locker room over a year ago. I wanted to pull that woman out of her, scare the hell out of her, ravish her and make love to her, and fucking cherish her, the way she deserved to be cherished.

I wanted to promise her the moon and the fucking stars, and come hell or high water, I wanted to deliver them.

I just needed to figure out how. I knew one place to start that was as good as any. I slipped up behind her and made good on my self-imposed vow to give her the affection she so seriously craved, putting my arms around her and pulling her back against my chest.

The smile that lit her beautiful green eyes made an answering smile appear on my face. She leaned back into me and cuddled into my arms, and she fit so perfectly there, our difference in height tucking her just so perfectly into the front of my body, under my chin.

"Ready, baby?" I asked her, and she huffed out a sigh tinged with contentment.

"Yeah," she said.

"We'll follow you," Marcy said with a smile, and she and Tom got into their car.

"You doin' okay?" I asked Hayden and she leaned her head back against my shoulder and rolled her bright green eyes to meet mine. Their jeweled depths were steady and filled with a mixture of sadness and something else.

"Yeah, let's go," she said and smiled with a false bravado.

I nodded slowly. She was going through so much all at once and I wasn't helping. I sighed, her mercurial moods were to be expected. Riding always helped me when I felt like shit. When the world was full of confusion and it felt like the bits and pieces of me were being torn off and blowing away in whatever shit storm had come my way, riding had always brought me clarity. I was hoping the same would hold true for her so I helped her into her helmet and once we were both situated started up Baby and pulled us out of the drive. I followed Hayden's directions to the freeway, and from there, followed the historical marker signs to our destination.

The lighthouse was impressive. Tall and painted in classic barber-pole red-and-white, except the red had faded some in the punishing Florida sun to an orangey color. I backed Baby into a parking stall next to a yellow crotch-rocket and shut her off. Hayden had ridden beautifully, her slender arms locked around me, her body snug against mine the whole way. Her expression in the side view had gone almost meditative about ten minutes into the forty-five minute or so ride, and now she looked up at the lighthouse from beside me, her face completely unreadable; her eyes hidden by her too-large sunglasses.

"It's big," I said, and she handed me her helmet, smoothing her pixie cut across her forehead, and nodded.

"It's the second-tallest lighthouse in Florida," she said and automatically took my hand once it was free. Marcy and Tom had found parking and were coming across the lot.

"I thought you weren't a couple," Tom called and Hayden's face fell; she tried to take her hand back but I wouldn't let it go. I gave Tom an unfriendly look which lost some of its fierceness to my own dark lenses.

"Baby, if it makes you feel better to hold my hand, you don't ever have to let go," I murmured before the other couple drew close enough to hear me. She nodded and took her hand back anyway, and I tamped down the urge to kick Tom's damn teeth in. His wife Marcy was looking at him with the tried-and-true wife's "I can't believe you just said that" look.

I plastered on a fake smile, deciding that Hayden didn't need me acting like a dick, that it would just make things more uncomfortable for our final day or so at the bed and breakfast. I followed her up the cement steps and across the sweeping cement slab leading up to the lighthouse. When we stepped inside it was immediately apparent that this was more a museum than a functioning lighthouse anymore.

Off to our right, the archway leading into the light keeper's quarters opened up into a gift shop rather than a home. I looked up the long sweeping set of spiral stairs and nearly got a case of vertigo from it. Hayden was looking up as well, her green eyes luminous with curiosity, her sweet, full, sexy lips curving slightly at the corners in a mysterious little smile.

God, she drove me wild. I could look at her all fucking day and night and never grow tired of the subtle nuanced expressions she wore. An older woman appraised us from over in the corner as we all four looked up the stairs. We could see people above us through the steel grating of each step. The flicker of movement and flashes of color through the black steel... or was it iron?

"How old is this place?" I asked and, cue the older woman, wearing a sweatshirt with the lighthouse on it and a name tag that said "Gladys", to come forward.

"The Acantilados Cortos, or Short Cliffs, lighthouse was built in 1878," she told me kindly.

I smiled down at her stooped frame and cap of snowy-white hair. "Thank you, Ma'am."

She smiled up at me with soft blue eyes and said, "Oh please, call me Gladys! You folks interested in going up to the top?" and we all exchanged looks.

"Does the Pope... uh, wear a funny hat?" I asked. Hayden and Marcy burst into a fit of giggles and Tom grinned.

"Well, as soon as the tour that's up there comes down, we'll go on up," Gladys said beaming. I spied the chain across the old iron steps. A painted wood plaque hung from it and declared 'Tour in Progress...' and below that, 'Please Visit Our Gift Shop'. I nodded.

"I think I'll take the sign's advice," I said to Gladys, and gave her my best charming smile. She reminded me of the grandmother I never had. I wandered with Hayden, Marcy and Tom into the gift shop and picked up some free pamphlets on the lighthouse.

I was midway through reading about The Wailing Gray Lady, the lighthouse's resident ghost when I caught Hayden at the register buying a few things. I wandered along the shelves and looked for something to take to my boy Connor, settling on a carved and painted wooden likeness of the lighthouse and a slim book on the building's history and its ghost.

An old brass ship's bell was rung out in the lighthouse and the people wandering the gift shop turned to look. Gladys stood in the archway and smiled sweetly.

"Next tour!" she called.

About seven total herded in her direction; I paid for my stuff and went out after Hayden who was standing in the front, rapt, the shine of curious excitement all around her. I smiled and Marcy stepped up beside me.

"You really do love her, don't you?" she asked.

"Yep," I said.

"But you were going to let her marry someone else?" she asked.

I sighed. I didn't know how to explain that it was really none of my business that Hayden had chosen her path, and as much as I'd wanted to complicate things for Andy, I didn't wish that for my girl. I smoothed my hair down and grunted noncommittally and went forward to stand with Hayden. She smiled up at me and I smiled down at her and there wasn't any more time for uncomfortable questions I didn't feel like answering because Gladys was welcoming us to the Acantilados Cortos lighthouse and was launching into her tour of the place with gusto.

The lighthouse was built in 1878 and rose to a height of 152 feet. The tower was conical in shape and mirrored the design of its big sister, the St. Augustine lighthouse, which was only a few years older. Gladys went on and on about the lighthouse's history: when it was built, how it was built, when it got its first lamp, when that lamp was replaced; when it went from being a manned lighthouse to being automated by the U.S. Coast Guard.

She told us about when it was declared on the National Register of Historic Places, how it narrowly escaped being torn down after it was decommissioned by the Coast Guard, and the grassroots effort that had been waged to restore it to operating conditions for the history tours today. Throughout the lecture we climbed and I was amazed.

For as aged and frail as Gladys looked she took the iron stairs like a mountain goat. Tom and Marcy and a few other younger people in the tour group were getting winded and Gladys just kept on gaily prattling on and she was doing all the talking. I grinned and had a new appreciation for our tour guide. Hayden was just in front of me and I could nearly feel the tension radiating off of her, bursting with the need to ask about her ghost, which Gladys hadn't even mentioned yet.

I put my hands on Hayden's narrow shoulders and gently dug my thumbs into the muscles on either side of her spine along her shoulder blades. The tightness there eased and she sighed out, and so

I continued my ministrations until we started to climb again. Gladys had a flair for this tour stuff, her voice dropping in tone but not volume as she launched into the family histories of the keepers of the lighthouse.

"It was nineteen twenty-six during the height of Prohibition when the lighthouse was being run by Matthias Toungstead. Matthias had a wife, Mary, and a daughter, Annabeth, and was an accomplished lighthouse keeper," Gladys was saying. Hayden was leaning forward slightly hanging on Gladys' every word. We were just below the room that housed the lighthouse's grand brass and glass lamp, just a few more steps and we'd be at the top.

"Now, Annabeth was a willful girl of seventeen; much like teenagers nowadays, she had a mind of her own and wasn't afraid to use it. Unlike today, things like that were frowned upon back then, especially by Matthias, who was raised in a strict Protestant household, the God-fearing son of a minister and a strict church-goer." Everyone was listening to the older woman, rapt, myself included.

"Annabeth spent a lot of time out on the beach and in town, and met a boy, Anthony Wilde, and Tony was wild. A trouble-shooter for the local speakeasy – that's a bouncer for your modern times– Tony was also neck-deep in rum-running. Well, you can imagine Matthias' protest at his only daughter spending so much time with a roustabout rapscallion like Tony. He would have none of it!" Gladys gave a melodramatic sigh.

"So Annabeth and Tony eloped, wed in secret, and Tony, well, he started rum-running harder than ever in order to buy a house for himself and Annabeth. In the meantime, though, Annabeth had to stay with her parents." Gladys' voice filled with regret.

"Matthias found out about the young couple and, boy, he knew just how to fix Tony. It was a particularly bad night on the water and Ol' Matthias made the long climb up here after having it out with his daughter. He knew Tony was out on the water and he knew just what to do to fix the man who'd stolen his child. Annabeth wailed and screamed and begged her father on her knees, but Ol' Matthias would hear none of it, and he came up here and snuffed the light." Gladys paused.

"Tony and his boys went down in the storm and Annabeth was inconsolable. She leapt from the lighthouse to her death on the rocks below. Still, on stormy nights, Annabeth's wailing and crying can be heard and she's appeared to some visitors and staff as an indistinct gray shade, hence her name as the Wailing Gray Lady of Acantilados Cortos." You could hear a pin drop as everyone stood and let the tragedy sink in.

I sighed inwardly and wondered what I would do if Hayden's pops had gotten in my way, if he'd been more like Matthias and less, well, understanding. I was pretty sure the minute we had departed Hayden's daddy had started making phone calls to vet me. Shit, if I had his money and connections and she were my daughter, I would. I wondered what kind of fallout from those calls I would face when I got back up north.

Gladys was telling us to take our time up here, exploring and checking out the view and that she'd be there for any questions we might have and our little band of folks dispersed throughout the confined space.

I was checking out the giant brass and glass monstrosity that was the lighthouse's original lamp, which had been lovingly restored and replaced to add to the building's value as a historical museum. The lamp was fully-functional and apparently something they lit on special occasions, at least the plaque nearby said so. I looked around for Hayden and spotted her near the window.

She stared out across the water that seemed to go on forever, dotted with bits of green and white, distant islands that were almost too far for the eye to see. Her look was stoic, her eyes far away as she stared off into space—or into herself, which was another very real possibility.

I slipped up behind her and became a presence at her back like I had been on the beach just hours ago, only this time I had to ask, "Hey, baby, what 'cha thinkin'?" She leaned back the fraction of an inch that it would take to come to rest against my chest and I put my arms around her.

She continued her sightless staring, her green eyes weighted with thought and said, "You're a force of nature, Reaver."

My eyebrows went up. "How do you mean?" I asked.

"I can't tell if you're the storm or my shelter from it..." she said and I felt my heart drop out the bottom of my stomach. Before I could open my mouth to apologize to her, to find out what she needed me to do, who she needed me to be to make things better for her she was going on.

"What I do know, is that when we're like this, you touching me, holding me, I feel okay, whole, safe, and loved and it's amazing, but it's hard too, because I thought this is what I had with Andy, I thought that he was my rock, my shelter... the person I could go to. But looking back on it, especially over the last year, it was you, wasn't it? You, Ashton, Trigger, and the rest of the girls, and the club. Always there to listen, to keep me busy when he was gone. But mostly it was you." She sniffed and I tipped a finger under her chin. She looked up and her eyes, made so much brighter, so much greener by her tears, tore through my heart like it was a wet paper bag.

God, she was fucking gorgeous when she cried, but at the same time I didn't want her to cry. Not like this, not from the hurt that was her crushed and broken heart. I wanted my Hayden back. The bright, vivacious spitfire that had my balls in a vice the second I laid my eyes on her. I wanted her laughing, I wanted her dancing, and the only time I wanted to see her cry was from the intense-as-hell things I did to her in the bedroom.

"Baby, don't get me wrong, you're hot as fuck when you cry, but please don't. Not for him, not for what was or what could have been, you're okay. It's okay." I gave her a watery grin. "You may be a little late to the party, sweetheart, but I promise you, it's only fashionably late, isn't that what you rich folks do?" She laughed, and swallowed her tears and her smile was the way Trigger explained Ashton's to me once, like the sunshine coming out from behind the clouds after a long absence from the rain.

I bent and impulsively kissed away her tears, and with the salt of them still on my lips, covered her mouth with mine. I felt her delicate fingers touch the side of my neck and my pulse throbbed, jumping up to meet them.

I kissed Hayden gently, sweetly, the way she should have been kissed, the way she should have been cherished from the beginning. She sighed out and went boneless against me, her back easing that much further into my chest, my hands settled on her trim waist and it was a moment that was perfectly captured with a click of Marcy's cell-phone camera.

Hayden startled and the moment was gone.

Marcy looked sheepish and asked me, "What's your number? I'll text it to you." She stood, thumbs poised, the bag from the gift shop downstairs dangling around her wrist. I gave her my number, completely aware of Hayden's vivid green gaze roaming my face. A moment later my phone buzzed and a moment after that it buzzed again. I pulled the phone from the inside pocket of my cut and held it so both Hayden and I could see.

The first text was the picture as it had been taken, in full color. It was taken from the waist up, vertically and it was something I would likely treasure forever. My eyes had been closed for the kiss and Hayden's had too. The lovely lines of her face were smooth with peace and serenity when I kissed her. Her body lax against my own, I held her, fiercely protective, and my own face was just as peaceful as hers.

I flicked to the next image and I gotta say, I liked this one much better. Through some magic on her phone, Marcy had removed all the color, and the image of Hayden and I locked in our embrace was so much more powerful in the stark black-and-white image. I looked up at the woman and smiled.

"Thank you," I said and I meant it with my whole being. Marcy smiled and nodded and went back over to her new husband who was watching the whole exchange from over by the lighthouse's lamp with some kind of fascination. Marcy murmured to him and showed him the picture and he smiled and kissed her like she was his whole world. He looked at me and an understanding passed between us, which was kind of cool.

Hayden was staring at the picture on my phone. Finally, she looked up at me and blinked owlishly.

"Is that really how you feel about me?" she whispered, and let her eyes roam my face before turning back to the photograph. In the picture, the hard lines and edges of my general look, of my personality, was markedly softened by her presence.

"Yeah, babe. That and so much more, that no images or words could convey." I pressed a kiss to the top of her head and saved the images to my phone, texting the black-and-white one to Trigger and Ashton for safekeeping before putting the device away. Hayden sagged into me further.

"I've always dreamed of being loved like that," she whispered. Her gaze returned out over the vast ocean.

"Like this..." I corrected her.

"What?" she asked, voice far away.

"You always dreamed of being loved 'like this', baby. There's no 'like that'. That's past tense and there's no past tense here. There's just the here-and-now, right here and right now. I love you like this." And to prove it I kissed her all over again, and she let me.

I drew back from her and smiled at the shine of tears in her eyes. She smiled up at me tremulously and I did a little victory dance in my head. Those were the kind of tears I wanted from her. I thumbed one out gently from beneath her eye and she smiled.

"Sorry," she said, "I'm such a sap." I smiled at her, a genuine grin.

"Don't ever be sorry about these," I said, wiping another away and sucking it from my thumb. She gave a little gasp of surprise at the action and I put my lips close to her ear.

"You are so fucking pretty when you cry," I growled, and I nipped the shell of her ear. She jumped in the circle of my arms and I smiled.

The brass ship's bell downstairs rang twice and we looked back over our shoulders to Gladys who smiled and announced that was our cue to head back down. We filed down the spiral stairs, our descent much quicker and easier than our ascent had been. When we reached the bottom steps an eager, bright-eyed, small crowd of tourists stood listening to another tour guide begin the story of the lighthouse's history.

I slipped my shades out of the inside pocket of my cut, the opposite side of where my phone rested. It had started buzzing insistently midway down the tower and I smiled to myself. No doubt Trigger and Ashton were blowing me up wanting to know what the fuck. Marcy was speaking softly to Hayden and I let them talk, pulling out my phone to see what was what.

Trigger: Didn't see that coming at all ;)

Trigger's Girl: Reaver OMG I thought you were going to look after her!?

I responded to Trigger's text first.

Sarcastic bastard.

Then to Ashton's.

Baby girl I am taking care of her. Look at the picture again.

Trigger's text came back first.

Trigger: LOL U now it.

I shook my head; he needed to learn how to friggin' spell.

Trigger's Girl: Okay. I see what you're saying, just please be careful with her. She's my best friend. *kisses*

I smiled and Hayden's voice brought me back to the here-and-now.

"What's that look for?" she asked softly, curiosity coloring her tone.

"Ashton says she misses you and hopes you're okay," I said. Hayden smiled.

"Tell her I miss her too and I'm okay," she said. I looked at her and smiled, tucking my phone away.

"Yeah?" I asked her.

"Yeah, I think so," she answered. I hooked an arm around her shoulders and neck and pulled her into my side. She brought her hand up and linked her fingers with mine where they rested at her shoulder and we walked like that back to the bike.

"Where are you off to next?" Marcy asked.

"Gotta meet up with Cutter," I said.

Marcy frowned. "Where do you get these names?" she asked, and Tom put his arm around his wife. I shrugged a shoulder indelicately.

"Cutter's the president of the local motorcycle club, the Kraken," I said.

"They tend to be named after certain physical or personality traits, sometimes mannerisms." Hayden said.

"Do you have time for lunch?" Tom asked, looking his wife over.

"Sure," I said. We didn't have to meet Cutter until four and it was barely noon. Marcy smiled and Tom smiled back indulgently.

"You mind if we do lunch in town?" Hayden asked, "I really want out of long pants in this heat and humidity." She gave the three of us a hopeful look and Tom and Marcy agreed whole-heartedly.

"Sure! Sure! We'd like to drop off our gift shop buys at our room anyways," Marcy said and smiled brightly.

Hayden smiled, and with plans set, we went back to the B&B. Hayden ran upstairs and I followed. We kept buying shit so I figured it was best to put the saddlebags back on the bike. I did that while Hayden slipped into some short white shorts that made her legs seem long. We left our clothes for the next day in a neat pile in the room's wing back chair and packed everything else carefully into the saddlebags.

I swapped out of my jeans and into my old-ass army fatigue cutoffs I'd picked up at some surplus store or another when I'd been out with Trig. I put the bags back on the bike and Hayden came back out in her running shoes; she'd stashed her white flip-flops on top so when we stopped she could ditch the hot sneakers in the saddlebag and swap out to the cooler sandals. I'd done the same. I switched into my white Adidas with the shorts; I wasn't about to ride in flip-flops. I didn't have 'complete moron' stamped on my forehead, just 'idiot' for bein' on the back of a bike in shorts in the first place.

Tom suggested this little seafood shack on the beach. It didn't take much to figure out that it was close to the marina Cutter had texted me the night before. Of course, the town wasn't that big. I followed Tom and Marcy this time and Hayden and I switched out to the more fashion- and temperature-conscious footwear when we reached the little open-air faux-grass-roofed establishment.

We were pretty quickly seated across from the other couple, and Marcy was eyeing me with unabashed curiosity.

"I'm pretty sure Reaver doesn't bite, babe. You should ask your questions," Tom said, perusing the menu.

I raised an eyebrow at Marcy. "What questions?"

She looked a bit embarrassed and nervous.

"Marcy is an anthropologist. She studies human behavior," Tom explained.

"Oh, that's interesting!" Hayden cried and leaned forward to listen.

"Uh-huh," I said, catching on. I was her new favorite science experiment, The Badass Biker. Marcy blushed and looked like she was afraid I was offended. I gave her one of my panty-dropping grins. "Ask your questions," I said and she glowed with excitement.

Out came a journal and a pen from her purse and I blinked. Damn, didn't think shit was that serious! Okay. I steeled myself.

"How did you get the name Reaver?" she asked.

I grinned. "My brothers gave it to me," I said. That was easy.

She frowned. "Your brothers growing up?" she asked and Hayden laughed lightly.

"I'm an only child," I remarked.

"He means the other men in the MC," Hayden said.

"MC, motorcycle club?" Marcy asked.

I nodded. "Yeah," I said.

"What does it mean?" she asked.

"My name?" I asked. Marcy nodded enthusiastically.

I gave Hayden a sidelong look and she smiled at me and shrugged. "YOLO." she said and I laughed.

Marcy frowned again. I looked at Tom and gave a one-shouldered shrug and before either of them could blink, I had slipped one of my knives out of my cut and flicked the handle, the blade springing free. Marcy jumped and this time, Tom frowned.

"I like knives," I said, and to make the point stick home, I slipped three more stilettos, two throwers, and a butterfly knife out of their hiding places, showing them and slipping them back into place in the blink of an eye each. I had more, way more, but the waitress came by to take our food order, stopping my little sleight-of-hand blade show.

Tom looked unsettled, but his wife Marcy was fearless; she leaned forward and asked, "So are all road names based on the kind of weapon you like?"

I laughed a little.

"Well there's me, and Trigger... he's a Marine Corps sniper; then there's our P., Dragon. Not sure how his came about but I have a few guesses. Then there's our VP, Dray, which is what he's always been, that's short for his given name, Draven. Uhhh..." I thought about it.

"There's Doc, he's an ER doc by profession; then there's Data, our resident tech-nerd. We got three prospects; Loyal, who is as his name implies but we're on the verge of patching him in and when that happens, it's bound to change..." Marcy held up her hand.

"Patching in, what does that mean?" she asked.

I explained what it meant, that Loyal would get the large center patch of our MC's colors and the square MC patch on the back of his leather vest. Right now it was just a top and bottom rocker, no colors. No name patches on the front.

Marcy was writing all of this down, though truth be told, she could find it all on Google for the most part.

Hayden placed her hand in mine under the table. I glanced in her direction and Marcy's next question brought with it the sound of screeching tires and breaking glass.

"What do the knife patches on the front of your vest mean?" she asked.

I turned my killer on her, the cold filling my eyes, my face shutting down, becoming expressionless. Tom's back went up, but Marcy simply looked at me with mild curiosity.

"I'm not going to answer that," I said, flatly.

"Why not? You've been very forthcoming about everything else. I don't see the big deal–" Tom put his hand on hers where it clutched her pen and she looked at him sharply.

"Leave it alone, babe," he told her, and she startled and looked at me again, I mean –really– looked. If she had any sense, she'd feel the cold radiating off of me. Hayden did. She shivered by my side and held very still, like prey when a predator goes by. Marcy blinked.

"I'm sorry I asked," she said finally, and I nodded once, my mask of charming personality snapping back into place. She was lucky she was getting anything out of me. If it hadn't been for that damn picture she'd given me at the lighthouse she wouldn't be getting shit, but she had no clue just how damned much that image meant to me.

We resumed talking but we avoided any more talk about the club, Tom carefully steering the conversation away from it. Marcy let him. Turned out she was an anthropologist and he was a historian, and they'd met in some kind of educational capacity or other. She asked us how we met and I was content to let Hayden tell the story.

I laid an arm across the back of her chair and leaned back in my own, listening to the story from her point of view, rapt, trying to glean anything and everything I could from the telling. She thought I'd been sweet and charming; she blushed as she told Marcy and Tom things that I knew, and some that I didn't, and I filed it all away.

She glossed over hiding Ashton and I went back to the conversation that had precipitated her agreeing to hide Ashton and I realized that I had some questions about it. Usually when it came to the dirty shit, the deeds better left buried, the ones better locked away in some internal vault never to see the light of day ever again, I could just walk away. Something nagged at me about this one, though.

I ate mechanically and replayed the phone conversation with Hayden all those many long months ago in my head…

"Ashton, hi!"

"Not Ashton, baby."

"Oh… Who's this?"

"Reaver, you remember me?"

"Of course I remember you! You're hard to forget."

"Good to know."

"Why are you calling me from Ashton's phone, is she all right?"

"No, babe, she's not. She's hurt pretty bad."

"Oh my god! Where is she? What can I do?"

"Hayden, Ashton's going to be okay, but there's something I need you to do. Can you do it?"

"What do you need?"

"Hayden, do you trust me?"

"..."

"Hayden?"

"..."

I sighed.

"Yes." Her voice soft, barely there. I let out a slow breath I hadn't realized I'd been holding.

"Okay, this is what I need you to do..."

"Reaver, are you all right?" I came back to the present at Hayden's panicked tone. Tom and Marcy were both staring at me, a little wide-eyed.

"What? Yeah! Yeah, I'm fine. Just got a little lost inside my own head for a minute there, Doll. What'd I miss?" I took a drink of my soda and gave her my full attention.

"Where did you go?" she asked. I licked suddenly-dry lips.

"You remember the first time I called you?" I asked, and gave her a meaningful look. Her brow furrowed and then understanding dawned in her bright green eyes, the fine line between her brows easing.

"Yes," she said carefully. I nodded.

"That's where I went," I said and carried on eating. She quietly changed the subject with the other couple.

"I don't understand how you aren't together. You both obviously have a long history. You've known each other, by all appearances, for years..." Marcy was saying. Hayden and I looked at each other, surprised.

"We've known each other one year, three months and two days," I said. Tom laughed.

"Can you give us hours and minutes?" he joked. I thought about it.

"What time is it?" I asked.

"One thirty-two."

"Two hours and eighteen minutes," I said. Tom laughed and I leveled a stare at him. He stopped laughing when he realized how serious I was. Hayden was staring at me open-mouthed.

"That's amazing," Marcy remarked.

"I remember the important things," I said around a mouthful, and swallowed.

"What else you have timed down like that?" Tom asked.

Every man I'd killed, the birth of my son, and the minute that Aimee walked out the door... I'd started calculating these things the day I got sober. When you went sober, counting the days suddenly became important. Like my knives, it had become an obsession. I looked at Hayden.

"Rick, the others, the birth of my son, and the moment Aimee walked out the door... and the moment you did too, right behind Ashton," I said, and her expression was soft with wonder.

"Who's Rick and the others?" Marcy asked.

"That's all I'm going to say. She knows what it means and that's enough. I'm done talking about me. Pick another subject..." I tried to soften the hard attitude by adding a belated "Please."

Our table was silent for a long time before Tom cleared his throat and turned the topic of conversation back to the lighthouse we'd just been to. Marcy's journal and pen disappeared back into her purse and I smiled, warming back up again. We chatted amicably, the tension smoothing out over a few minute's time.

"Well, I have to say you're a very interesting person, Reaver," Marcy said after a lull in the conversation. "Thank you for being so candid," she added and I took a swallow of my soda.

"Uh, sure, no problem. Sorry if I was a dick," I said. She and Hayden laughed.

"I'm sorry if I made you uncomfortable," Marcy said, shifting in her seat. Tom gave her a look of simple adoration and I nodded.

"It's good for me every once in a while," I said and she smiled. I cut a glance over at Hayden and felt my eyes widen some in surprise. She had a look on her face that was just a hair off from Tom's and she was looking at me with it. I searched her face and her expression changed to one of doubt.

"What?" she asked.

Marcy shot a knowing smile across the table and she and Tom stood.

"Well, thank you for a lovely first part of the day. See you at breakfast?" she asked.

"Maybe, depends on where the rest of the day takes us," I said. A beach party with an MC probably involved alcohol at the very least, a late night for sure. If we slept through breakfast we slept through it. Hayden had been around Sacred Hearts for enough weekly meet-ups and late nights out to know the name of the game. She nodded along with what I was saying.

Tom and Marcy went up to the front after more polite goodbyes and paid their half of the bill. Hayden was roaming me with her green-eyed gaze.

"What was that look for?" she asked me.

"For the way you were looking at me!" I said and laughed.

"Oh, and how was that?" she asked.

I let my own gaze roam over her lovely features.

"Don't know how to explain it, Doll," I said and it was half the truth. I didn't but I probably could have if I put enough brainpower into it. I just didn't want to. Hayden sighed but she was smiling a smile that said she was going to let me get away with that half-assed answer.

"So what now?" she asked, and I smiled faintly.

"We're gonna be early if we go to the marina now," I said.

"So what should we do?" she asked.

"I'm game to sit and talk," I said quietly.

"You want to talk?" I grinned. I could see her confusion, after all, wasn't that what we'd just been doing?

"I like talking to you, Doll," I said, stretching.

"Why?" she asked. Again with the why! Always, always, always needing to know why. I chuckled under my breath.

"I don't know. You see me and don't run screaming?" I said. She scoffed but I could see the understanding in her light green eyes.

"Reaver, you've never done anything to hurt me, or Ashton, or anyone else that I've seen or heard of that didn't deserve it," she said quietly and it brought me back to the questions I had earlier.

"Hayden," I said quietly and she looked up at me, cocking her head to the side at the seriousness of my tone.

"Yes?" she asked. So formal, so polite... so inquisitive.

"Remember when I called you?" I asked.

She was very quiet. I almost didn't hear her above the din of the fish shack when she said, "The first time you ever called me?" I nodded, keeping her under my watchful gaze. I didn't want to blink. I didn't want to miss any subtle nuance that said my questions unnerved her or distressed her.

"Yes. I already told you I remember. Why?" she asked, brow furrowing. I quirked a smile.

"Why'd you trust me?" I asked her quietly. She'd had no reason to. We'd barely crossed paths on anything more than an acquaintance level a handful of times.

She let out an explosive breath, her gaze far away as she turned inside of herself, going back.

"When you asked me if I trusted you, I hesitated... I mean, I didn't really know you, but when you sighed, it sounded just so defeated, and it was Ashton. I'd seen the bruises, you know... that first day in the locker room and I knew what that monster was doing. I had a friend in college whose boyfriend hit her. You sounded, I don't know, desperate to help her and I wanted to help her too, and I figured the least I could do was hear you out. So I did." She looked down at her hands.

"I didn't know about your friend," I said quietly.

"She got away. She was okay, but when I saw Ashton... I had to help any way I could and you were just asking me to hide her. I think I knew what was going to happen to her husband," she said, her voice low and careful, looking around to make sure no one was listening.

"But you helped us anyways," I said.

"I couldn't just sit by and not do anything," she said and I found myself nodding. The woman had a warrior's spirit hidden inside that slight body of hers.

"What about the rest? After you knew what I'd done?" I asked her, low and careful myself. Her luminous green eyes widened. It was the first time she'd ever heard anything even close to an admission of guilt out of me.

"I didn't know that you, personally, had done anything..." she said, but I could see she'd always suspected. It was written in the lines of her posture.

"Do you want to know?" I asked her solemnly. She gazed up at me.

"You would tell me?" she asked, incredulous.

"If you wanted to know," I admitted, but secretly begged from the bottom of my soul that she wouldn't ask. She closed her mouth.

"I trust you, Reaver," she said finally.

"I know, babe," I said, confused.

"It's good that you trust me too, but I... I don't think I need to know. Safer for all of us," she said and I nodded.

Good. Because I did not want to tell her about how Dray and I had broken into Chadwick's house. How we'd disabled and reset alarms, how we'd spent the entire spring day holed up in the man's own panic room. How we'd waited until deepest night until he was asleep, safe and sound in his bed.

I didn't want to tell her how I'd scored heroin off my old dealer the night before. How Dray and I had crept into Chadwick's room, how Dray had held the man down in his own bed while I'd shot him up. How I'd been jealous about the sweet oblivion I'd put him into.

I didn't want to tell her how Dray and I had drawn him a hot bath. How we'd stripped him buck-naked and got his incapacitated ass into the tub. How I'd sat on the tiled edge and told the man why it was he was going to die that night. How killing Chadwick Granger had meant absolutely nothing to me.

How I had felt cheated as I drew the razor down the insides of his arms from elbow to wrist. Not cheated because the task had fallen to me to take him out, but cheated because he was so doped out of his fucking head he'd smiled as I'd done it. Not a trace of fear in him or on him. It was probably the kindest murder I'd ever committed and that rankled me more than anything.

I was a fucking monster. My psyche was cracked right down the middle to a point where not even therapy, or the love of Hayden Michaels would fuse me back together. It would be like putting a Band-Aid on a severed artery. Useless... but having her green eyes fill up with horror, having her turn from me and leave, that was a devastation I didn't think I would be able to come back from. I needed Hayden to know about the monster in my head but I never wanted her to see it. Not if I could avoid it.

"Reaver, what's wrong?" she asked me startled.

"Why?" I asked and let my puzzlement show. Her slender arms went around me and she hugged me tight. Her voice, when it came, was muffled against my shoulder.

"You looked so incredibly sad just then..." she said, then asked, "What were you thinking?" I closed my mouth, and opened it to speak, then closed it again. I must have looked like a landed fish. She turned her face up to mine, her bright green eyes glimmering with worry as I debated what to tell her. I sighed out in semi-defeat. Lying had gotten me nowhere with Aimee and I didn't want to commit the same mistakes twice, but the truth could net me the same result here.

I took a deep breath and spoke my last thought aloud, a bid for the truth. No lies, not anymore...

"I was thinking I need you to know about that stuff, know it's there, never forget it but, babe, I never want you to actually see it." I looked at her solemnly.

"Why does that make you sad?" she asked but I could see she suspected she knew the answer already. Some of us just needed to hear it anyways.

"Because the thought of you seeing it for yourself... I'm afraid you couldn't handle it. That you'd walk and you wouldn't look back. That kills me just thinking about it," I confessed.

"You remember when you asked me to promise that..." she paused and bit her lower lip, blushing hard.

"Just tell me, baby. No need to be embarrassed," I said.

"Remember when you cut off my pajamas, the conversation after?" she asked boldly, a stubborn set to her chin. I smiled. There was my spitfire girl. I curved my arm around her shoulders and gave her a squeeze.

"Yeah, but you might have to remind me of some of the finer points," I said gently.

"After you asked me to promise you that you didn't mess our friendship up," she said. I nodded.

"Yeah." I said carefully, feeling like I was on dangerous ground all of a sudden. Where was she going with this? I felt my knee begin to bounce with nervous agitation under the table. She looked up into my eyes with such a serious look my heart seized in my chest.

No. No, no, no, no, don't do it babe. I silently begged in my head.

"You know what my first thought was when you asked me?" she asked.

I shook my head, not trusting my voice.

"My first thought was that if I had to choose a life with you in it versus one without, that it wasn't really any choice at all. That I'd rather walk out into the surf and drown myself than live a life without you in it," she said and I felt like I had taken a very real blow to my gut. I stilled, the air leaving my lungs in an explosive breath and no matter how hard I tried I couldn't draw another one until her words finished soaking into my brain. That had not been what I was expecting and I suddenly felt giddy, like a normal kid on Christmas.

I don't think Hayden realized what she'd just told me. I don't think she'd processed the feelings fully herself but her words... reading between the lines I looked down at her and pulled her tight against me. She fit in the curve of my arms, beneath my chin so perfectly, as if she were made for me. Meant to be there.

She'd rather drown than not have me in her life. If that wasn't love, I damn sure didn't know what was. She drew back and looked up at me.

"Say something, please?" she begged and I felt my lips curve into a smile. I didn't have words, and I'd rather show her instead anyways so I did.

I bent my head and placed my lips against hers in a kiss, and I poured every ounce of love, affection, desire, and need I had in me through that kiss and into her mouth, and let her drink it down, and the way she kissed me back told me more than anything that she was thirsty for it.

All the confusion, all the pandemonium going on inside her pint-sized package could be sorted through at her leisure. I didn't need any more validation than she had just given me. Though it would be nice to hear the words from her lips at some point, those three simple words that I gave her so freely, I didn't need them.

I broke the kiss and she smiled up at me, high spots of color on her cheeks.

"Wow," she said a little breathlessly, "What was that for?"

I just smiled at her, my most enigmatic smile and held her close.

8

H ayden...

"Hey, good to see you! Glad you could make it, man." Cutter strode across the parking lot of the small marina and clasped hands with Reaver, who sat astride Baby. I sat behind him and smiled politely in Cutter's direction. When he leaned down and kissed me on the cheek, I jumped and laughed, startled at the unexpected gesture.

Cutter gave me a grin and winked from behind his black wrap-around sunglasses, the corner of one eye twitching before smoothing into lines of laughter. I blushed. He was very handsome in his own way. Not as breathtaking or intense as I found Reaver to be but attractive none the less.

"I got a garage, follow me over and I'll open 'er up for you so you ain't gotta worry," he said and gestured to a line of small garages, like you would find in an apartment complex if we were back home in our land-locked state. I looked around and wondered where the housing was. All I saw was the marina office and it did look to have some kind of living quarters on the second story, though there were easily a line of twenty single-car garages, each with a number stenciled in white on the bright blue metal roll-up doors which were set in gray cinderblock walls.

Cutter was striding down the length of the structure and Reaver idled the bike along after him. Cutter stopped at number eight, and unlocked a sturdy padlock and rolled up the door to reveal his motorcycle backed into the single-car structure, to one side.

"Hop down, babe?" Reaver asked, but he didn't need to, I was already doing it. He backed Baby into the garage beside Cutter's black and orange Indian motorcycle. I handed Reaver my helmet after he shut off the bike.

The small garage was lined with flippers of every size and hooks and fishing poles and scuba tanks and all manner of things related to the sea. The bikes both barely fit. Reaver tossed my flip-flops on the ground at my feet with a loud slap. I toed out of my running shoes and shrugged my feet into the sandals, balancing on one foot, then the other, so my feet wouldn't come in contact with the scorching cement.

Cutter put out an arm to steady me and I gripped his muscled forearm with a little laugh and a grateful smile. I looked at Reaver, and he was watching me carefully, considering. I pulled my hand away from Cutter's arm self-consciously. Reaver smirked and chuckled to himself and shook his head, switching back into his flip-flops on the cool cement of the garage floor. He pulled out my crocheted beach cover-up and two towels from one of the saddle bags and Cutter pulled a beach bag that looked like it had been made from fishing net off a hook on the wall and handed it to me. I stuffed the towels into the bag and said thank you. I handed Reaver my oxford shirt to stuff back into the saddle bag. He did, and I shrugged into my cover-up and sighed in relief. It was much cooler in the oppressive heat.

"Here, babe," Reaver said and held out a can of spray-on sunscreen. I added it to the bag and he checked for his wallet and phone, and pocketed his keys.

He closed up his bags, leaving the helmets on the bike seat, and stepped into the sunlight. Cutter closed up the garage and locked it and I looked around again.

"The boats, Li'l Bit," he said and I blinked from behind my over-sized sunglass lenses.

"Excuse me?" I said.

"The people who park in the garages live on the boats," he explained patiently and I nodded and blushed, suddenly feeling stupid for not realizing it.

Reaver pulled me into his side and I let my arm go around his lean hips, taking shelter against his hard body. I felt small and safe tucked into his side, and I decided I really liked the sensation.

"Welcome to my little slice of paradise," Cutter said as we followed him around the marina's office, which had a painted sign that said "Harbormaster's office" over a door. Another door in the building stood open. It appeared to have a full laundromat going, the door propped open to combat the heat from the driers that were spinning.

"Which one is yours?" I asked, shading my eyes, looking out over the rows of bobbing boats at the dock. There were powerboats, sailboats, luxury yachts, and at one end of the marina, obvious houseboats.

"Guess," Cutter said with a grin. I raked him with my gaze and clasped my lower lip between my teeth.

"Not one of the houseboats. Not one of the powerboats either," I said. Cutter crossed his arms, his eyebrows going up.

"I'm guessing sailboat," I said.

"Okay, sure, but which one?" he said with a lopsided grin.

"That one," Reaver said, pointing down a row. Cutter laughed.

"Mmm, you cheated," Cutter said. I frowned.

"How do you know?" I asked Reaver.

"He's flyin' his MC's colors." Reaver said with a grin of his own, and I shaded my eyes again, looking at the flags fluttering in the wind off the back of the boat, and, sure enough, there was a flag for the Kraken MC.

It was some kind of sailboat, but I didn't know one boat from the other so I couldn't tell you. It was white and wood and beautiful gleaming brass and bronze in the sparkling Florida sun. It looked well-cared-for.

"It's beautiful," I breathed.

"Happy to take you aboard later, Li'l Bit," Cutter said and smiled, his chest swelling with a bit of pride.

"Come on, beach is this way," he grunted and Reaver and I trudged with him to the end of the marina and down some steps. He led us out to the beach, across the white sands. Some of his motorcycle club members were digging a pit in the sand, stacking the center with wood. They looked like a column of ants going back and forth from the parking area unloading trucks with wood, back and forth, back and forth, red-bronze skins glimmering with oil and sunscreen, deeply-colored from too much sun. Most wore shorts: board shorts, cut-offs, cargo shorts, but went shirtless beneath their cuts. Cutter was shirtless, his cut hanging loose from his deeply-tanned shoulders.

"Know what, not a bad idea," Reaver said and slid his cut from his shoulders. I fished the sunscreen from the bag as he stripped the snowy-white tee over his head.

"Whoa!" Cutter said, and put a hand up in front of his eyes laughing.

"Yeah, fuck you, buddy!" Reaver said, laughing. I sprayed him down paying careful attention across his broad, well defined shoulders and the back of his neck. He shrugged back into his cut and stuffed his tee into the bag. I slipped out of my cover-up and caught the appreciative curve to Cutter's lips as he raked me with his gaze. Reaver sprayed me down and I rubbed sunscreen across my forehead, cheeks, and nose.

We went down toward the water and set our stuff next to a pile in the sand, where Cutter indicated we should. Several surfboards were leaning against a rack much like a saw-horse set in the sand.

Cutter cupped his hands around his mouth and shouted out over the water. "Hossler!"

A blonde woman in swim shorts and a bikini top sitting on a

surfboard bobbed out in the surf. She whipped her head in our direction, then paddled out, leapt up and rode the next wave in. She was so athletic and elegant, riding with grace and ease. I laughed.

"That looks like so much fun!" I commented.

"Yeah? Good, 'cause I figured surfing today. A thunderstorm is rolling in tonight, tomorrow'd be better for snorkeling. We can get an early start and I can take you out to a great spot," Cutter said. I looked up at Reaver, nearly vibrating with excitement, and he smiled down at me.

"Rock on, brother, let's do it!" he said. The woman was running up the beach with her surfboard tucked under her arm. She reached us a little breathless.

"Cutter, what's up?" she gasped.

"Hayden, Reaver, this here is Hannah Hossler, one of the best surfers this town has got and one hell of an instructor," Cutter said.

"Hoss, this is Hayden and Reaver. Reaver is from the Sacred Hearts MC up north. Hayden's his..."

I looked up at Reaver and Reaver smiled at me, his beatific smile and said, "Friend. Hayden's my friend, before anything," he murmured.

I looked from him to Hossler, a faint smile on my lips. She was a beautiful girl, long blonde hair, athletic body, tall... way taller than me, which isn't hard. She was probably close to, if not, six foot to my five-foot-three. She had colorful tattoos up and down her arms. Flowers mostly, but the most impressive one was big and bold, a larger than life lotus blossom in the center of her chest, riding high just above and between her breasts, the petals pink and perfect on the outside, yellow on the inside, green vines and leaves curling prettily behind it.

The lotus blossom was flanked to either side by a red-and-yellow devil bird and above each red-and-yellow devil bird were blue-and-pink angel birds. Big and bold in the style that Squick, back home, drew... I believe he called it New School. The whole thing formed a chest plate of art that stretched from shoulder to shoulder from her cleavage up over her collar bones stopping just below the hollow of her throat.

One shoulder was taken up by a blue-and-red toy train engine and delicately flowing script, a memorial to someone she'd lost. A grandfather judging by the dates to either side of the train car. Classy scrollwork in black and white bracketing the image and words. Her other arm was a riot of color, a full sleeve of flowers from shoulder to wrist.

Her lower leg was a riot of color all the way around that matched her flowered arm and her chest, a larger than life dragonfly with blue daisies with bright yellow centers behind it. The dragonfly approaching a larger than life, bright fuchsia-and-white orchid. It looked like she was steadily working on getting both legs to match her sleeved arm.

She wore a shiny royal-blue bikini top that glimmered metallic in the sun and some very short cutoff denim shorts, the front pockets hanging soggy, dripping with seawater from below the frayed hem. The dripping water made a soft tap, tap, tap sound on the top of one of her perfectly pedicured feet. The nail polish was a metallic blue that matched her bikini top. The second toe of her right foot had a delicate silver toe ring on it. She held out her hand, no nail polish on her fingernails, and I took it and smiled.

"Hi!" she said. "Call me Hoss or Hossler." I shook her hand and she smiled, the ring through the left corner of her lip pulling slightly. The silver shone in the bright sun, the black bead glimmering. She had another ring in the eyebrow above the lip ring, slightly smaller than the lip's gauge but the two matched.

Hossler's energy was bright and vibrant and her positivity seemed positively infectious. I was smiling genuinely and she grinned and led me over to the rack of boards pulling one away she handed it to me.

"First things first, this one should work for you. Ditch the cover-up, keep the shorts if you want and let's get in the water! Cutter take McSexy over there," she said and I laughed.

"I'll be with you as soon as I see what I'm working with here," she said to Reaver. Reaver gave her the grin that always made me want to straddle his hips and do something naughty and I realized that the next time he gave it to me... I could act on those desires if I wanted. He would probably let me. I added my cover-up and flip-flops to the pile of our other belongings and filed that thought away for later... much later. Then I walked towards the water with Hossler, listening to her as she launched into some basic instructions.

An hour later we were sitting on the surfboards bobbing gently in the surf, I was soaked and had fallen in countless times. Reaver and Cutter were talking a ways from us. My arms were tired from paddling but I was having a blast and was determined to ride at least one wave most of the way in before I gave up.

"You got some amazing balance, girl," Hossler said, breathless.

"I do yoga," I explained equally breathlessly.

"Look, just stop overthinking it. You get up, you're pretty stable, then I see your brain starts to going and then you lose it. Just go with it. You can do it, you're one of the fastest learners I've ever had on a board." I smiled under her praise. Reaver was better balanced than I was, but he hadn't made it all the way in without falling either. He had, however, been able to stay up longer than me every time.

"You ready?" Hossler called.

"Yeah!" I called back and we lay on our stomachs and started to paddle as the water began to swell. I leapt to my feet, wobbling a bit as I got the feel for the board beneath me. I bent my knees like Hoss had told me and balanced precariously for a moment. I moved with the board, with the water, and smiled triumphantly. I shouted a whoop of triumph and glided onto the beach, leaping from the board and running along the sand. I stood for a moment, victorious, and looked back to see Reaver bobbing in the surf beside his board shouting and cheering, his arms raised to the true-blue sky.

I gave another whoop, jumped up and down, and did a victory dance in the soft white sand. Hossler and Cutter were cheering me too and I laughed and stuck out my tongue at Reaver who was striding out of the surf his board under his arm. I put my thumbs to my temples and waggled my hands and he looked at me grinning, seawater dripping from his sculpted cheekbones and along the bridge of his nose.

"Oh, really?" he demanded.

"Yeah, really! Did it before you! Nah nah nah whoop! Ah ha ha ha!" He'd dropped his board and was chasing me. I ran, but he swept me up from behind, I curled in on myself laughing and he nipped the back of my shoulder. He was laughing, I was laughing, the sun was shining and I felt lighter and freer than I had in years...

9

Reaver...

"She's somethin' when she smiles," Cutter commented. We were sitting on some driftwood logs near the fire pit. The sun was creeping towards the horizon. I'd changed from swim trunks back into some dry cargo shorts a little while ago. I could feel the tingle of an emerging burn across my nose and cheeks. My skin across my shoulders felt hot under the weight of my cut. I'd even applied more sunscreen after we'd gotten out of the water.

"She's somethin', no matter what. Smiling, crying; hell, she's exquisite when she cries," I said and felt a slight smile curve my lips.

"You're one of those, huh?" he asked.

"A sadist?" I asked. He nodded.

"Psychological mostly," I admitted with a sniff. His mouth turned down and his eyebrows went up and he nodded, his expression communicating that he wasn't exactly surprised, he just hadn't guessed my flavor of kink.

"So I gotta ask..." he drawled and I quirked an eyebrow at him. "Friends before anything else?"

I smiled. "Yeah," I said.

"Does that mean if I wanted to give it a shot, you won't try and cut my balls off?" he grinned and I smiled back at him, but just then my phone rang, saving me from having to answer. I plucked it out of my pocket and looked down into Ashton's smiling golden eyes. I answered it.

"Hey, Sunshine."

"Hey, Reaver, how's Hayden?" she asked and I smiled.

"Hold up," I said and switched my phone to the camera function. I snapped a picture of her laughing at something Hossler said and texted it to my best friend's girl.

"Should see for yourself any second now," I said into the phone.

"Okay," she said and a second later I heard a wooshed breath of relief.

"She looks like she's doing much better," she said.

"One day at a time, Sunshine Girl," I said and I could almost hear her smile.

"Reaver, I never got to say thank you for looking out for her like you did..."

"Ashton, baby, you ain't got to thank me for nothing," I said and her laugh was as soft as her voice.

"I know it's wrong but I'm almost glad he did it; she would have been miserable," she said, and I snorted.

"You don't know the half of it, baby," I said and she sucked in a breath.

"I knew it!" she said, low and vehement. There were no secrets between me, Ashton, and Trigger, so I didn't even bother to hide what was what.

"I don't know why she didn't tell you, babe, but yeah, she confirmed our suspicions on that one. He was cheating, her mom talked her into taking him back to save face. She's all kinds of mixed-up inside over it. I'm trying to sort through the tangle but honestly, I think at the heart of it all, her self-esteem is the most damaged," I said.

Ashton sighed. "I know how much you care about her, Reaver, and I'm glad you're there for her. Hayden's amazing and deserves amazing things. I know you'll be careful with her. I'm sorry if I implied anything else over the last few days–" I cut her off.

"Babe, it's cool. I understand. We all got issues and some of hers are tyin' in with yours. The whole thing is a big pile of ugly and I'm shoveling as fast as I can," I said.

"Well, don't you try and take everything on by yourself!" Ashton admonished.

"I'm not, baby. First things first, is getting her to remember what it is to be happy, I think 'mission accomplished' on that front by the way she's laughin' over there. Next thing I'm gonna do is get her to realize that she's fucking beautiful and attractive and I'm working on that... Douche-canoe did a number on the way she sees herself, I mean did you see the old-man pajamas she packed for her honeymoon?"

Ashton snorted. "I packed them remember?" she said.

"Yeah, well, I cut 'em off her and bought her something better," I said and Ashton started laughing hysterically.

"You did what?" she demanded.

"Yeah... I lost my shit a little bit," I said ruefully. I told Ashton all about it and she was very quiet for a very long time on the other end of the line.

"You didn't scare her, did you?" she asked quietly and I grinned.

"That was the whole point, babe, but it's all good. I think we get each other. She's fine," I said.

"You're never like that with me... I mean the times..." I stopped her.

"Naw, babe, I know where you come from, and I'd never do that to you. You weren't ready for it the first spring run you went with us, and since sharing hasn't really come up since, it was just a moot point. I don't need it all the time and with you it would have been torture and even as fucked-up as I am, I don't enjoy puttin' a real hurt on a woman. I save that shit for rat-bastards who deserve it."

She was quiet on the other end for a few heartbeats then finally said, "Thank you. You're a better man than you realize, Reaver." I gazed across the sparkling white sand beach to Hayden and sighed.

"Not good enough, Sunshine, but I'm working on that, as hard as I can," I said.

"You are who you are, Reaver, and I love you just the way you are, so don't try to change too much. Your ruthlessness has its place, don't forget. You keep us all safe. Me, Hayden, the MC... There isn't anything worse in the world than to love someone or something and to be powerless to keep it safe," she said and I swallowed, eyes misting some.

Ashton was small. Her ex had been cruel on more than just a physical front. There had been a point when he'd sent a couple of fake cops to Ashton's door, after she'd left him, to tell her that Trig had been killed while he'd been out on a run. I think that was where some of this particular conversation was stemming from. Ashton couldn't do anything physically to protect herself or us from her husband. So, I'd done it for her.

After I'd killed her ex for her, and trust me, if anyone needed to just fucking die it'd been him, she'd started going to therapy on Trigger's suggestion. He'd said it had helped him when he'd come back from pounding sand over in Afghanistan, had gone for a good long while when we'd been trying to get on the straight and narrow, and it had helped him. I couldn't afford it back then, and really couldn't afford it now, but Ashton had said if I wanted to go, she'd take care of it. I just didn't feel right taking her money.

Still, I got a lot out of when Trigger had gone from the long conversations we'd had about it, and had gotten even more out of Ashton going. We'd spent some afternoons curled on their living room couch while Trigger'd been out with Loyal doing whatever. We'd lain there, her slender arms around me, head tucked under my chin in a familiar, comfortable cuddle pile, and discussed things, her telling me about the abuse at the hands of her ex and what her therapist had told her and the conclusions she'd come to.

A lot of those conclusions I'd been able to mirror onto my own situation with the shit with Rick. It helped and I felt like I was growing, getting better. I'd definitely noticed I was less angry, that I was able to go further and further between needing to feed the monster in my head with the fear that I invoked during sex or with violence. The shit with Hayden, what was done to her, what talking to her was bringing up for me... That was making it harder to shove the beast back in its box.

"Reaver, are you there?" her soft voice asked me.

"Yeah, baby, I'm here. Sorry, you just got me thinking," I smiled.

"Ah, well, I'd gladly leave you to those thoughts if you'd pass the phone to Hayden," she said and I grinned.

"Anything for you, Sunshine," I said and meant it. I loved Ashton like I loved Trigger. She was my second-best friend behind the big man. That being said, I wasn't in love with Ashton. Nope, that was all for Hayden. I got up and trudged across the sand and held the phone down to my beautiful girl.

"It's for you, Doll," I said and she looked up at me, shading her eyes. No clue where her sunglasses had gotten to. She smiled and took the phone.

"Hello?" she said and I went back over to Cutter and dropped down next to him.

"That was an interesting conversation," he said dryly.

"Yeah?" I asked, eyeing him warily.

"Well, at least the one side of it," he said. I smirked.

"Sorry man, didn't mean to be rude," I said.

"Naw, naw, naw! Not at all, brother, you got a life up north, a club, people who care about you, and people you care about. I get it man, look around me. I'm surrounded by much the same," he said. "I'm king of my very own little paradise kingdom out here and I wouldn't trade it for the world. Still, a king does get bored from time to time," he grinned in my direction.

"Let me guess, and then this fine little princess comes into town on the back of a black steed and the King's no longer bored for a minute," I said.

Cutter grinned, flashing very white teeth in his tan face. "So back to what we were talking about before you were saved by the bell..." he said.

"What? About me cuttin' your balls off?" I asked with a grin. He shoved me over, planting a hand in my shoulder. I went over easily and laughed.

"All seriousness, she's fucking gorgeous and I'm gonna sound like a barbarian here but I wanna tap that. Or at least I want to see if she's down for it. What I don't want to do is offend my guests or step on your toes. You're a cool dude, Reaver. I like you." He looked me over, brown eyes sparkling with calculation and intelligence.

I let out a breath I didn't realized I'd been holding and we both looked over to Hayden. She was looking over at the both of us, my phone pressed to her ear, her lower lip clasped between her teeth.

"She's so just... crushed, right now," I said. Hayden bowed her head and nodded saying something into the phone.

"Gimme the full Monty and we'll see what's what," he said, and it was so like something Trigger would say when we strategized or planned about anything, that I found myself spilling it. Cutter nodded and listened and said, "Lemme think about this for a bit. She's coming this way."

I looked up and Hayden held my phone out to me. Her eyes sparkled with good humor still but there was a bit of considering weight behind them. I smiled up to her and plucked the phone from her hand, making sure to graze her fingers with my own.

"Hossler is going back out," she said and dropped to the sand beside me.

"Doesn't surprise me!" Cutter said. "Swear to God that girl is half fish."

"So, what happens now?" Hayden asked.

"Well, pretty soon the grill gets fired up, Pyro will start the bonfire, we eat, we drink, we get some music going and, if you're up for it, Reaver, we'll bust out some targets. Get some knives out and see what you got when it comes to throwing." I felt a slow cold smile curve my lips, the warmth seeping out of my eyes.

"Oh, I think I'd like that. I think I'd like that a lot," I said. Cutter was giving me a calculated once over.

"Prospect!" Cutter shouted and a kid that looked like he wasn't even out of high school came jogging over.

"Yeah, Cap'n?" he asked and I felt my eyebrows go up. They called their President Captain. Interesting, but given where we were, not out of place.

"Set up the targets over yonder," Cutter said with a wave of his hand.

"Aye, aye, Cap'n!" The kid ran off and a few minutes later, there he was, wrestling a plywood cut out the height and shape of a man out a ways.

"You okay, Li'l Bit?" he asked and I turned to Hayden who was shading her eyes and watching everyone, a faraway distance to her gaze.

"Reaver is really good," she stated simply.

"How do you know that?" I asked. She'd never seen me throw, had she?

"Last summer at the clubhouse I watched you throw out in the back against some of the Sacred Hearts from out of town. You were so drunk you couldn't stand up straight, you didn't even remember you'd been throwing the next morning, you were so black-out drunk, but you hit the target with every knife on every 'X' marked out as a killing blow." She turned her green eyes up to me.

"Trigger and Ashton said you almost threw better drunk than you did when you were sober and I figure they would know." She gave an indelicate one-shouldered shrug. Cutter looked in my direction.

"This I gotta see," he said, grinning.

"Hey, Doll?" I said.

"Yeah?" she asked.

"Next time, do me a favor, and record that kind of shit," I said and grinned, and she laughed.

"I did. You threw my phone in the ocean," she said. I hung my head, shaking it and she laughed, high and long.

"Son of a bitch!" I swore.

"That's what you get!" she said, wiping tears from her eyes.

Cutter was grinning and cocked his head to the side.

"Lady has a point," he said.

"You would take her side," I said grumbling, getting to my feet and dusting off my ass.

"She's prettier 'n you," he said. Hayden snorted.

"I don't think so," she muttered under her breath. I smiled. She thought I was pretty. Huh.

The sun was over halfway down behind the horizon now. Cutter looked over.

"C'mere, you two, wanna show you somethin'," he said. Hayden and I exchanged looks and shrugged. He sat us down facing the water. The sun was going down at a pretty good clip.

"Wait for it and don't blink. At the very second the sun goes down behind the horizon, it hits the water just right and if you're lucky..."

A blinding green flash lit from the sun just as it dipped below the horizon. I smiled at Hayden's little startled "Oh!" of surprise.

"What was that?" she asked.

Cutter grinned. "That was science, Li'l Bit," he said, and explained to us both about the curvature of the earth, atmosphere, and light wavelengths as we stood up, dusted off, and went back toward where Pyro was lighting up the bonfire.

We ate and listened to the Kraken swap stories, laughing and smiling and just generally chillin' out. Hayden dug her cover-up out of the fishnet bag and shrugged into it, wrapping it around her slender shoulders. I got up and sat behind her, curving around her, warming her back against my body while the fire warmed both our faces.

"Storm should be rollin' in around midnight or so, kids. So enjoy it while the getting's good." Cutter called.

"Ow! Ow! Ow! Somebody piss on it!" Hossler cried from the surf and several of the Kraken erupted into howls of laughter.

Hayden and I turned; Cutter went running out in her direction, laughing. The look on her face was fury mixed with pain and Hayden got to her feet, I rose with her, and we went to investigate.

"It's not fucking funny, you assholes! Hurry up, Cut! Jesus Christ, it hurts!" she cried. Cutter unzipped his fly and Hossler held out her leg.

"Fuck, girl! You got too many goddamn tats! Where is it?" he demanded, she pointed, and he peed on her leg.

"What are you doing?" Hayden asked, aghast.

"Stung by a jellyfish, it fuckin' works. Easy, Hoss." Tears stood out in Hossler's eyes and she tried to hold still.

"You gotta go? I'd really appreciate it," she said to me, and I laughed.

"Never been asked to piss on someone before," I said.

"Cross it off your bucket list," she growled. So I did what the lady asked. Hayden's bright green eyes were wide and she was trying not to laugh.

"Hey, Li'l Bit, get me a few bottles of water to rinse off?" she asked.

"Uh, um, sure..." Hayden went back to the fire where a couple of bottles of water were handed up to her. She came back at a swift walk as I tucked myself back into my shorts.

"How does that not gross you out?" Hayden blurted. Hossler was staring at the sky making an inarticulate noise of frustration and pain.

"It hurts so bad!" she complained.

"I know, baby just give it a few minutes," Cutter said. She took in these short panting breaths and the kind of discomfort she was in, well, there was nothing hot about it, it did nothing to trip my trigger. I just plain felt bad for the girl.

"Li'l Bit, dump those out on the ground and fill 'em with seawater, dumping fresh on it is just going to make the barbs fire more venom. Seawater's best," he told her and she went to comply.

"Thanks, guys, it's easing off some. Goddamn, fucking, son of a bitch!" Hoss swore.

Hayden returned and Hoss took the bottles from her and rinsed off her leg.

"It hurts that damn bad, you'll do anything that works, girl. Trust me," Hossler said.

"Hey, Hoss! Heard you'd like to raise the Sacred Heart guy's trouser snake! How's that working out for you now?" someone yelled from the fire.

"Fuck you, Gator! You better watch your ass or I'm going to put a mess of my snakes in your bed and a few rats in your club room!" she yelled back.

"Hossler breeds and raises snakes and by default, rats to feed 'em, for a living," Cutter explained.

"Sweet!" I said.

Hayden's eyes were wide. "What kind of snakes?" she asked.

"Constrictors," Hossler answered shortly, limping towards the fire with us. She propped her board on the rack which had been moved inside the circle of light cast by the blaze.

I touched Hayden and she jumped. I frowned. She smiled up at me and said, "Sorry, still getting used to the whole casual-touching." She smiled and leaned into me and I pulled her close, an arm around her shoulders. Cutter raised an eyebrow at me and I shrugged a shoulder.

Hayden stayed near Hossler, who was getting better, the more time went by. Still, she would grab Hoss whatever she needed, food, beer, that sort of thing, until the lines of pain faded completely from her face. She'd pulled her blonde hair into a messy knot high on her head and stuck a couple of chopsticks through it. Where the hell she'd gotten those, I couldn't tell you.

"So, Reaver, you got any on you, other than what's inked under your skin?" one of the guys asked me. I glanced down at the stilettos inked into my inner forearms.

"Always do," I said.

Hayden watched me from across the fire, a faint smile gracing her lips, a bit of pride shining in her eyes and I smiled for her.

"Except when you came to the clubhouse. Didn't find a one on ya," Tiny said. I looked over at him and Cutter saw it before his Sergeant-at-Arms.

"Shit, you did, didn't you?" His brown eyes turned stormy, his mouth down at the corners. I nodded reluctantly. I felt bad for Tiny, I really did, but I liked Cutter, he was a cool cat and he ought to know.

"How many?" he asked.

I got up and stepped just to the edge of the brighter circle of light.

The target was at the very edge of where the fire illuminated, two tiki torches lighting it up to either side.

"A demonstration," I said. Cutter nodded.

"I got one more knife on me than I did the day I showed up to your MC," I said and swallowed. I got some skeptical looks, standing there in just my shorts and my cut. Better to just show them then. I slipped my first thrower free and let fly, then the next, and the next, and the next; one right after the other, each one finding the target out in the gloom, one after the next. I never stopped moving, when I was out of the short throwing blades I let fly with the stilettos, and let me tell you, getting a throw right on one of those slender, unbalanced blades had taken a shit-ton of practice.

Eight blades in all were sunk into various killing and seriously maiming points on the target and I straightened and wracked my neck. I didn't have a blade left on me and I felt naked as the day I was born.

Cutter's gaze had gone flat but he looked on me with some mad respect. There were a lot of stunned and incredulous looks from his people but you know, I got that a lot. I shrugged and smoothed my hands down the front of my cut. They tingled with apprehension and a desire to do more. I looked across the fire to Hayden, her shining eyes danced with firelight and an edge of fear that made desire uncurl in my chest. Her lips curved in a smile that spoke of deep, quiet pride in my ability to stun the men around us and I felt an answering cocky smile of my own start to spread across my face.

"That was nice, that was real nice," Cutter said and I heard the slight edge of sarcasm in his tone. He was looking square at Tiny, not me, and I realized he was impressed with my abilities, but not so much with his man. Tiny looked at me murderously.

"Hey!" Cutter barked, and Tiny looked to his President.

"You don't get to be pissed at him for your fucking ineptitude!" he said and people were pointedly looking away from the big man and their pres. I retrieved my knives.

"Look, man, I didn't want to make anybody lose face or nothin'.

I'm happy to show your man where I hid 'em. Sacred Hearts, we're a crafty bunch," I said.

"It's true," Hayden said softly, and several men turned in her direction, "They are." I felt something in my chest loosen, she thought I was in some sort of trouble, and it was true, things could swing that way, but I didn't get that vibe. Cutter was pissed, sure but it wasn't all at me. Still, she'd thought I was in some kind of trouble, I could see it in her eyes, in the stiff set of her body, and still she'd spoken, drawn the focus away from me and on to herself. Terrified, but fucking fearless.

"You worried for your man, Li'l Bit?" Cutter asked with a one-sided grin and his pleasantness was back in place. Shit, we were a lot alike, he and I.

"Yes, but Reaver isn't mine," she said quietly and cast her eyes to the sand.

"Yeah, I am, Doll," I said with a smile. Her gaze flicked back to mine and I could see a war in her eyes. She nodded slowly but was quickly lost inside her own head. I sighed, her happy reprieve had been far too short. Cutter's gaze flicked between us and finally settled on me. I could see he wasn't happy and I sort of felt like a puppy being scolded for shitting on the rug with that look he was giving me. I buried my hands in my pockets. He stood up in one fluid movement.

"Tiny," he said and the other man got up. Hayden got to her feet and looked dubious.

"Relax, Li'l Bit. Everything's cool," Cutter reassured her. She remained standing as the two men approached me.

"A word over here, man?" Cutter asked and I nodded, not entirely sure I wasn't about to have my ass beat. Hayden looked a touch frantic and I tried to calm her with my eyes.

"If Cutter says everything's cool it is," Hoss said, reaching up and taking Hayden's hand. Hayden looked so torn it was almost a little heart-rending. I smiled at her reassuringly and stalked across the sand back towards the target with the two men. Once we were out of earshot of the rest of the party, Cutter looked at me.

"Show him, and Tiny, by fuck, you'd better be paying attention," Cutter said. Tiny's eyes widened.

"Yeah, Cap'n," he said. I showed him the special pockets sewn in along the seams of my cut that held the stilettos, causing just a bit more bulk in the leather. I had four, two each side.

The throwing knives were ranged on the inside of the front of my cut, flat and secure between the leather and the patches. Cutter gave a low whistle.

"Where you get hardware like this?" he asked, finger-fucking one of my throwing knives.

"Got a blacksmith buddy of mine, backwoods fella, forges the throwing knives for me. They're thinner than what you can buy online, balance is a bit off, but compensation is easy, concealment is what I was after, though. Only thing I can't beat is an x-ray or a metal detector. Pat downs are a cinch," I explained.

"Tiny, I take some of it back buddy. I might have missed some of these," Cutter said carefully, and I saw him taking mental notes for himself.

"You got a badass setup," Tiny said, with no little awe in his voice.

"These the real deal?" Cutter asked, flicking a switch on one of my stilettos. He was handling the blade with reverence and I smiled. Finally, a dude that really knew his knives!

"It's a Panak," I said with pride. "All my babies are."

"Shit," Cutter said. I looked towards the fire; Hayden was watching us, her slight shoulders slumping in relief. I could see her drag in a deep breath and she trailed a toe in the sand. She looked up sharply and out over the water and started walking out towards it as if drawn by strings or a music we couldn't hear.

"Your girl all right?" Tiny asked, and he won points with me for asking.

"Yeah, let her think," I said and watched her go.

Cutter looked at me and nodded Tiny off. Tiny went, looking like he'd narrowly avoided the executioner's axe, a close shave rather than having his head lopped off.

"Mind if I butt in with my two cents?" Cutter asked.

"Naw, go ahead, man, I got mad respect," I told him and it was true, he ran a tight ship with his crew. He wasn't playin' at this.

"Seems to me that's all Li'l Bit's been doing is thinking. She's wearing herself ragged turning the same things over and over in that pretty little head of hers." He raked over me with his gaze. I smoothed down my hair and twisted my lips and thought about it some. He had a point.

"Lemme ask you somethin', Brother," he said.

"Shoot," I said.

"Why ain't you tapped that?" he asked and I barked a laugh.

"She's been wrung out psychologically and emotionally," I said and he raised his eyebrows as if to say 'So?' I palmed the back of my neck and I sighed.

"I want her scared and trusting underneath me more than words can say, but at the same time I don't want to scare her away. I'm afraid I'm gonna overwhelm her and that'll be it," I said truthfully.

"You didn't scare the gold-eyed girl. I heard you tell her on the phone," he said.

"Ashton was different, she's my best friend Trigger's girl, and is pretty much afraid all the time anyways, or she was when we shared her," I said and shrugged.

"You don't mind sharing?" he asked.

"Not every once in a while, for sex only. I'm not a poly kind of guy, just a freak in the sack. I told her, she should rebound off of you or one of your crew down here, get some of her physical needs met. Her intended hadn't touched her in forever." I was looking out at her small figure standing on the shore as she stared out over the water.

"Shit, no wonder she flinches every time she's touched, then goes all in as soon as she knows who it is. She's not used to being touched, and at the same time is starved for it." His gaze followed mine.

"Yep, that about covers it," I said.

"She wants you," he stated flatly.

"Yeah," I said.

"You want her," he said.

"Yeah," I agreed again.

"I don't mind sharing," he said and I glanced at him.

"She needs to feel good, about herself, her looks... She needs some serious attention." I thought about it. I could keep myself in check; she would probably be more comfortable with me... Hmm.

"She knows about you and the other girl, the one who belongs to your best friend," he stated.

"How you know that?" I asked.

"When she was on the phone at dinner last night. Remember? The girl on the phone..."

"Ashton, Sunshine." I supplied.

"Sunshine said she'd be willing to share her Viking and Hayden didn't as much as flinch or blink. Just politely declined. She's thought about it," he said with certainty.

I was thinking about it now.

"Let me go talk to her?" he said and I glanced his way. Why not? I was right here, she was safe enough. I frowned as light glimmered on the horizon.

"Storm is coming in," he said, and I realized it was lightning I was seeing, out over the water, in the distance.

"What do you think, man?" he asked. I nodded and he put a hand on my shoulder.

"Be right back," he said and strode out across the sand toward the woman holding my heart.

10

Hayden...

I watched the trio of men walk across the sugar-fine sand back towards the target Reaver had pulled his knives from. They stood in a huddle, going through Reaver's cut as he showed them how and where he had all of his knives hidden. Even I had been surprised at how many he had stashed away, but I shouldn't have been. Reaver was like that. Beautiful, dangerous, deadly, and apparently, mine.

The tension and my fear for Reaver's safety drained out of me so very slowly, ticking down and away like grain after grain of the same fine sand we stood on through an hourglass. I palmed the back of my neck and huddled miserably in my thin cover-up. The fire was warm at my back and conversation among the Kraken had picked up, though softer, more muted, and less boisterous than it had been.

Reaver was watching me, a faint reassuring smile painted on his lips. I watched them and when several minutes went by with no violence I let out a breath I hadn't realized I'd drawn and held. A glimmer of light out of the corner of my eye had my head whipping round. I watched and another flicker came a few moments later.

I looked back to the men who were obviously talking about the knives and rolled my eyes. The three of them looked like a trio of boys discussing their favorite GI Joe action figures now, a child-like gleam of wonder in their eyes, and I moved off towards the water to think. I stood and stared as lightning glimmered and flickered in the distance. It was so beautiful where it reflected off the water.

I wanted Reaver. I finally admitted it to myself. I wanted him to hold me, scare me, kiss me, thrill me in the way only he had ever been able to do. I wanted it with a deep and abiding ache and talking to Ashton that afternoon made me realize it.

The phone had been warm when he'd set it in my hand, it could only be one person, so I'd greeted her by name.

"Ashton."

"Hey, you! You sound better. Happier!" she'd said and I'd told her about the lighthouse and the surfing lessons. I really did feel better, lighter than I had in days.

"Soooo, Reaver sent me a picture of the two of you this morning," she said and my heart froze in my chest for a moment. I looked over at the man in question who was deep in conversation with Cutter at the time.

"You aren't mad, are you?" I asked meekly.

"Hayden, are you nuts?" she'd asked me. "I can't ever be mad at you, not for letting Reaver take care of you. Honey, you were miserable with Andy, you can't deny it..." she sighed. "You two... you know?" she asked.

"No, uh, not yet," I said, very conscious of Hossler beside me.

"'Yet' being the operative word," Ashton said and I smiled.

"I don't know if it's such a good idea so soon... you know?" I said.

"Worried about what people will think?" she asked and I was taken aback. Was I? I mean, was I, really?

"I didn't think I was," I told her honestly. It was always truth between us besties.

"Okay, are you worried about what people will think or what your mother would think?" she asked, and I think she hit the proverbial nail right on the head.

"Wow," I said into the phone.

"Hayden, we love you. Me, Trigger, Reaver especially, and the whole MC... You're family to us. Family that doesn't judge you! We love you for who you are, not for who we want you to be, not for who you're with, just you!" she said and I smiled a little sadly.

"You're the best, Ashton," I whispered, "I still worry about my dad, though," I confessed.

"Honey, Reaver talked to your dad. Your dad gave him his blessing to take you down there," she said.

"What?" I asked confused.

"Everett heard the whole thing," she said matter-of-factly. I looked over at Reaver and chewed my bottom lip.

"My dad knows I'm here with Reaver?" I asked just to make sure I was hearing things right.

"Yep." she said. I sighed. We talked for a few minutes more and I hung up, then dialed my daddy's number, which I knew by heart.

"Hello?" he picked up on the fourth ring, just when I thought it was going to kick to voicemail.

"Daddy?" I asked.

"Peanut! How are you doing?" he asked.

"I'm so sorry, Daddy..." I started and he hushed me just like he used to do when I was a child.

"No, no, no, not your fault, Baby," he said, "None of this is your fault." He sighed. "I owe you an apology, Peanut. I never should have left you alone with your mother for as long as I did. I realize that now."

"You're not disappointed in me?" I asked, tears welling up. Hossler put an arm around me and I sniffed.

"No, Baby, not one bit," he'd said and I sighed out in relief.

"Is that young man Rhett taking care of you?" he asked. I frowned.

"Rhett?" I asked. "Don't you mean Reaver?"

"Ah, yes, I looked into Mr. Butler, his first name apparently is indeed Rhett. Is he taking care of you, Hayden?" he asked, and his voice was full of concern like I had never heard it before.

"Daddy, he's really amazing," I said, adding, "He's taking very good care of me." I looked over at Rhett Butler and stifled a giggle.

"He has a past, Hayden. I figured he did when I saw the tattoos, but I never imagined–" I stopped him.

"What, that he was addicted to heroin at one point? That he has a son and an ex that he is paying child support to? That for a long time the motorcycle club he belongs to weren't the best of people?" I asked gently, slightly exasperated, but understanding full well that I was still my daddy's little girl. Of course he would check on me, into who I was with.

"He told you?" my father had asked, incredulous.

"Reaver doesn't lie to me, Daddy. It's not all pretty, sunshine and roses, but he doesn't lie. Not once, not ever," I said softly. There was a long silence on the other end of the line.

"He's suspected of murder, nothing they were able to prove," he said. I sighed.

"Daddy, I know about that too," I said gently.

"Hayden, you're bright, my little girl is so smart... Are you sure?" he asked me.

"Are you sure about Mom?" I asked and I know it was a low blow. He sucked in a breath.

"I never regretted marrying your mother. Not for one minute, Hayden," he said and I heard in the steel of his voice that he meant it. "Not until I walked into that house and heard her talking to you that way." Tears sprang to my eyes. "She wasn't like that when I met her, when she had you... I don't honestly know what happened. Maybe it's my fault, maybe I was away too much... I don't know. What I do know is that I loved your mother very much but after your wedding..." he trailed off, silent for too long.

"Daddy?" I asked, and he sucked in a shuddering breath.

"Peanut, you take as much time as you need," he said, and I realized my father was crying.

"Daddy?"

"I'll see you when you get home. I love you, Hayden, and I'm so very sorry for everything," he said.

"Daddy, I love you, too." My voice cracked and the pent-up tears spilled over.

"See you soon, Baby," he said and hung up. I swallowed and dashed at my eyes. Reaver was deep in conversation with Cutter and I sighed, wondering when this emotional roller-coaster would end, but I had had to admit to myself then, as I had to admit to myself now, that my conversation with my father had lifted quite the burden off my shoulders.

I sighed out and came back to the present, watching the lightning flicker over the water. I listened to the waves crashing upon the shore, felt the breeze tickle across my skin, and let some things go. Warmth enveloped me from behind, the still presence that had become so familiar folded around me and I leaned back into a muscled chest. I closed my eyes and sighed again and cuddled back into Reaver.

"I'm tired of thinking," I said.

"That's what I told your man. You've been thinking too much." I startled, hard, and the arms tightened around me.

"Easy, Li'l Bit. He's watching us, he's just back yonder. You're safe." I put a hand to my face and bowed my head.

"I'm sorry, I thought you were him, you have that same stillness..."

He chuckled. "Stillness, huh?" he asked, and I craned my head back to look up at him. His eyes smiled as much as his mouth did, jovial lines fanning out at the corners of his eyes and bracketing his mouth. I'd never been much for men with facial hair, but on Cutter, his close-clipped beard looked right. I didn't think he would look complete without it.

"Your man and I have been talking," he stated dryly, settling me more comfortably in his arms. I let him. It was growing chilly as the breeze grew stronger. I looked out over the water at Mother Nature's light show, which grew closer as the minutes passed. It still seemed a long way off yet, though.

"Oh? About what?" I asked, genuinely curious, but knowing the answer.

"About you, beautiful," he said.

"What about me?" I asked softly.

"About what you need, and the best way of gettin' it to you," he said.

"And what do you two think I need?" I asked, already knowing the answer to that, too, but wondering to myself if they weren't wrong.

"Baby, you know as much as we do what you need. You're getting a taste of it right now and you're drinking it up like it was the last drop of water in an eternal desert," he said.

"What are you talking about?" I asked, genuinely perplexed.

"I'm talking about this," he said, and gave me a little squeeze.

"This?" I asked.

"Touch, affection... love, at least from Reaver anyways," he said. I frowned and looked up into his tan and handsome face; some tendrils of his long brown hair had come loose from his ponytail and artfully framed his face in these fine curls that whipped sideways in the coming wind. He looked suddenly solemn.

"Let us take care of you tonight... What do you say, Li'l Bit?" he asked me.

I looked back behind us at Reaver whose expression was carefully schooled into a blank mask, giving nothing away. I beseeched him with my eyes and he started across the sand towards us. I looked up at him when he drew even with us.

"Cutter says I should let you both take care of me," I said. Reaver's smile was patient and kind and held just the barest hint of sadness.

"I think that's a fine idea, don't you?" he asked me. I tipped my head up and he brought his lips to mine, a careful, chaste press of lips.

"I don't know what I'm doing," I said, softly, against his mouth.

"You don't have to do anything, baby," Cutter said. "That's the whole point. Let us take care of you, let us spoil you, and hold you," he pressed a light kiss to my shoulder, "and make you feel good," he finished.

"Let us show you how beautiful you are to us," Reaver murmured and he kissed me again, only deeper this time. I kissed him back and gasped into his mouth when Cutter lightly nipped the side of my neck.

"Say yes," Cutter pleaded, and I looked into Reaver's eyes, silently asking if this is what he really wanted, because I was pretty sure it was what I wanted.

"I want you to feel good, I want you to be happy, I want to show you a good time tonight and later, much later, when we're alone I want to show you what it's like to play on the darker side of things, like I started to before." He swallowed hard. "I just want you to be happy, Doll. I want you to look in a mirror tomorrow morning and see what we see every time we look at you." I gazed up into Reaver's so-blue eyes, the firelight dancing along their icy depths. "Let us take care of you?" he pleaded and I nodded.

"Okay," I said, heart in my throat. That sensation you get, not when you're afraid, or terrified of doing something wrong, but rather the one you get when you're in the front car of the biggest tallest roller-coaster you've ever seen, poised at the top looking down that long stretch of track just before you go over the edge and your stomach drops out. It was like that. It was like that, a lot.

We went by the fire and collected our beach bag of things. Cutter instructed his people to pack it in in the next thirty minutes, that the thunderstorm was coming in faster than expected. He and Reaver walked with me between them, safe in the curves of their arms, Reaver's across my shoulders, Cutter's around my hips.

Cutter led us back to the marina, keying us inside one of the gates and down a long gangway onto one of the docks. We walked to his slip and he said to us, "Welcome aboard," leaping up onto his boat. Reaver handed me up to him and leapt up after us.

"I hope I don't get seasick," I worried and Cutter laughed.

"Shouldn't be too much wind, just a shit-ton of rain, thunder, and lightning," he said. "Water shouldn't be too choppy, not going to be smooth though, either." He led us belowdecks into a very nice living room with deep brown leather furniture.

"Make yourselves at home," Cutter said, "I'll, uh, be back in a sec," and he disappeared into a narrow hall toward the front of the boat and off into a narrow doorway to one side, the bathroom, I think. Reaver and I were alone.

"I talked to my father today," I said suddenly, looking at Reaver. He stilled and frowned.

"What, after you got off the phone with Ashton?" he asked.

"Yeah," I said.

"What did he have to say?" he asked and I gave him an impish grin.

"Really?" I asked.

"Really, what?" his frown deepened.

"Rhett Butler?" The look on his face was priceless, his blue eyes got wide and wider and his face just fell. I started to laugh but caught myself in time, and it died before ever making it past my lips.

"You gotta understand, my mother was thrilled when she realized my biological father had knocked her up. She thought they were going to get married, have the white picket fence, the whole nine yards. She was a die-hard *Gone with the Wind* fan, so it was just a bonus that his last name was Butler." He swallowed hard.

"He ditched her when she was six months pregnant. She had me, named me Rhett, put his name on the birth certificate and was just sure he'd come back. He never did. She crawled into a bottle, met Rick, and called me her biggest goddamn mistake of her life." He smoothed down the front of his hair. "Only name I hate more than Rhett is the name Butler," he said and I went to him, wrapping my arms around his waist, pressing my ear over his heart. He held me back.

"Not even Trig knows my real fuckin' name," he said and I was surprised.

"I thought the club gave you the name Reaver," I whispered.

"They did. I was Tweak before that, 'cause of the meth habit before I went chasing the dragon." He crushed me to him and kissed the top of my head. I turned my face up to his.

"Your secret is safe with me," I whispered and he kissed me. We stood inside the circle of each other's arms and kissed in Cutter's living room, the boat gently swaying and rocking. Hands descended onto my shoulders and I startled. Reaver pressed a hand to the back of my head to keep me from breaking the kiss. Cutter smoothed my beach cover-up off my shoulders and kissed from one shoulder to my neck, a line of soft, sweet presses of his lips to my skin.

"Off," he whispered in my ear and I unwound my arms from around Reaver's neck and let him slip the cover-up off my shoulders and down my arms. Reaver broke the kiss and looked down into my eyes, his blue ones soulful and deep, and the warmest I had ever seen them.

"You're going to let us take care of you tonight, right Baby?" he asked me. I nodded.

"Wanna hear you say it, Li'l Bit," Cutter said against my skin, breath warm against the back of my shoulder. I swallowed.

"Yes," I said and swallowed again, my heart beating a fierce tattoo against the inside of my ribs. Reaver's hands cupped my face and he leveled his clear, still, blue gaze at me.

"Do you trust me?" he asked me with a tremulous smile, and all of the tension eased from my body.

"Yes," I said. Steady, calmer.

"Good," he whispered.

"Tonight's not about fear, or kinky reindeer games, Li'l Bit. Tonight's about making you feel good and giving you what you need." Cutter's hands massaged my neck and shoulders, skin on skin, my bikini top leaving nothing in the way of cover on me. He bent and laid a line of gentle barely-there kisses on the back of my neck, taking his time to trail them, softer than a touch of butterfly's wings, down my spine. I shivered, my body breaking out in a sweep of goose flesh.

"Come on back to the bedroom," he said softly, getting back to his feet.

Cutter took my hand and led me down the narrow passage to the front of the boat. Reaver trailed right behind me, a warm comforting presence at my back, his energy still and content. His hands rested warm on my shoulders, his thumbs stroking lightly at the base of my neck.

Cutter opened the door to his small bedroom looked inside curiously. The bed was right up against the door so that you had to climb up into it and was much larger than I anticipated it would be. Cutter grinned. It was easily big enough to hold the three of us and must have been custom-made because it was triangular in shape, filling the space wall-to-wall, following the natural shape of the bow.

"You don't need these anymore," he said, his fingers tugging the button on my waistband free as he brought his mouth to mine; the material of my shorts gave a little cloth sigh of relief as he lowered the zipper.

He fed at my mouth, his tongue warm and sure in its strokes against mine. His kiss was different from Reaver's but no less enticing. There was something more demanding about Cutter's kiss, less controlled than Reaver's.

I whimpered as Reaver's long sure fingers unclasped my bikini top at the back of my neck. He trailed his fingertips down along the surface of my skin from my neck, between my shoulder blades, lower, until he reached the clasp at my back. He unhooked that, as well and whisked the top away, the warm sultry air spilling across my breasts, the nipples hardening to sensitive peaks.

"You got an incredible body, Li'l Bit," Cutter breathed. He shrugged out of his cut and hung it on a hook just inside the door and held out his hand past me. Reaver passed his cut to Cutter, who hung it on another hook on the other side of the door. I gasped and shivered as Reaver gently set his teeth into that sweet spot where my neck met my shoulder.

Reaver's hands rested high on my hips, his thumbs pressing into my lower back just below the waistband of my shorts and bikini bottoms, massaging, his skin smooth and warm against mine. Cutter's hands had returned to my breasts, his mouth to mine, and he eased his hands down my ribs in a silky smooth caress. I sighed and gave myself over to the sensation of their hands on my body.

Cutter drew back from kissing me, and his hands slipped from my body going to the worn brown leather belt holding up his cargo shorts. I let my gaze roam his body, specifically over the large tattoo that spilled over the right side of his ribs. It was a pirate ship in full sail that started just below his armpit, the keel or bottom of the ship disappearing into his shorts, waves licking just over his hip and waistband.

The leather of his belt gave a little moan of protest and the buckle jangled, and he let the shorts drop. He bobbed, long and perfect, in front of me and I reflexively wrapped my fingers around him. His penis almost burned to the touch where it rested, hard, against my palm. I teased the engorged head with the pad of my thumb and he sucked in a breath and shivered, his brown eyes on mine. I swallowed hard and he captured my wrist in a light grip and moved his hips back from my hand. I let him go.

He put his hands back onto the mattress and hoisted himself up and back onto the bed, beckoning me forward. Reaver was warm and close against my back, pressing against me, grinding his hips forward into my ass. I felt the hard press of him through our layers of clothes and reached up and back, palming the back of his neck.

He bent his head and kissed my waiting mouth, hungry for it, his hands slipping around my waist. He delved his fingers into the front of my bikini bottoms beneath my shorts and slid the offending scraps of material that covered me from their sight down my legs. I moaned into Reaver's mouth, a desperate plea for him to touch more of me and he smiled against my mouth. He broke the kiss and turned me around to face him.

I caught a glimpse of Cutter fisting his cock, rubbing up and down his length with sure, slow, firm strokes as he watched me and Reaver together and I felt a little thrill of something other than anxiety. Desire pulsed at the apex of my thighs and I let my hands go to Reaver's waistband. His blue eyes held mine and I couldn't turn away if I wanted to.

His gaze telegraphed so many things as I worked the buttons of his fly. Heat and desire flickered in their depths, as the lightning did out over the sea. His eyes also spoke of deeper, darker things, but for the most part, all I saw when he looked at me was just how in love with me he was, how beautiful he thought me to be and just how much he wanted to be near me, and it was so beautiful, so precisely what I wanted, what I needed, that I felt tears of joy spring to my eyes.

Reaver smiled that panty-soaking boyish grin of his that made my heart leap into my throat and my pulse quicken. I slid his shorts to a puddle on the floor and ran my hands along his hips, following the carved 'V' of his hip flexors with my fingers, to the prize at the end.

"I want you in my mouth," I whispered and he smiled even broader in the dark hallway. I wrapped my fingers around him and looked down and smiled. The tattoos I had glimpsed earlier were on full display in the dim blue-tinged light coming through the portholes in the doorway behind me.

Lightning flashed, much closer this time, and I could see the rounded loops of the throwing knives inked under his skin, the points begging me to look at what I had in my hands. Reaver put his hands on my hips and lifted me up and back so I sat on the bed. He prowled forward like a caged panther and covered my mouth with his and leaned me back. I was forced to let go of him and push myself back further still, as he crawled up after me.

"Oh, damn, that's a beautiful sight," Cutter breathed and I smiled against Reaver's mouth.

"Lay down, baby, close your eyes," Reaver whispered, and I did as I was told, the laying back part, at least. The men knelt to either side of me, the ceiling barely clearing their heads. Cutter swung the door shut and we were suddenly in a very intimate and very enclosed space. The three of us could lay comfortably on the large bed, but there was very little room for anything else. It was close, and with as close as we would be entwined it was incredibly intimate.

Cutter lay on his side facing me, his head propped in his hand, and Reaver mirrored him. They trailed their fingertips of their free hands across my skin and I shivered, which made them both grin. Cutter reached to the side and flipped open a compartment.

"Condoms, lube, massage oil... what do we want to do to her first?" he asked. Reaver grinned.

"You do come prepared. I like that. Condoms needed for sure..." They discussed my safety and well-being for several moments as if I weren't nude between them, their hands touching me everywhere, and I was surprised to find I didn't mind. I let my eyes drift shut and simply concentrated on their roaming hands and just how aroused I had become.

"Hayden, have you ever tried anal?" Reaver asked me, and I looked at him with uncertainty.

"No," I answered, honestly.

"Do you trust us, angel?" Cutter asked and I chewed my bottom lip. I nodded apprehensively.

"Doesn't it hurt?" I asked.

"Not if it's done right, baby," Reaver said and leaned down for a kiss. I turned into him and his arm went around my waist holding me, my front against his front, his erection pressing hot between us, into my stomach. Cutter kissed and nipped along my back and I groaned, it felt just so good to be touched.

I reached behind me and wrapped my fingers around Cutter and stroked up his length. I didn't want him to feel like I wasn't here for him too, because, I was startled to realize, that as much as I wanted Reaver, I wanted Cutter, too, even if my desire for him was much less. They were both so sweet, so kind, and so giving; and now that my mind had fallen quiescent, like my constant frantic jumble of thoughts had been switched off, I found that my body craved so much to be touched and I wanted all three of us to enjoy it as much as I was.

A hand palmed my breast and tweaked my nipple and I gasped. Another hand skated down over my ass, the fingers dipping into the crevice of my thighs to graze my vulva.

"Oh, man, she's wet!" Cutter said in a deep, husky tone filled with his desire.

Reaver's hand left my breast and trailed down my body to see for himself. He broke the kiss and Cutters fingers were at my chin tilting my head back to claim my mouth. I cried out around Cutter's tongue as it massaged my own when Reaver slid the long middle finger of his hand up inside me.

"Oh, yeah, baby. Hang on, I'm gonna make you come," he said, his voice husky with promise and dominance. He placed the pad of his thumb against my clit and felt around inside me until my hips jerked of their own accord and I gave a pleasured, involuntary cry. Cutter broke the kiss and nipped my bottom lip.

A slow, heavy sensation began low in my body as Reaver's hand moved in me and against me. I gasped, breaths coming in steady pants. I squeezed my eyes shut and so I felt, rather than saw, the smooth head of Cutters cock graze my lower lip. I opened my mouth and took him in and, oh, god, I loved the feel of a man in my mouth.

I felt my pussy throb around Reaver and he spoke, encouragingly.

"There you go, baby, yeah, almost there aren't you? Come on, Hayden, let go, come for me, Doll." I felt myself tighten around his fingers, two now, stretching me, filling me, but not too full, not to the point of pain, no, this was just intense, purest pleasure.

Cutter was thrusting into my mouth, sure, short, little strokes, going deeper every time. I let him glide across my tongue, timing my breathing for every time he hit the back of my throat, drawing breath every time he drew back. Reaver changed the way he stroked over that spot inside me and I cried out around Cutter. I felt my pussy contract around Reaver's invading fingers and then I was flying apart.

I was vaguely aware of a hand on my pelvis keeping me pinned to the sheets as Reaver knelt and worked my body into wave after wave after wave of pure sweet bliss that went singing sweetly through every vein, every nerve, every fiber of my being. Lightning flashed and there was no distant rumble of thunder, it cracked overhead, and the heavens opened up and we were surrounded by the dull roar of the rain pounding on the deck overhead.

Cutter laughed, "A few seconds earlier that would have been perfect," he stated dryly.

"I know, right?" Reaver said, and his hand slipped from me. Cutter slid himself free from my mouth and Reaver touched my face lightly with his fingertips. I turned my head towards him and he kissed me. I kissed him back languorously.

"How you feel, Doll?" he asked me and I thought about it.

"Warm and glowy and good," I said with a shy smile. He smiled at me.

"Hand me a condom?" he asked Cutter and I was vaguely disappointed I hadn't gotten to taste him.

I heard the plastic wrapper tear and watched as he rolled the condom down his length. There was always something just so erotic to me about that sight, about the anticipation it caused. I swallowed and captured my bottom lip between my teeth. I felt a slight pang of sadness that my first time with Reaver wouldn't be just ours, that it was a shared thing, and I felt a little bad about the selfish attitude. Cutter's voice was soft and nearly drowned out by the overhead rumble of thunder.

"Your first time together, isn't it?" he asked in an echo of my thoughts.

"Yeah," Reaver said, positioning himself between my thighs.

"Then if you don't mind I'm going to sit out for a bit and just watch you two. I'd appreciate it if you would take the time to make love to her good. Something incredibly hot about watching two people love each other rather than just fuck."

I looked over at him, startled, and he backed away from us, laying down on his side, head propped in his hand like before.

"Thank you." I murmured and he winked at me.

"Hayden, Baby, look at me," Reaver said and I looked up from where I lay on my back, up the long length of his torso, my eyes skipping from the swollen condom-covered head of his cock, bobbing long and full between us, skating across the throwing-knife tattoos on the insides of his hips, over the cobblestones of his abs. He had a beautifully-done lifelike gray-scale image of the Sacred Hearts MC logo on his right pectoral, taking up most of the flat expanse there. It was a match for the one I'd seen on Trigger last summer. They'd gotten them together.

My eyes roamed hungrily up over the sharp jut of his collarbones and up the sweep of his throat, his Adam's apple bobbing slightly as he swallowed. His lips were neither smiling nor downturned, just lush and still as my gaze traveled ever upwards, stopping at his eyes, which were so full of desire and heat, I gasped from their intensity. I'd never had any man look at me with such naked longing and desire before in my life. The look in his blue eyes had me reaching for him and he came to me gratefully, his lips soft against my own as I cradled him against me.

We kissed, taking time and care in the exploration of each other's mouths. The fingers of my left hand curled in the softness of the short hair on the back of his head as I pressed his mouth to mine. My right hand smoothed down the warm skin of his back, riding up and over the ridges of scar tissue which were slick beneath my hand. I gripped his ass with my right hand and urged him to take me, my legs winding around his lean hips in invitation.

He groaned into my mouth and propped himself on one arm rather than two as he held his full weight off of me. He gripped himself between us and slicked the head of his cock through my folds, just flirting with the notion of entering me for several passes until I cried out into his mouth. I felt him smile against my lips and he broke the kiss, drawing back so he could look me in the eyes.

"I want you to look at me, baby," he said when I made a small mewling sound of protest. "Look at me when I make love to you," he said and it was the most beautiful, most perfect thing I had ever heard, and then he made it even more perfect by pressing himself inside of me. I arched into him as he filled me slowly, my eyes growing hooded, but never leaving his. His expression was so somber, so careful, and I realized he worried about hurting me.

Reaver was so long, impossibly long; I had never felt anything like it. It was as if he glided into me forever and he filled me out so well; finally his body met mine and he was fully seated inside of me and I panted from it. Oh, my god, he fit me so well, as if his body were made for mine, as if we were two halves of the same whole and it were the most natural thing in the world.

The feel of our bodies melding together was the most beautiful thing I had ever felt and I was so overcome by such deep emotion at our coupling, at the expression of love, devotion and tenderness in his eyes, that I felt tears come into my own. As my eyes welled and the hot tears spilled down my temples, Reaver smiled the most beautiful, beatific smile I had ever seen. My smile. His smile that I realized would only ever be for me.

"Oh, yeah, that's it, baby. Cry for me," he said and pressed his lips to mine and he began to move.

I wrapped my arms around him and clung to him as he rocked into my body with the gentle swaying of the boat. Our breaths came in unison, gasping, moaning as he probed for and found that sweet spot with his thrusting. I cried out and spasmed around him and he bowed his head touching his forehead to my own.

"You're so fucking pretty when you cry," he grunted, and captured my lips and tongue in a punishing kiss that left me gasping and wanting more. One of his hands trailed down my body, grasping my thigh and pulling my leg higher up along his flank. I cried out as he found that slightly deeper angle. His eyes slipped shut and he turned his head to the side, giving himself over to the sensation of riding me, buried deep inside of me, being one with me and it was one of the most heart-rending, beautiful things I had ever seen in my life, just how completely he loved me.

I squeezed down tighter around him and pulled myself tighter against him, and moaned my pleasure to the deepening night and the boat's small cabin. The sound was very nearly swallowed by the pulsing rain.

With every push of his hips, I felt full and fuller, the warm glowing pulse of orgasm growing with each thrust. I cried out and gasped for air, the sound high and breathy.

"Oh, god, Reaver, I'm going to come again!" I cried in a high little voice and his eyes flashed with victory and his lips curved in triumph. He pinned me with his gaze and he growled, his face barely an inch from my own.

"Come for me, baby, let it go. I wanna feel you," he said and his words were the final push I needed, right over the cliff, right over the edge, and then I was plummeting, falling, arching across the sky like a shooting star before finally crashing back down to earth, back into my body, only to find I'd been writhing safe and sound beneath my lover's body all along, warm and safe in the hard-muscled cage of his arms.

Reaver's teeth were set in a stinging arch low, just beyond where my shoulder met my neck and I realized that we'd come apart only to be remade together. I'd never come with someone before, I didn't think it was possible, I mean, really, it had ever only been one or the other of us, never both at the same time... things just didn't work that way in the really-real world, did they?

Reaver brought his face up to where I could see him, his blue eyes glazed and languid with pleasure. He gave me a loving, satisfied, and lazy smile and we kissed. I could feel my body pulse around his in time with my heartbeat and it felt so relaxed and just so damn good.

"That was probably the deepest, most beautiful thing I've ever seen two people share," Cutter said, his voice tinged with awe. I startled, I'd forgotten completely that he was there. Reaver and I turned our heads, Reaver's smile sexy, satiated, and triumphant. I flung out my hand and Cutter caught it around my wrist, cradling the back of my hand in the palm of his. He smiled, his brown eyes warm and full of heat and he laid a gentle kiss in the center of my palm.

"That an invitation, Li'l Bit?" he asked and I smiled, still drugged with the pleasure Reaver had given me, but why not? Cutter deserved to feel this good too.

Reaver reached down between us to secure the condom but he needn't worry. I was on birth control, got a shot every three months. He slipped from inside me and I shuddered with little aftershocks.

Cutter swung open a cupboard to reveal a trashcan and Reaver climbed over my prone body. He and Cutter moved around each other and Cutter snugged himself up against me, Reaver behind him. I lay still, floating on cloud nine. Reaver handed Cutter a condom and the man looked over his shoulder and grinned.

"Thanks," he said and turned those warm chocolate-caramel brown eyes on me.

"You up for it?" he asked me softly and I smiled serenely, both touched and pleased that he would ask.

"Take down your hair?" I asked softly, and he smiled and pulled out his ponytail, his hair falling like a curtain around his face.

"Better?" he asked and I nodded, combing my fingers through the thick strands. Whereas Reaver's hair was sable-soft like a bunny rabbit's fur, Cutter's hair was warm and thick and silky, almost like a living being of its own. He bent his head to kiss me and the silky strands tickled across my body when he did it. I buried my fingers in it and held it away from our faces as we kissed. He knelt at my hip, bent awkwardly over me to kiss me, as he ripped open the condom with deft fingers.

My pussy still vaguely pulsed and tingled from Reaver and I found myself blushing hotly that I would allow another man to enter me so soon, one right after the other. I decided strongly to not think about it, to just let go of all the societal preaching on normal versus the obscene and to just revel in my sexuality. I pulled Cutter's mouth tightly against my own and kissed him harder with my determination to fly in the face of what was proper and to just cut loose and enjoy being irreverent and hedonistic. Cutter chuckled against my mouth and pulled back, his eyes smiling.

"A little eager are we?" he asked, and I nodded and let him believe that was what it was. I caught the smile on Reaver's face as he lay the way Cutter had moments before, head propped on his hand, watching us, and his smile and the sparkle in his eyes told me that at least he knew exactly what my feelings had been. He winked at me behind Cutter's back and gave me a slight chin lift and his odd sort of blessing on the situation put me at ease.

Cutter got between my thighs and suckled one of my nipples into his mouth. I arched, my blood zinging through my body like it had suddenly turned to soda pop, sweet and sticky and fizzy, from my breast, sweeping down and out through my fingers and toes. My pussy twitched deep inside and caused me to moan a little with the pleasurable little throb.

Cutter fixed his eyes on mine and backed off my breast, his tongue flicking out, teasing the nipple, the air slightly cooler on my damp flesh than his mouth had been. Lightning flashed and cut across his wicked teasing grin as he straightened.

"Going to be hard-pressed to top your man, sweetheart," he said, wrapping his arms around my thighs. He dragged me across the bed bodily, bringing my vagina closer to his straining condom-covered cock.

"I'm still gonna try though," he said, and he entered me with one strong, sure thrust. I arched and raked my nails down his forearms, his hands gripping my hips. He lifted my ass off the bed and settled it on top of his muscular thighs. This was going to be different.

I gripped his arms as he started in with these wicked short thrusts, barely withdrawing before surging forward, his body meeting mine with sharp little reports of flesh meeting flesh. I gasped as he adjusted angle a few times and yowled with pleasure when he found that fucking sweet-spot deep inside me. He gave a savage grin of triumph and looked down on me. It was intense and almost over-whelming, so soon after the earth-shattering orgasm beneath Reaver. I reached out and Reaver grasped my hand, grounding me, holding it as if we were about to arm-wrestle.

Cutter smiled and thrust harder and I felt that warm glowing weight begin to grow in my lower belly. I cried out in evenly-spaced rhythm with his thrusts, and he closed his eyes and turned his head, the way some people do when they are listening to the sweetest music they have ever heard.

"Oh yeah! I love that sound," he said, voice low and rough with passion. He slid his fingers across the dip in my pelvis and buried his thumb in the top of my sex. He rubbed small intense circles over my clit and I howled as everything coiled tight and tighter and grew more intense. Reaver's hand squeezed my own in reassurance as Cutter mercilessly teased me to a fever pitch, both inside and out. I was close, so close.

"I'm close!" I cried, and he bent over me and crushed his mouth to mine, and I exploded around him, screaming my release into his hot mouth. He swallowed my screams, rolling them around his mouth like candy first, and before I knew what was happening, we were rolling and suddenly I was on top of him, his arm behind my lower back keeping me crushed to his chest, his other arm cradling my upper back, his hand pressed to the back of my head to hold my mouth to his.

He said something to Reaver but me in my orgasm-induced fog, I couldn't make sense of it. Cutter continued rocking his hips, his penis thrusting tight and hard up into my wetness, he was bottoming out, bumping my cervix in that half-pleasure-half-pain sensation that, given enough time at it, could go either way.

I felt the bed shift, or was it just the boat? Reaver's hands cupped my hips and smoothed up and down my back. I startled at the unexpected touch, and Cutter's arms tightened around me, holding me. I eased into the embrace and his thrusts slowed down, becoming almost lazy.

"You got it?" he asked and I heard Reaver say "Yeah," before he spread the cheeks of my ass. I jerked and Reaver's hands smoothed up and down my back. Cutter stopped thrusting all together and simply held me.

"Do you trust me, baby?" Reaver asked gently and I relaxed. Of course, I trusted him.

"I need to hear you say it, Hayden," he said, his voice low and intense, and nearly swallowed by the storm.

"I trust you," I said, and something cold spilled down the crack of my ass. I yipped and jerked.

"Cold!" I cried and Cutter laughed.

"Did some awesome things around my cock when you did that, brother," he said, and Reaver chuckled. I went very stiff and very still against Cutter at the first gentle probing touch of Reaver's fingers against my asshole.

"Relax, baby," Cutter breathed against my hair. I did my best, trying to relax my muscle groups one by one.

"Deep breath, Doll..." Reaver said, and I took in a deep breath. I yipped as he forced one of his fingers inside of me to the second knuckle. I felt my vagina spasm around Cutter's invading cock and it felt delicious; my back broke out in a wave of tingling shivers. This was okay, this wasn't so bad… Reaver worked the lone finger back and forth, working the lubricant in and out of me.

"Push out, Doll, I'm going to add another finger," he said and the sensations were so delicious that I didn't argue, I did what he told me. I had never done this before and I was a little sad that I'd never gotten to experiment with it because so far, this felt incredibly good and not just because it was considered naughty or forbidden.

Reaver added another finger to my ass and I wriggled, and pushed out like he'd said, and doing so alleviated some of the sudden discomfort. My anus burned slightly from the unfamiliar stretching. He added more lubricant and the cool slick feel eased things too. I rested my head against Cutter's chest and listened to the thud of his heart. He held me close and still, tight against him.

"Oh, yeah…" he said and took several quick breaths, I felt so relaxed and languid, Iike I couldn't move even if I wanted to.

"She's coming, man, I feel it around me…" he sucked in a long breath and kissed the top of my head.

I felt so wet and slick where Cutter rested inside of me. I closed my eyes and relaxed into him, the sensations Reaver wrought with his probing fingers relaxing me, immersing me in a river of pleasure where I felt like I could just float forever. I don't know how long he teased my anus, five minutes? Ten? But suddenly it stretched even more, almost to the point of pain.

"Relax, Doll, easy, relax, push out, come on, baby, do it for me…" Reaver's voice was slow and patient and soothing and I did what he said, and the unpleasant sensation eased and nothing but a pure shining pleasure was left behind.

"Good girl, good…" he said and it didn't sound condescending at all; if anything, he sounded both relieved and pleased.

""K, man, go easy," he told Cutter and Cutter began to move inside of me once more and oh my god… I'd never felt so full or so amazing in my life, like I was flying or like I was completely ethereal, like my bones and muscles and skin no longer held me together in physical form. I moaned and realized Reaver was inside of me too, that both men were fully seated in my body and taking turns thrusting into me, and it was the most incredible sensation I had ever felt in my life!

They held me on that shining edge of the fall and kept me there, where it felt so, so, good until I could no longer form coherent thought. It felt powerful and wonderful to listen to their heavy breathing and muttered curses of ecstasy. I was so wet and slick and ready for them and I never wanted this to end. I kissed Cutter soundly and felt Reaver's hands on my hips, smoothing over my ass.

"God, you're so fucking tight, you're so perfect," I heard one of them moan and it thrilled me to no end.

"Hang on, man," I heard one say and by the vibration of it through my chest it was Cutter. I felt him delve a hand between us, down the front of our bodies until he found that sensitive bundle of nerves.

"I'm getting close," he told Reaver, and Reaver said, "I'm not, but go ahead."

I closed my eyes and Cutter teased my clit a little more which was easier said than done. I felt like a raging inferno had taken up residence low in my body, building in intensity. I felt like I was filling with light, slowly, steadily, the quicksilver of orgasm nearly upon me. I could hear a high sweet voice crying out over and over with each deep thrust and before it fully came to me that the voice was mine, the light flared out through every nerve ending in my body and my whole world exploded until all that was left of me was this fine shining, burning thing. I was a creature forged from purest grace and the gentle, loving patience of the two men sharing my body.

I came back to myself slowly, limp with satisfaction, cradled lovingly against one man while Reaver continued to work himself in and out of my ass. Cutter had withdrawn from my body, so I didn't feel as full, which wasn't either good or bad, just a different sensation. Reaver slowed and added more lubricant, and picked up his pace again.

It still felt so incredibly fucking good that I didn't care. I wanted him to come. I wanted him to feel as good as I did. I heard him give a hoarse cry and his thrusting faltered for a second. Cutter's hands smoothed up and down my body in these firm caresses, touching every bit of exposed skin that he could reach. Reaver worked himself in and out of my body, and with a final cry lost any sort of rhythm or synchronicity, bucking wildly against me once, twice, before stilling completely.

He knelt, breathing heavily, my body trembling finely beneath him, before slowly, almost reluctantly, he withdrew from my body, discarding the condom in the wastebasket in the cupboard. He stretched out beside Cutter and me and held out his arms.

"Give her here..." he said gently, and Cutter turned on his side and I slipped gently into Reaver's arms. I still didn't feel like I was capable of forming coherent thought and I was completely okay with that.

"You doing okay, Doll?" Reaver asked me, kissing gently every bare inch of skin close enough for his mouth to reach.

I gave a slight little blissful moan and Cutter laughed, stripping the condom from himself. I was a mess below the waist and so was he, moisture from my body glistening along his smooth tan skin.

"She's more than good, I think," he said, and Reaver chuckled.

"Hold her, I'll be back in a minute," Cutter said, scooting to the edge of the bed and letting himself out into the narrow passageway.

"I love you, Baby," Reaver breathed into my ear and I struggled through my lethargy to cuddle closer to him. I managed to twist so I could lay my head on his chest.

"Thank you..." I breathed.

"For what, hmm?" he asked.

"For loving me... I'm pretty sure I'm falling in love with you too," I murmured. He kissed my forehead and I honestly don't remember anything else after that. They exhausted me just so well.

11

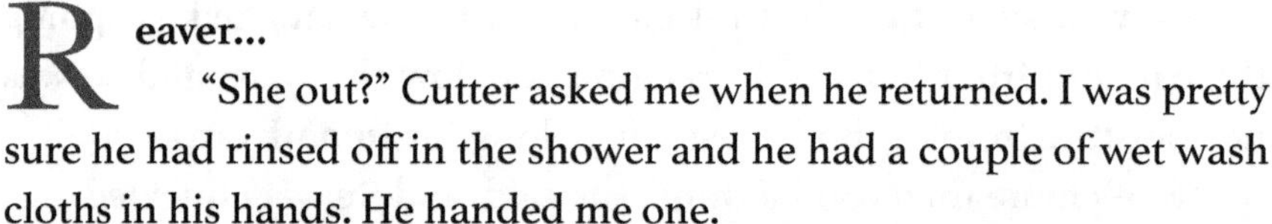

Reaver...

"She out?" Cutter asked me when he returned. I was pretty sure he had rinsed off in the shower and he had a couple of wet wash cloths in his hands. He handed me one.

"Yeah. Mission accomplished, I think," I said and cleaned myself up, which granted, there wasn't much for me to do on that front. He gently wiped Hayden down watching for any signs of discomfort or that he was causing her to stir, but she was just so much dead weight in my arms, against my chest.

She felt so incredibly good there too. Deeply unconscious, sleeping the sleep of the truly exhausted.

"We wore her out," he observed with a smile. I kissed her hair absently.

"I've never seen anything like you two," he said, smoothing a hand up and down Hayden's body in a tender touch. Lightning still flickered outside, but the storm was dying down, moving off from over us. I watched the light cast deeper shadows under her eyes, making her skin glow with an ethereal light.

"Your connection, your energy..." he sighed. "I would kill to have a woman look at me the way yours looks at you." He kissed the back of her shoulder and I smiled at the reverent gesture.

"Thanks, man," I said softly and he choked on a laugh.

"Thank you, both of you, for letting me join you. That had to have been one of the most profound sexual experiences of my life." He propped his head on his hand and continued his idle caressing. I didn't mind. Hayden deserved all the love and gentleness she could get. I sighed.

"What was that for, man?" Cutter asked me.

"Ahhh," I made a slightly frustrated noise and sighed again. I had a sudden wish that he were Trig, but Trig was hours away and working... besides, Cutter had earned a bit of my confidence. He might have a decent bit of advice, who knew?

"I'm not always like that with women. I'm afraid I'm gonna break it. Scare her away with how intense I can be..." I confessed.

"Mind if I make an observation, Brother?" he said and I nodded that he should go ahead.

"Your little woman is pretty fucking fearless," he said and I frowned. I mean I got what he was saying, Hayden was fearless in a lot of ways, but maybe he was picking something up I wasn't.

"How do you mean?" I asked, wanting to hear what he had to say.

"Not only was this her first threesome, her first time even trying anal and not only did she let us? She let us double penetrate her too, all without batting an eye? C'mon, man, how many girls you know like that? That wouldn't freak or have any misgivings?" I was silent for long moments, listening to the thrum of the falling rain on the ship's deck overhead while I contemplated his words. "I think she trusts you," he said after I'd been silent too long. "More 'n that, I think she would follow you to the ends of the earth if you'd only just ask her," he said and placed another reverent kiss on her shoulder. She shifted slightly in her sleep and we both went predator-still so as not to wake her.

We looked at each other over Hayden's body, her shoulder gently rising and falling as she drew breath. When I was sure I wouldn't wake her, I spoke.

"I hear you," I said, but I didn't know what to do with it. I closed my eyes and he shifted restlessly on the other side of my girl.

"Hope she's not sore in the morning," he said and I smiled.

"Still a little unsatisfied?" I asked and he smiled at me.

"Yeah," he said.

"I don't swing that way, or I'd help you out," I commented. He laughed a little but didn't comment back. Hayden shifted and sighed out.

"Baby?" I asked softly, to see if she was awake.

"Mmm..." she sort of replied.

"You awake, Li'l Bit?" Cutter asked quietly. Her steady breathing was her only reply.

"Shit out of luck," he grunted and I smiled.

"You never know, she might be game in the morning," I commented dryly. He sighed and it was a wistful sound.

"I could be so lucky," he muttered and lay back. He still idly touched Hayden who let out a contented sigh. I held her body close in the curve of my own and closed my eyes, a bit touchy about really sleeping with Cutter nearby. I didn't think we'd have a problem but I needed to really trust someone to be at ease sleeping around them. The fact that Hayden could get up and move around a room I was sleeping in without waking me was a testament to how I felt about her.

I laid a gentle kiss against her forehead. She'd been incredible, so open and trusting as I'd made love to her, and without a doubt that's what I'd done. I'd poured every ounce of my heart and soul into loving her body, the world around us falling away until it'd been just me and her and the quicksilver coursing through our veins, passing between us where our bodies touched.

Cutter settled, his hand resting on the swell of her shapely hip and I settled too, but while he closed his eyes, mine remained wide open, drinking in her face in the dim light. I had a feeling I'd be up before either of them in the morning, despite lying awake longer.

I fell into a light sleep to the sound of Hayden's even breath, the distant thunder and thrumming rain, jolting awake a few times in the night, mostly whenever Hayden moved or Cutter did. I kept replaying the feel of being deep inside her lithe small body over and over in my head when I'd wake. I was looking forward to making love to her again, though next time we wouldn't have anyone else but us. The final time I woke up, the sun was streaming through the two portholes in the bed cubby and Cutter was sitting up, gazing at the fall of light across Hayden's nude form.

"She's fucking spectacular," he murmured.

"Yeah, she is," I agreed, smiling slightly, a little uneasy that he'd been awake while I'd slept on. Old ghosts tried to fight their way free of the vault inside my head.

I hadn't been a heavy sleeper since I was a young kid. Not since Rick, getting piss-drunk and pissed-off about one thing or another, started coming into my room to drag me out of bed to put a beating on me. Which I guess was still preferable to what'd been happening to Shells a few trailers over. I fought to swallow the bitter memories down. The bright clean Florida sunshine pouring through the two round windows in the room helped with that; so did the fact that the most beautiful woman I'd ever seen remained resolutely in my arms.

"C'mon, man, let's let her sleep. I wanna take you guys out. You can help me cast lines." He slid off the bed and pulled on his shorts out in the hall. It sounded good to me, so I eased out from under Hayden who shifted to get more comfortable. She was still dead to the world, though the shadows under her eyes were less than they'd been last night. She was getting some good rest finally.

I pulled on my shorts, checking for the knives in them. Reassured they were there, I turned in time to see Cutter lay an orange tee shirt out on the bed for Hayden to use when she got up. He handed me my cut, shrugged into his own, and picked up Hayden's discarded clothing from the night before, folding it neatly and leaving it on the small couch in the living area of the ship.

I found my sunglasses in our borrowed beach bag while he did that, and he pulled a pair off a rack of 'em by the door and put them on his face before we went up and out into the bright sun. Even with the lenses on my face, my eyes watered from the bright light.

"What do you need me to do?" I asked, once my vision had cleared.

"Take this," he said and handed me a length of rope. He went up by the wheel and turned a key; the boat's deck began to rumble faintly beneath my feet. The man ran around and leapt over things like some kind of monkey, unhooking this, unraveling that. Finally, he jumped off the side and landed on the dock with a hard thump. He unhooked ropes from the dock and threw them up to me, where I caught them and coiled them.

Before I knew it, he was up at the wheel again and talking into a radio. A voice squawked, indistinct through the other end, and Cutter laughed and spoke into it again before setting us to moving. I worried vaguely that we were going to wake Hayden but she seemed to slumber on.

It barely took any time at all for Cutter to get us out onto the open water. I'd joined him up at the wheel and sat on a bench made for it behind him and to the side as he navigated us out of the marina, watching everything he was doing with an open curiosity. I'd never been on a boat like his before, just small motor boats on the lake back home, and a rowboat or two when we were on lake runs to set up the sniping targets, and even that had been more 'n a minute ago.

"What do you think?" he asked me as he killed the engine.

"She's beautiful, that's for sure," I said.

"Yeah, she's a grand lady. Restored her myself. You should have seen her when I first got my hands on her," he said ruefully.

"Bad shape?" I asked, as he set about unhooking the sails.

"The worst, man. She was about to be scrapped but I just couldn't let it happen. I saw so much promise in her... She was just as busted up as me and I wasn't ready to give up on either of us," he confessed, and it was such an extreme pronouncement it left me frowning and trying to figure out how to ask.

"You ex-military?" I asked, noting some of the tattoos high up on the swell of his shoulder. One was a tattered American flag and below that a row of numbers.

"Naw, man, once a Marine, always a Marine," he said with pride. My eyebrows went up.

"Shit, man, no wonder I like you. My best friend, Trig, was a Marine Corps sniper; one of our prospects was his partner over there," I said.

"No shit?" Cutter stopped raising the sails.

"Here, you do this," he said. I took over the cranks, aping what he'd done.

"What unit your buddy serve in?" he asked. We traded information and he gave a choked laugh.

"Shit, me an' your boy pounded some of the same sand over there," he said, and nodded to himself.

"You know, we got our summer lake run comin' up in about three weeks. It's around four hours south of us, about halfway four, maybe five hours for you guys. If you can do it, you should come join us," I said.

"You got the authority to be invitin' folks to something like that?" he asked.

I pointed to my Treasurer's patch.

"I'm solid on our council of five," I said. "Besides that, we got another crew, the Suicide Kings, coming down with us this round. You wouldn't happen to have any beef with 'em, would you?" I asked.

"Now, why would you ask a thing like that?" he asked me, as the sails began to fill with the light wind, unfurling and snapping full under the bright blue sky. I looked up and watched the canvas fill, a little impressed that I'd help make it happen.

"They're off to a rocky start," I said, and told him about last fall and how one of their young buck punk-ass members had shot Irish, our VP's girl, in the leg, during the course of trying to rob the coffee stand she worked at. He gave a low whistle.

"Damn. You handle it?" he asked.

"Naw, I was mostly out of that one. The Suicide Kings handled it themselves. Shot him back and put him out of their club on bad terms. They didn't even want to fuck with us." I felt a nasty smile curve my lips. Our reputation from the bad ol' days still served us pretty well. The thing was, even though we'd gone straight, even gone further than that, atoning for and righting some past wrongs under the radar, we held true to that old reputation. We weren't afraid to get violent and get nasty to protect what was ours. Especially now with people like Sunshine, Shells, Irish, and my Doll, Hayden, under the club's umbrella.

"Yeah, the way I hear it, you fuckers don't play," he said with a grunt, and steered us across the waves

"No, we do not," I agreed. We were silent for a few moments.

"Where we headed, anyways? I asked.

Cutter grinned. "Sweet spot for some free-diving and snorkeling. Killer scallops nearby, too. As long as you don't have any moral qualms about poaching," he said and I snorted.

"You gonna eat it?" I asked.

"Yep, and you are too," he said, grinning.

"Then, nope," I said and smiled back. We were out on the water for a good hour before he looked around us and nodded. An island was nearby; it didn't look like it had anybody livin' on it, too small for that, but there were some darker scars on the sand, and I realized they were charred piles of wood, so, big enough to party on, apparently.

"This is it," he declared and took down the sails, dropping anchor.

I looked around us and over the side of the boat. The water was crisp and so fuckin' clear you could see the bottom. It was shallow where we were at and I asked, "How are we not touching bottom?"

Cutter chuckled, "There's a good fifteen or twenty feet under us, don't worry."

He moved around the boat and stripped off his cut, hanging it off a hook set in the mast. He opened a hatch on the deck and pulled out swimmer's fins, a mask, and a snorkel.

"I'm going in," he said and I watched as he pulled out a wicked-looking dive knife in an oddball sort of sheath, the nylon straps too short, to my eye. He saw me eye-fucking his knife and grinned. He handed it to me while he pulled out a mesh bag and a belt full of what looked like weights. I slid the knife out of its sheath. The hilt had a good weight to it and the blade was strong and wicked sharp.

"That's not too shabby." I commented.

"One hundred percent titanium blade, double locking sheath, the serrated edge is a built-in line cutter. We use the knob at the end here to bang on tanks..." Cutter rattled off the different specs for the knife. I was just impressed. If I had one of these, I'd never have to swim without a knife again, which would be kind of nice. I didn't know why I'd never thought of it before. He wound down on what was quickly becoming a sales pitch and he strapped the knife to his lower leg along the outside. The strapping on the sheath suddenly made a whole lot more sense. I nodded, impressed.

"Where can I get me one of these?" I asked. Cutter grinned.

"I've got one below decks still in the package if you don't mind blue on black for the handle," he told me.

"Hell, no, sounds good to me. I'll buy it off ya."

"No, consider it my gift to you. Not many dudes as gifted with a knife as you are. Consider it something to remember your time in Florida by." He strapped on the weight belt and put on the mask, leaving it high on his forehead like a pair of glasses. His sunglasses he handed me.

"Be back in a bit, bro," he said and fitted the mask in place, carried his flippers over to the edge of the boat and jumped in the water. I propped a foot on the edge and leaned over.

"Shit! Can you toss me the bag?" he asked.

"Yeah!" I went back and picked up the nylon mesh bag and returned to the edge of the deck. He was already treading water, flippers in place, mask over his eyes and nose.

"Cool, thanks!" he said as I tossed the bag down to him. He clipped it to his belt and put the snorkel in his mouth and with a thumbs-up, he slid under the crystalline waters and made for the bottom.

I sat down and gazed out over the water, letting the gentle lap against the side of the boat, the rustle of the canvas in the breeze, and the cry of the sea birds nearby filter across my senses. It was warm and it was rare that I got these quiet moments to myself. I felt almost as calm as I ever had, thanks in part to the environment, but mostly thanks to Hayden, who still slept below-deck.

Hayden. I couldn't stop the smile from curving my lips. I smoothed my hair down in front and bowed my head, watching Cutter swim along the bottom, indistinct through the glassy waters. A little over a year ago Hayden had been this dynamic powerhouse of a woman, a force to be reckoned with, a fierce glint in her light green eyes. Then, the more time her ass-bag fiancé spent away from home, the more uncertain she'd become. I wanted that fierce little woman back. I wanted her to fight back, I wanted to take the hurt and replace it with pissed and I just... I just didn't know how to do that for her.

A splash. Cutter surfaced.

"You good?" I called down to him.

"Yeah!" he called back, replaced the snorkel in his mouth, took a visible deep breath and kicked his way back to the bottom. I continued my silent introspection and gazed out over the cool aquamarine waters. I took a deep cleansing breath and let it out slow.

I tried not to feel nervous. I had no idea where to go from here with Hayden. I had no idea how she was going to feel, what she was going to do with what we'd done last night. I wracked my neck from side to side and twisted my upper body to get the same crunch out of my lower back. I felt a little looser, and that was good, but it did nothing to ease the tension I was feeling on the inside. Cutter surfaced again and called out. I went over to the edge of the boat.

"Yeah, man, what's up?" I asked.

"These fuckers are a bitch to catch!" he said and spit seawater that had splashed into his mouth.

"What do you mean?" I asked frowning.

"Boat's not going anywhere and neither is your girl! You might as well get down here so I can show you a thing or two!" he called out.

I raised my eyebrows and laughed. "Oh, you're going to show me somethin', huh?" I asked.

"What, you don't know how to swim? I can teach you that, too! Grab some gear. Spare knife is in the cabin on the galley counter.

Help yourself!" he called. I laughed and hung my cut off another hook in the mast and went below-deck. I spotted the dive knife he was talking about but bypassed it to check on Hayden.

She lay on her stomach amidst the light-blue, crisp cotton sheets, the golden light from outside bathing her nude form until it glowed and I got so fucking hard looking at her. I breathed out and leaned in the doorway and just watched her sleep. Her breathing was deep and the line of her back was smooth and perfect where it dipped before the swell of her lovely ass. God, she had felt so fucking good there last night. I shuddered and fought the urge to drop my shorts and crawl in there with her.

Instead, I went back above-deck and opened up the dive knife. I really, really liked it and got a certain pleasure strapping it to my leg for the first time. The sheath was this weird double-locking thing that took a bit of getting used to, but at the same time, it would hold true and I didn't have to worry about losing the blade. I took up a mask and fins and went over the side. Cutter came up.

"'Bout time you got out here," he said.

I pulled on first one fin and then the other. "Yeah, had to check on Hayden."

"She cool?" he asked as I pulled the mask on.

"Yeah, should see her! The light's perfect and it's making her just glow," I said.

"Damn, man, you got it bad!" he grinned and treaded water; I grinned back and did much the same for a moment.

"No argument there! So, what are we doing?" I asked.

"Well, come on down, and I'll show you." He put his snorkel into his mouth and bent, submerging himself, his fins rose smoothly out of the water, and with a deft kick he went under, making his way to the bottom.

I'd never really swum in the ocean before. Plenty of times in the lake on lake runs and in pools and rivers and shit. One of the things my Aunt Jen, Shelly's mom, had done for us growing up was take us both to swimming lessons at the local pool. It had been more for Shells than me but I'd benefited from it too and I was grateful. Time at the pool had meant time out of the house away from Rick and my drunk-ass mom.

I pulled myself down through the water and felt the pressure in my ears. I made them pop and continued to the bottom, where Cutter held himself suspended over a patch of short, waving seagrass. He reached into it and a rock shot up and waddled away. I blinked. What the fuck? I swam closer and he grabbed for another one and held it out for my inspection. I took it from him and realized that it wasn't a rock but a barnacle-crusted clam thing, the kind with a shell shaped like a fan and ridged like a Ruffles potato chip. He pointed to the grass and took the thing from me and shoved it in his bag.

I searched the grass and found that the whole bottom was littered with the bastards! They were hidden in the wavering green and yellow like fuckin' Easter eggs. I reached for one and it snapped closed and shot out away from me, swimming in that weird waddle to a clump of grass nearby. Could these fuckers see me coming? I kicked for the surface to get some air, Cutter following me up.

"What the hell did you call those things?" I asked.

"Scallops!" he said and laughed a little.

I'd eaten scallops before, the round white meat was succulent, and good in this pasta dish I'd had in this Italian joint back home, that I could remember, but I'd never seen 'em in their raw state before. Cutter held one out to me and I took it. It looked like a clam, only with a fancier shell, and I said as much. He laughed at me, and I had to admit, out here I was definitely some podunk hick from a landlocked state, so I couldn't bitch much.

"How many we need to feed the three of us?" I asked.

"Pick up the biggest you can find. I'll let you know when we're good."

I shrugged, gave a look towards the boat, and dove again. It sounded good to me and it kept me busy, kept my mind from worrying about Hayden and what her reaction would be when she finally woke up. Catching the scallops proved to be both easier and more difficult than I expected. Problem with the damned things were when they leapt up and took off, you had no idea which direction they were gonna go in. You almost would have better luck with a catcher's mitt than anything else when it came to harvesting 'em. Still, it was a hell of a lot of fun. Finally, Cutter gave me a thumbs-up and jerked the digit skyward. We kicked for the surface and bright sunlight, and both sucked in great gouts of air when we broke through to open air.

"Got enough?" I asked.

"Yeah, should be. Now, we gotta clean them. Come on, I'll show you how." I nodded and we swam for the ladder off the side of his boat. So far, this was a lot of fun.

12

Hayden…

I woke alone, the sun shining brightly through the port-holes on either side of the bed. I pushed myself up into a sitting posi-tion and bit my lower lip, trying to figure out if I were sore or not, and decided that, surprisingly, while I was a little stiff, it wasn't too bad. I sat for a long time staring at the sunlight as it crawled lazily across the light-blue sheets. I could smell them both on my skin and, in fact, pressed my hands and the light top sheet to my nose to breathe them in.

There was the familiar cool scent of Reaver, the smell of clean laundry and of his cologne, which I had long ago identified as Acqua di Gio. Underlying those, the ever-present edge of cold steel. It was an amalgamation of both comforting and crisp, scents both modern and familiar, that he wore well and that I had begun to equate with safe harbor, not just since the beginning of this trip, but really, since the first time he'd touched my face and asked in that even timbre if I trusted him. While the smells should have clashed, should have been confusing, they were so much a part of Reaver that when I smelled any one individually, I thought of him, but together like this, I don't know… It had this strange calming effect.

Waking surrounded by them, I felt secure despite having woken up alone.

Stronger, and a bit less comforting, was the smell of Cutter, of Old Spice, open water and salty air. His smell held its own appeal in some ways, though it barely compared with Reaver's in my mind. I cast my gaze around the cozy space and my eyes immediately went to the bright splash of orange at the foot of the bed. I picked up the orange tee and held it up so I could read the black writing. *Ander's Elite Maritime Salvage* was emblazoned on the back, while on the front was a caricature of a ship being dragged down by a giant octopus or squid and another boat, that looked like it was a marriage between a ship and a tow-truck, that was latched onto the sinking vessel and had popped it mostly free of the giant beast's flailing arms. I bit my lip and smiled. It was cute.

A thump from outside made my head come up. I heard a masculine voice, then Reaver's familiar tones, muffled and indistinct, returned the first voice's query, and I felt myself relax that much more. The boys were up. I slipped the shirt over my head, the hem pooling in my lap and slipped off the end of the bed into the narrow hall. The shirt fell to my mid-thigh and covered me better than my bikini and shorts would have. Still, thinking on last night, on letting the two men share my body so thoroughly, I felt myself blush and, despite the covering, felt as naked as the day I was born.

I was a little worried about how I would be received by them. Would they look at me as something less? Was I something less for what I'd done? I stood in the hall and chewed my lower lip, contemplating my sudden onset of nerves, and decided that I was doing it again – that somehow I was thinking with the wrong set of filters, that I'd been thinking with the wrong set of filters for a very long time. Rather than deciding how I felt about last night, I was thinking about how I would be perceived by others for what I'd done. I hugged myself and closed my eyes.

How did I feel about the two men? Honestly... I felt okay about Cutter. He'd been respectful and we'd had a good time. The cold knot of fear sitting in the pit of my stomach, that was all for Reaver. I really did worry he would think of me as something less. I didn't want that. I didn't want that at all. I suddenly had to know, needed to know, would this be a walk of shame or would things be okay between us?

Oh, my god… What did it say that my feelings on if he would care or not were that strong? I closed my eyes and breathed like I did during yoga. Deep, even, controlled breaths. This sudden realization that it mattered so very much what Reaver thought of me was terrifying in its own right. Just days ago I was set to marry Andy! I was left slightly reeling, my feet carrying me unbidden above-deck and into the bright sunlight. I squeezed my eyes shut against it and halted, unable to see to move forward.

"Hey, look who's up!" Cutter's friendly voice came. "How'd you sleep, Li'l Bit?" he asked. I blinked my watering eyes and was mercifully cast in shadow. I looked up into familiar cool blue eyes and felt myself relax. Reaver's hands palmed my shoulders, his long fingers kneading the backs.

"You okay, baby?" he asked me, concern radiating from him.

"Kiss me," I said and he smiled, his eyes thawing, warming, just for me. He lowered his mouth to mine and kissed me carefully, then more soundly when my arms wrapped around his neck. His arms snaked around my back and he straightened, lifting me. I held onto him and put everything I was feeling, the awe, the confusion, the hurt and the wonder, the depths of my heart and the things that, after Andy, I was too afraid to speak out loud, into that one kiss and I wanted it to go on forever, because Reaver kissed me back with all of that and more!

Reluctantly, we broke apart and the smile that he graced me with reassured me more than anything else that he was as he'd said so many times on this trip. Reaver was truly, madly, deeply in love with me and I–

"Wow, you two never stop amazing me." Cutter's voice, gruff with wonder and emotion, broke my reverie. We both turned to look at him.

"Do you need a kiss, too?" I asked, teasingly.

"You going to kiss me like that, Li'l Bit?" he asked me and his warm chocolate-caramel gaze was speculative.

"I don't know if I can," I said shyly, afraid of hurting his feelings, "But I'm willing to try." Reaver slid me down the long hard length of his body, the orange tee damp where it had touched his skin and turned me so my back pressed to his front. He kneaded my shoulders and Cutter came forward, a predatory glint in his eyes similar to one that Reaver sometimes had in his. He stopped in front of me, our bodies nearly touching, and looked down at me while I looked up at him. He smiled and brought his lips to mine and kissed me almost chastely.

"Naw, baby," he murmured against my mouth. "Wasn't even fair of me to tease you like that," he said but I still felt bad. I cupped his face in my hands and kissed him and put everything I felt about him and about last night that I could into it. I kissed him gratefully, sweetly, and tried to communicate with lips, tongue, and teeth how very special he made me feel. He sighed a contented sigh against me, his breath warm and ghosting in a delicate blush against my mouth and throat. When he drew back, his eyes were sparkling with happiness and mischief.

"You fancy a round two, Li'l Bit?" he asked me, and I smiled.

"I'm not terribly sore…" I said and decided that alone, with these two, I could unleash my inner wanton sex goddess to play. Both of them, the way they looked at me, the way they touched and kissed me, allayed any fears I'd woken up with.

Cutter looked over my head at Reaver and grinned. "Ever make love to a woman outdoors on the open water?" he asked, and it was about this time I looked at our surroundings, startled to find we weren't anywhere near the marina, or another living soul for that matter. I thought about it for a second and smiled up at Reaver who was smiling down at me with a sheen of pride in his eyes.

"Sounds fun," I said, the familiar feeling of my old impish grin curling my lips, and we did just that.

We spent the rest of the day swimming, snorkeling, and sailing, feasting on what the boys had caught that morning, and again on fresh grilled fish that Cutter caught spear-fishing while we were snorkeling. Finally in the late afternoon, early evening we motored back into Cutter's slip at the marina. I was almost sad to say goodbye when he hoisted his garage door open. Reaver's bike, Baby, was just as we'd left her.

"Thank you for such a lovely time," I said to him and he bent and snatched another kiss.

"Naw, Li'l Bit, I'm the one who should be thanking you," he said and smiled, resting his forehead against my own. "You take care of her, bro." he said to Reaver and I went to him, twining my arms around his lean hips.

"You don't have to worry about that," Reaver said quietly, and I smiled up to him. I wanted desperately to be alone with him at this point and couldn't wait for our last night alone together at the bed and breakfast. We rode back to the little Victorian and slipped upstairs to our room. He shut the door behind us and a silence descended between us as we regarded one another from several paces apart; the air grew thick and heavy between us, crackling with emotion.

"I need a shower," I said softly. Reaver's cool blue eyes slid over my skin from head to toe and suddenly the air conditioning seemed positively frigid and I wanted to turn it off.

"Things are different," he said quietly and I knew what he meant. They were different between us, and while things seemed clear and concise earlier today with Cutter in the mix, now they were much less so.

"Yes," I said, and my voice rang hollow with fear, things were different, and that meant change. I was afraid though. Did Reaver want that change? Did I? Were we going to be okay or was this something that was going to break us apart? Would I be able to handle this? Were my insecurities going to destroy us somehow?

"Doll?" Reaver said, and my eyes snapped up to his questioning look.

"Yes?"

"What have you got chasing around in that pretty little head of yours?" he asked me.

"I'm scared…" I said and he chuckled.

"I can see that, it's turning me on," he said and I gasped. It had almost been easy to forget about that part of him. I swallowed.

"Talk to me, baby," he said and I was surprised to find he was still several paces away, giving me space, giving me room to breathe and collect my scattered thoughts. I opened my mouth, closed it, and opened it again.

"I'm afraid I'm going to ruin this, whatever 'this' is, with my insecurities," I said and it was the most honest thing I think that had ever come out of my mouth. Reaver's stance and expression softened.

"What else? I can see there's something more." His voice was gentle, coaxing and I found his asking, his genuinely wanting to know so compelling, so freeing.

"I'm half-afraid that I'm not going to be able to handle it," I said, referencing his darker nature. He nodded gravely at this and looked so carefully withdrawn that I pressed on. "I'm also half-afraid I might like it too much," I said and shuddered, hugging myself. He searched my face and the little spark of hope I saw in his deep blue eyes made me want to try so badly but I was being honest and part of that honesty meant admitting to myself that I really had no idea how deep the rabbithole went, when it came to his needing that edge of violence in the bedroom.

"I felt so vulnerable when you were," I swallowed and pushed past my trepidation at talking about this out loud, "when you were cutting the clothes off my body." I met his eyes and he was as closed-down as I'd ever seen him, not giving a single thing away.

"You trust me, Doll?" he asked me, and my breath caught in my throat, because I knew that this time, this time it really, really mattered what came out of my mouth because this time, there was no going back. I didn't answer him right away. I thought about it, I really thought about it, the conflict raging in my heart and my head. I let my breath out slowly. This was it, he was going to show me the monster in his head and it was written all over his face, if I couldn't deal, if I couldn't handle it, he would take me home and never darken my door again and that I just couldn't have because I loved Reaver and even though I wasn't ready to admit that out loud, this I could…

"Yes. I trust you," I said and his head cocked to the side, all the warmth that his eyes could hold simply gone, his gaze as desolate as an arctic tundra. He slowly and deliberately reached into his cut, my eyes following the movement, tracking along as he withdrew one of his switchblade knives. Fear trickled along my skin as I stared at the folded knife in his hand. Long moments passed, my chest feeling like it was caving in on its self.

"'No' isn't going to make me stop," he said, and I swallowed hard, transfixed by the glitter of light along the silver fittings. "You want me to stop, you say 'Icarus'. You get me, Hayden?" he asked.

"Yes," I croaked.

He voiced everything I saw play on his face moments before, "You say it, we're done, baby. I'll take you home and I'll leave you be with my heartfelt apologies," he said softly. I nodded, eyes still on the knife clutched in his long fingers, more afraid of what I'd see in his eyes if I looked.

"Say it for me once, Hayden, so I know you're with me, you want me to stop you say…"

"'Icarus'. I say 'Icarus' if I want you to stop…" but I didn't want him to stop, not if it meant having to say goodbye permanently. I prayed silently that this would be something I could do, that it would be something I could deal with.

The blade snicked free of its handle and I jumped, fear crushing my throat closed. I prayed harder than I ever have in my life before, one thought turning over and over in my head.

Oh my god, what is he going to do?

Reaver...

I didn't want to break her but she needed to know and I needed this, I so needed this. I depressed the little button on the handle of my knife and the blade flicked free. She jumped, visibly fucking jumped, the fear sliding through her pale green eyes, perfuming the air subtly around her. She stood stock-still and I closed the gap between us in a rush. She gasped but held her ground; she didn't run. I was right up in her personal space, the point of my blade against the jumping pulse-point in her neck. I looked down into her timid green gaze, she didn't have any idea what I would do, her fear was of me, the unknown, and I loved it, reveled in it and cherished the trust she put in me.

"You know what would happen if I pressed just a little bit harder?" I asked her.

"No," she said, voice high and breathy with fear.

"It takes very little pressure to pierce the skin, piercing it here wouldn't be so bad on the surface, but once I start cutting, I have a hard time stopping." I trailed the point of my knife slowly from her throat down the inside of her button-down blouse over the swell of her breast. Her eyes slipped shut and she shuddered against me.

"Like that?" I asked.

"Yes."

"Would you like it if I cut you, spill some of that rich warm red across your lovely skin?" I gauged her reaction and it was priceless. My cock grew stiff in my shorts as her eyes flew open wide.

"Please, don't..." she moaned.

"Please don't, what?"

"Please, don't cut me."

"Baby, I'm going to cut you if I want to." I slipped the sharp blade between the button holding her oxford closed and the thread holding it on and flicked it; the button fell to the carpet between us and the shirt gaped a little more. She shuddered.

"Do you trust me, Hayden?" I asked her again.

"I'm still here, aren't I?" she asked, some of her old fire peeking through.

"I'm going to cut these buttons off one by one, and you're going to let me do it, aren't you?" I asked.

"If it's what you want," she said, swallowing convulsively.

"Mmm." I flicked my knife, severing another button, and another. I had her backed up against the neatly-made bed, pinning her with my body, a knee between her thighs. I cut every one of the buttons holding her shirt free and slipped it back off of one shoulder. I lowered my mouth to her skin and pressed a kiss there as a reward for her trust, then straightened.

"Now what are you going to do?" she asked and she seemed calmer. I couldn't have that. I put my lips against her ear and whispered harshly,

"Whatever the fuck I wanna do, you're my Doll." She gasped and I swallowed it, crushing my mouth over hers, forcing my tongue past her teeth and claiming her mouth for mine. Her hands came up and pressed against my chest, pushing, but I'd told her the rules; she knew she had an out if she needed it. She struggled against me and I held the knife carefully out and away from her. I only needed her afraid; I didn't want her damaged.

She leaned back and I moved with her, she thought she'd be clever and scooted up on the bed. I pinned her hips with mine and she gasped when she could feel the hot hard press of me through our clothes.

I pulled my mouth from hers and growled, "Stop struggling, or I'm going to hurt you for real."

She instantly stilled, her green eyes wide and frightened.

"You wouldn't..." she said, certain, then more uncertainly, "Would you?" I had her right where I wanted her and felt the slow cold grin take over my lips. Tears sprang to her eyes and I brought the knife around cleanly slicing through her swimsuit top beneath the shirt which was pinned beneath her ass, her arms bound to her sides where the shirt had slipped from her shoulders and rode around her elbows. Her lip trembled and the tears poured faster.

I gave a contented sigh. I needed to pull her back from the brink; she was too close to breaking, thinking I'd actually hurt her, damage her. I knew what would do it, so I asked her, "You still trust me, baby?" Her breath stilled, confusion clouded her pretty little face, not trusting her voice; she nodded carefully. I trailed my blade in a barely-there touch down her ribs, using the cool metal pommel rather than the edge, giving her the sensation of cold steel without the sharp cutting edge. Her eyes, locked on mine, grew wide and wider still. I smiled and pulled it away, doing the same up her leg until I reached her shorts, where I switched to the blade, slipping it between her skin and the cloth, carefully cutting up the leg of the short-shorts, the material parting like water.

Her breath came in short little pants as if she were afraid to draw a full one, and I liked that, I liked that a lot. I cut her clothes from her body slowly and deliberately, keeping eye contact the whole time, drinking in her fear and uncertainty like fine wine paired with a delicate cheese. She was everything I wanted, everything I needed and craved in those moments, and when I roughly pulled her shredded shorts and bikini bottoms out from under her and let them fall to the floor I was pleased to see her wet and glistening. Ready for me. I smiled cruelly and shrugged out of my cut. I folded the blade of my knife away and set it aside, within reach. I ground my lower body into hers, holding her deftly while I stripped my shirt off over my head and worked my belt and shorts off.

I put a hand to her lovely throat, not squeezing, not choking, just holding her there and didn't even ask. I didn't care. She knew she could stop this at any time. I roughly pulled her to the edge of the bed and fit myself inside of her. I wasn't gentle. Her eyes dilated, a heady mixture of fear and passion as I seated myself deep inside her body. God, she felt amazing skin-on-skin! So hot and wet and perfect around my shaft.

"Wrap your legs around me," I ordered and she complied. I smiled a slow curl of lips and set a punishing rhythm, a rough fuck that had her crying out, her head tipped back, the most feral and lovely sounds pouring from her throat, spilling from her mouth. I lifted her from the bed and turned, sitting on the edge so that she rode me, sitting in my lap.

"Feel good?" I asked her, she nodded, a helpless, inarticulate sound escaping her. She was slick with her arousal, her eyes hooded with it as she looked at me. I smiled a much less wicked smile and kissed her throat, the side of her neck, laving my tongue over the fluttering pulse-point there. The shirt that had been binding her arms whispered over my knees and shins as it went to the floor, and her slender arms twined around my shoulders. She held herself to me and I rocked up into her, awkwardly due to the angle.

She leaned back so she could look me in the eyes while I fucked her. I liked that, too. I fished beside me for the folded knife and the blade snicked free. Hayden gasped and her pussy constricted around me. Oh, that was nice, that was really nice. I held the blade where she could see it, glittering razor sharp in the overhead light.

"I wanna see you bleed a little, baby. Can I have that?" I asked her. She nodded, her eyes welling a bit, and I smiled, a wicked, cruel curve of my lips. She thought I was going to cut her bad. No. Not my thing. I thrust up into her until her eyes slipped shut and her head dipped back. I placed the very point of my blade against the front of her left shoulder beside her collarbone and moved my hips searching for that wonderful place of hers inside. I felt a surge of triumph when I found it and Hayden gave this little broken moan, and I struck, nicking her shoulder in a barely-there cut about half as wide as her little fingernail. Tiny. Almost not even there.

I let the knife clatter to the bedside table and watched the tiny cut well ruby red against her peaches-and-cream skin. I continued to fuck her, my body almost on autopilot, hips surging as I watched the crimson bead slide down her skin. With a groan, I covered the tiny cut with my mouth, sweet copper pennies exploding across my tongue. Hayden cried out and spasmed around me. The monster went back into its box. It usually did when it was sated, when the thrill was gone. Hayden's eyes had become glassy, and I was flying high, drunk off her submission.

Now it was time to make it up to her, to reward her for giving me what I wanted, what I needed. Now it was time to give her what she needed.

"Hold onto me, baby," I crooned in her ear and I stood up, awkwardly walking us up onto the bed on my knees. I slipped from her and cursed that, before laying her gently into softness of the bed. I found purchase, slipping back into her, and with more freedom of movement than I had before, I started doing her gently.

"Look at me, Hayden?" I asked, and she squeezed her eyes shut tighter and shook her head.

"Please, baby, I'm back, I promise, just look at me," I whispered, and it was suddenly very important that she look, that she see me. She shivered beneath me and opened her eyes. I smiled down at her tenderly and moved gently inside her. She gasped, a little broken sob welling from her chest, her hands cupped my face, and she shuddered in relief beneath me. I felt a pang of fear and loss in my chest and stilled my movements, resting my forehead on hers.

"Please don't stop," she begged, her voice small and I drew back and searched her face.

"I didn't break you?" I asked half-afraid.

"I don't think so."

"Tell me what you're feeling, Doll," I ordered, but with none of the harshness of before.

"I don't want to feel anything but you right now, Reaver, just hold me and love me," she said, and I complied. Who the fuck was I to argue over such a request?

14

Hayden...

That hadn't been so bad. Truth be told, I hadn't known what to expect, I didn't enjoy the cold and vacant predator's look coming from Reaver's face, I hadn't known what to expect when the knife came out, and it scared the ever-living shit out of me not having any say or control... but I wasn't sure that was a bad thing. When Reaver had let himself go, I had too, in a way. All my jumbled thoughts, all my cares, all my worries and constant over-thinking things had spiraled down to nothing in the face of that cold and calculating part of him and all that had remained was the flick of the knife against my clothes, and the fear my skin would be next.

He'd been so rough when he'd taken me, and I was acutely aware we used no protection but I didn't want to. I was on birth control and I knew I could have stopped him with one little uttered word but I didn't want him to stop. I didn't want to stop. I wanted to be for him what he had been for me these last several days. I wanted to give him what he needed, and I wanted desperately to be able to embrace every part of Reaver.

He'd asked me if he'd broken me and I marveled at the question.

If anything, Reaver had picked up the broken pieces and glued them back together! His darker side wasn't as bad as I'd thought it would be in the bedroom, and I wasn't sure what that said about me. Truthfully, right now I didn't care. Right now, the tender side of Reaver was back, he moved inside me slowly and gently, and looked at me with such sweet tenderness that fresh tears, happy tears slipped into my hair.

"Tell me what you're feeling, Doll." His voice was soft, and held none of the sharpness of before. He'd found that place deep inside me and stroked over it, coaxing my body to life, and so I asked him for what I needed and didn't feel a bit of shame doing it.

"I don't want to feel anything but you right now, Reaver, just hold me and love me." He smiled beatifically and his eyes went from the cold of winter to the color of warm spring skies. I felt an answering smile of my own paint my lips and he bent, I cupped his face in my hands, and we kissed, carefully, sweetly, as if either of us were made of thin glass and apt to break with too much force.

"You're so fucking perfect," he whispered, and my breath caught in my throat. He thought I was perfect?

He came down over the top of me, engulfing me in his warmth and I couldn't be sure, but I think we stayed like that for hours. There was nothing rushed about this time, there was no immediate need to climax or even a desire to. He just felt so good, in me, on me, around me, that I just drifted in a state of euphoria for the longest time... like I was drunk or drugged. When I did finally come, it was a gentle thing, sweeping through my body from head to toe and back again. It seemingly went on forever. I shivered beneath Reaver and felt my body gently pulse around him, in time with my languid heartbeat.

"Oh, god, Hayden," he gasped and bowed his head, gently kissing the side of my neck. I shivered again, and wrapped my legs around him as he shuddered once, violently. He pulled himself from my body and his orgasm spilled up over my hip, hot and wet, and I closed my eyes and moaned, finding the sensation completely erotic.

Reaver kissed me once, then twice, and searched my face. I lay placid beneath him, safe and secure within the cage of his muscular body. He smiled serenely, an expression likely mirrored by my own.

"You look high, Baby Doll," he murmured.

"High off you." I quirked a smile.

"How do you feel?" he asked, and I had to work to pull any coherent thought together.

"Warm, safe, like I'm floating or falling..." I frowned slightly. How could you feel like you were falling but feel safe at the same time? That didn't make sense. Reaver chuckled and it was a rich sound that coated the senses like warm chocolate, thick and decadent.

"Enjoy it, Hayden, stop overthinking it," he murmured, and to make his point, he kissed me and took his time doing it until I sighed and relaxed that much more beneath him. He withdrew from the kiss slowly and got up off of me.

"Where are you going?" I didn't want him to go anywhere.

"This is a little beyond a wet washcloth, babe, I'm going to start the shower. Be back in a flash." He disappeared into the bathroom and the shower started and, as promised, he returned. I sat up carefully and Reaver chuckled.

"Still a little disconnected?" he asked me.

"Yeah." I smiled and he lifted me in his arms. I let him, not quite trusting my legs yet. I still felt drunk or drugged and I wasn't sure how it was possible. "Am I okay?" I asked him, and he laughed a little.

"Baby, you're more than okay. I'm beginning to think I'm the only man to ever love you right." He set me on my feet and opened the shower door for me. I stepped in and he followed close behind. It was a tight fit for the both of us, but I didn't mind; I don't think he did, either. He turned me into the warm shower spray and I tipped my head back and closed my eyes, letting the water sluice across my skin. He washed me, his touch careful and gentle. I flinched a little when he washed me between my legs.

"Sore?" He had a pinched look on his face and I nodded reluctantly. I was really sore.

"I guess you can have too much of a good thing," I said and giggled. He smiled and huffed a short laugh.

"You okay?" He looked like he was afraid of the answer. I placed my hands on his shoulders and tugged insistently. He bent so I could wind my arms around his neck. He put his arms around me and pulled me in against him, and I smiled against his shoulder.

"Whenever you do this, it seems like everything is okay. Even when the rafters are dripping from the shit that hit the fan."

He laughed and hugged me tighter. "God, you're such a delicate fucking flower! I love it!" He laughed, so wild and free it made my heart so glad to hear it. He finished washing me and wouldn't let me wash him, stating gravely that this was his time to take care of me. He dried us briskly and pulled back the covers on the bed. I crawled up into the fluffy cloud – and his cellphone rang. He retrieved it from his cut and hung the vest from the bedpost, answering the phone as he got into bed with me.

"Hello?" He raised an arm and let me settle against his chest. I sighed out and closed my eyes.

"Yeah?" He listened for a long time and, though he was incredibly warm where I touched his skin, he grew coldly still beneath me. Had I looked, I was sure his eyes had grown distant and icy.

"No. I'll take care of it. Gibson Drywall is the name of the company. Tell them Reaver sent you, they'll give you a fair price. The rest I'll try to handle when I get back." He sounded irritated. I looked up at him and he was looking down at me, a glint of something undefinable under his carefully-schooled blank veneer.

"Yeah, we're headed back tomorrow." A long pause as whoever was on the other end said something. "Probably sometime after breakfast, it'll take us about nine hours, probably more, with stops." He smoothed a hand up and down my nude back and I hummed with contentment.

"I'll take her to Ashton's." he said and I frowned. Why did I need to go to Ashton's? He sighed a harsh exhalation of breath.

"I'll just bet he does," he muttered. I pushed myself up and looked at him.

"What did he do?" I asked, in a harsh half-whisper. I wasn't stupid. That comment coupled with my apparent need to go to

Ashton's rather than home equaled one thing and one thing only: Andy had done something to my home.

"Call you in the morning, Sir," he said, and with a quick goodbye, hung up the phone.

"You gonna torture yourself all night and get no sleep if I tell you?" he asked.

"Probably," I said, then, "Tell me anyways."

"Promise me something, first." He leveled a serious look at me.

"Depends on what it is," I ventured cautiously. He grinned ruefully.

"Promise me you'll let me take care of it. You're going to have enough on your plate with getting back to work and things." He searched my face and my heart sank a little, the easy euphoria of our lovemaking quickly seeping from my body as my muscles tensed in preparation for the bad news.

"What did Andy do?" I asked hollowly.

"He moved his shit out like we told him, but left the job in the care of his butt-buddy groomsmen. One of them took it upon himself to move all of Andy's crap, and I think some of yours, out of the place, then he put an ad on Craigslist pretending to be you, stating you were moving out of the country and didn't want or need anything in the townhouse. He left the door unlocked and turned it into a free-for-all. Everything is gone, babe: the appliances, the furniture, clothing, jewelry; what's more, they punched holes in a bunch of the drywall and tagged the inside of the house. One of your neighbors got suspicious about the comings and goings and called the police, but the damage was done when the cops got there. Your pops was called when they couldn't reach you by phone, because his name is on the paperwork, too." I stared wide-eyed and devastated at Reaver and felt twin scalding-hot tears trail salty-slick down my cheeks.

I wasn't hurt... well, okay, I was hurt, but more than hurt, I was angry, and after days of moping, hurting, and just generally wallowing in self-pity, being pissed-off felt really, really *good*.

"What are you thinkin', Doll?" he asked me, smoothing the tears away with his thumbs. I swore to myself right then and there that those twin tears were the last Andrew Richardson was going to get out of me.

"I'm thinking that I am way beyond pissed-off," I answered truthfully and sniffed. Reaver pulled me down against his chest and gave me a squeeze, kissing my forehead.

"That's m'girl," he murmured.

"Shit, my whole life was in that townhome, things I'm never going to get back! All my clothes, all my photos and memories, my paintings!" Some more tears slipped free. "My laptop! It was at the wedding, I don't know who has it!" Reaver placed a hand over my mouth to silence me and tapped at his home screen. He placed a call, the phone ringing loud on speaker between us.

"Hello?" Ashton's ethereal and melodic voice came over the line, music from the tattoo shop blaring in the background.

"Hey, Sunshine, do you happen to know what happened to all of Hayden's stuff after we bolted from the wedding? Her laptop specifically." Reaver asked. I waited with bated breath.

"Oh, yeah, Ethan and I have it at the house, why?" she asked. I breathed out a sigh of relief. Reaver filled her in.

"They took her car, too?" Ashton cried.

"Baby, they took all of it," Reaver grunted.

"I have some clothes at the cleaners," I informed them. "It will get me through the next day or two, but I'm going to have to go shopping." I sighed.

Ashton giggled. "Hell of a way to get a shopping spree!"

I felt myself smile. "True enough," I agreed and tried very hard to find the humor in it. I managed after a short internal struggle. Everything was gone and there wasn't any way to get it back. I found myself thanking my lucky stars I was fairly well-off in my own right, and that in my fierce independence, I hadn't put Andy on any of my bank accounts.

I would recover from this. I needed to return to being that fierce girl who had hidden away her friend, lied to the police, and helped the man who held me now get away with vengeance at the way

Ashton had been treated. I kissed Reaver's chest and snuggled against him tighter. I groaned.

"I have so much more to do now than I thought!"

"It'll be fine, Hayden. Reaver, you bring her straight to me and Ethan!" Ashton ordered and it was cute how much she had the men wrapped around her little finger.

"I will, but not because I want to, Sunshine. I gotta head to her place and check out the damage. I told her dad to hire my company to fix it, mostly because I want to see it done right," he said.

"Good." Ashton sounded resolute.

"I don't know how bad it is yet," I said, "but maybe it's not such a bad thing doing a little remodeling. Make the place feel like mine instead of what it was when Andy was there." I was desperate to grab onto anything positive at this point and I caught Reaver smiling at me, a little sheen of pride in his eyes.

"Maybe so. Just come home and get here safely, you two! I have to go, customers are coming in." We heard the little shop bell ring.

"Bye!" Reaver and I both chorused and he hung up. I slumped against him.

"This is some bullshit," I declared.

"Yep. Fucker's going to pay for it too," he said, darkly.

"Just don't get arrested. I need you," I admitted and he gave me a squeeze.

"I need you too, Doll," he said and I sighed. I was pretty sure I knew what the fluttery feeling my heart made meant, but after saying it so many times to Andy and having it returned as a lie, I wasn't ready to go there yet, so instead I melted into Reaver's side and closed my eyes.

"It'll all get taken care of, Doll. I promise," he murmured, and I believed him, I really did. Mostly because Reaver had never let me down in the entire time I'd known him. I mean sure, reality dictates, it was bound to happen at some point, but that point had yet to arrive, and I didn't have time to worry about any 'what if's' right now. No, I was firmly in crisis-mode, my mind whirling and clicking away at how to best go about keeping up appearances for the über-elite; my career somewhat depended on it.

Reaver held me, lightly stroking my skin, fingertips drifting in lazy, nonsensical patterns across my back and down my arm, making sweeping circles on my hip. I closed my eyes and tried to shut my mind off, to sleep. It was hard, but the light caresses he made along my body with his fingertips helped immensely. I finally drifted off to sleep.

15

———————

R eaver...

    We woke up late for breakfast. I didn't care. A good night's sleep was more important. We dressed and packed, and our stay was already paid for, so with a quick adios to Miranda, the innkeeper lady, we mounted up – but didn't exactly ride out. We went into town first for some food and ended up at a little diner about a block up from Sultry Nights, the lingerie store. Hayden excused herself and went towards the bathroom once we were finished eating, and I nodded absently as she got up from the table, my phone buzzing in my cut. I took it out.

"Yellow?" I blurted my typical phone greeting without looking at who was calling first. My mistake.

"Where are you?" a female voice demanded and I closed my eyes.

"None of your business, Aimee, why?" I asked. She stopped cold on the other end of the phone. I'd never spoken to her that way before. Well, before Hayden. After ten years, I think she was used to being my one-and-only. Even after she married Mark, I'd always been as patient and as kind as I could with her, but even I couldn't deny that Aimee had turned into a total bitch where I was concerned, a condition that only seemed to get worse as time dragged on.

"Did you forget that this was supposed to be your weekend with Connor?" she demanded. Bullshit, my weekend with Connor was next weekend and I called her on it.

"Next weekend. I told you two weeks ago that I had a friend's wedding to go to, you agreed that I could trade this weekend for taking him the next two. Connor knows it, too, now that he's old enough, so what the fuck are you playing at?" I demanded. Silence met me on the other end of the line, a silence so complete I had to check and make sure she hadn't hung up. "Aimee?"

"What's gotten into you?" she demanded suspicious.

"Rough weekend, now why are you trying to fuck with me, this time? Are you bored?" It'd been building for a long time. She could never accuse me of not paying my child support so she would always taunt or threaten me with the next best thing, which was being able to see my son on a regular basis. I understood why she had hated me; what I didn't understand was why she still hated me with such a fiery passion after doing so much better with Mark. He loved her and he loved my son, which sometimes didn't sit well with me as he overstepped once in a while, but for the most part we were cool.

"Connor needs a father who is going to be there for him, not one who disappears on the weekend he's supposed to have him," she snapped and ouch, okay, I got it but at the same time, I hadn't missed a weekend or rescheduled a weekend with Connor in years, so what the fuck was the deal?

"He misbehaving or something?" I asked quietly. Something wasn't right, I just couldn't put my finger on it. Aimee gave a long-suffering sigh.

"The police brought him home. He was caught shoplifting candy and soda from the corner store." Ah-ha… so this was more about 'like father like son'. I'd done a lot of stupid shit when I was a kid, was constantly in trouble. What most people didn't know was the shoplifting I'd pulled was so I could have something to fucking eat. You couldn't survive off booze, black coffee, and cigarettes in junior high. Shit. Connor was well-fed and well-looked-after, though, which made me want to know what this was all about.

"I'm in fucking Florida," I grunted.

"Florida? I thought the wedding was at that race horse farm out on State Route 62!"

"It was, long story, we're headed back today–" she cut me off.

"We? Does this have something to do with that stupid motorcycle gang you're in? I swear to God, Rhett," I grimaced at the use of my name, "if you skipped out on your son for that club of yours and used some stupid wedding as an excuse–"

"Aimee, shut it. It's not like that," I said. Silence on the other end of the line, stunned this time.

"What did you say to me?" she sounded incredulous.

"That's better," I said. "Now, I'm headed north as soon as I get off the phone with you. I'm not with the MC, I'm helping out a friend." The word 'friend' as I applied it to Hayden left an oily film of deceit in my mouth once it was spoken. Hayden was way more than a friend but I didn't want to set Aimee off any worse than Connor already had.

"How long will it take you?" she asked.

I did the math in my head: about nine hours or so, with stops I'd push that to ten, getting Hayden set up with Ashton and Trig... "About twelve hours. You want me to come by and talk to him tonight, or you want it to wait until morning?" I asked.

"It's going to have to wait until morning, I let the police take him. He's in juvenile lock-up," she said and had the motherfucking audacity to sound smug.

"I'll see you in twelve hours, and you had better have my son out of that place. You don't know what it's like in there. You are fucking unbelievable! Twelve hours, Aimee or I swear–"

"You swear what? Rhett? I'm his parent! Me! You're just the unlucky sperm donor! If I say he needs to be in jail for what he's done, then that's where he's going to be! I will not have him turn into a worthless druggie gang-banger like you! I will not let my son ruin some other teenage girl's life! You hear me?" she yelled into the line and never in my life had I been angrier or more defeated.

Where the hell was Hayden? I frowned realizing she should have been back from the bathroom by now. I swallowed hard.

"Twelve hours, Aimee. You have every right to be pissed off at me, but I'll be fucked if you're going to take that shit out on our ten-year-old boy. As for the rest? Okay, I'll take that. I did ruin you for a while, but if you can't see what you've got right in front of you, with Mark and our beautiful boy, well... Jesus, I don't even know what to say. I'm speechless." I smoothed my hair down between my eyes and closed them.

"He's staying right where he's at, Rhett. It'll be good for him," she said quietly.

"Okay. Sure. Whatever you say, Aim's." I hung up the phone on her and sucked in deep breath after deep breath, resisting the urge to chuck the glass-and-plastic slab against a wall. I closed my eyes and retreated to the quiet place where I killed, shutting down the emotions as fast and as hard as I could. I needed to think, I needed to be clear-headed, *where the fuck was Hayden?*

I called Trig.

"Yo, what's up?" he asked by way of greeting. I spelled it out for him. There was silence for a time and he gave a low whistle.

"You want me to try and go get him?" he asked.

"Yeah. Call me if there's any trouble. I don't think they'll let you have him. Take Sunshine with you and try to look respectable. Might help. If you can't get him out, at least try to get in to see him, hell, fuck, I don't know..." I felt my knee bouncing under the table with my distress. The bell over the diner's front door chimed and I looked up, and felt my face collapse into a frown. Hayden slipped into the booth a second later.

"Just get back here, Sunshine and I will do what we can," he grunted.

"Thanks, Trig. I owe you another one."

He snorted. "Bullshit. We're family, and family takes care of each other. We don't keep score." He hung up on me. I slipped the phone back into my cut and raked my gaze over Hayden.

"Where the fuck were you?" I asked, and she turned wide green eyes up at me.

"Something wrong?" she asked and raised an eyebrow, and I cursed myself silently.

"Yes and no," I told her, then asked her again more gently, "Where did you go?" She looked out the window, refusing to meet my gaze but she spoke.

"This trip has meant more to me than I could possibly... I didn't know how to..." she exhaled harshly and held out her tiny fist towards me. I bumped it with my own and she laughed.

"No, hold out your hand," she said, and she was smiling from ear to ear, her light green eyes dancing. I held out my hand, palm-up and she dropped a necklace into it. Not just any necklace either, but one of those old-ass coins, the silver edged in gold. A white gold chain, fashioned to look like rope, ran through the loop at the top, and pooled warm from her body's heat against the palm of my hand.

"Hayden, I can't take your..." the words died on my tongue as I caught the glint of the coin she'd bought the other day, on a shorter but similarly-fashioned chain, the coin resting alluringly in the hollow of her throat where her collarbones met. I stared at it for long moments and curled my fingers around Hayden's gift.

"I know it's sappy and maybe even a little silly. I mean, matching necklaces," she laughed mockingly, "who even does that anymore?"

"Hayden, baby, shut up," I said and she immediately went silent. "I love it." I pulled the chain over my head and the coin settled just above Trig's dog tags. I pulled the black cords containing other various charms off and looked through them, for the pewter sword my son had bought me with his allowance for father's day when he was five, and put it back on. The others were meaningless, and so I stuffed them carelessly into the hip pocket of my jeans. Hayden's lips were curved into a subtler smile as she watched me, her hallowed green eyes lingering on the coin where it rested against my tee.

"Come here, so I can kiss you," I said. She slipped around the table and onto the bench seat of the booth beside me. I kissed her, a long lingering touch of lips, deepening it with a sweep of my tongue and I poured my appreciation and love for her into it. A soft sound of surprise escaped her lips, followed by a contented sigh of relief, her warm breath fanning across my face.

"You do the most perfect things at the most perfect times without even realizing it," I told her. She smiled and blushed a little at the praise.

"You like it, then?" she asked.

"No, Doll, I love it. 'Like' isn't a strong enough word." She smiled and I pulled her against my chest in a fierce yet gentle hug.

"Ready to go home?" I asked eventually.

"No... but yes, if that makes sense?" She looked up at me, resting her chin on the swell of one pectoral.

"Yeah, it does. Come on, baby, we have a long ride." I let out a great exhalation of breath that ruffled her chestnut hair which looked and felt much softer without all the crap she usually smeared in it to keep it in place.

"Okay, let's go." She got to her feet and I followed her. We paid at the front and started the long ride home.

Unlike the ride down here I made stops for her to stretch, get a drink, and hell, even use the bathroom. We stopped maybe six times on the way back; one of those times was for a late lunch/early dinner and was only a couple of hours out from home. We were at least back in the 'ol home state.

"How are you holding up?" I needed to know; she looked tired and I was a little afraid she was going to try and fall asleep on me like she had on the way down.

"I'm okay, really not used to this, but it's not so bad the second time around." She smiled, but it was a bit wilted around the edges.

"We need to get you an energy shot or something?" I asked. She considered it half a second too long, because despite her shaking her head no, I pulled off at the next convenience store and got her one. It helped but not that much. By the time I pulled into Sunshine and Trig's driveway, Hayden was flagging pretty hard.

Ashton had her front door open, the hulking figure of my best friend looming in the rectangle of light behind the diminutive woman. I helped Hayden down and Ashton swallowed her whole in a big hug. Trig was at the edge of their cement drive on this side of their white picket fence, arms crossed, his face schooled and carefully neutral. I raised my eyebrows, hopeful, and his came down slightly. He shook his head almost imperceptibly and my heart sank.

That fucking cunt left my boy in there. I shook myself out of my black thoughts, a little shocked at myself for thinking about the mother of my child that way. That had never been me before… I got the saddlebags off of Baby handing them over to the big man.

"Go ahead, Doll, let Ashton get you settled, I'll come say goodbye in a minute." Hayden nodded, a furrow between her brows as she regarded me and my bestie, before reluctantly letting Sunshine guide her into the house.

"Spill," I told him.

"Went to see him, they at least let us do that. He was crying a lot. He's scared as hell. Some of the other kids are bein' hard on him. You can go and try and get him out but this time of night, I'm not sure you'll have much luck, especially with Aimee behind tellin' 'em to lock him up." He took a drag off his e-cig, the tip flaring blue and let out a plume of vapor, then crossed his arms over his black tee and cut. I unconsciously mirrored him, my leather jacket creaking.

It was damn near ten o'clock at night on a fucking Wednesday, but fuck it, I was gonna go. I jerked my head in the direction of their small two-story cottage and Trig fell into step beside me.

"Did you fuck her?" he asked and I huffed a laugh, remembering a time when I'd asked him the same exact thing about Ashton.

"No, but yes." I said darkly. Trigger raised a blonde eyebrow, his silvery-blue eyes searching my face.

"What the fuck kind of answer is that?" he asked.

"A truthful one," I said, circumspectly. I'd fucked her, but I'd loved her more. He laughed.

"Seriously man, what happened between you two?" he asked, stopping. I stopped with him, just shy of the steps leading to his front porch.

"Okay, super condensed version: met up with the local MC down there, good guys, invited them up for the summer lake run in a few weeks, shared Hayden with their Pres., made love to her, then the next night I fucked her, and then loved her damn near into a coma. I think that about covers it," I thought about it some, nodded once, and looked at my best friend in the world who looked absolutely poleaxed, e-cig dangling forgotten between his lips and I grinned. I patted him on the shoulder twice and went into the house. I don't think he moved for a long minute from that spot.

I found Ashton in the master bedroom upstairs, the shower was running and I felt my shoulders drop. I wanted to get to my kid, but bailing now would be a bad idea. Hayden had been bailed on enough. I was relieved when the shower shut off before I could say anything. Ashton was watching me curiously with her golden gaze.

"I suppose you wanna know what's up, too?" I said and she gave me this heart stopping little smile.

"Oh I'll know, trust me. Hayden's my BFF after all." She smiled bigger when I stuck my tongue out at her.

Hayden stepped out of the bathroom in the purple nightgown I'd bought her and I swear my cock leapt to attention. She stopped and smiled, a glint of her old self in her eyes.

"Have to go?" she asked.

"Yeah, babe, I do," I said gently. She nodded and I could see it in her eyes that she both understood, and at the same time didn't want to let me go. That warmed a part of my heart, it really did. It warmed me even more, knowing that I could confide in her on the way up here, tell her what was going on, be totally open, and not feel guilty about it. I'd never had that before.

"Go get your son," she breathed gently, and whatever guilt I'd been harboring over leaving her like this was absolved. I went to her and bent, kissing her softly.

"I'll call you," I murmured, and she smiled this little crooked smile that said she didn't believe me.

"You tossed my phone. I have to get a new one," she reminded me.

"We'll do that tomorrow," Ashton said gently, reminding us she was there. Looking into Hayden's bright green eyes it was too easy to forget my surroundings, forget about everyone else...

"Like I said, I'll call you," I said softly. "After I get things settled."

"Okay," she said sweetly, and it was one of the hardest things I have ever done, leaving her there like that, with so much in her life unsettled like it was. I ducked out into the hall and took the stairs as fast as my feet would carry me out the front door. If I stopped now, I wouldn't leave her, but my son was –and always would be– the priority in life.

Trigger was sitting on the porch swing, the end of his e-cig flaring bright blue, a captured star under the eaves in a night that I realized was full of them when I looked up at the sky. I let out an explosive breath. Trig chuckled at me and I shot him a narrow-eyed glare.

"Don't get your panties in a wad," he started.

"Hard to when I don't wear any," I grated and he laughed.

"She'll be here tomorrow, and the day after that, and the day after that, I reckon. How bad is her place?" he asked.

"Dunno, haven't seen it. Look I gotta go get my kid, bro–" I started apologetically.

"Yeah, no, go! We're always here for you, too. You know that." Trig waved me off casually. I cracked him a smile.

"Thanks for having my back in all things baby-mama-drama," I said, and his expression darkened a bit.

"You running out of guilt yet?" he asked.

"With this, yeah, I think I am," I said.

"Good, it's about fuckin' time you kept Aimee from running rough-shod all over your ass. It isn't pretty," he said, and that's what I liked about Trig, he spoke the truth but always did it in such a way as to take the bite out of it. He always managed to give it less sting, some-how. By now I was sitting astride my bike, and as I mulled over what he was sayin', fixing my helmet onto my head. I tightened the chin strap to where it was comfortable and slid the safety glasses over my eyes to shield them from the wind. The night was warm, and just this side of becoming uncomfortable in my leathers, but once I started moving that should ease off.

"Thanks, man," I grunted and he nodded.

"Keep the shiny side up, Brother," he said, and I fired Baby up and carefully backed her out of Trigger and Sunshine's driveway.

"Take care of my girl," I shot at him over the rumble of the engine.

"Like she was my own!" he called back.

I couldn't help it, I gave him a rakish grin and said, "Keep it in your pants, buddy!" and he barked a laugh.

"I got my own for that!" he called at my retreating back, and I almost didn't hear him from my engine and the wind.

16

Hayden...

My shoulders slumped a little as I heard the growl of Reaver's bike grow more distant. Ashton caught it and gave me a sympathetic look. We'd moved from the master bedroom into her guest room and she was sitting on the bed, watching me go through the saddle bags Reaver had left behind. Mostly, I was trying to take inventory of what I had versus what I didn't, and trying like hell to remember what I'd had packed for the honeymoon and what might be at the cleaners. Ashton huffed impatiently and got up.

She went to the closet and opened the doors. My wedding dress hung forlorn, by itself. My suitcase sat forgotten on the floor at the opposite end; I seized up my laptop bag and crushed it to my chest.

"I love you so much for rescuing this, Ashton, I can't even begin to tell you. All my clients, all my notes, all my designs, everything is in here and I have an online backup, I know, but even with that it wouldn't be the same and just so much has happened, so much has changed..."

Ashton knelt beside me and wrapped her arms around me hugging both me and the laptop case as one. "Hayden, what happened?" she asked me, and I took a deep breath and let it out slowly, and tugged back from the embrace.

"I'm not even sure," I told her and I started from the beginning, going way, way back, all the way to when Andy first started to grow distant, through when I caught him cheating, through him and my mom convincing me to take him back, through the process of he and I rebuilding the shattered pieces, to when Ashton and I met, then the engagement... just all of it.

Ashton sat and listened patiently and I startled when a glass of water appeared over my shoulder, just when my mouth had begun to go dry and my throat get scratchy from just so much talking. I looked up at Trigger, who arched a blond eyebrow, the silvery-blue of his eyes startling surrounded by the pale yellow mane of his hair. He'd pulled off the elastic that held it back and it framed his face in thick yellow waves. I took the glass gratefully from him, and tried valiantly to remember the man didn't at all match his imposing packaging. Still, his sheer size and breadth of shoulders was intimidating as hell.

I drank the contents down and he took the glass from me and returned to his self- imposed post at the door, leaning his broad frame nonchalantly against the door jamb, his arms crossed loosely, the cotton of his tee straining across the back and the swell of his biceps. He smirked at me and I shook my head to clear it and went back to my story.

"I thought we were okay, Ash. I thought we were fine, and then we're standing at the alter and he's looking at me like I'm Rosemary's baby and is telling me that he can't marry me. I thought that was the worst thing, I was so wrong because the next morning, in Florida, he called while I was on the beach and told me he didn't know if he had even ever loved me." I chewed my bottom lip and sighed out a little in relief. Just talking this all the way through with Ashton listening was already taking some of the edge off my burden. Still, I missed Reaver's patient questions and warm embrace just the same. When he held me, the whole mess seemed somehow less, more tolerable; I could be angry about it, instead of just hurt.

"Is that when he tossed your phone?" Trigger asked from behind me. I startled, not expecting him to speak.

"Yeah."

He grunted, "Good man."

"Agreed. We'll get you a new one in the morning. It was worth the expense if it gave you a few days of peace." She smiled at me and I felt myself blush to the roots of my hair. Ashton looked past me to her man and said, "Okay, out now. This is all girl time from here on out." I looked at her, my mouth agape, and turned to see Trigger grinning from ear to ear, his hands upraised, palm out. He backed out of the guest bedroom and closed the door with a soft click behind him.

"You're kind of incredible, you know that?" I asked.

"Yeah, well, he knows whenever we girls talk about sex, he gets it, and it's usually incredibly hot, so he's not one to complain." Ashton smiled conspiratorially and I laughed.

"What do you want to know?" I asked quietly, fully aware that she and Reaver had... well... at least once that I know of. I wanted to say that made me feel uncomfortable and it did a little bit until I thought about why it made me so.

"Why are you frowning?" she searched my face, her golden gaze concerned, and I smiled.

"I was thinking I should feel uncomfortable with the fact that you and I both have slept with Reaver but lately I've been taking the time to analyze why I think or feel certain ways," I confessed.

"Why?" She tilted her head curiously.

"Because a lot of what I have been thinking or feeling lately has been heavily influenced by my mom or Andy and I don't know, Ashton, I feel like I should be upset or grossed out that Reaver's slept with us both, but that's my mom talking. Truth is, Reaver gave me a beautiful and amazing experience and made it not-weird for me and it felt like..." I thought about it for a long minute before putting it into words, "It felt like he brought me back a little from whatever weird rabbit-hole I'd gone down with my mom and Andy. I came back feeling more like the girl you met back when I had a backbone." I nodded, thinking that was as close as I was going to get to putting it into words. Ashton was grinning.

"Good, I'm glad you feel that way, that you're back together a bit, but what was with that kiss? Reaver sent me a picture of you two. Where were you guys?" she asked.

"Oh, the picture?" I asked.

"Yeah."

"That was the Short Cliffs lighthouse, but that wasn't the first time we kissed." I told her about the conversation on the beach, about how he'd asked to kiss me before opening up about himself and about why he'd asked to kiss me, that he was afraid once he'd told me that he would never get another chance. We shared a moment of quiet sadness over that for Reaver, and I didn't disclose anything he told me, just that he had been very up front and honest about some darker aspects of his past and how he felt like he had a monster inside his head. She nodded and no more needed to be said.

I told her about how he'd cut the pajamas off of me and she and I both swooned a little over how hot it'd made me feel. She didn't seem to be bothered at all about that. I told her about Cutter and Reaver sharing me and how beautiful that experience had been for me, how they had made sure of it, and she smiled sweetly, fondly, and shared some of her own memories of the time she'd been shared by Trigger and Reaver.

I couldn't help myself, I had to ask her. "Was that the only time?" she nodded silently.

"There's been plenty of opportunity for it to happen again, but Reaver was having such a hard time with even considering another girl the more you and I started to hang out after Chadwick died. He's only had eyes for you for a long time. Hasn't even looked twice at any of the club whores," she smiled and I chewed my lower lip thoughtfully.

"I'm not sure if I should say 'I'm sorry' or not." I looked at her and she burst out laughing.

"No, most definitely not!" she said and hugged me.

"My time with Reaver and Ethan was a one-time thing and I was happy with it being that. My question to you is how are you feeling? I mean, if it came up would you do it again?" she asked.

"You know I think if the opportunity came up and Reaver were okay with it, I would but only with Cutter. I wouldn't be comfortable with anyone else."

She raised an eyebrow at me. "Hayden, just say what you mean," she said and I blushed.

"Doing it with Trigger is a total turn-off no-go for me, because you two belong to each other!" I blurted, as if saying it faster would take the embarrassment out of it, and I still slapped a hand over my mouth when I finished. I mean it wasn't anything on Trig! He was a beautiful specimen of what a male should be, but he was Ashton's and I didn't want to mess with that, like... at all. Ashton smiled wide, her golden eyes sparkling.

"That's another reason I never went there with Reaver again. Whether you knew it or not, he was yours, and leading all the way up to and after what happened, I sort of had my fingers crossed for you two." Her confidence of her secret hopes surprised me and I didn't know how to take it. Instead I filed it away to look at when I wasn't so tired. I mean, right now I was in negative-Nancy mode, and tired, and it sounded to me like my best friend had just told me she'd hoped my relationship with Andy would fail! I couldn't put it down, so I asked.

"I didn't want it to fail; I wanted him to treat you better. I wanted him to be there for you and do what he was supposed to do in a rela-tionship. I wanted him to stay home more, and plan the wedding with you, I wanted him to be excited to be with you and love you and make you happy, and he was doing none of those things!" She looked more than a little put out by it too, before she went on. "So I guess when he didn't and I was absolutely sure he wasn't going to, yeah, I secretly started wishing he would go away so that Reaver could do what I knew he was desperate to do from the moment he laid eyes on you. He wanted to be all of those things to you and more. What a real man should be to his woman. What Ethan is to me..." She smiled with pride at the last and I smiled with her, happy as hell she had that with Trig. She deserved it after her douchebag ex. That, and of course, when she put it that way, I could see her point when it came to me and Andy, and decided that I couldn't be angry with her. After all, the feelings weren't coming from a bad place, but rather a good one.

I finished telling her about Florida, about last night, which after the long, exhausting ride of the day, seemed like ages ago rather than just last night. I told her about Reaver letting his darker side out to play with me and how it had scared me, sure, but more so it had secretly thrilled me because I knew deep down in my heart of hearts that I could trust Reaver implicitly and that I had an out if I needed it. That one little word would have stopped the ride. Ashton's eyes were a little wide.

"I had no idea," she murmured and I could see she was thinking back to the lake run of a little over a year ago. She smiled then and it was both sweet and a little sad, not for herself but for Reaver, I think.

"What?" I asked her.

"I'm glad you could give him that, Hayden. I don't think it's something I could do," she said at last, and I held her hands in mine and gave them a little squeeze. She searched my face and whatever she saw there caused her to nod.

"Bedtime. You're exhausted and I'm pretty sure Ethan is waiting for me. We can sort this in the morning. You gave yourself a day of being back before any actual appointments with clients, right?" I nodded wearily.

Ashton's spare bedroom was decorated like something straight out of *Phantom of the Opera*. I'd helped her decorate the room and it had turned out nice. It was tastefully Victorian without being garish, which had been hard to do. It was like once you opened the door to this room and stepped inside, you stepped into another era, which had been the goal from the start.

The wallpaper on the wall behind the bed was a black and gray damask pattern, the queen-sized bed robed in rich black satin sheets, the comforter a deep, rich red with a raised diamond pattern on it. Seed beads like pearls were sewn where the lines crossed at every point. An antique writing desk was in one corner, the wood rich and dark, complementing the two nightstands and the tall four-poster bed.

I got to my feet, my legs sore from sitting on them so long. She helped me sort out the sea of decorative pillows at the head of the bed and I climbed into it.

Ashton had wanted at least one fun themed room in the house and she'd gotten it with this one. Trigger hadn't said a word about it. In fact when we'd asked he'd locked Ashton in an intent gaze and said to her that he hadn't cared what she'd done with the house at all, as long as he'd be coming home to her every night.

"Get some sleep, Hayden. I love you," she said, and flipped out the antique brass-and-crystal light fixture overhead, plunging the room into darkness. I sighed and closed my eyes. It was after two in the morning; we'd talked longer than I'd thought. I settled into the soft bed and slept like the dead, too exhausted to do anything else other than capitulate to my body's demands.

The next morning I woke later than I would have liked, by like, a lot. I groaned, and got up and padded down the hall to the restroom in the master suite. Ashton and Trigger's bed was already made. The house was always perfect, a throwback and testament to Ashton's beginnings. I would be jealous, if I didn't know the sobering and sinister connotations behind it. Still, if there was a habit she should keep from her days with her abusive ex, I suppose there were worse ones than keeping her house clean and perfect. I went back to the guest room and knelt by my piles of things to sort through them. I found that my dirty laundry from Florida, at least the pieces which had survived Reaver's knives, was missing.

That didn't leave me much to choose from. I went downstairs and found Ashton and Trigger in the kitchen; she poured me a cup of coffee without being asked, and I made a noise of approval. It was all I was capable of before that first sweet hit of caffeine. I hopped up on the barstool beside Trig's and sat at the counter with him. Ashton moved, wraith-like, through the kitchen fixing breakfast. After I had a few swallows of coffee, Trig slid a box across the granite countertop at me. I picked it up.

"You guys bought me a phone already?" I asked.

"Nope. Reaver brought it by with Connor this morning. It was the first thing he did after he got his boy out of Juvie." I nodded and tried to force down my disappointment that he didn't come see me. He had Connor with him, of course he couldn't, the fact he brought the phone... he shouldn't have, not with his other responsibilities.

"Your carrier would sell it to him but wouldn't connect everything until you came in, in-person. Account confidentiality and all of that." Ashton made a face and I grinned.

"How was Connor?" I asked, and both of them were very subdued. Trigger unlocked his phone and slid it across the granite at me. I picked it up and went out onto their back deck for some privacy before making the call.

"Hayden?" His voice came across the line by way of greeting.

"Yeah," I said, and couldn't keep the smile out of my voice.

"You were out when I got there this morning. I didn't want to wake you, did you get your phone?"

"Trig gave it to me, and you shouldn't have. I heard you had Connor with you. Is he all right?" I bit my lower lip, afraid of the answer.

"He's scared; they wouldn't let me have him last night. I slept on the bike in the parking lot and got him out first thing this morning. Some of the bigger boys gave him a rough time. He came out with a busted lip and a black eye. He's asleep right now. I think he was too scared to last night. He took some other things other than just soda and candy. A couple of prepaid cellphones and some of the minute card things. I asked him about it. Some of the neighborhood kids convinced him that if he did it, they'd let him be a part of their little club. When the cops brought him home, Aimee had a shit-fit and refused to pay for the things he took. The shop owner's tired of the little thugs stealing from his shop, and the items were just over the amount, so he wanted to prosecute and Aimee told the cops to take him. Even the cops were confused by her reaction. They'd never seen a mother want to throw the book at her own son. I think it made a little more sense to them when they saw me." He sounded rueful at the last, and throughout the entire telling had sounded just so tired... my heart went out to him. I wanted to fix it but I didn't know how.

"So, what happens now?" I asked, softly.

"Now I have Connor, and I'm not taking him back to his mom until I'm sure everything is straight. Might be a few days; might be a few weeks; I don't know, babe. It's summer vacation, so I don't have to worry about getting him to school which is a bonus. I'm going to have a talk with the shop owner, take Connor with me. I'm hoping I can sort everything out. Get him doing some community service, that sort of thing before his court date, which is in a week and a half. I don't want my boy to be like his old man." His voice became gruff, as if he fought down tears.

I said gently, "I don't know, Reaver. I wouldn't trade Connor's old man for anything in the world. I like you just the way you are."

We were both quiet for a long time and he said finally, "I don't deserve someone like you."

I laughed a little. "That's funny, I keep thinking the same thing about you! You've been so amazing these last few days." I heard him smile.

"I love you, Doll," he said, and I bit my lip.

"I trust you, Reaver," I said softly, reluctant to tell him I loved him back, but not because I didn't... I did, didn't I? I sighed inwardly and felt my shoulders drop. Truth was, I didn't know. I thought I'd loved Andy, thought he'd loved me too... but that had ended rather badly. One thing I knew for absolute certain was I trusted Reaver, like I could never trust Andy, and in some ways I think that was worth more. Wasn't it?

"I get what you're saying, Doll, and I don't blame you one bit. Maybe someday you can say it too, but I know plain as day how you feel about me I see it in your eyes, see it..." he paused as if checking on something, and maybe he was, I didn't know where his son was in relation to him, "... in the way you move under me and 'round me. Words are kind of pitiful in the face of all of that." I heard the chime of metal against metal and could envision him picking up the coin out of the necklaces he wore and smiled. My hand was clenched around the one I wore.

"I miss you," I said. "Is that pathetic?"

"Nope. I miss you too. I wish I could say 'I'll see you tomorrow' or give you some kind of time frame but…"

"No, don't worry about any of that. You take care of your son. Text me when you can, call me when you can, I understand and it will be enough," I assured him.

"I want you to meet him someday, just not now. I don't want to overwhelm him with too much new. I've never, you know, been with anybody that he's ever gotten to meet. I'm afraid with everything that too much change would be just that, too much."

I swallowed hard. He wanted me to meet his son? That was a bit overwhelming for me right now. I didn't even know what we were doing. Still, I was touched, honored that he would place me before any other woman he'd had in his life up to this point.

"Okay," I said. I heard a sound, like shifting. and a boyish moan.

"I gotta go, babe; Connor's having a nightmare." Reaver sounded distressed.

"Okay, I'll call you when I can," I said.

"Okay."

We hung up. I sighed and tipped my face up to the warm sun, closing my eyes, letting the light from our daytime star paint my vision in a fiery wash of red through my eyelids as I soaked in the warmth. It was almost as warm as it was in Florida but had none of the oppressive humidity, for which I was grateful. I breathed slow and deep and heard the slider open and close behind me.

"Yoga?" Ashton asked.

"Sounds like a really fine idea," I answered.

We did a lot that day. Yoga first, then we got my cellphone up and running. I had Andy's number blocked by my carrier. I didn't want or need to hear anything from him, ever again. Paying the monthly fee was going to be worth it to never have to hear another lie or lame excuse. After that, we stopped at the cleaners, where I was grateful to find that I had at least two complete outfits that were appropriate for my work. One of them happened to be my favorite, which helped brighten me up a little bit. We stopped by this little boutique where they had a killer shoe sale going on, so I could pick up some shoes to go with my meager stack of salvaged clothes. I bought two pairs and a new purse, so that helped me brighten up just a little bit more. I ended up with one appointment that day, and it was the last, and the hardest, stop. I had to meet with the contractor that employed Reaver about my townhome and see the damage for myself. Ashton and Trigger both went with me.

It was so deceptive. The outside of the townhome was as it had ever looked. The small patch of neatly-trimmed yard, the little lights lining the drive up to the garage, marking out the border between the concrete and the grass, were all as they should be. I got out of the back of the Jeep and Trigger followed me and Ashton up the walk. Ashton held my hand and I didn't realize I had hers in a white-knuckled grip until she winced.

I knocked on my own front door and a man in his late forties or early fifties answered. His salt-and-pepper hair peeked out from a scuffed and dirty white hard-hat. He wore one of those neon-yellow tee shirts with the silvery reflective bars on it, and a pair of sturdy white pants. His boots were steel-toed and brown, spattered with paint and white dust. He had an ample beer gut that hung over his belt, but his blue eyes sparkled jovially, wrinkles from smiling and laughing fanning from the outside corners of his eyes.

"Ms. Michaels?" he asked and stuck out his hand. I took it and shook back.

"That's me," I said.

"I'm John Gibson, of Gibson Drywall and General Contracting. Sorry about you having to knock on your own front door. Here are your keys. We changed the lock for you. No charge. It's a damned shame what happened here."

I took the keys gratefully. "Thank you, you didn't have to do that," I said and meant it.

"Yeah. Yeah, I did. Come on in, I'll show you what needs to be done." He wasn't smiling anymore and I quailed a bit inside. The damage was stark and immediate the second we stepped through the door.

"They damaged just about every wall in the place. Some of 'em worse than others but I'm afraid it's more than that. They ripped out the walls to get to the wiring. Copper goes for a lot of money in the scrap business."

"They stole my wiring?" I asked, incredulous.

"Afraid so. Is there any place you would like to start?" he asked.

"Upstairs," I mumbled.

It was horrible. It looked like a bomb had gone off in my house.

The whirlpool bath, the shower doors, even the shower-head were all gone, the tile broken and smashed in places in the master bathroom. They'd even taken the toilet and sinks! The counter had been smashed to facilitate removal of the sink basins.

In my bedroom, there were gaping holes in my carefully-painted walls and long tears in the drywall between them where the wire had been ripped free. The carpet was even gone in here.

"Have you done anything?" I asked.

"Like what?"

"Like, take up the carpet?"

"No, honey, they stole that, too."

I nodded and chewed on my bottom lip.

The guest room had its carpet but the wall damage was much the same.

Downstairs the bathroom was mostly intact. No holes, but the toilet was missing as was the sink.

In the kitchen the stove, fridge, dishwasher, just —everything— was ripped out. The hardwood floors were streaked with splintered gouges both there and in the dining room, where the heavy appliances had been dragged through. The kitchen floor sported broken tile and the walls were much the same as the other rooms. I don't think a single wall remained intact.

The living room was bad. The carpet was gone and the walls were wrecked. Swaths of fresh primer, hastily-applied, striped the walls where they didn't have holes, and I pointed to it.

"What was that?" I asked.

"I did that. You didn't need to see what they spray-painted up there," he said.

"What was it?" I asked, dully.

"Miss, you really don't need to know," he said and the sympathy in his gaze did me in.

I felt hot tears mist my eyes and strong hands fell onto my shoulders, kneading them comfortingly. I sniffed, and Ashton came around and hugged me from the front. I hugged her back tightly and stared at the fresh gray blank slate of primer on my wall, and gave in to the deep well of self-pity that was finally boiling over.

I let myself ask, *why was this happening to me?*

17

R eaver...

"She keeps calling out that she's fine and won't come to the door, but I know better; she's in there crying and hasn't stopped since we got back. I'm not sure what it was about the primer on the wall, but it hit her hard somehow," Trigger said into my ear. I pinched the bridge of my nose between my eyes and looked over at my sleeping son. We'd spent the day together and had done a lot of talking. I'd been sad to realize just how much Aimee fucking hated me. I'd been sadder still that I hadn't realized how it had been affecting our son.

I scraped my bottom lip between my teeth and told Trig, "Let me call you back."

"'Kay, man. Sorry to be the bearer of bad news," he said.

"Better to know than be kept in the dark, Bro," I said, and meant it.

"True enough," he agreed, then, "Later."

"Later." I disconnected the call and scrolled through my contacts.

"What up cuz?" Shelly shouted into the phone, by way of greeting.

"Need your help, Shells," I grunted and I swear I could hear her face fall through the line.

"What's wrong? You never ask me for help," she said.

I laid it all out on the line, the shit that was going on with Connor, and she listened intently, which wasn't like Shells if it were anybody else, but it wasn't just anybody else, it was me, so she listened.

"I just need to go out for a few hours. Maybe 'til morning. Can you watch him for me?" I pleaded.

"I was just going to do homework, and was going to take a shot at taking a ride on one of the new guys, but I can do homework there and Zander will still be there tomorrow or the next day," she said.

"Loyal still shooting you down?" I asked, and I swear I could see her in my head, rolling her eyes in that way that was purely my cousin Shells.

"Loyal is such a goddamn prude, it's driving me crazy!" she exclaimed.

"You ever think he's just that into you? That he's waiting for you to come around and see that he wants you and only you and isn't on board for anything less in return?" I asked her. She was silent for far too long.

"Yeah, well, we both know I'm not any good for that, Reav. So let's not pretend I'm not damaged goods and pretty much no guy would touch me with a ten-foot pole if they knew," she said quietly. I opened my mouth to retort, to deny her crazy fucked-up view on her status as desirable because of something she'd had no control over, but she stopped me by saying, "Be there in ten," before hanging up on me.

Fuck. I could only carry so many people right now. I looked over at Connor, who was pretty much wracked out from an exhausting day of moving and shaking. As soon as he'd gotten up, we'd gone to Mark and Aimee's. Aimee had had a goddamn conniption fit when she'd seen I'd gotten him out of Juvie. I'd told him to stay in the truck and gone in and packed him some clothes. All the while Aimee was screaming at me and Mark stood silently by, his arms crossed, and stared at her like he'd never seen her before.

Finally, when she'd realized she wasn't going to get a rise out of me, she'd gone somewhere in the house and into a room, slamming the door behind her like some petulant fucking child. Mark and I had stared at one another for a long time while I'd waited for him to start in on me.

"For what it's worth," he'd said, "I agree with you." Since Aimee was out of her fucking mind, he and I agreed that it was best Connor stay with me for a while.

After that, we'd gone to the shop he'd stolen from and I'd talked the store owner down some. I'd called Dragon and we'd set it up so the prospects and him would run a protection of sorts, just without the extortion of the bad ol' days. We'd rotate in and out of the corner store when the kids were likely to come around with their thieving ways and scare the shit out of them, if the owner agreed to take my money and drop the charges. I also set it up with him that Connor would be doing his bitch work for five bucks an hour all the way up until the matched amount of the debt was paid, and then some. The shop-keep was impressed with me. My son, not so much. Boo fucking hoo, he shouldn't have had sticky fingers.

After the beat-down in Juvie I spared him from having to pick his own switch, old-school style, and I told him he'd best be grateful for that. I think that was what finally put the fear of God into him. I'd never, not once, no matter how badly he behaved, ever hit him or even threatened to. The fact that I hinted at it now had him being a pious little angel. The really exhausting shit came during lunch when he'd cried his fucking eyes out over his mom going on about how much she fucking hated me and in the next breath telling our son how much he looked just like me and it was true. He did. Still, that didn't give her the damned right.

Mark, the only other rational fucking adult in all of this, had agreed to meeting up and talking about Connor and some of Aimee's malfunction later on when the dust settled some. Aimee was going to be pissed off if she found out about Mark going behind her back, but somehow I didn't think Mark was going to care.

Shelly showed up, as promised, and I let her in to my small trailer.

She took one look at Connor and said, "Awesome. Homework it is," and sat down at the little table by my kitchen.

"Thanks, Shells. I owe you." I whispered to keep from waking him, but the kid was sleeping like the dead.

"No worries, Reave, you've done so much for me this doesn't even come close to evening the odds." I kissed the top of her head and she hugged me awkwardly because of our positions in the extra small space.

"Be back as soon as I can," I promised.

"Go do whatever needs doing," she said, waving me off. From experience, she knew better than to ask me what I got up to late at night.

I left the trailer and pushed my bike out to the road. I didn't want to fire it up too close and wake my boy. The ride to Trig's was around a half hour and felt just too damn long. The front door was open, a rectangle of light spilling into the warm summer night. The bright blue tip of Trig's e-cig signaled his position on the porch swing. He let out a cloud of vapor as I shut off the bike and approached.

"Still cryin'?" I asked. He nodded and I handed off my helmet and glasses, which he set on the swing beside him.

"Go get 'er, tiger," he said and I gave him the finger over my shoulder. He chuckled and I couldn't help but smile. Ashton was curled on the couch with a book in her hands.

"Hey, Sunshine," I said as I went for the stairs.

"I'm glad you could come," she said as I hit the bottom step.

"For her, always."

I took the stairs two at a time and stopped outside the guest-room door. I could hear her faint sobbing from inside and it hurt my heart a little. I tried the handle but it was locked. Not for long. I flicked open one of my thinner blades and worked it between the jamb and door. It was an old lock you could jimmy with a credit card, but this way was more fun. I tried the handle again and it turned, smooth as butter. I went into the room.

Hayden lay curled on her side, a pillow hugged to her chest, just weeping her heart out. Again I was struck by that odd twisting feeling in my chest and the desire to stop her pain mixed with that stirring in my pants, the extreme lust that I just about always had for her unfurling at my center. It wasn't fair. She was just so fucking beautiful when she cried.

I toed out of my Adidas and took off my jacket and cut, hanging them on the back of the desk chair and got onto the bed behind her. She startled, giving a little shriek when the bed dipped, and oh, god, that flipped my switch. I took her wrists gently in my hands and turned her onto her back. She calmed some when she saw me.

I asked her, "Do you trust me, Hayden?" and I could see the relief wash over her, the relief – and something else entirely. She sagged and let me pin her wrists to the mattress.

"Yes," she said and I settled between her thighs. She wore the satin I bought her in Florida, the purple just darker against the already-dark coverlet. The two narrow windows to either side of the bed didn't let in much light. I ran the tip of my nose along her tear-slicked cheek and licked the salt from her skin. She sucked in a startled gasp.

"Why you cryin', Doll?" I asked her in a low murmur.

"Just giving into the despair, I guess," she whispered, brokenly.

"See, I don't like that, baby," I said. "I mean, I love to see you cry, but not over that douchebag or anything that his douchebaggy little friends did. No, if you're gonna cry, I want it to be because I make you cry," I told her. I kissed her gently and she made a little startled noise of surprise. "You're so fucking pretty when you cry, and it's been a really shitty day." I pressed my forehead to hers and I sighed out, drinking in her sorrow and her light edge of fear.

"What do you need?" she asked me, and I felt terrible that I was making this about me when it so clearly needed to be about her, but I couldn't help myself.

"I need to fuck you," I whispered next to her ear, then switched sides and whispered into her other ear, "What do you need?"

"I... I think I need that too," she said with a trembling sigh. I let go of her wrists and placed my palms flat to either side of her head.

"Undo my pants," I ordered coldly and she immediately moved to comply, her fingers deft in the dark. I sprang free of my jeans immediately.

"Can I touch you?" she asked.

"Baby," I growled, "You never have to ask me that." Her hands cupped my face gently and her light green eyes, made colorless by the diffuse light, searched my face.

"What are you waiting for, Reaver? I thought you needed to fuck me," she murmured and I felt a cold, nasty smile curve my lips. She needed to be fucked as much as I needed to fuck her; well all right!

I let myself collapse onto her, my lips grinding harshly over hers. She wasn't wearing panties under the nightgown, and while she was growing aroused she wasn't quite wet or ready for me. I didn't care. I needed to be inside of her with such a savage intensity I fit myself into her anyways and thrust hard and deep. She cried out in pain and I swallowed it, striking up a rhythm that wasn't exactly punishing, but wasn't easy for her, either. Her hands wound into my hair and her legs around my hips. She used her whole fucking body to pull me into her and I was lost. Lost in her kiss, lost in her eyes, lost in her ragged breathing and drowning in her delicate smell. She'd found whatever it was that she used, soap, perfume, or whatever and so she smelled like she always did, fresh and clean like a salty sweet ocean breeze overlaid by a delicate tropical flower smell and I couldn't get enough of her. She ripped my shirt over my head and I let her. Her small hands smoothing up and down my ribs, my back and my chest, just touching me wherever she could reach.

Her body had caught up with the program and she was sliding slick, hot, and wet around my cock, her body opening up a little more but still so damned tight, gripping me with fervor and a need to have me there. I palmed the outside of one of her thighs and hauled her leg up higher on my body, changing the angle, making my thrusts go deeper. She cried out her pleasure in the change in tactic and broke our kiss to do it. I nipped her lower lip and she pressed her forehead to my shoulder.

"Harder!" she cried, and I was honestly thinking the same thing. I pounded the shit out of that pussy, drawing back as far as I could without leaving her body all together, before letting my body weight drive me back in to the hilt. I could feel her tightening up around me and I knew she was close. So was I, which saddened me a little, I mean, this was going to be way faster than I wanted it to be, but that was okay. I had a pretty quick recovery and the next time I would savor it, drive her nuts, make her cry her beautiful tears for me for a whole different reason, a much better reason.

Her breathing became more ragged, took on that desperate, frenzied cadence that told me she was about to sail over the edge and I wanted it, I wanted it so fucking bad! I needed her to feel good, I needed to feel good, my god, she made it so fucking hard to think, she felt so damn amazing. I bowed my head over her and thrust once, twice, and she came apart beneath me. I was dimly aware of her nails biting into my ass as I drove into her violently one last time. Her body convulsed underneath me, squeezing down around me so sweetly it took everything I had to ride her orgasm out without coming myself. Her body went lax beneath mine and I thrust a few more times, drawing out her aftershocks before I pulled out to come, myself. Hayden lay gasping beneath me and laughed a little into the dark.

"You know that method doesn't work right?" she asked, and I smiled. All trace of sadness had been whisked away.

"I know just something incredibly hot about watching myself spill up over a woman's hip. Doing it up over yours, is just out of this fucking world."

I lay beside her and she stayed on her back, trying to keep from staining the comforter, if I had to hazard a guess. I whisked my tee shirt off the bed beside us and cleaned her up. I could borrow one of Trig's, it wasn't a big fucking deal.

"Let's get the rest of this crap off," I suggested and tugged on her nightgown. She slipped it up off over her head and I sucked in a breath as her silky skin was revealed. She positively glowed in the night, and I couldn't move for a second while I drank the image in. I shoved my pants and socks off and kicked them off the bed, pulling her against my body.

"What had you so upset, baby?" I asked.

"I don't know... I guess it was the fact that I didn't ask for this – any of this – to happen. I did everything right, I forgave him, I loved him no matter what and still, someone felt the need to write something so horrible on my wall your boss, or whoever, felt the need to cover it up and wouldn't tell me what it said. It just all came crashing down, became real, you know? Whatever wall was holding everything back just crumbled and I sort of lost it." She sounded a little miserable; 'embarrassed' may be the better word.

"Hey," I said and tipped her chin with my finger, forcing her to look at me. "None of this is your fault, none of this should be happening, and I'm amazed at how well you've weathered the storm, not only from what these assclowns have been putting you through, but me, too." She searched my face and pushed herself up into a sitting position. I raised an eyebrow and she made an exasperated noise and threw a leg over my hips, straddling me.

"What is your middle name?" she asked me, and I laughed and told her the truth.

"Kinnicutt."

She opened her mouth and then frowned, closing it.

"Wait, seriously?" she asked.

"Just like the character," I affirmed. She wrinkled her cute little nose at me.

"Well, that ruins it," she complained, then shrugged and slapped my bare chest.

"Oh ow!" I said and putting up my arms and rising off the bed. I was laughing, though.

"Rhett Kinnicutt Butler!" she exclaimed anyway. "Don't you fucking get it?" she demanded, hands on her hips, the image of an irate housewife, except, you know, nude and perfect and fuck! Even mad, she was getting my dick hard.

"Get what?" I asked, genuinely confused.

"Being here, like this, in your arms, just in your presence, is the only time I feel like myself any more. Like its okay to be me; the 'me' I used to be. I don't know what you do to me half the time. You turn me upside down, inside out, and confuse the hell out of me, but so far I like it. You feel good," and she slipped me inside of her as if to prove her point. She bent at the waist still riding me and put her lips against mine.

"I have a hard time saying it, but I believe you. That you..." She faltered.

"That I love you?" I supplied for her, letting my arms go around her, cradling her against my chest.

"Yes," she said and bowed her head, resting it against my shoulder as I lazily thrust myself up inside her with some long, slow strokes.

"I'm glad you believe me, baby," I murmured and turned my head to kiss her ear. She drew in a shuddering breath and pushed herself off my chest, I groaned as it seated me deep inside her and was a little frustrated it stopped me from moving.

"Stop, I'm trying to tell you something important," she said and her tone made me go stock-still. Whatever it was, it was important, at least to her, and if it was important to her, then it meant the world to me, so I listened with rapt attention.

"Go ahead, babe," I said when she didn't immediately speak.

"I figured something out, after Andy, in Florida, with you," she said quietly.

"What's that?" I asked.

"That there's something even more important than love; that if you can't trust someone, you can't love them completely," she said and I watched her, my face carefully neutral. I nodded carefully and I thought I knew what she was about, but then she leaned forward again, oh, so carefully.

"What I had with Andy wasn't love, at least not completely, because I couldn't trust him as far as I could throw him," she said, a little sadness in her voice. "What I'm trying to say is 'I trust you, Reaver'," and she kissed me, long and slow, our tongues mingling, and, dumb ox that I am, I still got it. She'd said the words 'I love you' to that sod countless times and when he'd said them back they were nothing but hollow empty lies.

Hayden was telling me in her own way that she not only trusted me, she loved me, and her choice of words was something stronger, truer, than anything she had ever felt before. If I were head-over-heels in love with the woman before, I was ass-over-teakettle drowning in my love for her now. I crushed her to me and flipped us so I was riding between her lovely legs. I thrust into her slowly, drawing out our mutual pleasure.

"God, I love you, Hayden."

"I trust you, with my life and with my heart," she whispered back and it was the sweetest, truest, most amazing thing any woman had ever said to me in the history of, well, fucking ever!

I made love to her until we both saw stars, then after a short rest I did it again for good measure, partly because I didn't know when I would get to see her again and partly because I just needed to.

She slept soundly against me and with great reluctance I had to let her go. I tucked her safe and sound into the blankets and kissed her softly. She didn't so much as stir while I got dressed and slipped out. I went into Trigger and Ashton's room where they were busy doing it and asked Trig for a shirt.

"Help yourself!" he said with a grin and made Ashton cry out with his thumb on her clit. I laughed under my breath and shook my head ruefully. It wasn't a regular occurrence, walking in on them having random sex, but the few times it did happen, they didn't bother stopping on account of me, or anyone else, if it was their own house or the club. If anything, it added to it for them. I pulled a shirt from the drawer and shut the door behind me. I heard Trig's deep voice, muffled and indistinct through the door and heard Ashton's high, musical laugh in response. I found myself chuckling the whole way down the stairs.

18

Hayden...

I woke alone the next morning, Reaver's scent lingering on my skin. I smiled to myself and stretched luxuriously before starting my day. I met with six clients and was basically fired by three, on the grounds that they wanted to 'distance' themselves from the scandal my wedding had caused. I wasn't exactly devastated, more pissed-off, and I hurriedly made notes to blacklist them. I would rather die than work for one of them in the future. I wish I could say that there were three or four more right there to take their place but, unfortunately, this was the really-real world, and shit just didn't work that way.

My day went from bad to worse when I met with John Gibson and the electrician that he contracted with. The repairs to my townhome were going to be far more costly than I had imagined and I may make my own money; I may be really good at what I did, but not to the extent the repairs to my home were going to be. I was forced to call my dad and I hated calling my dad for money. It felt like I couldn't handle myself and I really, really loathed that.

"Pumpkin?" he answered the phone.

"Hey, Daddy," I said.

"What's wrong?" he asked, and I told him. He laughed.

"Oh, Baby. You get what you want. You remember what I used to tell you when you were little?" he asked.

"Out of everything negative there's at least one positive..." I recited.

"That's right," he said. "What would one be out of this one?" he asked, and even though he was talking to me like I was eight again, I humored him.

"I can redo this place however I want, the layout will be the same but everything else can be different, new, my own and not 'ours' anymore. A fresh start," I said, when really all I could think about was Reaver, and his hands on my body, the feel of him as he moved inside of me. Reaver was the real positive out of all of this.

"Oh, Hayden," my father said, "I am so proud of you." I hugged myself and smiled. That meant a lot to me, it really did.

"I love you too, Daddy," I said and meant it. I trusted him, too but that would just be awkward to say. We chatted for a little bit, discussed what needed to happen for the lawyers and some other matters pertaining to my home that was simply just ruined around me. The contractors waited patiently outside while I made my call, and when I stepped out into the summer sun, I felt marginally better about things. Especially after talking about the lawyers. When you grew up in an affluent home, it really was "just money", but I hated being that way, more now than I ever had before, since spending so much time with the hard-working men and women of the Sacred Hearts MC.

Still, talking about the lawyers, and documenting the damage, and receipts, and figuring out how much everything I had owned and lost had been worth and so on, made me realize I wasn't really spending my daddy's money, more like just borrowing it until we sued the pants off the bastard who'd done this. I was suddenly ever so grateful I had had the insurance company appraise and document all of the antiques. I had a record of just about everything that had been lost and that was a very good thing. It was integral to getting my revenge in the long run.

"Ms. Michaels," John greeted me as I approached them.

"When can you start?" I asked.

"Tonight, I reckon," John said.

"Can you please start with the master bedroom and master bath?" I asked. "I can't live with my best friend for the whole duration of the repairs. I love them dearly but I don't want to impose."

The men exchanged looks.

"You want to live here while the repairs are being done?" the electrician asked.

"You won't even know I'm here," I said, calmly.

That had been a week and a half ago. I had picked out new everything, and the men had installed it all, and painted the room to my specifications. Ashton and I went furniture and linen shopping, and my bedroom and master bathroom were livable again. What wasn't livable was that I had to spend all of it away from Reaver, except for stolen phone calls late at night and the occasional daytime text. He worked, but it was late at night when Shelly could watch Connor. When I came home the first night that my room was livable I had caught the faint whiff of his cologne in my entryway and had quickly gone through the house, greeting the men who worked, hoping against hope that he was there, but he wasn't.

So, imagine my surprise, when I dragged myself through my front door, my feet absolutely aching in my heels, and saw him, his back to me as he smeared mud on a seam of the drywall in the living room. He had headphones in his ears and I simply stood there and watched him for long moments, my pulse quickening, my blood zinging through my veins. I set down my laptop case and slipped off the shoes which were hurting me so badly, and straightened, half-afraid he was a figment of my imagination.

I wanted to go to him but I didn't want to startle him. Something told me that would be bad. I shifted from foot to foot and watched his long-fingered hands smooth over the wall with the metal bladelike tool and it made me smile.

"Yo! Reaver!" someone called from behind me and I jumped, smoothing my gray pencil skirt. I turned back and cool blue eyes, the hue of a winter's sky, were locked on me. His face was somber, unsmiling and my heart dropped. He set the trough of mud and blade aside on a temporary table made of plywood over two sawhorses and I looked him over, concerned.

"Hey," he said, and pulled the headphones out of his ears. Why was this so awkward all of a sudden?

"Hi," I echoed back.

"Reaver?" someone called from my kitchen.

"In a minute, Buck!" Reaver called out, harshly.

"What's wrong?" I asked softly.

"Had to take Connor back to his mom's," he muttered and I felt my shoulders drop. I went to him and wrapped my arms around him. His curved around my shoulders and he held me tight to his body.

"Stay with me tonight," I whispered, and I felt, rather than saw, him nod.

"I got three more hours. I'll come up when I'm done," he murmured against my hair.

"Okay," I agreed.

"What's your safeword?" he asked, and I looked up at him sharply.

"What?" I asked.

"The word I told you in Florida," he reminded me gently.

"Icarus?" I hazarded. He nodded.

"Will you go away for good if I use it?" I asked. I could tell something was different this time. He shook his head 'no'.

"Just get ready for bed, go to sleep, I'll be up when I can," he murmured.

"Okay."

"Reaver... Oh, sorry, Ms. Michaels, didn't know you were home." I turned to see one of the workmen, Buck, standing beside my pile of forgotten things.

"It's okay, Buck. I was just about to head upstairs." I looked up at Reaver, searching his face, which was back into its crafted mask of neutrality. His eyes, though, his eyes were downright tempestuous. I stood up on tip-toe and kissed him softly, which I think startled him. I smiled my best impish smile and reluctantly withdrew from his arms, wincing a bit when I lowered myself back flat-footed. Reaver frowned.

"What was that for?" he demanded.

"Breaking in new heels, my feet are a little wrecked," I answered.

"Buck, do me a favor and grab my girl a chair?" Reaver said.

"Uh, yeah, sure, no problem," Buck sounded a little flabbergasted and it made me smile, almost as much as hearing Reaver call me his girl did.

Buck wheeled a dusty black office chair in from another room and I dropped into it. Reaver took a knee in front of me and lifted one of my feet onto his leg, pressing his thumbs into the bottom and kneading. I groaned and dropped my chin to my chest. That was pure bliss!

"What did you need, Buck?" Reaver asked, but didn't stop what he was doing. That was okay. I was on board. Like completely... Oh, god, that felt good!

Buck was saying something about a tricky installation of some sort or another when it came to a certain kind of patch or this or that. I couldn't follow, and after my day I didn't want to. One of the projects I had been working on, the material the client wanted had been discontinued and we were just a smidge short but she just had to have that particular flooring or the whole project would be ruined. It was just plain draining working for Francesca, but as one of my better clients I supposed I should just be grateful she hadn't fired me like some of the others. Reaver started in on the other foot and I'd like to have died and gone to heaven.

I let my mind drift while the two men talked about putting the humpty-dumpty that was my house back together again, and missed it when Buck left and Reaver called my name. His hands stopped and came to rest on my knees and he tried again.

"Hey, Doll..."

"What? Sorry... my brain went out to dinner without me. You are way too good at that." He smiled.

"Go on up to bed, baby; you're tired. I'll be up in a few hours," he said gently, and I wasn't about to argue.

"You better be," I told him. "I've missed you." He smiled and swept me with his cool blue eyes before standing up.

"Missed you, too, Doll. More than you can know," he said.

I nodded and went back up the step from my sunken living room to my entryway and gathered up my things. I padded up the stairs in my smoky pantyhose, and by the time I got to the top, declared them dead from too many snags. I figured it was a valiant and acceptable death and well worth not having to put the heels back on. I opened my bedroom door and it was like stepping from a shattered and war-torn landscape to a peaceful and borderline-opulent oasis. I shut out the ruin of the rest of my house by simply closing the door.

My bedroom and master bath were worlds away from what they had been. Before, they had been done in subtle pastels of lilac and lavender tones that were reminiscent of time spent in the country. Now they were done in whites and cool, soothing blues that reminded me of two things, the beaches and ocean we left back in Florida, and Reaver's eyes. Sappy and lame? Yeah. Did I care? No.

The bathroom was spectacular. It not only had a glassed-in shower that was walled in beautiful light sandstone, but also a raised bath, big enough to fit three people. The bath was white and a whirlpool, and was just the thing after a long day spent in heels having to deal with exhausting clients.

The wall opposite the shower and bath held the sinks and counters. The counters, also sandstone, had his-and-hers sinks, and, closer to the closet, a lower counter with a small bench in front of it and a lighted mirror on the wall, specifically so that I could sit and do my makeup each morning. The closet was closed off by white floor-to-ceiling doors that resembled shutters. There was a window over the bathtub; the stained glass in it had been butterflies and purple flowers before it was stolen. Now it was a design of shells: sand dollars and scallop shells and even a conch. Also on the wall over the tub were two perfectly square shadowboxes framed in white; inside were two perfect scallop shells I had saved from our meal on Cutter's sailboat. They were as big as my hand and patterned so beautifully, I hadn't been able to resist. I'd wrapped them carefully in my swimsuit cover-up and packed them in carefully with my things. I smiled and switched out the bathroom light and went into the bedroom.

The carpet was plush and off-white, very similar to the white sand beaches we had enjoyed. The wall behind the bed was blue, the rest of them crisp and white.

The bed was a queen, and set high, high enough that a wooden step was set on the side so I could get up into it. The step matched the four thick, square pillars making up the head- and footboard's four corners. The headboard was higher than the footboard and had bronze metal scrollwork set in an expanse between the wood.

Tall end tables were on either side of the bed; I could reach the lamps on them whether I was in or out of the bed. The tables matched the satiny wood of the bed frame; lamps with scrollwork that matched the headboard and natural-fiber shades matching the creamy carpet lived on their tops. I switched one of these on.

I had found an antique dressing table that matched closely the color of more modern replica furniture and it sat in one corner. An antique dresser sat along the wall between the bedroom door and the doorway to the closet area, which also acted as an entryway into the bathroom.

I got out the black nightgown Reaver had bought in Florida and put it on. It wasn't actually that bad. It was held up by thin spaghetti straps and plunged low in the back. The front hugged my body, subtly flaring at the hips and ending mid-thigh. Two panels ran along my ribs that were made of sheer lace, hints of my skin peeking through.

I pulled some of the decorative pillows from the bed and turned back the white comforter, revealing sheets the color of Reaver's eyes. I got up into it and stared across the room at the wall opposite the bed and the large framed picture there.

Bronze sconces bracketed the sixteen-by-twenty-inch frame. The frame itself was a very modern black, the mats around the photo were white, then gray, and the picture in it was the black-and-white photo Marcy had taken of us in the lighthouse. Reaver had sent the image to Ashton, and I had asked for a copy. She'd given it to me and

I had it professionally printed, as large as I could make it without it distorting. Never had I been more grateful for the increasingly good quality of smartphone cameras.

I settled back into the bed and switched out the lamp. The ambient light from my bedroom windows was enough to study the photo by. I wondered briefly what Reaver would think, but I didn't get to wonder long because I fell fast asleep.

I woke sometime during deepest night to Reaver snugging up tight to my back, pulling me back against his chest. He paused, his hands sliding over the lace panels of the nightgown, his lips, where they were pressed against the back of my shoulder, curving into a gentle smile. He breathed me in and settled into the bed with his arms around me.

"You picked a damn comfortable bed," he whispered and I smiled.

"It was okay," I said, snuggling back into him. I was acutely aware of the way he spooned me, and just what my satin-covered ass was wiggling against. He let out a groan as my body made more contact with his. I let out a happy sigh and told him, "–Now– it's comfortable. I always knew it was missing something." Reaver chuckled.

"Love you, Doll," he murmured.

"Mmm. Are you okay?" I asked softly.

"I miss him. I guess Aimee and her husband Mark have been disagreeing on some things. Not sure why, or where, or how, but she somehow got it into her head that they wouldn't be fighting if Connor weren't misbehaving, but honestly, up until the whole 'stealing' thing, Mark says he's just being a typical ten-year-old." Reaver was quiet for a time.

"What do you think it is?" I asked.

"Honestly, I don't think Aimee ever got over the idea of 'us', even after she moved on with Mark. I think it doesn't help that the more Connor grows up, the more he's starting to look and act like me and I think that drives her nuts. She's got a lot of pissed-off and confused going on. Some of that's my fault but only part of it. I screwed up. There isn't a day that goes by I don't regret those mistakes..." I hugged his arms where they were around me and twisted in his embrace to face him.

I could feel the tension radiating through his body and it felt all wrong. I cupped his face in my hands and pushed his damp hair off his forehead. He'd showered before he'd come to my bed.

"What aren't you saying?" I asked him gently.

"She tells my son she hates me and in the next breath tells him how much he looks like me." He shuddered from head to toe and I couldn't tell in the dark, but if I'd had to guess, I would put my money on it was to suppress his anger at the situation. God, how terrible for Connor!

"Sounds like Aimee is tearing pages out of my mother's parenting playbook," I said softly and Reaver barked a bitter laugh and crushed me to him.

"I have to follow the custody agreement when all I want to do is rip him away from her, take him far away where he doesn't have to put up with that shit. He's ten, Hayden. He's ten and ought to be able to just be a ten-year-old boy, without his parents bleeding their fucked-up issues all over him." He sounded savage and I clung to him, holding him as much as he was holding me.

"I don't disagree," I said softly. We held each other in the dark for a long time, and he absently kissed my hair from time to time.

"I have him again this weekend. I want you to meet him," he said softly, then, "Next weekend is the summer lake run; I want you to go with me."

I nodded against his chest.

"Are you sure about me meeting your son?" I asked, tremulously.

"Never been more sure of anything in my life. Trig and Sunshine are having a barbecue at their place, I figure it'd be good neutral ground."

I relaxed marginally. "Yes, okay, that would be good," I said and he gave me a little squeeze.

"Thank you," he breathed. We were silent for another stretch of moments.

"Reaver?" I asked.

"Mmm?"

"What are we?" I asked.

"Dunno, baby. Never been much for labels. Why don't you pick one, and we'll go with it," he said. I laughed.

"Just like that, I just say what I think we are and you'll go with it?" I had a hard time picturing Reaver going with just anything. He was always his own man, doing his own thing and this was no exception. He rolled lightning-quick and pinned me to my bed.

"Baby, I love you. I belong to you. I'm your very own monster on a leash in a lot of ways. I'll guard you, I'll protect you, I'll love you, and sometimes," he nipped my shoulder playfully, "I'm gonna bite you, but never for one minute think that any word you put on us to define us to other people makes a bit of fucking difference to me. I know what we are, what I feel like when I'm with you, what I feel like without you… If calling me your lover, your boyfriend, your friend, your plaything, your anything, makes your life easier with the hoity-toity bunch or makes you feel more secure, then label away. I'm a big boy and I can take it. Whatever you pick, I've been called worse things."

I melted a little inside at his words, tears springing to my eyes. No one had ever said anything so beautiful to me, ever.

"Kiss me," I begged and he did, long and slow and sweet, and I let the issue lay fallow. Defining our relationship suddenly became a moot point. I mean, honestly! How do you define the undefinable?

19

———

Reaver...

"I can't get over how much he looks like you," Hayden murmured for like the thousandth time. Trigger and my boy were going at each other with Super Soakers down in the grass, along with Chandra's grandkids. Dragon was manning the grill, Dray and some of the other guys were playing poker, and Sunshine and the rest of the girls were putting out side dishes. Ashton was slowly but surely trying to organize some club events where the families could be more involved. She said the MC was the family she'd never had the chance to have and she wanted everyone else to feel the same, so, in the last year, get-togethers like these started happening.

"Yeah. He's mine through and through," I agreed. I was sitting on top of one of the picnic tables on Trig's back deck sipping a cold beer. Hayden was sitting on the bench beside my feet, a cold glass of her sweet tea in her hand. We watched my skinny little rebel, barefoot and shirtless in a pair of red basketball shorts, charge after my best bud with a yell, firing a stream of water at will. All the kids were ganged up on Trig, and he was fairly out-matched. Hayden laughed.

"He's got your hair and eyes," she mused, again, not for the first time. I smiled down at her.

"Hey, Dad!" I looked up and Connor trudged across the deck, dripping water and out of breath.

"Yeah, Bud?" I asked.

"She your girlfriend?" he asked, and indicated Hayden with a wave of his watergun.

"Why don't you show some respect? Get over here and introduce yourself, and stop talkin' about her like she's not here! Then you can go ahead and ask her!" I hooked Connor around the neck and pulled him into my side, planting a kiss on his temple.

"Ugh! Dad! I'm not a kid anymore!" he protested and shoved away from me. I grinned ruefully.

"Hi, I'm Connor." He stuck out his hand at Hayden after wiping it on his shorts. Hayden shook it with a grave expression on her face.

"I'm Hayden. I'm pleased to meet you, Connor." She smiled her sweet, charming smile and Connor grinned.

"So, are you my dad's girlfriend?" he asked her and I couldn't help it, I held my breath as she turned her bright green eyes up to mine.

"What makes you ask, Connor?" She turned to my boy and looked at him.

"You're pretty," he said and she laughed softly. "And my dad looks at you the way he used to look at my mom," Connor looked at me.

"How's that, Bud?" I asked, taken aback.

"Mmm," he shrugged, uncomfortable.

"Connor, what's the rule?" I asked, and he made an exasperated noise.

"Don't open your mouth unless you're gonna commit. Say what you mean and mean what you say," Connor recited for me. Then he committed and I almost wished he hadn't. "You used to look at mom like she mattered, like you missed her and wished we could be a family, the three of us together... now, you don't. Now you look at her that way." He waved his watergun in Hayden's direction again.

Fuck.

Fuck fuck fuckity fuck.

Hayden murmured "Excuse me," under her breath and got up and moved off towards Ashton, giving us privacy. I pulled Connor forward, my hands on his narrow shoulders, and sighed. Truth was best here.

"I love your mom," I told him honestly.

"But...?" he asked. My boy was smart, ten and he already knew when a 'but' was coming.

"But, your dad did some stupid sh... stuff and your mom, well, she had to do what was best for you at the time, Buddy, and what was best for you was to not be around me. I'm sorry for that, but what I did... Your mom had to look out for you and that meant we couldn't be together and then she found Mark, and Mark was good for her and for you... It just took me a little longer to really realize that and let her go." Adrenaline was racing through my veins while I watched him mull this over.

"I think mom's mad you don't love her anymore," Connor said, looking at his feet.

"Your mom has a lot of reasons to be mad, but I do still love her, she gave me you Bud. How could I not love her? I just love Hayden too..." I held my breath and Connor pretty much leveled me with my own gaze.

"Think I hurt her feelings?" he said, looking over his shoulder at Hayden and Ashton. I waved Hayden over.

"She doesn't bite, Buddy, why don't you ask her?" I said as Hayden approached.

"Do you love my dad?" he asked her.

"Yeah, I think I do." She smiled her perfect smile.

"You think or you know?" he asked, and Hayden laughed and shot me a look over his head. I shrugged a little helplessly; the direct third-degree shit, well, that was all Aimee's DNA.

"I know I do. Why?" She retook her seat by my legs and Connor twisted his lips back and forth in indecision.

"My Dad is a good guy and I want good things for him, too. Not just my mom," he said finally and I was surprised yet again. Where the hell did he get this stuff?

"I love your dad very much," she said softly, and I felt like the whole world just clicked into place. I was pretty sure this was the happiest I remembered being in a very long time. "You know," Hayden said, "I want the very same thing." She and my son exchanged smiles and she tipped her head to the side.

"You still didn't answer my question," she said.

Connor snorted. "You didn't answer mine, either!" he shot back.

Hayden's smile got bigger. "Fine, I'll go first. Yes, I'm your dad's girlfriend. Now, what made you ask?" She looked at him and Connor grinned.

"You guys have the same necklaces. It's what the girls in my school do," he said and Hayden laughed, wild, high, loud and clear. Connor laughed with her and even I joined in and dared to hope a little.

"You got one more hour, Buddy, then I got to take you back to your mom," I told him and Connor grinned.

"'Kay, Dad!" and he let loose a stream of water, right into my face. Hayden howled and I grinned. Oh, it was on!

"Come here, you!" I said, and went after him.

I couldn't think of a more perfect Sunday afternoon, playing with my son under a summer sky at my best friend's place while my girl sipped sweet tea and looked on. It was the closest thing to normal I had ever had in my life and I would do anything to keep it that way.

Later that night, after I'd dropped Connor off with his mom, I returned to my girlfriend's house. I'd been replaying the exchange between Hayden and Connor a lot in my head and it never failed to make me smile. I pulled my bike up into her driveway, glad to be out of my truck. Connor, by his mother's decree, wasn't old enough to ride and I could respect Aimee's wishes on a lot of things. That was one of them. As soon as I'd dropped him off, I went back to the trailer, packed my saddle bags for another week, and went straight for my girl.

Her place was almost ready for paint. The electricians and building inspectors had held up a lot of the drywall repairs. We'd been busy in the kitchen first, trying to get all the basic amenities up and running for her. She could now eat, sleep, and shower in her own home versus just sleeping and showering, and since the first night she'd come home and asked me to stay with her, the only nights I'd spent away were with Connor and goddamn, I'd missed her body snugged against mine the last two nights.

I'd been shocked as hell that first morning when I'd woken up to that picture of us hanging on her wall and even more shocked when I'd seen the scallop shells in their picture frames over the tub when I'd gone to take a leak. The little sculpture of the lighthouse she'd bought was perched on the edge of the tub in the corner. An alabaster vase held fronds of the long, waving, golden sea grass we'd seen along the beach in the opposite corner. The woman knew how to decorate. The bed and bath looked like something out of a magazine to the point I even picked up after myself.

"Hayden?" I called. I could hear running water upstairs and she called down.

"Up here!" I took the stairs two at a time and went into the master bedroom. Candles glowed in the little votive sconces to either side of our picture and I smiled. I ducked past the closet and into the master bath and found more fat white pillar candles surrounding the tub on the step and the edge. The bath was nearly filled with water and bubbles. A silver bucket of ice sat on the creamy carpet with a bottle of wine and around three of my favorite beers sticking out of it.

"What's all this?" I asked, smiling. Hayden sipped white wine out of a large wine glass and shrugged one shoulder up out of the bubbles.

"Thought you might like to relax with me before we go back to work tomorrow," she said.

I snorted. "You thought right!"

I hung my cut on the hook by the shower door and got naked in a real damn hurry. Hayden watched me over the rim of her wineglass, eyes alight and smiling.

"What?" I asked stepping into the tub with a mild curse. That was hotter 'n hell!

"I love watching you get naked," she said and I choked on a laugh. She was pretty much back to the girl I'd met a year and more ago.

Confident. Sexy as hell, and fuck if she wasn't finally all mine. I pulled a beer from the bucket and twisted off the top with a hiss and a click. Hayden moved across the giant tub and settled between my legs, her back to my front, with a contented little sigh, and sipped her wine.

"Good surprise?" she asked.

"Best fucking surprise ever," I said gravely.

"I missed you," she confessed and I slid a hand down her arm, beneath the water and held her to me.

"I missed you, too," I murmured into her ear and kissed the edge. She gave a little shiver against me and I smiled.

"Cold?" I asked mock-innocently. She made a rude noise and laughed.

"You suck at being Little Miss Innocent," she said and sipped her wine. I poked her in her ticklish spot and she jerked to the side with an indignant squeal. We laughed together and she settled down against me and turned on the jets. The water frothed and the bubbles grew and she shut them off.

"Why'd you do that?" I asked.

"The bubbles will overflow if you leave them on too long," she murmured.

"What, no foam party?" I mocked and took a pull off my beer.

"I just had this carpet installed," she said and leaned her head back against my chest. We were quiet for a time.

"Do you think he liked me?" she asked, her insecurities peeking out.

"Who, Connor? I know he did," I said.

"How?" she asked.

"He asked about a million questions about you on the way home. If he didn't like you, he wouldn't care," I said.

"Oh," was her only reply.

"He wants to know if you can hang out with us weekend after next." That made her perk up.

"Really?"

"Yep. I said I'd ask, but to not get his hopes up." She smacked my leg under the warm soapy water, which I only now realized smelled like some kind of herb or flower.

"Of course I will!" she protested.

"Hey, I had to ask first," I said in my defense. She let out a long breath and sipped her wine.

"Should have seen it when we got to his mom's house. She opens the door and he marches up to her and says 'Dad's got a girlfriend' and walks right on past her. High-fived Mark and went straight to his room and shut the door."

Hayden barked an incredulous laugh.

"Yeah, I know right? Like father, like son," I said ruefully and took another sip of beer, the crisp, hoppy flavor flooding my mouth and going down smooth.

"How did Aimee react?" she asked and I could feel her tense with nerves. I brought my hand up and kneaded her shoulder and neck with it.

"She looked at him, then looked at me, and said 'Really?' in the snottiest tone."

"What did you do?"

"I told her about you. She wants to meet you. She doesn't believe you're not a club whore, and wants to know who her son is hanging around. I told her I'd talk to you and see if you'd be willing to come with me the next time I picked Connor up. Really, it's up to you, babe."

She was quiet, mulling things over, so I told her the rest. "I also told her that she didn't run Mark by me first and that it was up to you; I told her she'd best keep her bitch mode to a minimum; and that you weren't going away."

She snuggled back into my chest. "Can I think about it?" she asked.

"Shit, yeah. I would be surprised if you agreed right away, this is kind of a big deal."

She trailed her fingertips idly up and down the top of my thigh beneath the water, knee to hip, hip to knee, rinse and repeat, over and over again while she thought things through. I finally couldn't take it anymore.

"What're you thinking about so hard, Doll?" I asked her.

"About what's best for Connor, really. The picture you've painted of Aimee isn't exactly an entirely stable one lately," she murmured.

"True enough," I felt bad about that. I really did, but nothing I'd said was untrue. I sighed.

"What are you thinking about?" she asked, and it was the perfect opportunity for a change of subject.

"The red menace stopped its march yet?" I asked her, and she laughed.

"I've never heard a woman's period put that way, but I suppose it fits!" she said. I smiled and bit my lower lip to keep from laughing.

"You didn't answer my question."

She gave a long-suffering sigh.

"Yes," she giggled.

"You little shit!" I nipped her shoulder and she laughed.

"We should probably be a little more careful. Birth control isn't one-hundred-percent." She stretched a leg up out of the water, the candlelight gleaming along her silky smooth wet skin, tantalizing me.

"Yeah?" I was secretly disappointed, but if she wanted to use more protection, then I could understand it. I'd be an asshole not to.

"Mmm, this is all still so new, and I'm just not ready for children," she said softly.

"Do I need to run to the drugstore?" I asked.

"No. I bought some; they're in the bedside table."

I smiled. "Should I go get one?" I asked and she leaned her head way, way back and smiled at me, lifting one of the pillar candles within reach. There was a condom underneath. That was my girl, always overthinking things, which, admittedly, made her prepared for anything.

20

H ayden...

Reaver set his beer down on the sandstone with a click. He took my wine glass from my hand and did the same. I turned and straddled his lean hips and brought my lips to his. His hands disappeared beneath the water and kneaded my ass and I couldn't help but groan into his mouth. He leaned up and forward and I held onto him. He sat up on the edge of the tub out of the water and continued to kiss me like I might disappear any moment. I loved the wild desperation with which he held me and kissed me most often times. His hands roamed my body, slick with water and suds from our luxurious bubble bath and I couldn't help but kiss him with a wild desperation of my own.

Over the last few nights we had just seemed to click, connecting on a fundamental level like I had never connected with anyone else before. Having Reaver live with me had been so much warmer and more comfortable than having Andy here had ever been, and I knew it was wrong to compare the two men, but I couldn't help it, and the one thing I always ended up circling back on in my head was that Andy wasn't even close to Reaver's league. Reaver could go scary sometimes, but those times seemed to be getting further and fewer between. It was like we balanced each other out somehow; like I shared some of my warmth and humanity with him and he shared some of his killer's practicality with me.

I lost myself in his hands on my body and tried very hard to touch every inch of him myself. I slipped off his lap and into the water on my knees between his thighs and gazed up at him with a smile.

"What are you doing, Hayden?" he asked me, but he already knew the answer. I'd been wanting to do this for a very long time but we either never seemed to have the time or Reaver was too much in the driver's seat to let me have my way. Well, damn it. I was going to, whether he liked it or not! I stroked up and down his length a few times with my hand. He closed his eyes and tipped back his head letting out a pent-up little gasp of a moan. I smiled and gently kissed the tip, flicking my tongue against the head to get his attention. He looked down at me with those cool, blue eyes and I looked back and took him into my mouth, so very careful of my teeth.

"Oh!" He cried out and sucked in a breath between his teeth as I worked him into my mouth, the tip of him resting at the back of my throat. He gripped the edge of the tub and thrust forward a little with his hips. I held them with my hands, his skin warm and damp from the bath, my thumbs caressing the throwing knife tattoos as I worked my mouth over him, bobbing my head, tasting every last delicious inch.

I loved how responsive he was. His grip, white-knuckled on the edge of the tub; eyes, closed; head, bowed; lips, pressed together; chest, rising and falling with deep unsteady breaths: everything about Reaver's reactions said that he was enjoying what I was doing to him and that he wanted more, and I was happy to oblige. I sucked him, rolling my tongue around him like he was a piece of candy, and I loved that it caused him to gasp, his head thrown back as he tried so very hard to hold still, to not thrust like I knew he wanted to do.

"Baby! Baby! Baby, stop!" He scooted back, and I drew off of him, letting him pop free of my mouth with a smile.

"What's wrong?" I asked playfully and he looked down at me. That switch inside his head that controlled his humanity was still flipped to the 'on' position but I could see the struggle. He tore open the condom and I watched him roll it down his length.

"Come here," he said and I got up, standing carefully. The water sloshed and he hit the drain plug with his heel. The water began to drain and he grabbed my ass, pulling me up against his ridged body, my thighs to either side of his, pressing us tight. We kissed as he searched blindly, moaning into my mouth triumphantly as he slid inside of me. A smooth and perfect fit. I ground against him, moving him inside my body, and pleasure radiated out from my core. He was so perfect, so deeply-seated, made for me and touching all the right places. I broke our kiss so I could throw back my head and give a throaty moan, quickly swept up in the euphoria that was making love with this man. With Reaver.

He held me close, his own breath coming in barely-controlled pants, as we moved against each other. While it felt so incredibly good, our position wasn't going to get either of us to climax, but rather held us both maddeningly on the cusp, on the very edge of spilling over. It was beautiful and amazing sharing that headspace with him for so very long but eventually something had to give, for one of us, for the both of us, and it was Reaver that broke first. His long-fingered hands gripped my hips, stilling my movements.

"Off," he growled and I complied, shivering with a mixture of cool air on heated skin and the anticipation of what he had planned for us next. I slipped off his lap and stood, shaky but carefully in the empty, but still slick, bathtub. Reaver stood too, keeping my hands in his. He stepped out of the bath and down the two steps onto the carpet and I followed suit.

"Bedroom," he murmured and I turned and walked out of the humid master bath and into the cooler bedroom. I looked over my shoulder, his hands resting on my hips and he crooked a grin at me and gave me a little shove towards the step. I got up into the high fluffy cloud of my bed and he followed, covering my body with his.

We kissed, one of those long and slow and perfect ones that lingered in all the right ways, tongues performing that slow, erotic dance. We took the time to explore one another's mouths while he nestled himself between my thighs and sought purchase once more. He found it and stroked into me, slowly and deliberately. There was nothing rushed about our joining this time, nothing hurried, just a slow buildup of heat and love and longing between us.

The pleasure that mounted between us, oh, God, how do I describe it? It was like pouring a slow trickle of water into a chalice. The rate unbelievably slow, a thin stream just enough to keep the flow steady, keep the stream from breaking. The cup growing fuller and fuller until for the longest, most agonizing moment, the only thing keeping it from spilling its edges was the surface tension of the water. Reaver was a master of my body like no one had ever been before, or likely, ever would be again.

He kept me in that agonizing state of between, where my cup was over-full but not quite spilling, not quite at the release I so craved from him, and he kept me there for what seemed like hours until finally with one of his beautiful beatific smiles, he twitched just so, riding over that spot, and the waters carrying my orgasm spilled over the rim of the vessel that was my body and my muscles seized, my back bowing off the bed, my body pulled as if by strings, strings that Reaver was fully and undeniably the puppeteer of.

I came back to myself slowly, panting, warm and safe beneath him, supported on what felt like cloud nine. I smiled and laughed through my gasping breaths and heard him chuckle beside my ear. He withdrew from my body with a laugh that broke on a lilting moan and lifted himself over my leg to stretch out beside me, staying close so the long line of our bodies remained touching.

"That was..." I panted, "Wow." He chuckled and pulled me tight against his warmth. We lay atop the covers and let the air-conditioned air swirl against our heated skins, the sweat dampening us assisting in the cooling effort.

" 'Wow' is a good way to put it," he agreed jovially. We lay together for a long time, basking in the afterglow and I rested my head on his shoulder.

"You're stuck with me now," I said, smiling.

"Sounds good, but why do you say it that way?"

"Because you've thoroughly spoiled me and ruined me for any other man out there. I'm pretty sure no one can measure up to your talents." I turned onto my stomach and laid an arm across his chest, resting my chin on my arm.

"Good," he said, a hard glint in his eyes.

"You're incorrigible," I said, wrinkling my nose and grinning.

"Yeah, Ashton had to explain that one to me, kind of a big word. I have to pretty much say that it was invented specifically to apply to me," he grinned.

"Is that so?" I exclaimed, laughing.

"I'm pretty sure, yep!"

I laughed and we cuddled and I thought to myself just before he got up to clean up and get us tucked in that –this–, this is what happiness felt like. When it was you and someone you loved and everything felt right with the world, no matter how topsy-turvy everything around you was.

If only it could be this way, stay this way, forever.

21

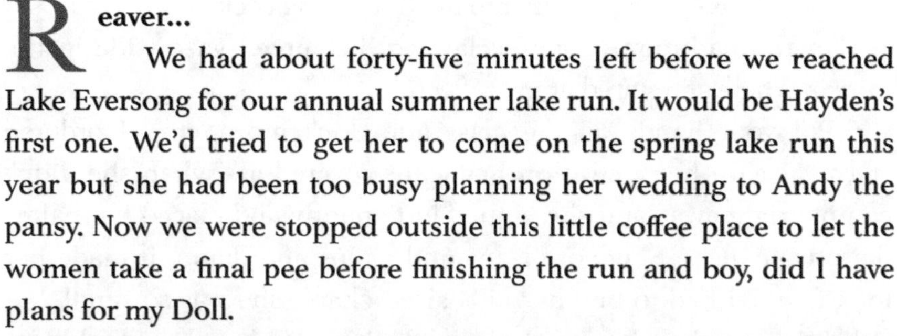

R eaver...

We had about forty-five minutes left before we reached Lake Eversong for our annual summer lake run. It would be Hayden's first one. We'd tried to get her to come on the spring lake run this year but she had been too busy planning her wedding to Andy the pansy. Now we were stopped outside this little coffee place to let the women take a final pee before finishing the run and boy, did I have plans for my Doll.

I'd been going easy on her when it came to some of the kinky stuff and I'd been feeling the right kind of ornery this morning so, before leaving, I'd stuffed a particular toy and some of those packets of lube into my jacket pockets in anticipation of this specific stop. I grinned as I pushed through the café and went for the back hall where the bathrooms were. Hayden had gone in with Irish and Sunshine a while ago and I figured they'd had enough time to do what needed doing.

I schooled my face into my scariest 'don't fuck with me' look and pushed open the door to the women's room. Hayden was at the sink washing her hands, Sunshine and Irish standing behind her, laughing and chatting away.

"Out," I ordered them. Ashton's golden eyes widened and Irish's steely blue ones narrowed, but they complied. Hayden's bright green gaze was wide in the mirror where she stared at my reflection and the bewilderment and edge of fear turned me right the fuck on. God, I loved every subtle nuanced expression this woman made and she had a million and one little tells for her fear. It made things way more exciting. I shut the door behind Sunshine and Irish and locked it. I checked the bathroom stalls and grinned when I found them empty. Hayden watched me from the sink, her eyes a little wide. I went to her and grabbed her by the front of the shoulders, firmly.

"Do you trust me, Doll?" I asked her and she nodded carefully, eyeing me with suspicion. I grinned my wicked-evil grin and she gasped, but it was too late. She'd nodded, so let the games begin! I spun her and shoved her up hard against the sink counter. Fucking perfect, it caught her right at the hips and she bent forward slightly, her delicate ass pushed back into my hardening cock.

"In the bathroom?" she exclaimed, her green gaze wide in the mirror, where she stared at my reflection.

"Put your hands on the glass and don't move 'em," I ordered sternly. I gave her a swat on her jeans-covered ass when she didn't comply right away and she yipped indignantly and placed her palms flat on the glass. She wore jeans and chaps and damn, it made her look fine. I'd had to buy her kids-sized chaps, she was so small, but hell, it had worked. I pressed a hand flat between her shoulder blades on her new vest. We'd had to buy them for the girls since we were running with the Suicide Kings and the Kraken. We didn't want to take any chances. Hayden's read 'Property of Reaver' and I liked that, I liked that a lot, no, more than a lot. I fucking loved seeing it on her.

She bent over the counter and I reached in front of her and unsnapped and unzipped her jeans. They fit her like a second skin and so it took some work to peel them down over the perfection of her ass. I took the scrap of black lace that passed for her fucking panties down with them and she closed her eyes and moaned. She was wet, her cunt glistening in the dim light of the bathroom, which was mostly done in mochas and brick reds.

I smiled inside that I would think in those terms. Before Hayden, I would have been like any other dude, and said 'red' or 'brown', but the fancy-ass differentiation of colors was important to her and her career, and somehow it had happened that I had started thinking in broader terms when it came to them too.

I kept her pinned to the counter with my body and kneaded her ass a little and smiled at the pure perfection of it.

"What are you going to do?" she gasped, and I shot a stern look into the reflection of her eyes, which widened.

They got wider still when I said, "I'm going to do whatever the fuck I wanna do. You're my Doll," which was the name-patch that was sewn to the front of her vest. 'Doll.'

I pulled out a packet of lube from my coat pocket and tore it open at the corner with my teeth. She gasped and squirmed when I let it drip onto her tight little asshole and I grinned. She was stuck fast between me and the counter and was going nowhere.

"Reaver!" she cried quietly when I worked a finger in and out of her there.

"Relax, babe. Push out," I ordered. She squirmed, but when she realized I wasn't going to relent, she did as I told her and submitted to my probing fingers so beautifully.

I smiled and praised her as she stilled. "That's my girl. Almost there," I said and pulled the anal plug from my other pocket. She couldn't see it; I kept it too low for that. A blush painted across her nose and cheeks and she looked a seriously-conflicted combination of embarrassed and aroused. I moved my fingers and pressed the plug to her ass, and she yelped.

"Easy, Doll," I soothed, and pressed it in. She made a noise like it was too much just as the plug crested its widest part and slipped into place. I smiled. It was only slightly smaller around than my dick, and I so planned on going there when we got to our room at the lake. I hadn't taken Hayden's ass since Florida, and it had been one of the sweetest fucking rides then. I wanted that experience again. I pulled up her panties and pants.

"You seriously can't expect me to ride behind you like this!" she cried, and I gave her a withering look.

"I can. I do, and you will," I told her and started to button and zip her up. Her eyes glistened with embarrassed tears and the blush that had been a dusting of pink before suddenly intensified to near-neon intensity. She took a step back, taking the task out of my hands.

"I think I hate you," she whispered, but she finished zipping up and buttoning her jeans.

Someone tried to come in the locked bathroom door and I called out, "Occupado!" I washed my hands in the sink while Hayden glared at me mutinously.

"I can't believe you," she said and her eyes glistened with angry tears, *holy hell that was hot* and it made me smile, which made her cross her arms.

"Don't look at me in that tone of voice, Doll," I said ripping off some paper towels to dry my hands. "Ain't nobody out there have to know what you got going on down there but us." I winked at her.

"How do you expect me to ride behind you like this?" I winked at her again and went up to her; she tipped her head back to look up at me and I let my fingers slide along her lovely throat, my thumbs caressing the underside of her jaw and she sighed out, a little calmer, which made my smile bigger.

"You trust me, don't you Baby?" I asked her and she nodded, eyes closed. "Then come on. Let's go." She went in front of me, her gait just a little bit off at first, but then she squared her shoulders in determination and slipped on her sunglasses and plastering an award-winning smile on her face, unlocked the door, and went out. I followed, my hands possessively on her narrow shoulders, a surge of pride tickling the center of my chest from the inside out.

Sunshine and Irish stood together between Dray and Trig's bikes, their conversation dying on their lips as they shot Hayden questioning looks. Hayden waved at them and turned to look at me. She shot me the dirtiest, most pissed-off look I'd ever seen, and I laughed, which only made her flip me the bird, which only made me laugh harder.

Dragon got astride his bike; my cousin Shelly was riding with him. I frowned at her. She had refused a 'Property' vest, on one of her self-destructive downward spirals again. When I'd tried to argue with her about it, she'd turned on me.

"What do you care? I'm the Sacred Hearts' pet slut, Reaver. I'm cool with it, now put on your fucking big-boy pants and deal with it," and she'd turned on her heel and walked away.

I'd blinked stupidly after her and demanded loudly, "What crawled up your ass and died?" and she'd shot me the middle finger over her shoulder, but her eyes had drifted to Loyal. Ah. Maybe it wasn't me, then.

I got astride Baby, and Hayden got on quickly behind me, a little more intrepidly than she ever had before, and I smiled a secret smile I was sure she couldn't see as we put on our helmets. I slid on my wraparounds with the ice-blue lenses and fired up with the rest of my brothers and, oh, my god, the look on Hayden's face was fucking priceless as the bike thrummed to life beneath her little bottom.

"Still hate me?" I asked and she smacked me on the shoulder in reply. I revved the engine and sent some vibrations through the plug in her ass and her face paled. She closed her eyes and a blush swept up her pretty pixie features and I told her, "You better hold on!" Her arms snapped around my waist and I pulled out into my place in the line. For the first twenty minutes she squirmed behind me and I couldn't stop laughing. Finally she settled down but about five or so minutes out she started squirming again.

"You all right?" I called over the wind and thrum of engines.

"This is starting to get really uncomfortable!" she called back after a minute or two.

"It's right there!" I pointed at the sign for the lodge and Dragon turned off. "We'll get you square in a minute or two!" I shouted but she was stretching up straight like a meerkat, her attention rapt on a flag on the back of a bike in a line of them up ahead.

"Reaver, is that the Kraken?" she called, suddenly excited.

"Surprise!" I called, and she squealed with excitement, her discomfort momentarily forgotten. I pulled the bike to a stop as the line started to back into places and Cutter turned around, phone pressed to his ear. He grinned when he saw us and I kept us balanced when Hayden launched herself off the bike. She ran up to Cutter with an excited yell, and he dropped his phone, opened up his arms, and caught her.

"Hey! Li'l Bit!" he crowed, spinning her around. She laughed.

"I didn't know you were coming!" she cried. "Reaver didn't tell me!"

"If I told you, it wouldn't be a fucking surprise!" I called after her, backing Baby into place. She stuck her tongue out at me.

"Does this mean I'm forgiven?" I asked.

"No!"

"Why's he need forgiving?" Cutter asked.

"Reaver's being mean to me," Hayden sulked.

"Oh, how so?" Cutter asked. She tugged on his cut and he leaned down so she could whisper in his ear. His eyes shone and he burst out laughing.

"Fuck! You're being mean too!" she cried, and pouted so pretty.

I went up to them and took her into my arms. "Aw, Doll, you suffer so beautifully," I murmured and kissed her and she kissed me back. I was forgiven, all right. Her kiss would like to set me on fire. Someone cleared their throat and I turned to see Dragon, Dray, Irish, Trig, and Sunshine standing close, all of them watching me, Cutter, and my Doll.

"Shit. Yeah. Cutter, here, is the Prez for the Kraken; this here is Dragon, Sacred Hearts' President; Dray, our VP... Irish is his girl. Then, this here is my best friend, Trig, who's our Sergeant at Arms and his Sunshine Girl." I made the introductions and hands were shaken all the way around.

"Thanks for having us." Cutter grinned. Hayden was tucked under my arm; she had an arm curved low behind my back up under my cut, her other hand fisted in the front of my tee shirt.

"Let's all get settled and we can do formal introductions at the cabin," Dragon grunted. "Reaver explain how this works?" he asked Cutter.

"Yeah, somethin' about Presidents stayin' in the cabin with your cabinet, the rest of my cabinet having rooms at the lodge. Sounds good to me. I'm game." Cutter slung a pack up onto his shoulder.

"Trigger's my head of security; he'll get your boys and their ol' ladies settled in the lodge. Reaver–" Dragon started, and I grinned.

"Come on, Doll and me are happy to get you settled," I said, clasping hands with Cutter. Ashton was murmuring with Hayden at my side, and I shook her a bit to get her attention. Her green eyes snapped up to mine.

"Ready?" I asked her, and she smiled with a touch of gratefulness that her torture was coming to an end.

"Absolutely," she said. I slung my saddlebags over my shoulder, and we three traipsed down to the cabin. I took Cutter to his room.

"Dump your shit," I said, with a wink, and he did. Hayden looked up at me questioningly. I bent near her ear and whispered. "You up for a round with the both of us?" Dawning realization shone on her face. Cutter was looking from one to the other of us with a raised eyebrow. Hayden scraped her bottom lip between her teeth. Finally, she smiled her impish trouble-making smile.

"What happens at lake run..." she started.

"Stays at lake run," I affirmed, and she laughed.

"Where's our room?"

Formal meet-and-greet couldn't happen until the Suicide Kings arrived. They apparently had some club business to attend to that would make them late, so we had some time to kill. We didn't waste any. As soon as we were in my room, I started to strip her while Cutter claimed her mouth in a fierce kiss.

"Fucking hell! Shut the damned door before you get..." Dray snarled, but then stopped and watched for a second. "Didn't know you had it in you, girl. Good on yah!" The door slammed shut and we all heard him exclaim 'Ow!' before a decidedly-strong Irish accent started chewing him a new one. Cutter pulled his mouth from Hayden's and laughed.

Hayden's shirt and bra were off, the fullness of her breasts weighting my hands when the door swung open again and Trigger's deep voice started to ask, "Reave, Sunshine wanted to know... Whoops! Shit. Sorry!" The door shut and it was Hayden's turn to laugh.

"What?" Cutter asked.

"Ashton was with him, she gave me two thumbs up. Didn't you see it?" she asked.

"Mmm mmm. I have the most perfect pair of tits in front of me, kissin' this girl with the most vivid green eyes... I only got eyes for you right now, baby," he'd said and it made me smile. We took my Doll every which way from Sunday after that.

All of us were cuddled, her sandwiched between us while we came down from our high, when there was a pounding at the door. About time someone fucking knocked.

"Yeah?" I called out.

"You fuckin' decent?" Trig called out.

"Has it ever mattered before?" I called back, and the door opened and he and Ashton scooted in. I took one look at her and said, "Not like you weren't doing the same thing like five seconds ago." I recognized her freshly-fucked look anywhere. Trig snorted and Ashton giggled. Hayden blushed and held the sheet to her chest.

"So you're Cutter," Ashton said in her quiet ethereal voice, and looked the Kraken's leader over.

"I'm Cutter," he affirmed and gave her a sweep of his eyes right back. Ashton wore one of those flowy Hawaiian-patterned sarong things, like a dress, white with bright white and yellow flowers set against bunches of green leaves. She had another of them in her hands and smiled at Hayden.

"He don't bite unless you ask nicely," I teased her and Ashton came forward and sat on the bed by my hip.

She and Hayden laughed over the awkward and she held out the sarong to her best friend. "It's hot out there, thought you could use this."

Hayden took it with a smile and said a murmured thanks.

"Might want to get out here. Suicide Kings just showed up," Trig's mouth quirked up at the corner. He was gettin' Cutter's measure.

"You one of Uncle Sam's Misguided Children?" Trig asked, and I looked up from trying to untangle myself from the sheet.

"Yeah, I thought I told you, Cutter here is a Marine, too. Cutter, Trigger, Trigger, Cutter..." I freed myself from the sheet and pulled a pair of white basketball shorts out of my saddlebag and put them on. I held up an itsy-bitsy jade-green bikini and Hayden nodded. I flung it over to her like a rubber band and Ashton laughed. Trigger and Cutter were trading info on units and battalions or some shit like they were trading baseball cards, oohing and ahhing over locations I'd never even heard of, don't even ask me where they were on a map.

"Shit, yeah, I spent time in Kandahar Province!" Cutter said and got up, pulling on his clothes.

"We pounded some of the same sand over there for sure," Trig said and his look wasn't entirely happy, the ghosts of memory sinking their teeth into some soft bit of his brain. Sunshine went over to him and wrapped her slender arms around his waist and he smiled down at her, the clouds chased away.

I held the sheet for Hayden so she would stop struggling to pull on the bathing suit underneath it using only one hand and she shot me a grateful smile. Despite her bold and adventurous nature, my baby doll was still modest as hell. I guess just because she could do it with two guys didn't mean she was comfortable being naked in front of just anybody. I know Ash had seen her change so that meant it was Trig makin' her uncomfortable. I caught her exchanging a look with Ashton and something passed between them. Chicks, man. I'd probably understand 'em about the time hell froze over. For real. I resisted the urge to roll my eyes.

I shrugged into my cut once Hayden got up. She tied the wrap around her trim waist and looked like some kind of goddess. I had to suck in a breath. That swimsuit of hers, the color, did some strange things to her eyes, making them stand out in high relief. She shrugged her feet into some white flip-flops and tossed mine down on the floor near my feet for me to do the same. Cutter was dressed and we were ready to go. Well, except for one thing.

"You girls might want to put on your cuts. We don't want any misunderstandings," I said and Ashton looked to Trigger. He nodded and she scooted off to their room to change. Hayden slipped hers on without a word over her bikini top and I smiled. I loved that she trusted me so much. She was right; it meant as much, if not more, than love to trust someone so implicitly. She looked up at me through her lashes and I bent to kiss her. Cutter smiled at us both.

We went out to the lakeshore, the Sacred Hearts' red-white-and-blue mingling with Kraken orange-and-brown and Suicide Kings yellow-white-and-red. There was a small stage erected near the dock and Dragon was up on it, Dray beside him. Cutter and his VP –I think his name was Marlin– were up there, and Sparks and his VP, Griz, were making their way up. I kissed my Doll's temple and dropped her with the other Old Ladies from our crew. Irish smiled knowingly at her and bumped shoulders with her. I went up to stand with the rest of my club's cabinet, drawing up even with Doc and Trig.

"Welcome to the Sacred Heart's annual summer lake run!" Dragon boomed out over the crowd. There were shouts, and cheers, and whistles. "Eat, drink, have a good fucking time! Only rules are the rules we all live by anyways. RESPECT! Always. And don't touch what ain't yours!" He scanned every face in the crowd with his smoldering dark gaze then repeated, "Have a good fucking time!" The crowd went nuts, he shook hands with Sparks, then Cutter, and spoke with them briefly and then all the P's and VP's went up to the cabin.

I gave a short wave to Hayden and fell into step by Trigger in our President's and guests' wake.

"Sparks look a little twitchy to you?" Trigger asked, out of the side of his mouth.

"Doesn't look happy. Wonder if it had something to do with why his crew was held up."

The Suicide Kings were supposed to ride out with us, but the night before the ride, Sparks had phoned Dragon and asked if it would be cool if they came down later on a count of club business that had to be handled on their end. Of course, being the generous hosts we were, what the fuck were we going to say? 'No, piss off, you ride with us or you don't come'? Pssht!

So here we were, the leadership of three separate MC's, gathered around the fucking kitchen table; a bottle of Patrón had its seal cracked and shots were passed all around. I raised an eyebrow at our VP, Dray, who looked like he was smellin' something bad as he put his down.

Griz, the Suicide Kings' VP, laughed, a booming crack of thunder that filled the cabin's large open front room to the second-floor rafters. "Never met a Mexican that didn't like his tequila," he commented, and Dray gave him his award-winning scowl that was enough to scare the pants off a lesser man, but then grinned, showing a whole lotta teeth, and said nothing. 'Respect': I could see that was the only thing that held our second in check, but it wasn't respect for Griz; more for his old man, because that's where his eyes cut to next. Trig and I saluted our Vice President with our shots before putting them down ourselves. Mmm, smooth as silk.

We traded all the necessary pleasantries and talked some about what the weekend was all about, the friendly competitions and the like. The big topic of discussion was the main event for the Sacred Hearts the next morning.

"Just lettin' y'all know we and by 'we', I mean the Sacred Hearts, are gonna be up early tomorrow. Sniping tradition, but more'n that, we're patching in a new member. Don't feel the need to get up on our account, just lettin' you know we're gonna be up and moving around at first light to set shit up," Dragon said.

The men of the Kraken and the Suicide Kings nodded.

"Good deal, man, thanks for the heads up," Cutter said.

"Yeah, sorry, I plan on partying hard tonight so I probably won't be up that early, but more power to y'all. Congrats," Sparks said, and the bald and scarred president of the Suicide Kings stretched.

"Cool, all right, well, the food is up, the booze is out, let's go join our brothers and have a good time!" Dragon said, and we all nodded and joined the rest of our folks outside. I was looking forward to watching my old lady soak it all in, and the questions I was sure were going to come. Trig slapped me on the back of my cut and grinned, and I grinned back. This was going to be awesome!

22

Hayden...

It was early, the windows barely lighting with the first hint of dawn when I woke to Ashton shaking my shoulder.

"Hayden, Hayden, wake up!" she whispered excitedly. I jolted and turned, and I realized Reaver's side of the bed was not only empty, but stone-cold when I swept an arm over the sheets where he should be.

"What time is it?" I moaned.

"Time to get up! It's that time," she whispered excitedly, and I sat up.

"Oh, right!" I exclaimed and dressed quickly, pulling the tags off the short denim shorts before yanking them up my legs. I didn't bother with a bra; instead I pulled a ribbed Sacred Hearts tank top on and pulled on my leather vest that proclaimed me the property of Reaver. Ashton giggled hysterically and I looked at her, I mean, really looked at her, and I burst out into a fit of giggles of my own.

As I snatched the binoculars Reaver had packed for me out of the saddlebag and hung them around my neck, I heard Everett say dryly, "Apparently we've adopted a Sacred Heart's Old Lady uniform code." She was standing in the doorway. Ashton and I looked over and then all three of us cracked up. We were all dressed the same, by happy accident.

We heard a muffled –and very unhappy– male voice shout from the couch in the common room, "Shut up!" and we all giggled again, stifling it with our hands stuffed in our mouths. I shrugged my feet into my flip-flops and we made our way out of the cabin.

Apparently we'd been admonished by the Suicide Kings' VP, who lay face down on the couch, his denim cut much the worse for wear. "Fucking females," he muttered as we went by, and I saw Everett's mouth turn down at the corners, an expression I knew I had mirrored on my face. Ashton's golden eyes went wide and she hugged herself, tiptoeing as quietly as she could past the couch between Everett, who led the way, and me, bringing up the rear. I placed my hands on her shoulders and she jumped. Old habits brought about by old ghosts... I sighed.

We made our way quickly up the steps to the deck on the back of the lodge and I smiled. Everyone was here! Ashton, Everett, Chandra, Shelly, Doc, Dray, Dragon, Data, Gypsy – everyone except Reaver, Zander, and Squick, who were on the opposite side of the lake. Trigger and Loyal, who wouldn't be called that much longer, were hoisting the long picnic table up against the railing. Ashton had described in detail how they went about preparing to shoot and I raised the binoculars to my eyes. Sure enough, there was Reaver, Zander, and Squick across the water. The targets, sturdy crossbeams of wood with watermelons and cantaloupes set on top to act as heads, were lined up in the sand, and Reaver was waiting for some kind of signal. Dragon and Dray were standing off to the side with binoculars of their own to their eyes.

"Mind if I watch the fun?" I heard from the top of the stairs, and smiled. Cutter stood and waited to be invited the rest of the way up.

The men of the Sacred Hearts exchanged looks. Dragon looked to Dray and something passed between father and son; Dragon raised an eyebrow, and Dray said, "Sure."

Cutter grinned and stood over behind me. He had a squat, round leather canister in his hands, and he snapped it open and pulled out a breathtaking wood, brass, and glass spyglass. He opened it up so it telescoped out and quirked a smile down at me. I leaned back into him and bumped against his tanned bare chest beneath his Kraken's cut and said, "Showoff."

His grin got wider. "You know it, Li'l Bit," he said, and everyone visibly relaxed around us. Dray slid his hand up under his hair, I caught a little blue light shining between the strands and grinned. I raised the binoculars to my eyes and picked out Reaver who touched the Bluetooth on the side of his head.

"Snipers take your marks, Loyal, you're up first," Dray said. Loyal settled behind the large scary-looking gun and Trigger spotted for him. I watched Reaver, who stood beside a target with white cue cards. A brand-new, fully-patched Sacred Hearts cut hung from the target below a watermelon. Even with the binoculars the name patch was indistinct and too hard to read.

Trigger was rattling off a whole bunch of tactical jargon and I heard Loyal exclaim, "What the fuck? No! Serious, you guys?" We all burst out laughing and Reaver dropped the first, blank card. We could clearly read the big letters.

Hey, Loyal...

"Next one," Dray said.

You've proven yourself, Brother.

"Next one."

You have one last test...

"Next one."

You want it?

"Next one."

You really want it?

"Yes, I fucking want it!" Loyal yelled, beyond excited. We all laughed. Reaver must have heard because he dropped the last card.

Then come and get it!

Loyal looked through the scope at the flash of movement and in a single fluid movement, no hesitation, bounded to his feet. He leapt off the picnic table and dashed wildly for the stairs, flip-flops flying; he didn't even care! He shrugged out of his prospect's cut and left it hanging over the railing haphazardly as he took off running full-tilt for the lakeshore to the track of our wildly-pealing laughter. He pulled his black tee over his head and let it fall to the ground and hit the water, wading in until it hit him at the waist, and then, elegantly, he bent at the waist and disappeared. For long moments there was nothing, and then his head and shoulders crested the water as he propelled himself forward with long, sure strokes of his arms.

"It's so far..." I said dubiously; it was a very long way to swim.

"He's a Marine, Li'l Bit," Cutter said, his hand dropping to my shoulder. "He can do it." I caught Trigger giving Cutter a look and craned my neck back. Cutter looked at Trigger with an equal measure of respect. They both nodded once, a sharp inclination of their head, and we all turned to watch Loyal swim like the devil was on his tail across the lake. It was still a long swim.

We all cheered, clapping and jumping as he trudged wearily up the beach on the other side. He went to the target and pulled down the leather vest and stared at it. He said something to Reaver, his chest heaving. Dray had his phone out and put it on speaker. Reaver's already was, on the other side of the lake.

"You good?" Reaver asked, laughing.

"Naw! I'm better than good, I'm great!" we heard Loyal cry and we all laughed and cheered. Dragon cleared his throat.

"Now y'all listen, and listen real fucking good. Loyal, you've been a boon to this club, worked hard, always been what your name implied, and persevered. You helped us save Trigger's Old Lady; you've been ass-deep in alligators with us; you've laughed with us, cried with us, and served us unquestioningly over this past year. You've fucking earned that cut like no other. Still, that being said, "Loyal" ain't no name for a biker. A prospect, yes, but "Loyal" is something you call your dog, as a general rule. So you go ahead and read the name patch on front o' that cut and tell us all who you are now," Dragon said.

"Ghost!" came Loyal's voice over the phone, his breath heaving. "It says I'm Ghost!"

"That's because you're one of the quietest motherfucker's we've ever seen. Lost count of how many times we've shouted 'Prospect' in the last year, only to have you right up on our ass," Dray grunted.

"No, thank you, I love it, thank you guys so much!" he said between breaths.

"Okay, now swim back," Reaver said and we all burst out laughing.

"Naw, just fucking with you man! We'll give you a ride back in the boat," Reaver said when Ghost turned to trudge back towards the water. We could hear Zander and Squick busting up in the background.

"Welcome home, Brother!" Dragon declared, and we all let out a cheer that carried across the water to Reaver, Ghost, and the two, as yet, prospects. It was a good way to start the day.

After the excitement of Ghost patching in, we all had breakfast, sitting together to eat. Everyone kept coming up to Ghost, clasping arms, hugging him and congratulating him. Shelly, though, she came to him and kissed his cheek and said "Congratulations" so softly, so unlike her spunky usual self, it took us all aback. She was almost sad somehow, and Reaver watched her with worry in his eyes as she disappeared into the crowd.

"What's wrong?" I asked him.

"She likes him," he said, and shrugged a shoulder.

I frowned.

"Then why don't they–" Reaver cut me off gently.

"It's complicated, baby, and it's not our deal. Just let them handle it." He kissed my shoulder and smiled down at me where I was cradled in his lap. I smiled back and sighed in contentment.

After breakfast, the boys went to play with their knives and guns while the girls went out on the lake with Hossler. She'd brought six strange-looking, oversized surfboards, strapped to a rack on the roof of the Kraken's crash truck.

"What are these?" Ashton had asked.

"Paddle-boards!" Hossler had beamed at her. Another girl who had come with the Suicide Kings was standing nearby. She wore a pair of capri pants and sneakers and huddled in an oversized sweatshirt.

"What do you do?" she asked. She was pretty, her hair a light brown with blonde highlights, cascading in perfect curls past her shoulders, a simple headband holding it back from a face free of makeup but simply beautiful. Bright, inquisitive hazel eyes watched us curiously.

"What's your name, hon?" Hossler asked.

"Tonya," the girl said shyly, and I caught Ashton looking at her with compassion in her eyes. I think my best friend was seeing something different than I was. While I was just seeing a shy girl, Ashton was picking up something different. I would ask her about it later.

"Well, come on, Tonya! I'll show you!" Hossler said, enthusiastically.

"I don't know how to swim but I'd still like to watch if that's okay," the girl said, with a shy and slightly-embarrassed smile.

"Sure! Hey, Doll, you remember how to surf?" Hoss asked me. I nodded. "Same principle..." and she showed us how to do it.

The surfing lessons gave me an inside edge; Everett, because of her dancing, was a natural when it came to balance; and Ashton, after a few tries, was able to get up, stand, and get the balance right. Shelly was doing her best, but kept getting frustrated, and gave up, choosing to read in the sun. Chandra kept Tonya company while Shelly brooded silently beside them. We paddled out onto the glassy surface of Lake Eversong, Squick and one of the Kraken prospects, a guy they called Jonesie, possibly in correlation with the Davey Jones myth, joining us. It was a good way to spend the day.

It was dinner before I saw Reaver again, but that was okay. We were sitting with Cutter at a table with Dray, Everett, Trig, and Ashton when Everett got up to get Dray a beer.

"Whoa, hey!" Cutter exclaimed, and hooked an arm around her waist, pulling her down onto his knee. He didn't mean anything by it, I knew that, he was just friendly. Dray stood up swiftly and the darkness in his eyes made me swallow hard, but Cutter didn't notice, his fingertips grazing the scar on Everett's thigh where she'd been shot.

"What happened here?" Cutter asked her and her steely-blue eyes were frosty.

"Get your hands off my Old Lady," Dray ground out, and Cutter put up his hands.

"Didn't mean anything by it. My honest and sincerest apologies," he said.

"I was shot, last fall," Everett said, standing up abruptly as soon as Cutter's hold on her was gone. She immediately went to Dray and took shelter in his arms.

"I think I remember you saying something like that," he said absently to Reaver. I knew Cutter's body, had seen the scar, I'd just never asked. He pulled his cut away from his side and showed the indentation on his front lower right ribs and turned so they could see the bigger one out the back.

"Sorry it happened to you, sweetheart," he said gently. "I know what a bitch it is. I really didn't mean anything by it, I'm just a friendly guy. No disrespect, sir," he said, addressing Dray at the last. Dray's gaze flicked to Everett's; she smiled at her Old Man and there was a collective sigh of relief at the table when Dray nodded.

"Just... hands to yourself and we're good. She's mine and no one else's." Then, as an afterthought, he added, "I don't share." I bit my lower lip and felt a blush of shame creep up my face, the first time the emotion had come up for me in regards to the times I had allowed Reaver and Cutter to share me.

"Hey, whoa, that's no slight on you, Doll! Don't go taking it to heart, it's just not my thing," Dray said, retaking his seat, with Everett sinking into his lap. She held herself to him, her arms around his shoulders while he clasped her around her waist. I pursed my lips and nodded mutely but couldn't make eye contact with Dray. Reaver gave his VP a chilly look and Dray shot an apologetic one back. I sighed, waged a short internal struggle, then looked Dray in the eye. I stuck my tongue out at him and the table laughed, including him, and the tension evaporated. I enjoyed my time with Reaver and Cutter. It was for me, I wouldn't let anyone else take that from me or step on that. I was okay with it and that was all that mattered.

I smiled at Reaver, who was smiling back at me, and he bent to kiss me. Cutter's hand smoothed up and down my back, a comforting, supportive, and decidedly nonsexual gesture, and I graced him with an appreciative smile. The rest of dinner passed without incident. After dinner Everett danced for us, and everyone went wild. Reaver had gone off with Cutter to grab us some drinks and I stayed to watch Everett. Nearby, the Suicide Kings' President and Vice President were standing near Dray.

I heard the President say, "I'm glad she's all right, for true man. She's got some talent."

Dray nodded. "Me, too, man. Me, too," he said.

"Sorry I thought she was a stripper," the Suicide Kings' VP muttered and I laughed. Three sets of eyes turned my direction and I colored and waved meekly. Dray gave me a warning look I couldn't decipher, then schooled his face into his cold hard mask of tough before the other two men caught it.

"Fucking bitches," Griz muttered, and Sparks grunted his agreement. I frowned but said nothing as Dray stared impassively in my direction. Ah. Warning heard, loud and clear. The Suicide Kings were apparently nothing like the Sacred Hearts when it came to their women.

A few minutes later Griz and Sparks moved off into the crowd and Dray came to stand near me. "Be careful, Doll. Don't let anyone know you're listening. Old Ladies, Bitches, and Club Whores are meant to be seen and not heard when it comes to a lot of other MC's. Some of these fuckers don't play," he said quietly to me.

Reaver returned and gave Dray an inquisitive look. Dray filled him in and Reaver held out his hand, they clasped them, and Dray and Reaver did one of those "pull each other into each other's chests and let go" things that was a hug without being a hug. I rolled my eyes.

"Thanks, man. Good lookin' out," Reaver said and I frowned. I hadn't thought it was that serious! Cutter handed me a hard lemonade and the look on his face, combined with Reaver's and Dray's, said I had dodged a bullet of some kind.

"If you were with the Suicide Kings, it would have been perfectly acceptable for Griz to backhand you into next week for that, Li'l Bit," he said gravely, and I think I looked stunned.

"You girls are considered spoiled by most MC standards," Reaver said solemnly. Dray nodded.

"We love you and wouldn't have it any other way," Dray said and graced me with one of his rare, full-on smiles before turning his attention back to his woman.

"I'm sorry," I said, and Reaver tucked me under his arm and pulled me in to his side.

"If he'd touched you, I would have carved him up, no question about it, baby. I'd have no problem starting a fucking war for you." His smile was cold, a wicked curve of lips and the monster in him was showing true. I shivered with fear at the cold, empty, and dead look in his eyes and his eyebrows went up, his lips parting slightly with his arousal at my fear. I wasn't sure I would ever quite get used to that but I could accept it. I had to, it was a part of Reaver. We watched Everett dance and I drank what Reaver and Cutter affectionately called my 'bitch beer'.

23

———————

R eaver...

The fire crackled warm and bright. I'd spent half the day with the guys throwing knives and talking about hand-to-hand tactics and the other half with Hayden, swimming, which turned into making out like a couple of teenagers, which turned into carrying her back to our room, her body twined around mine like a vine, so that I could make love to her. Now it was past dinner and past fight night and we were lounging against a fallen log that had been drug over to the beach. I had Hayden on one side, Ashton on the other with Cutter on the other side of Hayden and Trigger on the other side of his girl.

I had Hayden's head on my shoulder, a beer in one hand and Ashton's hand curled around my other one while she cuddled against Trigger. Cutter's arm was up over Hayden's shoulder along the back of the log and to see us, you would see exactly what it was: one giant-ass, comfortable-as-hell cuddlepile in front of the fire. Squick, the prospect under my mentorship, was staring thoughtfully into the flames, lost inside his own head. We'd discovered he wasn't a half-bad shot but he had a hell of a proficiency for knives some time ago. I guess it was fate that he ended up under my mentorship.

I felt a little bit guilty. Since hooking up with Hayden I'd been a shit mentor. Even if it had only been a gap of a month or so, shit, it felt like an age at this point. He and I had a heavy talk just after dinner about truth, honesty, and brotherhood. We all knew the kid was gay but he was fuckin' terrified. He was scared more about how we'd react if he came clean than what he should really be fuckin' afraid of: lyin' to his brothers. I'd tried to gently steer him in the direction of coming clean to the club on his own. We were a patient lot, but not infinitely so. If he wanted to ever patch in, he would need to learn to fucking trust us, trust that we had his back in all things, just as we needed to know we could trust him to have ours. I'd planted the seeds but it was up to fucking Squick to make 'em grow.

I kissed Hayden on the temple as she stared into the fire. I was slouched low and she was sitting up high, propped against me, curled up snug against my side and it was perfect. The back of her head was on my shoulder. Basking her slightly-sunburned face in the warmth from the flames, she drowsed against me like a sleepy but well-fed kitten, satiated for the time being. I smiled to myself a secret little half-smile; I was glad her sexual appetite was just about as ravenous as mine. It was nice to have a woman who could keep up. I shifted slightly, uneasily. That coldness that lived inside me was growing hungry again with the need to do violence, to hurt, to maim, all in the name of giving me my next fix of my real drug of choice: fear.

"Never met a couple of people I was really gonna miss. It more than kinda sucks y'all live so far away," Cutter commented. It was our last night at the lake. Time to go home tomorrow. I sighed.

"I hear you," I said.

"You should come visit," Hayden said with a yawn.

Cutter smiled. "Hell, if it weren't for me running my crew, I'd consider moving," he said in a low whisper only meant for us. I smiled.

"You have your boat," Hayden protested.

"Yeah, I could get a pretty penny for her. Take up a new project..." he mused aloud but then stopped. "I got people, though." He looked across the fire at a laughing Hossler.

"You two?" I asked.

"Yeah and naw. She's not one to commit, and right now, neither am I." He heaved himself to his feet. "Be right back, I gotta piss," he said and trudged off toward the cabin and the nearest bathroom. Hayden heaved a sigh.

"You okay, baby?" I asked her, lips against her temple; god, her skin and hair were silky soft and I loved the feel against my lips!

"Mmm... I just wish Cutter were happy like us; he seems restless, like he needs something to ground him," she said and I nodded. I had known the feeling, then this spritely little thing had bounded out of the locker-room door behind my best friend's girl and I was smitten. Bitten by the love bug something fierce. Cupid got me over a barrel when I'd seen Hayden, and I can't say that I was sorry. The monster inside my head had never been quieter than these last few weeks, even if it was rearing its ugly head. Something about Hayden just balanced me out.

We basked in front of the fire, content to listen to the conversation and laughter around us. My eyes were distant, slightly unfocused as I stared into the hypnotizing flames, which is why I felt rather than saw them coming. Like a thunderstorm rolling in across the sky, their energy crackled just the same. Dragon and Dray strode across the sand, expressions grim, eyes smoldering, fury swirling the air around them, a palpable thing, like if you put out your hand you would feel the press of it long before you touched one of them.

Dragon looked like shit. He and Zander had squared off in the fights a few hours ago, and they'd let each other have it. Zander had proven that he wouldn't or couldn't back down and had ultimately laid out our Pres., something that had never happened before. He'd helped Dragon to his feet after the stunner and Dragon had conceded the match, proclaiming that getting hit by Zander had been a revelation. Now he strode across the sand, anger crackling around him like a cloud, looking like he'd been through the wringer. Both eyes blacked, lips swollen, a cut over his eyebrow that had crusted to a scab, fists with the knuckles all swollen, he looked like he was comin' straight out of hell, but what's more he looked stone cold sober, which he never was after a good fight.

"What the fuck?" Trigger said out loud and I grunted. What the fuck, indeed. Hayden's eyes snapped open as tension radiated through me, my arms locking around her.

"Reave, Trig, you're needed at the cabin. Club business. Bring your women," Dragon said through his swollen lips, and my brows snapped down into a frown. We didn't involve the women in club business, ever, unless...

"Come on, baby. Up you go." I thrust Hayden to her feet and scrambled up after her. One of the girls had to be hurt. It wasn't Sunshine; and Dray looked pissed, but not like he was going to blow a motherfucking gasket. He wouldn't be standing here if it were Irish... that left Chandra and... My blood went cold and I picked up my pace.

"What happened?" I demanded, and Dray shot his Pops a look.

"Told you he'd figure it out," Dragon said sourly.

"What the fuck happened to my cousin?" I demanded again, and Hayden gasped. Ashton started running and then we were all running. Cutter was standing outside the front door talking to Tiny, who looked grim.

"Shelly!" I shouted and burst through the front door. She was sitting at the table, Doc was beside her, gently taking her blood pressure. My cousin was staring off into space, her eyes glazed, fixed on a point somewhere out in the ether. Her lip was busted and bleeding, her tank's strap torn on one side, a sheet had been draped over her lap. I fisted both hands in my hair. That fucking sheet! That goddamned fucking sheet!

I punched a wall and screamed. Hayden jumped and stared at me, wide-eyed and open-mouthed. I went to my cousin and knelt on the floor in front of her. Tears welled in her eyes, glistening, turning the blue of her eyes, so like my own, into twin glowing sapphires. They spilled over and tracked crystalline down her cheeks.

"Shelly, Shelly, Baby Cuz, who did this?" I asked. I took her hands into mine but she remained steadfastly mute. Broken. The screen door slammed closed behind me and jumped twice in the frame but I didn't turn.

"Shelly, come on, come on, Cuz, who did this? Please, baby, tell me who, I promise I'll kill him, I promise for you. I'd kill anybody for you. Come on, Shells, just a name. Talk to me, Shelly, please? Please!" I stroked my thumbs over the backs of her hands and her eyes flicked to mine.

"Reaver?" she asked, and sounded far away. She broke down in a sob and Irish was suddenly there, and Sunshine.

"Yeah, Cuz, I'm here," I said and she yanked her hands out of mine and clung to Irish and just, howled, weeping bitter, broken, wracking sobs, parts of her soul just pouring out her eyes and simply lost for fucking ever. Someone was gonna fucking die. Slowly, painfully and in a lot of fucking fear. The switch just flipped in my head, decision made, humanity just fucking gone. I instantly calmed and welcomed the monster, let him rush to the surface, all the anger all the pain suddenly just so much static inside my head. I turned slowly and Trigger looked resigned; so did Dragon and Dray. I smiled, at peace and with such serenity, now that there was no emotion getting in my way.

I took in a deep breath, in through my nose and out through my mouth, and was fully into that quiet place inside my head where I went when I killed. Question was, who was I killing?

"I want to know who did it," I said and my voice was calm – pleasant, even.

"It was Sparks." A quiet mouse-like voice, almost too quiet to hear, came from the doorway. All my brothers turned as one.

"Who the fuck are you?" Dray demanded.

"Tonya?" Hayden asked, "Honey, what do you know?" My woman went to the girl, who was bundled down deep into a sweatshirt too many sizes too big.

"He's been talking about her all weekend. About how he hasn't been able to get his mind off her since he first saw her. How he couldn't wait to–" Tonya sobbed. "I saw him grab her, I followed them into the woods but Sparks, he's big, he's mean, and he'd hurt me if he knew I was here!" I saw Tiny and Cutter through the screen. Cutter nodded once to me.

"You have the Kraken's backing. We'll be back," he said, and he and Tiny clattered down the steps. Ashton went to the woman, Tonya, and took her from Hayden. Irish was rocking Shelly, making soothing noises.

"Stay here with Doc," I told the women coldly, and went out front with Trig, Dragon, and Dray. Ghost, Zander, and Squick were coming up the path.

"Squick, stay with the girls. Shoot anyone not wearing Sacred Hearts or Kraken colors that tries to go in there," Dragon ordered. Squick nodded and went into the cabin.

"This is going to start a war," Dray said coldly.

"Do I look like I fucking care?" I asked, and everyone startled and looked at one another, then at me.

"Did I say I did? It's Shelly in there." Dray shifted uncomfortably. Shit, that's right, they'd gotten it on a few times back in the day. Before Irish. I sniffed and gave him a nod. He nodded back. Apology accepted now it was time to move the fuck on.

"Glad we're unanimous on this one. Reaver, she's your cousin, so you do the honors. When we find the son of a bitch, we'll gladly hold him down for you," Dragon said. There were grunts of agreement all around.

"What's the plan?" Trig asked wearily, pinching the bridge of his nose.

"Find him, separate him, fucking beat the shit out of him?" Zander asked.

"No, he's dying my way," I said.

"Hate shittin' where we eat, but there's a lot of woods and water out there. If ever there were a place to do a kill, it's here. Still, too fucking close to home for my tastes," Dragon said.

"He dies. Here. Tonight," Ghost said hollowly, and our eyes met. I nodded. Yep, if ever I had an ally in this, Ghost was it.

"Beggin' your pardon," we all twisted and took in Pyro standing at the edge of the path. "Got a present for you boys," he said coldly. We followed him.

Sparks was being held in a clearing against a narrow tree by several of the Kraken. Cutter smiled at me and I nodded back a cold thanks.

" 'Kay, boys. Our work here is done," he said to his crew. Dragon went forward and hitched Sparks' arms behind him around the tree and held him.

"Dray, get over here an' keep him quiet," Dragon ordered. Dray brought out a bandanna and wrapped one end around his fist. He stood taller than Dragon; he stood behind his Pops, looping the bandanna between Sparks' teeth before wrapping the other end around his other fist.

"See you back at the cabin," Cutter saluted and the Kraken left the clearing. Trig stood square at my back, arms crossed, and Zander mirrored him on my other side. Ghost went up to Sparks and spit in his face.

"You motherfucker!" he said, low and heated, and buried his fist in Sparks' gut but Sparks' eyes were on me, defiant. I smiled my coldest smile and slipped one of my blades free, flicking the switch. The snick of the blade coming free was loud in the quiet of the clearing.

"What did you think was going to happen?" I asked him. Dray took the bandanna from his teeth so he could answer.

"Fuck you! What's it to you, anyways? She's just some mouthy dumb club whore!" Ghost hit him, a stiff right hook and I think I saw a tooth fly. I laughed. Sparked glared at me, and I got up into his face.

"They say the eyes are the window to the soul, motherfucker. What do you see in mine?" I demanded and he looked, I mean really looked, and blanched. Oh yeah! There it was. He wasn't so defiant anymore. I drank in the first curling of fear that appeared in his eyes and smiled broader.

"She your sister or some shit?" he demanded, and the fear coming off of him lightly perfumed the air.

"Or something," I said enigmatically, and went to work. I sliced his thin tee down the middle, making slow work of slicing the material from his body, out from under his cut.

"What the fuck you gonna do?" he asked, his voice thick with false bravado. They always tried to act tough. It bored me some.

"I'm gonna do whatever the fuck I wanna do. You're mine, asshole," I whispered and chuckled.

"You're a sick fucker, ain't you?" he demanded with the same false bravado.

"You have no idea, princess," Dray grated, and I smiled wider. I think our VP was getting the hang of the whole 'fear factor' because Sparks visibly paled, sweat popping out on his brow.

"So what? You strip me, you beat me, what?" Sparks was way off-base.

"Nope. You touched her, you die slow," Ghost muttered coldly. Yeah, my brothers had my back in this. I let the monster out to play, I really did, no holds barred. I glutted on Sparks' fear.

"Get his pants," I said coldly and Sparks began to struggle. I mean, really struggle. Dragon had a good hold on him though. He opened his mouth to scream and fight as Ghost undid his belt and I jerked my chin at Dray. He pulled the bandanna tight between Sparks' teeth and the man's eyes got wide, real wide, showing too much white. I laughed, an icy, hollow, soulless sound, and gave myself completely to the darkness inside me. It was my atonement for not protecting Shelly. It wasn't enough. It would never be enough but still... Ghost pantsed the Suicide Kings' President and I stepped in close, our bodies nearly touching.

"First, I'm going to carve you up, let everyone know that you're a rapist piece of shit," I seethed and he shook his head. I stepped back and started my work, carving into the meat of his chest. It hurt, I know it hurt. He screamed around the bandanna in his mouth and thrashed in Dragon's hold. Ghost and Trig came up on either side and held him back against the tree by his shoulders. Zander acted as a lookout making sure none of his people happened upon us. Retribution would be fucking mine for what he'd done, come hell or high fucking water, and I would not be rushed.

I carved slowly, deliberately, blood running from the letters down his stomach, dampening the nest of curls his shriveled cock was trying to hide in. I'd get there too. Eventually. He slumped halfway through the 'I' and my shoulders dropped.

"Pussy," Ghost said, and he was heated. I had a solution, though. I used my blood-slicked fingers to pluck an ampule out of my cut and snapped off the top, waving the ammonia stick under his nose. Sparks came to with a jolt and a shout, and I smiled.

"Not done, sweetheart," I said, and resumed carving the word 'rapist' in big, bold, block capital letters. He squirmed, and he screamed through the gag, and he cried like a little bitch.

I wondered, had my cousin cried?

"Dray!" I barked, and he pulled the gag as Sparks threw up. Trigger and Ghost barely dodged in time. Sparks' head hung limp, lolling back and forth. He moaned and a whimper escaped him. I carved fucking deep. I know I carved muscle. I scraped bone with my blade. I folded the knife and gave it to Ghost, who plucked the bloody offering from my stained fingers. I slipped out my favorite blade and flicked it open. Time for the main event. I didn't want him to go into shock and die from the word before I had the chance to finish what I had in mind.

"You're never going to touch another girl again. You're gonna die here tonight," I whispered in his ear and his eyes flared wide. I grabbed him by his junk and he opened his mouth to scream but Dray was too quick with the gag. Sparks fought but I squeezed, and twisted a little.

His eyes rolled back in his head and I eased off, backed off on the twist-and-grip. "No! No, no! No. No passing out. Not now, not yet," I said, and I sighed happily when he stayed with me.

"Jesus Christ, just get it over with, Reaver," Dragon grated. I looked around me and noticed all my brothers were pale and looking a little sickly. I sliced into Sparks' ball sack and let his testicles drop free. He screamed, muffled by the gag, but still, it was this high-pitched little-girl sound that I found supremely satisfying. The deep woods night air carried the coppery tang of blood as I turned the fucker into a eunuch, taking off first one ball, then the other. Still not fucking satisfied, I savagely sawed through his cock and threw it to the ground in a mangled bloody heap. I stepped back, and when Dragon and Dray let him go, he crumpled to the ground, his severed manhood only inches from his face, and we all stood vigil as he bled and died.

I wiped my bloody hands down the front of my shorts. I hadn't been wearing a shirt, just my cut and the shorts. I stared indifferently down at Spark's cooling body. It still wasn't enough. It would never be enough. Fuck.

24

H ayden...

They were gone a long time.

Everett, Ashton, Chandra, and Doc were all in with Shelly. I didn't know what to do. I wanted to comfort Shelly but she'd flown into a fit when I'd tried to come near and had started screaming at me about how this was my fault, how, if Reaver hadn't been so wrapped up in me, this wouldn't have happened to her. It had hurt, it had made me feel bad and I had worried that in some ways she had been right, but I also understood that she was upset and traumatized and... I couldn't help but sigh. I didn't know, honestly.

The cabin was quiet now, oppressively so, and I slipped out onto the front porch where Squick stood vigil. He was on the porch swing by the door, and I sat down beside him. He had a mixed look of determination and nerves on him and a handgun balanced on his knee, one of his long-fingered artist's hands curled around it at the ready. I swallowed, but my mouth had gone dry.

"Hey," I said.

"Hey," he grunted back, and gritted his teeth, a muscle jumping along his jaw as he scanned the darkness outside the pool of light cast by the bare bulb of the porch light.

"What do you think is happening?" I asked softly.

"I couldn't say, Hayden," he said softly, and I wondered to myself, *couldn't* or *wouldn't*? Either way, it didn't matter. Whatever was happening was happening and in the universe's hands now. Somehow, whatever was going on in the dark, whatever the men had gone to tend to, I didn't think God had anything to do with it. I shivered and hugged myself.

"If you're cold, you should go inside," Squick said kindly, misinterpreting the movement. I wasn't cold; at least not the kind that a blanket could cure. I opened my mouth to tell him so, when voices in the dark had our heads snapping towards the pathway. I saw Trigger first, his bright blond head a beacon in the dark. He came into the light and I sprang to my feet; Reaver was just behind him. I started down the steps and froze, the blood draining from my face.

"Hayden! Baby, no! Stop! Wait, Doll!"

I backpedaled away from him but he was quick, dropping the bloodied leather vest that had belonged to the Suicide King who had hurt Shelly to the ground. His hands snapped out, his long agile fingers wrapping around my arm, just above my wrist. They were tacky, sticky with what looked like chocolate sauce in the washed-out porch light, but the overwhelming metallic smell, that cloying smell that invaded my nose and coated my tongue with bitter copper, told me what it really was. I jerked on my arm and leaned back.

"Let me go!" I cried, horrified.

"Hayden, baby, stop! Listen!" Reaver tugged on me, and in my imbalanced state, I pitched forward against him, my hand planted against the slick leather of his cut, over the felt patches of switchblades lined up in a neat column and I felt myself sob. I pushed away, but he'd captured my face between his hands. I jolted at the congealed feeling of his fingers against my skin, thick with blood that was beginning to, or had, dried to flaking patches on his skin. It was like something out of a horror movie. Trigger had a hand on Reaver's arm; Dray and Dragon were calling to him to stop.

"Please let me go, please let me go," I chanted.

"Dude! Reaver, stop!"

"You're scaring the shit out of her, man, let her go!"

"Reaver!"

I needed it to stop, I needed him to let me go! I looked up into his calm blue eyes, so full of sadness, so tormented, which turned serene when he saw how afraid I was, and I screamed. I screamed, sharp and loud, the only word I knew that might make him let go, might make him stop.

"Icarus!"

Everyone went silent around me.

Reaver's face crumpled in confusion, his expression undermined further by agony, and his tight hold on my face dropped. I threw myself backwards away from him, and hands-over-feet up the porch steps. I ripped open the screen door and stumbled, sobbing, through the front room. There was no one to see me, no one to care, and I was glad for that. I was really glad for that. I threw myself into the nearest bathroom and slammed the door, locking it behind me, and slumped to the floor, giving myself over to my despair.

I closed my eyes and tried to block out the image of his white basketball shorts smeared with bloody handprints, of the cracked and crazed look in his clear blue eyes, and most of all, of those beautiful hands of his, the ones he'd used over and over to hold and caress my body, to bring me to the height of pleasure, with blood caked around the nails, reaching for me like something out of a horror film. Except this was no film, this was real life, my life, our life... One thing played over and over in my mind... *What had he done? Dear God, he'd warned me, he'd told me, but what had he done?*

25

Reaver...

    Trig, my best friend, held me back from going after my girl. His arms locked around my shoulders and he lifted me clean off the ground; the rest of my brothers were shouting and calling my name, but it was Trigger's voice by my ear that made me go still.

"She's lost, Brother, and this ain't over yet! Just let her go for now. She's safe, she's in the cabin, and she's gonna be all right, but we gotta see this through!" He was right. Of course, he was right, but... I stared longingly after where she'd gone, her scream echoing in my ears like an accusation. *'Icarus!'* Shit. Fuck. Goddamn motherfucker! I stilled in Trigger's arms and wanted desperately for someone –anyone– else to cross us tonight. My blood-lust was at a fever pitch.

Trigger let me go slowly, cautiously, and I stood, chest heaving, staring at the ground for a long minute. I looked up and turned, to see almost all of my brothers looking at me with varying degrees of pity and concern, and some even with a touch of fear. Trigger's eyes were full of compassion and it calmed me down; I connected with my best friend better than anyone – well, before Hayden, at least. I glanced at the front of the cabin one last time and turned, giving our current situation my all.

"Reave, you good?" Dragon asked me. I gave our President my full attention, meeting his inquisitive gaze with my own and gave him a short nod. I didn't trust myself to speak, not yet, anyways.

"Zander." Dragon looked over to the stocky man and tossed him a set of keys. Zander caught them. "You know which one is his?" Dragon asked. Zander nodded. "Leave now. Trig will make sure your shit is taken care of. Take it to the clubhouse and make sure to lock it in one of the garages out back. You get me?" Dragon asked.

"Yes, sir. I get you." He took off at a jog for the line of bikes in front of the lodge, to ride Sparks' bike back up North. We'd part it out and dispose of the hulk later. Zander had driven the crash truck down with Squick, so his bike wasn't here to worry about. Guess Squick would be driving back solo.

"Squick, stay with the women, anything–"

"Not in Sacred Hearts or Kraken colors, shoot it. On it, Boss," Squick said with a faint smile, giving Dragon a little salute. Dragon gave him a steely look and a curt nod.

"Rest of you, arm up and're with me," Dragon said. Handguns, and in my case, knives, came out; for several seconds there were faint metallic clicks and the scraping of cold steel as everyone checked their weaponry for readiness. We went down the path towards the fires on the lake's beach and met Cutter and some of his cabinet on the pathway on the way down.

"Grizzly is makin' noises, wonderin' where Sparks got off to," Cutter said, falling into step beside Dragon.

"Got 'im contained?" Dragon asked.

"Did you one better, friend. Got 'em all corralled by the fires." Cutter grinned and slipped a couple of his own knives free, then he looked me over and stilled.

"Li'l Bit see you like that?" he asked.

"Later, man," Trigger grunted, and Cutter nodded, his face settling into unhappy lines. I appreciated that, that he'd worry for her, that he'd worry for us, but Trig was right. Now was not the time or the place. I didn't think I had much place prayin', after what I'd just done, but I did it anyways, sending up a silent plea for Hayden, that I hadn't damaged her psyche beyond repair, but I knew, without a doubt, it was over between us. I had to let her go. I braced my hands on my knees and dragged in several deep breaths before resolutely shoving my brain back into the game. We marched into the circle of light cast by the glowing orange flames and let Dragon take the lead.

"Congratulations on your fucking promotion," Dragon growled, and threw Sparks' bloody cut at Griz's feet. Griz scowled down at it.

"What the fuck?" he rumbled.

"What did I tell you fuckers?" Dragon bellowed, turning to take in all assembled. "Huh?" he demanded. Everyone went still and silent, the only sound the licking of flames and the crack of wood sending sparks dancing into the night sky.

"When you first arrived, I told you the rules! RESPECT! And to not touch what wasn't yours! Sparks broke both of them and he knew the consequences! He paid 'em!" Dragon's voice carried and when his words faded, the silence roared in their wake with their echo. All eyes were turned to our P.

"The fuck you sayin'?" Griz demanded.

"He took one of our girls by force. Raped her," Dray said and the look he gave was pure, heartless, killer, fierce-male-protector, and in that moment I knew that Dray had arrived. My respect for our VP crested at an all-time high.

"Now, anyone that doesn't want to end up the way of the dodo, I suggest you fuckin' leave," Dragon said.

"You gonna make us?" Griz demanded, holding out his hands and grinning. Guns pointed in their direction, both Sacred Hearts and Kraken, and that wiped the smile off of Griz's face.

"So that's how it's gonna be, huh? Over some dumb club whore? You guys are fuckin' pussy-whipped." Griz spit on the ground and I resisted the urge to bury one of my blades someplace tender on the bigger man.

"I suggest you leave, friend, before things get nasty," Cutter said and he was smiling an unfriendly and downright nasty smile. Griz took in the odds, the Suicide Kings outnumbered the Sacred Hearts alone, but not with the Kraken backing us.

"This ain't over." He pointed at Dragon, "You can't kill our P. over a fucking club bitch and expect that this ain't war," he said.

"Don't expect nothin'," Dragon said with a sniff. "Now get fuckin' gone."

We stood vigil and made sure they got while the getting was good. I got a lot of sideways looks from people at my bloodied appearance but I didn't care. All I could think about was how utterly I had failed all three of the females that really mattered in my life. I mean, Aimee was a lost cause, had been a lost cause for a long time. But Shelly... avenging Shelly wouldn't be enough to erase the hurt that had been put on her – and Hayden, losing Hayden...

"I'm gonna go check on Li'l Bit for you," Cutter murmured as we all wearily trudged back to the cabin after every last one of the Suicide Kings were gone.

"No offense, man, but I'd prefer if you didn't," I said. Cutter raised an eyebrow and followed my gaze where it was locked on the woods and the dark.

"Ah," he said, in understanding.

"I'll take care of it, Brother," Trigger said with sympathy in his eyes.

We went through the cabin door behind Dray, who exclaimed, "Fucking hell!"

"What now?" Dragon uttered.

"One of the Suicide Kings' bitches got left behind," Tiny muttered.

Tonya sat huddled on a dining chair.

I sighed, "Leave her alone, she sold them out."

"I just want to go home," she said.

"Where's home?" Dragon asked.

"Tallahassee," she answered.

"That, I can help you with," Cutter said, kindly.

"You seen my woman?" I asked her, and her eyes got huge at my appearance.

"Locked herself in the bathroom over there, a while ago, crying. Haven't heard anything in a while, and she hasn't come out," she murmured and I fisted my hair in my hands. Trigger put his hands on my shoulders and shook me a little.

"I got it, Bro, you get busy somewhere else." He gave me a meaningful look.

"Ghost, go help Reaver," Dragon ordered and I looked at him. "You got a mess to clean up." He arched a brow and I nodded. I was the best one of us here at body-disposal. I gave Trigger's back a lingering look as he rapped on the bathroom door.

"Hayden?" he called out, and Ghost gently gripped my elbow and steered me back out into the night.

26

Hayden...

    I cried my ugly cry until it faded into hiccupping sobs. I'd crawled across the bathroom floor and huddled, back against the wall, knees drawn to my chest, between the bathtub and the sink below the small frosted window to the outside. Once there, I gave myself completely to my misery. *Reaver had killed somebody.* There was a vast difference between hearing someone tell you they've done something awful and having that same someone come to you with actual blood on their hands. That wasn't all though. That wasn't what had terrified me or horrified me the most.

Tapping at the bathroom door. "Hayden?" Trigger's baritone voice. I didn't respond but hugged myself tighter, wincing at my stiffness, unsure how long I'd been huddled here, facing the disquiet of the stark reality: The man I loved and the man I trusted was a monster. My shoulders shook and I sobbed quietly.

"Hayden?" The knob turned, but I'd locked the door. I covered my face with my hands and something flaked under my fingers. I jerked my hands away from my face and stared, horrified, at the flaking patches of blood on my skin. I must have screamed or cried out because the door blew open on its hinges with a sharp crack.

I startled and tried to press myself back into the wall. Ashton's Ethan slid across the black-and-white tile on his knees, reaching for me, compassion in his silvery-blue eyes, which were warm, not cold like Reaver's but still, I cringed.

"Easy, easy, easy!" he soothed, then, "Aw, baby, let's get you cleaned up. Stay here." He hit the faucet on the sink, the sound of running water loud in the small space but drowned out by my keening wail and fresh panicked sobs.

Reaver had killed someone and his blood was all over my face, all over my hands!

Trigger wet a white washcloth in the sink and lathered it gently with a sliver of hotel soap. He knelt back down in front of me and gently captured my arm, just below the elbow and pulled it towards him.

"Aw, geeze!" came from the open bathroom doorway and I turned my blood- and tear-stained face up to Cutter.

"He killed someone!" I heard my heartbroken voice cry out as Trigger wiped at my hand with the washrag, like a parent cleaning up a toddler from a messy meal. The thought caused a hysterical little laugh to bubble in my throat.

"Go find Doc, she's shocky," Trig said and it made Cutter go away. I sniffed and he wiped at my face with the rag which was turning pink. I jolted back from it violently and gagged.

"Easy! Easy, Hayden, I'm tryin' to help. Let's just get you cleaned up. Okay? It'll make you feel better, I promise." He rinsed the washcloth in the hot water streaming from the tap and Ashton appeared in the doorway with a glass of water.

"Oh, no," she moaned, and knelt by me, too. "Here, honey. I need you to take this. Can you do that? Can you take this for me?" she murmured and held out her hand, a small white pill on her palm. God, yes, please! Anything to shut this out! I took the pill and put it in my mouth and swallowed three great draughts of water to ensure it went down.

"Help me check and make sure I got it all," Trig muttered, and

Ashton started checking me over. They were such good friends to take care of me. Me! There was nothing wrong with me, was there?

I shoved at Ashton. "Go take care of Shelly, she hates me but I don't hate her, she needs you more," I said and my words felt thick in my mouth.

"No, baby, Shelly has Evy, Chandra, and Doc. You're my best friend, let me take care of you for a change." She smiled sweetly.

"Mother to us all," Trig grunted and she gave him such a sweet and beautiful look, it made me break a little more because for a brief shining moment, I'd had that too, with Reaver, but then... but then...

"Oh, honey!" Ashton cried and pulled me into her arms. I didn't think I could cry anymore, but I was wrong. The next morning proved it. I woke between Ashton and Trigger in their room; my belongings that had been in Reaver's saddlebags sat in a neat stack outside the door. Ashton found a bag for them and we met with everyone to make the long ride home. Seeing Reaver hurt, unimaginably so. His eyes were shuttered and his expression cold when he looked at me. Shelly was near him and gave me an equally-cold look.

"Reaver?" His name escaped my lips unbidden, and he raked me with his gaze.

"You didn't trust me, Doll," he said, and mounted his bike.

"Reaver!" Ashton admonished him, but Shelly simply mounted the bike behind him and they fell into line. Trigger glared after his best friend and my heart ached with a sharp fierceness I'd never before known, as if my whole existence were being ripped in two. Cutter's hands descended onto my shoulders and I jumped.

"He's hurt, Li'l Bit. Give him time," he murmured. I had nothing to say and so I didn't say anything. Cutter kissed my shoulder where my tank didn't cover and murmured in my ear, "You need anything, you call me. Day or night, it doesn't matter. Okay?"

"What can you do?" I said and wiped at my tears.

"May not be able to do much, but I can listen." I looked up into his sorrowful brown eyes, sorrowful in the face of my pain, Reaver's pain, and nodded. He bent and placed his lips against mine in a soft, chaste kiss. A bike revved, loud and angry, and I jumped. We looked and Reaver scowled at us. I gave him the finger. He didn't get to do that! He didn't get to scare the hell out of me and then be mad when someone tried to comfort me! He didn't! It wasn't fair! I dissolved into more broken sobbing and Cutter pulled me against him, shushing me with a calm and practiced grace I didn't know he had in him. He helped me into the passenger seat of the crash truck beside Squick, who would be driving.

"You okay?" Squick asked quietly.

"I'm the furthest thing from okay that anyone could possibly be," I answered tonelessly, fixing my gaze out the window.

"Take care of her," Cutter said, and Squick nodded. I cried the entire four-hour drive back home. Squick was kind enough to peel off and take me home when we were close enough to the clubhouse, after calling Dragon and getting the okay first, of course.

When I went inside, it felt incredibly empty. The work had been finished but I hadn't furnished or decorated any of the other rooms yet. I shut the door on the outside world and slumped to my entryway floor and lost it all over again, with great noisy, racking sobs until I was completely empty, a hollow shell of the girl I used to be, before Ashton, before the Sacred Hearts, before Reaver.

Eventually, I heaved myself to my feet and moved about my empty home, numbly going through the motions of doing laundry, showering, and getting dressed in my nightclothes – which had me in tears all over again because all I had was what Reaver had bought me. Sometime around dusk there was a knock at my door. I went down and opened it to Ashton and Trigger, with cartons of Chinese food in their hands.

"Oh, I don't feel much like company right now," I said, and Trig barged his way past me.

"Too bad, Doll," he said and I flinched.

Ashton sighed. "He hit him, you know," she said, and looked sad.

"What?" I frowned.

"For what he said to you, Ethan hit him, as soon as were back at the club, off the bikes." I looked at Trig, who was in my kitchen, going through cupboards and finding nothing.

"I haven't finished anything," I said and let Ashton in.

Trigger was frowning. "He's hurt, I get that, and he's my best friend, but that was bullshit," he said. I didn't disagree but...

"I'm really tired," I said and sighed.

"I told you this was a bad idea," Ashton murmured.

"No! It's sweet, you guys, really, I'm just... I need to decompress," I finished lamely. Trigger smiled, opened my empty-but-working fridge, dumped the Chinese on the top shelf, and swung the door shut.

"At least you have dinner for tomorrow," he said, and I went to him and hugged him and then hugged Ashton.

"He really loves you," she whispered. I nodded mutely, not trusting my voice. That was the trouble... I loved him, too.

I went to bed alone that night and fell into a nightmarish sleep filled with bloody hands and Reaver's voice asking over and over again, "Why didn't you trust me, Doll?" I thought I did... Didn't I?

27

R eaver...

I couldn't stay away from her. I know, it was creepy as fuck, especially after my parting shot at the lake. Still, the night we came back, after I had made sure Shelly was settled, I went to Hayden. I broke into her townhome and slipped up to her room, where I found her sleeping. I pulled out the chair by the antique dressing table and set it beside the bed. I sat in it most of the night, my heels resting on the steps leading up to the bed, and I watched her. She looked haggard and worn, her sleep was restless, and I felt completely blasted apart and like a total raging cunt for what I'd said.

Ashton wasn't speaking to me, and truthfully, neither was Trig. In fact, when we'd gotten to the clubhouse, he'd strode over to me, put his hand on my shoulder, and with a look that was half pity, half something-else, had buried his fist in my gut. I'd doubled over, wheezing, and he'd kept me on my feet, and then, without a word, once he was sure I wasn't going to go over, he had walked away. Everyone else had given me nervous and silent looks, some were fear, some were pity, and some... well, some were just plain disgusted. I'd been assured that they weren't disgusted by the retribution I'd exacted out of Sparks. No. It was purely over what I'd said to Hayden.

Truth was, the only person who hated me more than her was me – and I wasn't entirely sure she hated me at all. I'd watched her toss and turn for most of the first night she was back and throughout the next and the next. I was making a habit of this and I knew it was unhealthy but, there it was. I loved her, she was my obsession, and I couldn't stay away. But I had to. I had to let her go and it killed me a little bit more with every day.

28

Hayden...

"How are you and that Rhett boy doing?" my dad asked. I paused for a little too long. "Oh... Oh, honey, I'm sorry..."

I put on a false smile and lied.

"No! Oh, no! It's nothing permanent!" I said with false brightness. "We both just have a lot going on and are taking a little bit of a break for a while, that's all." I didn't want my father to worry. He was quiet for too long on the other end of the line.

"Honey, do you love him?" he asked quietly, and I pinched the bridge of my nose. It had been a month since the Fourth of July 'Lake Run Of Doom', as Ashton and I had started calling it, and I had heard nothing from Reaver, though I had a funny feeling, a strange sense, that he had been near.

"Daddy, I thought I loved Andy and you saw how that turned out," I said, letting out an explosive breath.

"Hayden..." he said, with admonishment in his tone, "Don't you do this, don't you dare let what Andy and your mother did keep you from being happy. Granted, Mr. Butler isn't the kind of person who a father would want to see his daughter with, I mean, a biker, honestly... But if I have learned anything, it's that looks can be deceiving," Boy, wasn't that an understatement? "And I never saw you even a sliver of the kind of happy with Andy than I saw when you were with Rhett," he finished. I sighed, mostly because he was right. I pursed my lips.

"Reaver, Daddy. He hates being called Rhett," I corrected gently.

"Just... Just don't give up too easily, Baby," he said and there was something in his voice...

"Daddy, why are you really calling?" I asked softly. He let out a huge breath.

"Daddy?" I asked.

"I've asked your mother for a divorce," he said quietly, and I sat back in my office chair.

"Oh..." I said softly. I didn't know whether to say I was sorry or tell him congratulations. The last time I went to their house for dinner was the weekend after the lake run and I had left in silent anger. My mother had been in rare form and with everything happening with Andy, with Reaver, with my home... no. I hadn't been willing to deal with her. So I'd left, gone to Ashton's and let her and Trig get me drunk.

"It's time, Hayden," he said and sounded haggard.

"I agree," I said solemnly. We'd ended the conversation pretty quickly and I'd sat staring into space thinking for a very long time. I roused myself just in time to get down to the 'Y' and meet Ashton for yoga, my thoughts turning over and over everything that had happened since my failure of a wedding.

"Hayden, you all right?" she asked, as we were laying out our mats side-by-side.

"How's Shelly?" I asked quietly, trying to get the subject off of me. Ashton looked at me dubiously. She'd been there when Shelly had unloaded on me.

"She's not dealing with things; she's stubbornly pretending they didn't happen. When she's ready, I'm going to try and get her to go to therapy." Ashton gave me a shrug and cast her eyes to the floor and my heart ached a little for her, she was caught in the middle and I tried so hard not to put her in that position but... I sighed.

Shelly had resolutely made things my fault. I'd run into her once since the lake run and tried to say hello and she'd rounded on me and said some pretty horrible things, repeating what she'd said at the lake, about how if Reaver hadn't been so wrapped up in me that he'd have had her back and that she was glad he was rid of me; that she was glad he saw me for what I really was, in her words, a pansy-ass selfish bitch. I swallowed hard against the threatening tears that tightened my throat and we took our positions on our mats. The class greeted our instructor, who wasted no time in launching us into our first pose. I breathed deep the warm and humid air touched with the chemical tang of chlorine, and let the familiarity and relaxation that practicing yoga brought me take hold. I thought about Andy, my mother, and the wedding, and meditated on the entire sordid mess.

You didn't trust me, Doll...

Reaver's accusation rang in my mind, echoing over and over again as I breathed through yet another pose, another stretch. He was right; I'd listened to him, in my mind I had believed him, but in my heart, where it mattered the most, I'd failed him. I had listened, but I hadn't heard him and the moment it was thrust in my face, stark and horrifying and undeniable, I had panicked and run. I'd left him, probably at the point where he needed me to be as strong for him, as he'd been for me so many times in the last year and more, as he had been strong for me at my wedding, in Florida, and beyond. I had failed when he'd needed me the most and that was on me and no one else. Shelly was right in that regard. I was a pansy and I had been selfish to a certain degree as well, and I wanted so badly to be able to wrap my head around it, to be able to accept it, but I wasn't sure I knew how.

Next pose: arch, breathe, stretch, and hold.

I missed him. Every night when I went to bed I'd stare at the picture of us in the lighthouse. I would say a prayer that Reaver was healing, that he would be all right, and every night, I would cry myself to sleep and wish I could rewind and be what he needed me to be in that moment in the dark at the Lake Eversong cabin. But I couldn't take it back. I could forgive him, but I was too afraid that he would never be able to forgive me. Reaver wasn't the kind of man that was into forgiving.

Time to change pose, God, yoga was doing nothing for me today! My mind was suffering from too much unrest and I couldn't focus like I was supposed to. I suffered through the rest of the class and sat through the fifteen minute meditation when the instructor's silky, soothing voice interrupted my thoughts with her closing bit of wisdom.

"Today I leave you with a quote from Marianne Williamson," she said. "'Until we have seen someone's darkness we don't really know who they are. Until we have forgiven someone's darkness, we don't really know what love is.' " My eyes snapped open. Holy shit! Ashton was looking at me speculatively and I somehow just knew she had something to do with this.

"Namaste." Our instructor placed her palms together and bowed her head and the class did the same.

"Namaste," we chorused and I leapt to my feet and pulled on my sneakers.

"Hayden?" Ashton asked, but I scooped up my cellphone, wallet, and keys, leaving my towel and yoga mat behind, and ran for the exit.

I had to find Reaver. Had to. I couldn't stand it anymore! I needed to see him, to know for sure that I had done everything in my power, to know for absolute certain that we were lost, completely lost to one another. I didn't want it to be so, I didn't want this to be the ending to us or to our story because I'd seen his darkness up close and personal, in living color and still, I knew what kind of man Reaver was.

A good one.

One who would do anything to protect his family and the ones that he loved, and seeing Shelly that night, if it had been Ashton or even myself... I would have wanted him dead too. I did want him dead for what he'd done to Shelly, and so I could forgive Reaver's darkness. I had to, or I would have to face a life without him in it and after the last month... The last month of barely being able to concentrate, of being so lost and bereft I barely ate or drank, of nightmare-filled sleeps I had only been able to achieve through sleep aids and exhausting myself...

I didn't want a life without Reaver in it. I wasn't sure my sanity would take it and I missed him, with every fiber of my being crying out in despair and emotional agony. I was tired of being torn in two; I needed to see if I could be made whole again, and for that, I needed to see him.

"Hayden!" Ashton cried from the door to the pool area but I didn't turn; rather I broke into a run... but where there was Ashton, Ethan was sure to follow and I was suddenly stopped short by crashing into a solid wall of muscle. Trigger's hands closed around my upper arms.

"Whoa, Hayden, where's the fire at?" he demanded, and the desperation of my expression must have said it all because his face softened.

"Where is he?" I begged and the plea sounded pitiful even to me. Trigger opened his mouth and closed it, opened it again and sighed, and closed it resolutely.

"Are you sure?" he asked sympathetically.

"I need to know..." I said, and he nodded.

"He's working days over at that new office building going in on Grant Street. He's probably there – hey! Whoa! Hayden!" but it was too late, I had already jerked out of his grip and was halfway to the door.

I crashed down the front steps and dashed for the parking lot. I got up into my brand new Escalade and turned it on. My phone started buzzing, Ashton's face on the screen, but I tossed it onto the passenger seat, ignoring it, and threw the SUV into reverse. I drove quickly but carefully, and pulled into the lot on Grant Street. Reaver's bike was in the lot and my heart squeezed painfully in my chest. Moment of truth. No backing down, no going back. I got out of the SUV and went for the doors.

"Hey! You're not supposed to be in here! Hey! Hey, sweetheart!" I ignored the man and jogged from room to room, looking for Reaver's familiar build. I was out of breath, the dusty air sawing in and out of my lungs until my chest burned, when I skidded to a halt outside the door to a large room that looked like it was going to be a boardroom of some kind. I coughed from the dusty air and he turned around, eyes narrowing in suspicion.

"I…" Tears tracked down my face and his expression hardened. I didn't know what to say, I didn't know… I closed my eyes and swallowed hard and opened my mouth.

"I'm so sorry. I failed you when you needed me the most and I… I can't stand this. I can't do this anymore!" I sobbed and his expression softened marginally. "I miss you so much, and it's like I can't get any air and I can't breathe anymore without you and I feel so lost inside!" I put my hands over my heart and he dropped the tools that were in his hands with a loud clatter and rushed me. I jumped, not knowing what to expect, but held my ground because this was Reaver, and the Reaver of before, I knew would never hurt me but I'd hurt him, badly, I saw that now and I wasn't sure what that meant but I had to trust him, I just had to and… Reaver grabbed me and pulled me tight against his chest, his arms crushing me to his lean, hard body, and I sobbed, wilting in against him in total relief.

He didn't hate me.

"Shhhhh, I gotcha, Doll," he murmured into my hair and I felt him shudder against me.

"Yo, there she is! Reaver's got her," I heard someone say but I didn't care. I held onto Reaver and wouldn't let go, and wept a month's worth of pain, fear and apologies into his neon-yellow construction tee shirt.

"Baby, baby, baby, come on, you can't be in here." He pulled back and I nodded, and he walked me back out through the maze of corridors and to the parking lot, all the while keeping me in a death grip to his side. He walked me to my Escalade and took the keys gently from my hands, popping the locks. He opened up the driver's side door and lifted me into the seat, and planted his hands on my knees, his cold blue eyes, the warmest I'd ever seen them, locking with my own. I took several deep breaths and clutched his hands where they rested on my knees with my own.

"I missed you too, baby," was all he said, and he rested his forehead against mine. I closed my eyes and relished the contact, breathed deep his smell and let it calm me. He wasn't pushing me away, he said he missed me, but I didn't dare get my hopes up. He was being just so unreadable, cautious I think, that I didn't know where I stood, and while it bothered me, he wasn't pushing me away. He wasn't deriding me or telling me off or any of those things.

"We can't talk about this here," he whispered and I nodded against his forehead. I understood that. Believe me, I did.

"Come by the house," I said. "Please?"

"I can't tonight," he replied, jaw clenched in displeasure. "Tomorrow? Six o'clock?" he asked.

"Okay," I sniffed and he took his hands from mine and cradled my face in them, thumbing away my tears.

"I'm so sick of crying," I said with a broken, self-deprecating laugh.

"No more tears, at least not for now. We'll talk," he promised and I knew it was a promise that fell from his lips, even before he kissed my forehead.

"I'm sorry for coming at you like this."

"Don't be, babe. Just, I got to get back in there. Tomorrow night. Six o'clock," he intoned and I nodded.

"Okay," I whispered and he let me go, reluctantly. I turned my legs into the truck and he shut the door. He stood and watched as I pulled out, more than a few other curious faces at the door to the office complex as well.

I went home; there was no way I would be able to finish work, get anything accomplished, today.

29

———————

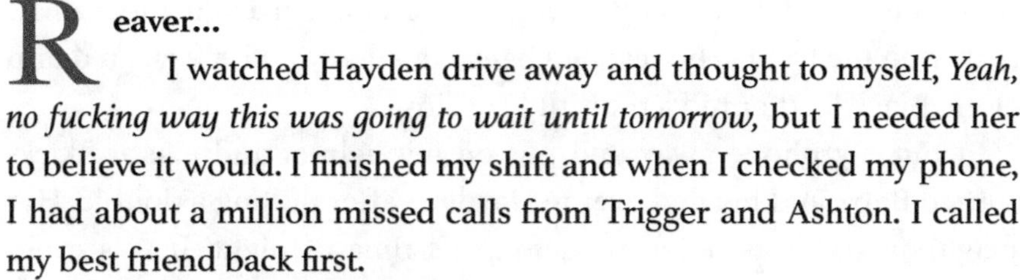

R eaver...

I watched Hayden drive away and thought to myself, *Yeah, no fucking way this was going to wait until tomorrow,* but I needed her to believe it would. I finished my shift and when I checked my phone, I had about a million missed calls from Trigger and Ashton. I called my best friend back first.

"Reave?" he asked, by way of greeting.

"What's up, Trig?" I asked.

"Hayden find you?" he asked. Ah-ha. Kind of figured that's how she knew where I'd be.

"Yeah," I said, carefully neutral.

"Dude, I didn't know what was up, but she had this look like the devil's own was riding her tail. She didn't even bother picking up her yoga shit, just took off like a bat out of hell. Wouldn't even answer Sunshine, just popped smoke, and that was it." He sounded worried and I frowned.

"She's okay," I said quietly, and Trigger held his breath.

"Yeah? Are you okay?" he asked, and I straddled my bike in the darkened parking lot and felt the first smile I'd had in over a month grace my lips.

"Getting there, I think," I replied and he was quiet for a heartbeat too long.

"Going to test your limits?" he asked.

"Have to. You know I have to," I bowed my head, smoothing my hair down in front, and sighed.

"You weren't there, Brother, you didn't see her in that bathroom. She was crushed, it scared the hell out of Sunshine and me both. I'm not sure how much more pressure she can take."

I smiled a little wider. "I know, Brother. I promise to be careful."

"You do that." He sounded grave. I wondered if he would beat my ass if I broke her. I hoped so. Actually, I kind of hoped that he would do worse. I pulled my cut out of my saddlebags and shrugged into it, smoothing down the switchblade patches, which now numbered seven. Somehow I'd managed to keep the majority of Sparks' blood on my hands and shorts; only a couple of small stains, that could have been mud or coffee for all anyone knew, marred the SHMC rocker on the front. The rest had been wiped away with a clean damp cloth. Black leather hid a multitude of sins.

I put my phone away and put on my helmet and glasses, kick-started Baby, and headed over to Hayden's after pulling a double. Her neighborhood was quiet, peaceful, this time of night. It was every night I'd been here. I killed the motor about two blocks away from her place and walked the bike the rest of the way. I didn't want to risk waking her. I did my check of the house, flicked open my best blade for B&E and let myself in her back slider off the kitchen. My tread was soft, and as I expected, I found her in the midst of one of her restless sleeps.

I took up my customary spot by the bed, settling my weight into the old wooden chair, only this time, I stripped off my socks and my boots. I needed to see for myself if what her eyes had implied that afternoon was true. I already knew my girl was an exceptional liar. She'd really pulled it out with the cops last year when it came to Ashton's ex. I knew Hayden was inventive and clever as fuck. I needed to know for sure. She hadn't trusted me, and so, no, I didn't quite trust her right back. I aimed to fix that tonight.

I stripped out of the rest of my clothing quietly and efficiently because I'd be lying to myself if I said I didn't want her. Difference here between me and Sparks was, if she wanted me to stop she knew what to say, and she knew that I would. I'd proven at least that much so far. I slid my favorite blade from my cut, which I hung on the back of the chair, and stepped up on the wooden stair. I drew back the blankets and sighed. At least her pajama preferences had gotten better; she wore a gray pair of cotton boy-shorts and a black cami to bed. Well. Not for long. I got up into the bed with her and put my hand over her mouth.

Her green eyes flared wide and she jerked, and I put my face over hers so she could see me. She froze, going very still beneath my body, beneath my hand, and waited. Her heart thrummed against the inside of her ribs faster than a hummingbird's wings.

"Do you trust me, Doll?" I asked softly, and she went limp with relief. Tears sprang from her eyes and leaked into the hair at her temples, and she drew in a shuddering breath through her nose. She nodded emphatically and I took my hand away from her mouth.

"Yes!" she cried and reached for me. I went to her and crushed my mouth over hers and drank in her sadness and her pain. I wanted to take it all back, take it all away, but I didn't really know how.

Her legs went around my hips, pulling me tight against her sexy-as-hell body and I'm sorry, but her clothes, what little there were of them, had to go. I flicked open my blade and she jumped at the sound but didn't stop kissing me, her hands in my hair, crushing my mouth to hers. I broke the kiss, savagely wrenching myself from her grasp so I could see what I was doing. I didn't want to hurt her, I didn't even want her fear, I just wanted her naked and writhing underneath me. I missed this. I missed her, and I didn't know how the fuck we were going to fix this but it was at least a place to start.

I cut some starts here and there and threw the knife onto the bedside table. It skittered across the wood surface and came to rest at the base of the lamp. I wrenched the cotton of her cami between my hands and it gave way with an angry snarl of ripping fabric. I gasped when the coin winked up at me from the hollow of her throat. She hadn't taken it off; I hadn't taken mine off, either.

She lifted her hips when I tore at her boy shorts and she was bare to me. I covered her body with my own and gasped into her ear, "I'm sorry!" before taking her in one long violent thrust. She called out, her back arching, and wiggled her hips to take me deeper, and I lost it. I set a punishing rhythm that barely allowed her the time to draw breath before I was surging up into her again. We came together in one of the most passionate explosions of emotion I've ever been a part of, and when we came, I saw stars, and not just in Hayden's eyes. I collapsed on top of her, breathing hard, cradling her against my body, and she held me right back.

"I missed you," she whispered against my shoulder and I kissed the side of her neck.

"I'm so sorry I broke us," I choked, and my shoulders shook and I finally let the dam break.

"I'm here, I'm right here, I was always here. I just didn't know how to handle it, but I love you. More than anyone, more than anything in the world, and I mean all of you. Not just the parts that make me laugh and smile, but the parts that scare the hell out of me and make me cry, too. I love you, Reaver, and I don't think I will ever be ready to let you go." She clung to me and we both wept. I'm not ashamed to say it. She was my balance, and holding her in my arms, I finally felt fucking whole again.

30

Hayden…

"Where are we going?" I asked, and Reaver smiled.

"If I told you, it wouldn't be a surprise!" he declared. I crossed my arms petulantly which made his lips quirk in that sexy secret-squirrel smile of his that always managed to drive me nuts. He was driving my new Escalade and I was in the passenger seat. It had been a month since the night of our reconciliation, a little over two since the disastrous Fourth of July weekend 'Lake Run of Doom', and now we were headed somewhere.

"Are we going to the clubhouse?" I asked, frowning. It was mid-morning on a Saturday and we'd skipped the party the night before in favor of staying in at my place. Reaver's lips curved even more. Sure enough, he pulled up into the gravel drive of the club and killed the engine. He turned to me, an enigmatic look on his face. It was still summer-like outside. An Indian summer, they called it, the forecasters saying it would likely be the end of September before the fall weather started showing up.

Reaver reached out and ran a delicate fingertip along the edge of the coin riding at the hollow of my throat. I reached out, too, and plucked at his in the nest of necklaces and charms at the center of his chest. He took a breath and then closed his mouth. I narrowed my eyes in concern.

"Reaver, what's wrong? Why are you nervous?" I asked.

"Just let me get your door," he said in a hushed tone and scooted out of the car. He came around and lifted me down, his hands lingering on my waist.

"Come on." He held out his hand and I took it, swallowing hard as he led me around the back of the club to the large open backyard. I gasped.

It was set up for a wedding.

"Oh, my god! Reaver! Who's getting married?" I turned back to him. He was on his knee.

"I don't want to wait," he said gently, taking me by the hands. "Hayden, I love you and I don't want to wait a minute more to show the world. I don't want to propose to you and spend a year waiting to make you mine, so…" he swallowed hard and I looked back at the chairs and aisle, the archway, and now all of our friends coming out of the woodwork. "Marry me. Here, now, today. Make me whole? I'm begging you." I stared, stunned, at the MC and Old Ladies, at my best friend, Ashton, and at Trigger behind her, hands kneading her shoulders. My eyes picked out familiar face after familiar—

"Daddy?" I whispered, as some of the happiest tears I had ever experienced spilled free. Reaver groaned and I looked back at him, heat, and love, and adoration radiating from him.

"You're so fucking pretty when you cry," he breathed for my ears alone. I looked at my dad, who was smiling, and I flung myself into Reaver's arms and breathed 'yes' into his ear. He crushed me to his chest and buried his face between my shoulder and my neck and lifted me, spinning me in a circle, and whoops and cheers went up around us. I laughed and he set me down and I was suddenly swamped by Ashton, Everett, Mandy, and Chandra, and ushered into the clubhouse and – I think –Dray's room; it was awfully black.

The girls did my nails and hair and put me into a white baby-doll dress and thrust a bouquet of white orchids with purple centers in my hands. Another of the blossoms tucked behind one of my ears.

Everett and Ashton each wore purple Havana dresses and clutched purple orchids in their hands. Chandra turned me and sat me in a chair and I looked up, bewildered, at Shelly, who wore another purple Havana dress and held a makeup kit in her hands. She chewed her bottom lip nervously and my eyes welled up.

"If you cry, I can't do your make-up." She sniffed and tears welled up in her eyes too.

"You're going to make yours run," I told her, and then we were reaching for each other and bawling.

"I'm so sorry for what I said to you!" she cried.

"It's okay, really! It's okay, I understand!" I cried back.

"You two need to stop!" Everett said with a smile, tears welling in her own eyes.

"There's a whole crowd of people out there waiting on a wedding to happen!" Ashton cried and sniffed back some tears of her own.

Shelly did my makeup and fixed her own while Ashton and Everett touched up theirs. Finally, I went out and joined my father.

"Are you okay with this?" I asked him as we waited to go down the aisle.

"Well, when Reaver called me and told me what he had planned, he did something Andy never did. He asked me for your hand and swore he'd do everything in his power to protect my little girl. He said there was no guarantee that you'd say yes to all of this, but he also reminded me that you're an indomitable spirit, Baby, and that you were going to do whatever it was you decided, regardless on if I were 'on board,' as he put it, and he's right. It is one of the things that makes me so very proud of you." He kissed the top of my head and I smiled, all out of tears for today.

Music started, and Trigger and Ashton went down the aisle, then Everett and Dray, then Shelly, who Reaver had partnered with Cutter, who looked only slightly uncomfortable in a shirt and tie. He'd come all the way up from Florida, just to see us married, which touched me deeply. The men wore their cuts over their white dress shirts and long, narrow, silvery ties. The sleeves of their shirts were rolled back smartly over their forearms. They were striking in their own way, and so perfectly Reaver that I adored the look.

My father and I stepped outside and I lost my breath at the sight of my man, dressed in silvery-gray slacks and wingtip shoes, his white dress shirt gleaming in the sun, a narrow blue tie the color of his eyes resting along his chest between narrow gray suspenders, our coin gleaming on its front. His gaze raked over me and a gentle smile curved his lips. He reached out and took me from my daddy and held my hands in his. His shirtsleeves were rolled back to his elbows, and I smiled at his stiletto tattoos. Dragon cleared his throat, and I smiled at him. He looked regal in all-black and his motorcycle vest as he stood with an open book in his hand.

"Now, y'all know, I've never done this before," he said and there were chuckles from the audience. Trigger winked at me from behind Reaver.

"Just be you, Prez," Reaver said gently.

"That I can do," he said under his breath. "Reaver and Hayden want to get married. I went on the internet and filled out some damned thing that says I'm a pastor and can officiate. I'm honored, but there isn't a damn thing I can think of to say, so Reaver, you go first, boy." There were some cheers and clapping and a whistle or two.

"Hayden," I looked up into Reaver's clear blue eyes and held my breath, "I've loved you from the moment I saw you. Your smile, your laugh, they were a lot like that lighthouse we went to... my beacon home, leading me to solid ground, which I don't think I've ever had to stand on. You're my light in the dark, and I love you. You don't know how much you balance my scales, and I don't want to ever have to imagine a life without you by my side." He swallowed hard and I let my gaze roam his face.

"I think it's your turn, sweetheart," Dragon said kindly, and there was some laughter.

"Reaver, I took you for granted in so many ways over this last year and I never want to be that person ever again. By your side and in your arms has been the safest I've ever been. When I'm with you, all the noise and the crazy and the busy just goes quiet and it's like I can finally breathe. If I balance you, then you, you do the same for me. I love you too, but more importantly, I trust you. You taught me what real trust is, the true meaning of the word, and I can honestly say, I trust you with everything that I am." His eyes softened and he pulled me to him and we kissed. Our friends and family went crazy with cheering, whistling, and applause, and we broke apart. Dragon cleared his throat and people settled down.

"You know, you were supposed to wait for me to tell you to do that," he grunted. There was laughter. "Hell, you two are gonna do whatever you're gonna do, whenever you're gonna do it!" There was uproarious cheering and whistling. "Rings!" he shouted and Connor came up and handed his dad a wedding set.

Reaver looked at me and slid the simple white gold band, crusted with diamonds, onto my finger, then he slipped a vintage engagement ring on after it. They were a matching set, and by the looks of it, antique as well as unique. The large center stone of the engagement ring was a blue diamond, the exact match for the color of Reaver's eyes. It was perfect, and I was momentarily stunned.

Connor nudged me and I startled. People laughed. I took the ring he handed me. It, too, was white gold, but set with a light emerald, I think to represent the color of my eyes. I stared at it for a long moment, then slipped it onto Reaver's finger, and he smiled at me.

"Congratulations!" Dragon roared. "Yer married!"

Reaver picked me up and kissed me soundly once more, and we were surrounded by applause and laughter and cheering. I laughed against his mouth.

"Ask me," I heard Ashton say, as she leaned back into Trigger's chest; he smiled broadly, but I didn't even have a moment to shoot her a questioning look. Flower petals were raining down on us from where our guests threw them. Reaver pulled on my hand and we dashed down the aisle under the soft rain and went over to where a marriage certificate waited.

"How did you–?" I asked, my eyes wide.

"That was me," my dad said, smiling. "I pulled a few strings." I hugged him.

Reaver picked up the pen and I considered him. "Wait!" I said before he could touch pen to paper. He stopped and looked at me, searching my face.

"Having second thoughts?" he asked, and I could see it pained him to do so.

"No!" I was horrified he would think so. "We get a free name change, don't you know?" He frowned and I smiled.

"Yeah..." he said but I could see he wasn't getting where I was going.

"We haven't done any of this in order. Why should we start now? Take my last name," I said gently and his eyes sparkled as his lips curved into a slow grin. He laughed.

"Can I get rid of the whole thing?" he asked.

"Oh, come on! It can't be that bad!" Ashton looked like she was dying to know.

"Rhett Kinnicutt Butler," he finally confessed. I swear to God, Ashton's eyes crossed as she processed what he'd said.

"You're right! Change it! Reaver Michaels sounds much better," Trig exclaimed.

"Dad, don't you need a middle name?" Connor asked, and Reaver smiled.

"Yeah, Bud. Can I have yours?" Conner lit up and he nodded enthusiastically.

And so Reaver changed his name to 'Reaver Connor Michaels', kissing me soundly once more before passing me the pen. I smiled against his mouth.

"I love you, Mr. Michaels," I said against his mouth, and the answering smile I felt against my own made all the bad that'd happened incredibly worth it, to have even a fraction of the good.

"I trust you, Mrs. Michaels," he said against my mouth, and the whole world fell into place for me and for us. I signed my name; I finally had everything I had ever been wanting, just slightly out of order!

ALSO BY A.J. DOWNEY

__The Sacred Hearts MC__

1. Shattered & Scarred

2. Broken & Burned

3. Cracked & Crushed

3.5 Masked & Miserable (a novella)

4. Tattered & Torn

5. Fractured & Formidable

6. Damaged & Dangerous

__The Virtues__

1. Cutter's Hope

2. Marlin's Faith

3. Charity for Nothing

__The Sacred Brotherhood__

1. Brother to Brother

2. Her Brother's Keeper

3. Brother In Arms

4. Between Brothers

5. A Brother's Secret

6. A Brother At My Back

__Indigo Knights__

1. Her Thin Blue Lifeline

ABOUT THE AUTHOR

A.J. Downey is the internationally bestselling author of The Sacred Hearts Motorcycle Club romance series. She is a born and raised Seattle, WA Native. She finds inspiration from her surroundings, through the people she meets, and likely as a byproduct of way too much caffeine.

She has lived many places and done many things, though mostly through her own imagination...An avid reader all of her life, it's now her turn to try and give back a little, entertaining as she has been entertained.

Stalker Information:
www.ajdowney.com